## About the

...thy Williams is a grea... ...severance as she had never written anything before ...writing career, and from the starting point of zero ...s now fulfilled her ambition to pursue this most ...joyable of careers. She would encourage any would-... writer to have faith and go for it! She derives ...spiration from the tropical island of Trinidad and ...om the peaceful countryside of middle England. ...thy lives in Warwickshire her family.

...ard-winning author **Jennifer Hayward** emerged on ... publishing scene as the winner of Mills & Boon's ... You Think You Can Write global writing contest. ...e recipient of *Romantic Times Magazine*'s Reviewer's ...oice Award for Best Mills & Boon Modern of 2014, ...nifer's careers in journalism and PR, including ...rs of working alongside powerful, charismatic ...Os and travelling the world, have provided perfect ...der for the fast-paced, sexy stories she likes to write.

...TA™ Award-winner **Anne McAllister** was born in ...lifornia and spent formative summer vacations on a ...all ranch in Colorado, where she developed her idea ...'the perfect hero", as well as a weakness for dark-...ired, handsome lone-wolf type guys. She found one ...n the university library and they've now been sharing ...happily-ever-afters" for over thirty years.

# Christmas in Paradise

CATHY WILLIAMS

JENNIFER HAYWARD

ANNE MCALLISTER

MILLS & BOON

First Published in Great Britain 2020
By Mills & Boon, an imprint of HarperCollins*Publishers*
1 London Bridge Street, London, SE1 9GF

CHRISTMAS IN PARADISE © 2020 Harlequin Books S.A.

*His Christmas Acquisition* © 2011 Cathy Williams
*Christmas at the Tycoon's Command* © 2017 Jennifer Drogell
*The Boss's Wife for a Week* © 2007 Barbara Schenck

ISBN: 978-0-263-29824-6

**MIX**
Paper from
responsible sources
FSC™ C007454

# HIS CHRISTMAS ACQUISITION

## CATHY WILLIAMS

# CHAPTER ONE

JAMIE was late. For the first time since she had started working for Ryan Sheppard she was running late due to an unfortunate series of events which had culminated in her waiting for her tube to arrive, along with six-thousand other short-tempered, frustrated, disgruntled commuters, so it seemed.

Wrapped up against the icy blast that raced along the platform—whipping her neatly combed hair into frantic disarray and reminding her that her smart grey suit and smart black pumps might work in an office, but were useless when faced with the grim reality of a soggy London winter—Jamie pointlessly looked at her watch every ten seconds.

Ryan Sheppard *hated* late. In fairness, he had been spoiled with her because for the past eighteen months she had been scrupulously early—which didn't mean that he would be sweetly forgiving.

By the time the tube train roared into view, Jamie had pretty much given up on getting into the office any time before nine-thirty. Because nothing would be gained from calling him, she had resolutely refused to even glance at the mobile phone hunkered down in the bowels of her bag.

Instead, she reluctantly focused her mind on the main reason why she had ended up leaving her house an hour later than she normally would have, and sure enough, all thoughts of her sister successfully obliterated everything else from her mind. She could feel the thin, poisonous thread of tension begin to creep through her body and, by the time she finally made it to the spectacular, cutting-edge glass building that housed RS Enterprises, her head was beginning to throb.

RS Enterprises was the headquarters of the massive conglomerate owned and run by her boss, and within its stately walls resided the beating pulse of all those various tentacles that made up the various arms of his many business concerns. An army of highly trained, highly motivated and highly paid employees kept everything afloat although, at quarter to ten in the morning, there were only a few to be glimpsed. The rest would be at their desks, doing whatever it took to make sure that the great wheels of his industry were running smoothly.

At quarter to ten in the morning, *she* would normally have been at her desk, doing her own bit.

But instead…

Jamie counted to ten in a feeble attempt to dislodge her sister's face from her head and took the lift up to the director's floor.

There was no need to gauge his mood when she pushed open the door to her office. On an average day, he would either be out of the office, having emailed her to fill her in on what she could be getting on with in his absence, or else he would be at his desk, mentally a thousand miles away as he plowed through his workload.

Today he was lounging back in his chair, arms folded behind his head, feet indolently propped on his desk.

Even after eighteen months, Jamie still had trouble reconciling the power house that was Ryan Sheppard with the unbearably sexy and disconcertingly unconventional guy who was such a far cry from anyone's idea of a business tycoon. Was it because the building blocks of his business were rooted in computer software, where brains and creativity were everything, and a uniform of suits and highly polished leather shoes were irrelevant? Or was it because Ryan Sheppard was just one of those men who was so comfortable in his own skin that he really didn't care what he wore or, for that matter, what the rest of the world thought of him?

At any rate, sightings of him in a suit were rare, and only occurred when he happened to be meeting financiers—although it had to be said that his legendary reputation preceded him. Very early on Jamie had come to the conclusion that he could show up at a meeting in nothing but a pair of swimming trunks and he would still have the rest of the world bowing and scraping and asking for his opinion.

Jamie waited patiently while he made a production out of looking at his watch and frowning before transferring his sharp, penetrating black gaze to her now composed face.

'You're late.'

'I know. I'm really sorry.'

'You're never late.'

'Yes, well, blame the erratic public-transport system in London, sir.'

'You know I hate you addressing me as *sir*. When I'm knighted, we can have a rethink on that one, but in the meantime the name is Ryan. And I would be more than happy to blame the erratic public-transport system, but you're not the only one who uses it, and no one else seems to be running behind schedule.'

Jamie hovered. She had taken time to dodge into the luxurious marble cloakroom at the end of the floor so she knew that she no longer resembled the hassled, anxious figure that had emerged twenty minutes earlier from the Underground station. But inside she could feel her nerves fraying, unravelling and scattering like useless detritus being blown around on a strong wind.

'Perhaps we could just get on with work and…and…I'll make up for lost time. I don't mind working through lunch.'

'So, if it wasn't the erratic public-transport system, then what kept you?' For the past year and a half, Ryan had tried to get behind that calm, impenetrable facade, to find the human being behind the highly efficient secretary. But Jamie Powell, aged twenty-eight, of the neat brown bob and the cool brown eyes, remained an enigma. He swung his feet off his desk and sat forward to stare at her with lively curiosity. 'Hard weekend? Late night? Hangover?'

'Of course I don't have a hangover!'

'No? Because there's absolutely nothing wrong with a little bit of over-indulgence now and again, you know. In fact, I happen to be of the opinion that a little over indulgence is very good for the soul.'

'I don't get drunk.' Jamie decided to put an immediate stop to any such notion. Gossip travelled at a rate of knots in RS Enterprises and there was no way that Jamie was going to let anyone think that she spent her weekends watching life whizz past from the bottom of a glass. In fact, there was no way that she was going to let anyone think anything at all about her. Experience had taught her well: join in with your colleagues, let your hair down now and again, build up a cosy relationship with your boss—and hey presto! You suddenly find yourself going down all sorts of unexpected and uncomfortable roads. She had been there and she wasn't about to pay a repeat visit.

'How virtuous of you!' Ryan congratulated her with the sort of false sincerity that made her teeth snap together in frustration. 'So we can eliminate the demon drink! Maybe your alarm failed to go off? Or maybe…'

He shot her a smile that reminded her just why the man

was such a killer when it came to the opposite sex. For anyone not on their guard, it was the sort of smile that could bring a person out in goose bumps. She had seen it happen any number of times, watching from the sidelines. 'Maybe,' he drawled, eyebrows raised speculatively, 'there was someone in your bed who made getting up on a cold December morning just a little bit too much of a challenge…?'

'I would rather not discuss my private life with you, sir—sorry, *Ryan.*'

'And that's perfectly acceptable, just so long as it doesn't intrude on your working life, but strolling into the office at ten in the morning demands a little explanation. And fobbing me off with promises to work through your lunch isn't good enough. I'm an exceptionally reasonable man,' Ryan went on, tapping his pen thoughtfully on his desk and running his eyes over her tight, closed face. 'Whenever you've had an emergency, I've been more than happy to let you take time off. Remember the plumber incident?'

'That was once!'

'And what about last Christmas? Didn't I generously give you half a day off so that you could do your Christmas shopping?'

'You gave *everyone* half a day off.'

'Point proven! I'm a reasonable man. So I think I deserve a reasonable explanation for your lateness.'

Jamie took a deep breath and braced herself to reveal something of her private life. Even this small and insignificant confidence, something that could hardly be classed as a confidence at all, went against the grain. Like a time bomb nestling in the centre of her well-founded good intentions, she could hear it ticking, threatening to send her whole carefully orchestrated reserve into chaos. She would not let that happen. She would throw him a titbit of information because, if she didn't, then the wretched man would just keep at it like a bull terrier worrying a bone.

He was like that—determined to the point of insanity. She figured it was how he had managed to take his father's tiny, failing computer business and build it up into a multinational conglomerate. He just never gave up and he never let go. His sexy, laid-back exterior concealed a strong and powerful business instinct that laid down rules and watched while the rest of the world fell into line.

She opened her mouth to give him an edited version of events, filtered through her strict mental-censoring process, when the door to his office burst open. Or rather it was flung open with the sort of drama that made both their heads spin round simultaneously in surprise to the leggy, blonde-haired, blue-eyed woman who literally flew into the office. Her big, long hair trailed wildly behind her, a thick, red cashmere coat hooked over her shoulder.

She threw the coat over the nearest chair. It was a gesture that was so wildly theatrical that Jamie had to stare down at her feet to stop herself from laughing out loud.

Ryan Sheppard had no qualms about bringing his women into the workplace once he had signed off work for the day. Jamie had always assumed that this was the arrogance of a man who only had to incline his head slightly to have any woman he wanted putting herself out to accommodate him. Why go to the bother of traipsing over to a woman's house at nine in the evening when *she* could traipse to his offices and save him the hassle of the trip? When things had been particularly hectic, and his employees had been up and running on pure adrenalin into the late hours of the night, she had witnessed first-hand his deeply romantic gesture of sending his staff home so that he could treat his date to a Chinese takeaway in his office.

Not once had she ever heard any of these women complain. They smiled, they simpered, they followed him with adoring eyes and then, when he became bored with them, they were tactfully and expensively shuffled off to pastures new.

And such was the enduring charm of the guy that he still managed to keep in friendly touch with the majority of his exes.

But there had never been anything like this, at least that she could remember in her brief spell of working for him.

She couldn't help her snort of laughter at the unexpected sight of some poetic justice being dished out. She quickly tried to bury it under the guise of coughing, although when she caught his eye it was to find him glaring at her before transferring his attention back to the enraged beauty standing in front of his desk.

'Leanne…'

'Don't you *dare* "Leanne" *me*! I can't *believe* you would just break up with me over the *phone*!'

'Flying over to Tokyo to deliver the news face to face wasn't an option.' He glanced at Jamie, who immediately began standing up, because witnessing the other woman's anger and distress was something she would rather have avoided. But Ryan nodded at her to sit back down.

'You could have *waited* until I got back!'

Ryan sighed and rubbed his eyes before standing up and strolling round to perch on his desk. 'You need to calm down,' he said in a voice that was perfectly modulated and yet carried an icy threat. Leanne, picking it up, gulped in a few deep breaths.

'Cast your mind back the last two times we've met,' he continued with ferocious calm. 'And you might remember that I *have* warned you that our relationship had reached the end of its course.'

'You didn't mean that!' She tossed her head and her mane of blonde hair rippled down her back.

'I'm not in the habit of saying things I don't mean. You chose to ignore what I said and so you gave me no option but to spell it out word for word.'

'But I thought that we were *going* somewhere. I had plans! And what—' Leanne glared at Jamie, who was focusing on her black pumps '—is *she* doing here? I want to have this out with you in *private*! Not with your boring little secretary hanging on to our every word and taking notes so that she can report back to everyone in this building.'

Little? Yes. Five-foot-four could hardly be deemed tall by anyone's standards. But *boring*? It was an adjective that would have stung had it come from anyone other than Leanne. Like all the women Jamie had seen flit in and out of Ryan's life, Leanne was the sort of supermodel beauty who had a healthy disrespect for any woman who wasn't on the same eye-catching plane as she was.

Jamie looked at the towering blonde and met her bright-blue eyes with cool disdain.

'Jamie is here,' Ryan said in a hard voice, 'because, in case you hadn't noticed, this is my office and we're in the middle of working. I'm sure I made it perfectly clear to you that I don't tolerate my work life being disrupted. Ever. By anyone.'

'Yes, but…'

He walked across to where she had earlier flung the red coat and held it out. 'You're upset, and for that I apologise. But now I suggest that you exit both my offices and our relationship with pride and dignity. You're a beautiful woman. You'll have no trouble replacing me.'

Jamie watched, fascinated in spite of herself, by the transparency of Leanne's emotions. Pride and anger waged war with self-pity and a temptation to plead. But in the end she allowed herself to be helped into her coat; the click of the door as she left the room was, at least, a lot more controlled than when she had entered.

Jamie studiously stared in front of her and waited for Ryan to break the silence.

'Did you know that she was coming?' he asked abruptly and Jamie turned to him in surprise. 'Is that why you chose today, of all days, to get here two hours late?'

'Of course not! I wouldn't dream of getting involved in your private life.' Although she had in the past: trinkets bought for women; flowers chosen, ordered and sent; theatre tickets booked. On one memorable occasion he had actually taken her to a luxury sports-car garage and asked her to choose which colour Porsche he should buy for a certain woman who had lasted no longer than a handful of weeks. He was nothing if not an absurdly generous lover, even if his definition of a relationship never contained the notion of permanence. 'And I don't appreciate being accused of...of... ever being in cahoots with any of your bimb—girlfriends.'

Ryan's eyes narrowed on her flushed face. 'The reason I asked was because you seemed to derive a certain amount of satisfaction from Leanne and her display of histrionics. In fact, I could swear that I heard you laugh at one point.'

Jamie looked at him. He was once more perched on his desk, his long, jean-clad legs extended and lightly crossed at the ankles. In heels, Leanne would have been at least six foot tall and he had still towered over her.

Jamie felt a quiver of apprehension race down her spine but for once she was sorely tempted to say what was on her mind.

'I'm sorry. It was an inappropriate reaction.' Except she could feel a fit of the giggles threatening to overwhelm her again and she had to look down hurriedly at her tightly clasped fingers.

When she next looked up it was to find that he was standing over her and, before she could push back her chair, he was leaning down, his muscular hands on either side of her, his face so close to hers that she could see the wildly extravagant length of his eyelashes and the hint of tawny gold in his dark eyes. He was so close, in fact, that by simply raising her hand a couple of inches she would have been able to stroke the side of his face, touch the faint growth of stubble, feel its spikiness against her fingers.

Assaulted by this sudden wave of crazy speculation, Jamie fought down the sickening twist in her stomach and carried on looking at him squarely in the face although she could feel her heart beating inside her like a jack hammer.

'What *I'd* like to know,' he said softly, 'is what the hell you found so funny. What I'd really like is for you to share the joke with me.'

'Sometimes I laugh in tense situations. I'm sorry.'

'Pull the other one, Jamie. You've been in tense situations with me before when I'm trying to get a major deal closed. You've never burst out laughing.'

'That's different.'

'Explain.'

'Why? Why does it matter what I think?'

'Because I like to know a bit of what's going on in my personal assistant's head. Call me crazy, but I think it makes the working relationship go a lot smoother.' In truth, Ryan didn't think that it would be possible to find anyone with whom he could have worked more comfortably. Jamie seemed to possess an uncanny ability to predict his moves and her calm was a pleasing counterpoint to his volatility.

Before he had hired her, he had suffered three years of terrific-looking fairly incompetent secretaries who had all developed the annoying habit of becoming infatuated with him. His faithful middle-aged secretary who had served him well for nearly ten years had emigrated to Australia and he had followed her up with a series of ill-suited replacements.

Jamie Powell really worked for him and it had nothing to do with the mechanisms of her mind or what she thought about him. But suddenly the urge to shake her out of her cool detachment was overwhelming. It was as though that shadow of a snicker that had crossed her face earlier on had unleashed a curiosity in him, and it took him by surprise.

He pushed himself away from her and walked across to the low sofa that doubled as a bed for those times when he worked so late that sleeping in his office was the easiest option.

Reluctantly, Jamie swivelled her chair in his direction and wondered how many billionaire bosses would be sprawled indolently on a sofa in their office in a pair of jeans and a faded jumper, hands clasped behind their heads, work put on temporary hold while they asked questions that were really none of their business.

Again that finger of apprehension sent another shiver down her spine. After a succession of unsatisfactory but emotionally important temp jobs, would she have taken this one if she had known the nature of the beast?

'I'm not paid to have thoughts about your private life,' she ventured primly in a last-ditch attempt to change the subject.

'Don't worry about that. I give you full permission to say what was on your mind.'

Jamie licked her lips nervously. This was the first time he had ever pinned her down like this, the first time he hadn't backed off when his curiosity had failed to find fertile ground. Now, like a lazy predator, he was watching her, gauging her reaction, forming conclusions.

'Okay.' She looked at him evenly. 'I'm surprised that this is the first time one of your girlfriends has seen fit to storm into your office and give you a piece of her mind. I thought it was funny, so I laughed. But quietly. And I wouldn't have laughed if I had left your office when I had wanted to, but you gestured to me to stay put. So I did. So you can't blame me for reacting.'

Ryan sat up and looked at her intently. 'See? Now isn't it liberating to speak your mind?'

'I know you think it's funny to confuse me.'

'Am I confusing you?'

Jamie went bright red and tightened her lips. 'You don't seem to have any morals or ethics at all when it comes to women!' she snapped. 'I've worked with you for well over a year and you must have had a dozen women in that time. More! You play with people's feelings and it doesn't seem to bother you at all!'

'So there's a lurking tiger behind that placid face of yours,' he murmured.

'Don't be ridiculous. You asked me for my opinion, that's all.'

'You think I use women? Treat them badly?'

'I…' She opened her mouth to tell him that she had never thought anything whatsoever about the way he treated women, not until this very moment, but she would have been lying. She realised with some dismay that she had done plenty of thinking about Ryan Sheppard and his out-of-hours relationships. 'I'm sure you treat them really well, but most women want more than just expensive gifts and fun and frolics for a few weeks.'

'What makes you say that? Have you been chatting to any of my girlfriends? Or is that what *you* would want?'

'I haven't been chatting to your girlfriends, and we're not talking about me,' Jamie told him sharply.

Her colour was up and for the first time he noticed the sultry depths of her eyes and the fullness of her mouth. She was either blissfully unaware of her looks or else had made a concerted effort to sublimate them, at least during working hours. Then he wondered how he had never really *noticed* these little details about her before. It occurred to him that they had rarely, if ever, had the sort of lengthy conversation that required eye-to-eye contact. She had managed to avoid the very thing every single woman he met sought to instigate.

'I treat the women I date incredibly well and, more importantly, I never give them any illusions about their place in my life. They know from the start that I'm not into building a relationship or working towards a "happy family" scenario.'

'Why?'

'Come again?'

'Why,' Jamie repeated in a giddy rush, 'are you not into building relationships or doing the happy-family thing?'

Ryan looked at her incredulously. Yes, he always encouraged an outspoken approach, both within the working environment and outside it. He prided himself on always being able to take what was said to him. He might choose to totally ignore it, of course, and did a great majority of the time, but never let it be said that he wasn't open to alternative opinions.

Except who had ever asked him such an outlandishly personal question before?

'Not everyone is.' But he was keen to bring the conversation to an end now. 'And, now that the cabaret show's over, I think it's time we get back to work.'

Jamie gave a little shrug and instantly resumed her professionalism. 'Okay. I didn't manage to find the time to look at those reports about the software company you're thinking of investing in. Shall I go and do that now? I can have everything ready for you by this afternoon.'

So, to Ryan's vague dissatisfaction, the day kicked off the way it always did: with Jamie working wonders with her time, sitting outside his office in her own private cubicle, where she did what she was highly paid to do with such staggering efficiency that he wondered how he had ever managed without her around.

His phone rang constantly; she fielded calls. The creative bods who worked on some of the games software three floors down burst into his office with some new idea or other, became over-exuberant; she ushered them out like a head teacher whose job it was to keep order in the classroom. When he made the comparison, his keen eyes noted the way she blushed and smiled, and then he grinned when she told him that she wouldn't have to play head teacher if he was a bit better at playing it himself.

At three, he grabbed his coat; he was running late for a meeting with three investment bankers. She told him at the very least to take off the rugby shirt and handed him something a little more presentable from the concealed, fully stocked wardrobe in the suite opposite his office. Everything was back to normal and it was beginning to grate on him.

At five-thirty, he got back to his office after a successful meeting to find her gathering her things together and slipping on her coat. About to switch off her computer, Jamie felt her heart flutter uncomfortably. She hadn't been expecting him to be back before she left.

'You're leaving?' Ryan tossed his coat over his desk and began pulling off the unutterably dull grey woollen jumper which he had obligingly worn for the benefit of the bankers.

Underneath, the white tee-shirt barely concealed the hard muscularity of his body. Jamie averted her eyes, mentally slapping herself because she should be used to all this by now and she wasn't sure why she was suddenly reacting to him like a complete idiot. Maybe it had something to do with her sister being back on the scene. There would be a psychological connection there somewhere if she could be bothered to work it out.

'I...I *would* have stayed on, Ryan, but something's come up, so I have to dash.'

'Something's *come up*? What?' He headed straight to where she was still dithering in front of her computer terminal and lounged against the door frame.

'Nothing,' Jamie muttered.

'Nothing? Something? Which is it, Jamie?'

'Oh, just leave me alone!' she blurted out, and to her horror she could feel her eyes welling up at the sudden intrusion of stress that had presented itself in her previously uncomplicated life. She looked away abruptly and began fiddling with the paperwork on her desk, before turning all her attention to her computer in the desperate hope that the man still leaning against the door frame would take the hint and disappear. He didn't. Worse, he walked slowly towards her and she felt his finger on her chin, tilting her face up to his.

'What the hell is going on here?'

'Nothing's going on. I'm just...just a bit tired, that's all. Maybe I'm...coming down with something.' She shrugged his hand off but she could still feel it burning her skin as she quickly stuck on her thick black coat and braced herself for the biting cold outside.

'Is it to do with work?'

'I beg your pardon?'

'Has something happened here at work that you're not telling me about? Some of the guys can be a bit rowdy. Has someone said something to you? Made some kind of inappropriate remark?' He suddenly blanched at the possibility that one of them might have seriously overstepped the mark and done something a little more physical when it came to being inappropriate.

Jamie looked at him blankly and shook her head. 'Of course not. No, work's fine. You'll be relieved to hear that.'

'Some guy giving you grief?' He tried to sound sympathetic but his imagination had broken its leash and was filling his head with all sorts of images that were definitely in the 'inappropriate' category.

'What kind of grief?'

'Has someone made an unwanted pass at you?' Ryan said bluntly. 'You can tell me and I'll make damn sure that it never happens again.'

'Why do you think that I would need help in sorting out something like that?' she asked coolly. 'Do you think that I'm such a fool that I wouldn't know how to take care of myself if some guy decided to make a pass at me?'

'Did I say that?'

'You implied it.'

'Other women,' Ryan said, his big body tensing, 'are probably just a bit more experienced when it comes to men. You… I may be mistaken, but you strike me as an innocent.'

Jamie stared at him. She distantly wondered how they had reached this point in the conversation. How many wrong turnings did it take to get from discussing a software report to her sex life—or lack of it?

'I think it's time I head home now. I'll make sure that I'm in on time tomorrow.' She began moving towards the door. She was only aware of him shifting his stance when she felt the hot weight of his fingers curled around her wrist.

'You were upset. Can you blame me for wanting to know why?' He gave a little jerk and pulled her towards him.

'Yes, I can!' Her mouth was dry and she knew that she was flushed. In truth, she felt as though her body was on fire.

'I'm your boss. You work for me, and as such you're my responsibility.' His eyes drifted down to her full mouth and then lower, to the starched white shirt, the neat, tailored jacket. He was aware of her breasts heaving.

'I am my own responsibility,' Jamie said through tight lips. 'I'm sorry I brought my stress to work. It won't happen again and, for your information, it has nothing to do with anything or anyone in this office. No one's been saying anything to me and no one's made a pass at me. I haven't had to defend myself but I'm just going to say this for the record— if someone *had* done something that I found offensive, then I would be more than capable of looking out for myself. I don't need you to step in and defend me.'

'Most women appreciate a man jumping to their defence,' Ryan murmured and just like that the atmosphere changed between them. He slackened his grip on her wrist but, instead of pulling away her hand, Jamie found herself staring up at him, losing herself in the depths of his eyes, mesmerised. She blinked and thankfully was brought back down to planet Earth.

'I am *not* most women,' she breathed. 'And I'd really appreciate it if you could let me go.'

He did, stepping aside, watching as she stuck on her coat and wrapped the black scarf around her neck.

She couldn't look at him. She just couldn't. She didn't understand what had happened back there but she was shaking inside. Not even the thought of Jessica could distract her from the moment. And she was horribly aware that he was staring at her, thinking that she was over-reacting, behaving like a mad woman when all he had done was to try and understand why she had been acting out of character.

She worked for him, and as her boss he had seen it as his civic duty to protect her from possible discomfort in her working environment, and what had she done in response? Acted like an outraged spinster in the company of a lech. She was mortified.

And then she had *stared* at him. Had he noticed? He noticed everything when it came to women and the last thing she needed was for him to think that she saw him as anything other than her boss, a man whom she respected but would always keep at arm's length.

'I've left those reports you asked me to do on your desk in descending order of priority,' she said crisply. 'Your meeting at ten tomorrow's been cancelled. I've rearranged it and you should have the new date updated onto your phone. So…'

'So, you can run along and nurse your stress in private,' Ryan drawled.

'I will.'

But she spent the entire journey back to her house dwelling on the tone of his voice as he had said that. She wondered what he was thinking of her. She didn't want to, but she did.

The barrier she had imposed that clearly defined both their roles felt as though it was crumbling around her like a flimsy pack of cards, and all because he had happened to catch her in a vulnerable moment.

Thanks to Jessica.

It was pitch-black and bitterly cold as she walked from the Underground station to her house. London was in a grip of the worst winter weather for twelve years. Predictions were for a white Christmas, although it had yet to snow.

In her house, however, the lights were on. All of them. Jamie sighed and reflected that, on the bright side, at least Jessica had managed to locate the key in its secret hiding spot under the flower pot at the side of the house. At least she had made it down to London from Edinburgh safe and sound, even if she brought with her the promise of yet more stress.

# CHAPTER TWO

'BUT you don't *understand*...'

Jamie took time out from loading the dishwasher to glance round at her sister, who was wandering in a sulky fashion around the kitchen, occasionally stopping to pick something up and inspect it with a mixture of boredom and disdain. Nothing in the house was to her taste; she had made that very clear within the first few minutes of Jamie pushing open the front door and walking in.

The place, she'd announced, was poky. 'Couldn't you have found something a little more comfortable? I mean, I know Mum didn't leave us with much, but honestly, Jamie!' The furnishings were drab. There was no healthy stuff in the fridge to eat and, 'What on earth do you do for alcohol in this place? Don't tell me that you while away your evenings with a cup of cocoa and a good book for company?'

Jamie was accustomed to the casual insults, although it had been so long since she had actually set eyes on her sister that she had forgotten just how grating they could be after a while.

Their father had died when Jamie was six and Jessica still a three-year-old toddler and they had been raised by their mother. Jamie had been a bookworm at school, always studying, always mentally moving forward, planning to go to university. She left Jessica to be the one who curled her

hair and painted her fingernails and, even at the age of thir-
teen, develop the kind of wiles that would stand her in very
good stead with the opposite sex.

Jamie had never made it to university. At barely nineteen
she had found herself first caring for her mother—who, after
a routine operation, had contracted MRSA and failed to recover—then, when Gloria had died, taking on the responsibility of looking after her sixteen-year-old sister. Without
Jamie even noticing, Jessica had moved from a precocious
pre-teen to a nightmare of a teenager. Where Jamie had inherited her father's dark looks and chosen to retreat into the
world of literature and books, Jessica had been blessed with
their mother's striking blonde looks. Far from retreating
anywhere, she had shown a gritty determination to flaunt
as much of herself as was humanly possible.

A still-grieving Jamie had suddenly been catapulted into
the role of caretaker to a teenager who was almost completely out of control.

What else could she have done? Gloria had begged her
to make sure to keep an eye on Jessica, to look after her,
'Because you *know* what she can be like—she needs a firm
hand…'

Jamie often wondered how it was that she hadn't turned
prematurely grey from the stress of it.

And now, after all that muddy water under the bridge,
stuff she still could hardly bear to think about, here was
Jessica, back on the scene again, as stunning as ever—more,
if that was possible—and already making Jamie grit her
teeth in pointless frustration.

'I understand that you have responsibilities, Jess, and they
may be getting to you but you can't run away from them.'
Jamie slammed shut the dishwasher door with undue force
and wiped her hands on a tea towel.

Dinner had been a bowl of home-cooked pasta with

chicken and mushrooms. Jessica had made a face and flatly refused to eat any of the pasta because she was off carbs.

'It's all right for you!' Jessica snapped, scooping up her poker-straight blonde hair into a ponytail before releasing it so that it fell in a heavy, silky curtain halfway down her back. '*You* don't have to deal with a bloody husband who works all the hours God made and expects me to be sitting around with a smile pinned to my face, waiting for him to return for a nice hot meal and a back massage! Like some kind of creepy Stepford wife.'

'You *could* get a job.'

'I *got* a job. I got eight jobs! It's not my fault if none of them suited me. Besides, what's the point me going out to work for a pittance when Greg earns so much?'

Jamie didn't say anything. She didn't want to think about Greg. Thinking about Greg had always been a downhill road. Once upon a time he had been her boss. Once upon a time she had fancied herself in love with him—a secret, pleasurable yearning that had filled her days with sunlight and made the burden of looking out for her younger sister more bearable. Once upon a time she had actually been stupid enough to think that he would wake up one day and realise that he cared for her in the same way she cared for him. Unfortunately, he had met Jessica and it had been love at first sight.

'Have you thought about volunteer work?' she offered, fed up.

'Oh, purr…leese! Can you *really* see me doing anything like that, Jamie? Working in a soup kitchen in Edinburgh? Or arranging flowers in the local parish church and doing fund raisers with the old biddies?'

She had dragged one of the chairs over and was sitting with her long legs propped up on the chair in front of her so that she could inspect her toenails which were painted a vibrant shade of pink.

'I'm bored,' she said flatly. 'I'm bored and I'm fed up and I want a life. I'm too young to be buried in the outskirts of Edinburgh where it rains all the time, *when* it's not snowing, hanging around for Greg, who only cares about sick animals anyway. Did you know he's got a fan club? The dishiest vet in town—it's pathetic!'

Jamie turned away and briefly squeezed her eyes tightly shut. It had been years since she had last seen Greg but she remembered him as clearly as if it had been yesterday. His kind face, the way his grey eyes crinkled when he smiled, his floppy blond hair through which he constantly ran his fingers.

The thought of her sister being bored with him filled her with terror. In the end, Greg had been her salvation. He had taken over the business of worrying about Jessica. Jessica might not need him, but she, Jamie, most definitely did!

'He's crazy about you, Jess.'

'Loads of guys could be crazy about me.'

Jamie felt her body go cold. 'What does that mean? Have you? You're not doing anything stupid, are you?'

'Oh, don't be such a prude.' But she sighed and leaned back against the chair, letting her head flop over the back so that she was staring glassy-eyed up at the ceiling. 'No, I'm not doing anything *stupid*, if by that you're asking me whether I'm having an affair. But the way I feel...'

She allowed that possibility to take shape between them and it was all Jamie could do not to slap her sister. However, years of ingrained caretaking papered over the passing temptation. This, she felt, was a subject best left alone in the hope that it might just go away. She was busy wondering what topic she could choose that might be safer when the doorbell rang.

'Someone flogging something,' she muttered, relieved for the distraction. 'Please, Jess, just give Greg a call. He must be worried sick about you.'

She left the kitchen to a disgruntled Jessica informing her that she had no intention of doing any such thing, that he knew perfectly well where she was, just like he knew that she needed some space.

Jamie wondered how long Greg would carry on waiting while Jessica hunted around for this so-called space she was intent on finding, and she was still chewing it over in her head as she pulled open the front door.

The sight of Ryan standing on her doorstep was so shocking that for a few seconds her mind went completely blank.

He had never, ever been to her house before. Not even when they had happened to drive out of London to attend a meeting. He had never picked her up or dropped her off. She hadn't even thought that he knew where she lived.

Eventually, her brain caught up with what her eyes were telling her, and she stopped gaping at him open-mouthed and actually croaked, 'What are you doing here?'

'You were stressed out. I was worried about you. I thought I'd drop by, make sure you were all right.'

'Well, I'm fine, so I'll see you tomorrow at work.' Belatedly, she remembered her sister scowling in the kitchen and she stepped outside and pulled the door quietly closed behind her, taking care not to shut it completely.

'How did you find out where I live?' she hissed under her breath. Under the lamplight, his face was a contour of harsh shadows and his eyes glittered in the semi-darkness. He was still in his work clothes, the jeans, the faded sweater, the trainers and the coat, which she knew had cost the earth, but which he wore as casually as if he had got it from the local Oxfam shop.

'Personnel files. It really wasn't too difficult.'

'Well, you have to go.'

'You're shaking like a leaf. It's cold out here—let me in for a few minutes.'

'No!' She saw his eyebrows rise fractionally and added, stammering, 'I mean, it's late.'

'It's eight-forty-five.'

'I'm busy.'

'You're on edge. Why? Tell me what's going on.' Ryan laughed. 'You're my indispensable secretary. I can't have you storing up nasty secrets and then suddenly deciding to walk out on me, can I? What would I do without you?'

'I...I'm obliged to give a month's notice,' Jamie stammered. Ryan Sheppard on her doorstep suddenly seemed to throw that all-important distance between them into confusion and she didn't like it.

'So you *are* thinking of leaving me. Well, it's a damn good thing I turned up here to get the full story out of you, isn't it? At least this way I can defend my corner.' For some reason he felt disproportionately let down by the thought of her just dumping a letter of resignation on his desk without any forewarning and then jumping ship. 'So, why don't you invite me inside and we can discuss this like two adults? If it's more money you're after, then name the amount and it's yours.'

'This is crazy!'

'I know. And I hate dealing with crazy.' He reached out and pushed the door open just as Jessica's petulant voice wafted from the direction of the kitchen, carolling to ask where Jamie was, because she really needed something to eat—and was there anywhere they could go for a halfway decent salad? She didn't fancy being cooped up for the rest of the night.

And then there she was, long and beautiful and blonde, and all the things that Ryan looked for in a woman, standing by the banister as Jamie turned around with a sigh of resignation. Stunningly pretty, stunningly fair-haired and dangerously bored with her husband.

If Jamie could have reached out and pushed Ryan straight back out of the front door, then she would have done so, but he was already inside the tiny hall, removing his thick coat while his eyes never strayed from Jessica.

'Well, well, well,' he drawled in a lazy undertone. 'What have we here…?'

'My sister,' Jamie muttered.

The glitter in Jessica's eyes mirrored his lazy speculation and Jamie felt a chill run down her spine.

There was no need for her to make introductions. Not when her sister was sashaying forward, hand outstretched, introducing herself—with, Jamie noted, her left hand stuck firmly behind her back.

'You never told me that you had a sister,' Ryan said, turning his fabulous eyes to Jamie.

Standing to one side like an uninvited spectator in her own house, Jamie's voice was stiff when she answered, 'I didn't see the relevance. Jessica doesn't live in London.'

'Although, I might just be thinking of changing that.'

Jamie's head whipped round and she stared, horrified at her sister. 'You can't!'

'Why not? I told you. I'm bored in Scotland. And, from what I see here, London certainly has a hell of a lot more to offer. Why did you never mention that you had such a dishy boss, Jamie? Did you think that I might dash down here and try to steal him from you?'

Jamie held on to the banister, feeling faint, and Ryan, lounging only feet away from her, took the opportunity to gauge the electric atmosphere between the sisters. Arriving unannounced on his secretary's doorstep had been a spontaneous decision which he had begun to regret on the drive over, but now he was pleased that he had made the journey.

'How long are you in London?' He looked at Jessica but his mind was still on Jamie and on that ferocious wall of privacy she had erected around herself. Purpose, he thought, unknown.

'She's literally only here for a day or two before she returns to Scotland. She's married and her husband will be waiting for her.'

'Did you have to bring that up?'

'It's the truth, Jess. Greg's a good guy. He doesn't deserve this.' *And* you *certainly don't deserve* him, she thought.

'I'm having lots of marital problems,' Jessica insisted to Ryan. 'I *thought* that I could come down here and find some support from my sister, but it looks like I was wrong.'

'That's not fair, Jess! And, besides, I'm sure Mr Sheppard doesn't want to stand here and listen to our family history.'

'Please, feel free to go on. I'm all ears!'

'You need to go.' Jamie turned to him. Every muscle in her body felt like it had been stretched to snapping point and the ground under her feet was like quicksand. One minute she had been on solid ground and then, in the blink of an eye, her sister was on her doorstep, Ryan was in her house breaking down her fortifications just by being there, and she was struggling in quicksand. 'And you, Jess, need to go to bed.'

'I'm not a kid any longer!'

'You behave like one.' In terms of condemnation, it was the first time Jamie had ever taken such a dramatic step. She had been conditioned to look after Jessica, to treat her like a baby, to make sure that her needs were met because she, Jamie, was the stronger one, the older one, the one upon whom the responsibilities lay.

In the tense silence that followed her flat statement,

Jessica hesitated, confused, then her lips pursed and she glared sulkily at her sister.

'You can't make me go back up to Scotland, you know,' she muttered.

'We can discuss this in the morning, Jess,' Jamie said wearily. 'I think I've had enough stress today.'

'And she *is* stressed.' Ryan inserted himself into the conversation and Jessica sidled a little closer to him, her body language advertising her interest in a way no amount of words could have done. 'She arrived late for work this morning.'

Jessica giggled and looked at her sister slyly. 'If you'd told me that you were running late, I would have got off the phone sooner. I know you're a stickler for punctuality. Don't worry. I'll be good as gold while I'm here, and you can be the perfect little secretary again and get in to work on time. Mind you…' She looked at Ryan coyly. 'If I had a boss like this one, I'd be getting in to work at six and leaving at midnight. Or maybe not leaving at all…'

Jamie turned on her heels and stalked off towards the kitchen. She knew how these conversations with her sister went. The slightest whiff of criticism and she would react with jibes below the belt that were designed to wound. Jamie had long discovered that the fastest way of dealing with this was to walk away from the situation, to treat her sister like a child who was not responsible for her tantrums. They blew over as quickly as they materialised and making herself scarce removed her from the eye of the storm.

She half-expected Jessica to linger on the staircase, turning on the full-wattage smile and bringing all her feminine wiles to play in an effort to charm Ryan. But, in fact, barely had Jamie sat at the kitchen table than Ryan appeared in the doorway and looked at her quietly, his hands shoved into his pockets.

An uncomfortable silence gathered around them which she broke by reluctantly offering him a cup of coffee.

She would cheerfully have sent him on his way, but there were things that needed to be said, and, reluctant as she was to open up any kind of discussion on her private life, she had no idea how she could avoid the issue.

'Where's Jessica?' she asked, standing up and moving across to the kettle.

'I sent her on her way.'

'And she listened?'

'I have that way with women.'

Jamie snorted, no longer bothering with the niceties that would have been more appropriate given that he was the guy who paid her salary. He had invaded her territory, and as far as she was concerned niceties were temporarily suspended.

'Now you know why I got in late to work this morning. Jessica kept me on the phone for nearly an hour. She was a mess. I only knew that she had decided to sort herself out by coming down here when she phoned me from the train.'

'No big deal.' Ryan took the mug she was holding out to him and sat down. 'Family crises happen. Why didn't you just tell me the truth this morning?' He watched her and re-alised that she was barely seeing him as she walked towards the kitchen table, nursing the mug in her hands. For a man who was fully aware of the impact he had on the opposite sex, being rendered invisible was a new experience.

He, on the other hand, keenly noted this new casual dress-code of hers, the one she used when she wasn't wearing her work hat. Lazy eyes took in the way her jeans clung to a body that curved in all the right places and the way her long-sleeved tee-shirt skimmed a flat stomach and lovingly contoured pert, full breasts. Even her hair looked differ-ent—less neat and pristine, more tousled, as though she had spent time running her fingers through it. Which, judging from what he had picked up of the atmosphere in the house so far, she probably had.

'I suppose because I happen to think that what happens in my private life is no business of yours.'

'Oh, for God's sake, I didn't even know that you had a sister! How much of a state secret could that possibly be?'

Jamie flushed and fiddled with the mug before taking a sip of coffee. 'I…I'm not really the confiding type.'

'Really? I'd never have guessed.'

'I didn't tell you about Jessica because the chances of you ever running into her were non-existent. I live in London, she lives just outside Edinburgh. She isn't a part of my daily life.'

'And that was exactly the way you wanted it until she had the misfortune to need your support.'

'Please don't presume to have any insight at all into my family affairs!'

'If you don't want me to presume, then you're going to have to be a bit more forthcoming.'

'Why? What difference does it make? I do a very good job for you and that's all that matters.'

'Why are you so uncomfortable with this conversation?' He could have let it go. She was right; she delivered the goods when it came to her job and whatever happened outside it was absolutely none of his business. But Ryan decided that he didn't want to let it go. It was as though a door had been partially opened and what lay behind it promised to be so intriguing that he was compelled to try and push the door a little wider.

'You don't understand. You're my boss, for a start, and like I said I'm not into confiding. I prefer to keep my own counsel. Maybe it's a reaction to having a sister like Jess. She always made so much noise that it was just a lot easier to keep quiet and let her get on with it.'

'Easier, but maybe not better. Forget for a minute that I'm your boss. Pretend that I'm just anybody—your next-door neighbour who has come over to borrow a cup of sugar, co-incidentally just at a time when you need a shoulder to cry on...'

'I'm supposed to think of you as my next-door neighbour on the scrounge for a cup of sugar?' She was momentarily distracted enough by the image to feel her lips twitch. 'What would you be doing with the cup of sugar?'

'Baking a cake, because I happen to be a kindly and caring neighbour who enjoys baking. It's my favourite pastime. Next to flower arranging and cross stitch.' She was relaxing. She was even smiling and he felt a kick of gratification that he had been responsible for that. For some reason, he didn't care for the idea of her stressed out, tearful and unable to talk to anyone about it. His experience of women was that they couldn't wait to pour their hearts out and confide in whomsoever happened to be willing to listen. He was the youngest of four and the only boy in the family. He could remember many an instance of sitting out one of his sister's ridiculously long phone calls, waiting impatiently to use the telephone.

This level of reticence was new to him. 'So...?' he prompted encouragingly.

'So, look, I'm not sure how to say this but...' Jamie sighed and adopted a slightly different approach. 'Now that you've met my sister, what do you think of her?'

'After all of my five-second acquaintance, I'm only qualified to tell you that she's very attractive.'

Jamie felt a stab of disappointment but she nodded sagely at him. 'She's always been the prettier one.'

'Hang on a minute...'

'Spare me the kindness. I'm stating a fact, and it's not something that's ever bothered me anyway.' But for a fleeting second Jamie wondered what he had been about to say. Of course, it would have been a polite lie, but nevertheless... 'Jessica's beautiful and she knows it. She's also married and going through a bit of a bad patch which will blow over just so long as...'

'As she's not offered any distractions by someone like me?' He looked at her coolly.

'I know what type of girls you go for—tall, blonde, beautiful and pliable. Well, Jess is tall, blonde, beautiful and at the moment she happens to be very pliable. I know you probably think that I'm being totally out of order in saying this stuff, but you chose to come here, and now that you're here I'm afraid I have every right to say what's on my mind.' She licked her lips nervously. 'I hope I'm not jeopardising my job by telling you this.'

'Jeopardising your job? What kind of person do you think I am?' He was outraged to think that she could even consider him the type of man who would penalise her for speaking her mind. Was that what she thought of him? Under her cool, dutiful exterior, did she think that he was some sort of monster?

'Don't worry, your job is perfectly safe, and if you're so obsessive about your privacy then I'm happy to walk out that door right now and leave you to get on with hiding behind your walls. As for your sister, she might be the sort of woman I date, but I don't date married women, even married women who claim to be unhappily married.'

He stood up and the colour drained from Jamie's face. She had enjoyed the free and easy way he had always had with her. It was all part and parcel of his unconventional personality, that curious, alluring mix of creativity, intelligence and self-assurance. Did she want to lose that? Did she want a boss who stuck to the rules and never teased her, or over-stepped the boundaries in asking about her personal life? That thought left her cold and she hurriedly got to her feet and reached out to put a restraining hand on his arm.

'I'm sorry. I know how that sounded, but I have to look out for my sister. You see...' She hesitated a fraction of a second. 'Our dad died when I was six, and when Jess was sixteen Mum died after complications following an operation. It was horrible. I was left in charge. Mum made me promise that I would look after her. I was about to go to university, but I found myself having to get a job and look after Jess.'

'That was a lot of responsibility for someone so young,' Ryan murmured, sitting back down.

'It wasn't easy,' Jamie agreed. 'Jess was boy crazy and I nearly tore my hair out making sure she showed up at school every day and left with a handful of qualifications.'

'What were you doing for a job?' he asked curiously, and was even more curious when slow colour crept into her cheeks and she looked down.

'Oh, just working at a vet's. It wasn't what I had expected to be doing at the age of nineteen, but I enjoyed it. The thing is...'

'What had you expected to be doing?'

'Huh?'

'Your plans? Dreams? Ambitions? What were they before your life was derailed?'

'Well...' Jamie flushed and hesitated. 'I wanted to go to university and study law. Seems like a lifetime ago! Anyway, that's not important. The important thing is that I just wanted to warn you off her.'

'Tough, having to give up on your dreams. There must be a part of you that resents her.'

'Of course there isn't! No one can help what life throws at them.'

'Noble sentiment. Alas, not many of us are noble creatures.'

'As I was saying…' Jamie chose to ignore the invitation to elaborate. 'I just wanted to warn you off her.'

'Because she's going to dutifully return to her husband and they're both going to live happily ever after?'

'Yes!'

'Warning duly noted.'

'What warning?'

Jessica was standing in the doorway of the kitchen, and with a sinking heart Jamie realised that she hadn't vanished because she had been instructed to vanish—she had vanished so that she could have a shower and resurface in the least amount of clothing possible. She was kitted out in slinky lounging culottes and a tiny vest, worn bra-less, that left nothing to the imagination. She had a stupendous figure and every inch of it was available for inspection as she walked slowly into the kitchen, enjoying the attention.

Through the thin, grey vest, Jamie could see the outline of her sister's nipples. Ryan would similarly be taking that in. Yes, he had told her that he would keep away from Jessica, but how strong was any red-blooded man's will power when it came to a sexy woman who was overtly encouraging?

'Well?' Jessica paused and leaned against the counter, legs lightly crossed at the ankles, her back arched so that her breasts were provocatively thrust forward. 'What warning?'

'A warning,' Ryan drawled, 'that I'm not to interfere and try and persuade you to return to your husband.'

Jessica looked at her sister narrowly. 'That true, Jamie?'

'Why would he lie?'

'So you don't mind me staying with you for a while? Maybe until Christmas is over? I mean, it's only a couple

of weeks away. I could help you decorate the tree and stuff
and by then I might have got my head together.'

Boxed in, Jamie had no choice but to concede defeat.

'Hey, we could even have a party!' She looked sideways
at Ryan and shot him a half-smile. 'I'm great at organising
parties. What are *you* up to at Christmas, anyway?'

'Jessica!'

'Oh, don't be such a bore, Jamie.'

'I'm in the country,' Ryan murmured. 'Why?' He had
already received so many invitations to join people for
Christmas lunch that he was seriously considering ignoring them all and locking himself away in his apartment until
the fuss was over.

'You could join us here.'

Adjacent to Jamie, he was aware of her look of pure horror at the suggestion. He nearly burst out laughing, but he
managed to keep a straight face as he appeared to give the
offer considerable thought.

'Well...' He hesitated. 'I am in the unique position of
spending Christmas day without my family.'

'Where are they?' Jessica strolled towards him, her
thumbs hooked lightly into the elasticated waistband of the
culottes so that they were dragged slightly down, exposing
a flat, brown belly and the twinkling glitter of her pierced
navel.

No wonder Jamie worried about her sister, Ryan thought.
The woman was clearly a walking, talking liability to anybody's peace of mind.

'They're in the Caribbean.'

Jessica's eyes rounded into impressed saucers and her
mouth fell open. 'You're kidding.'

'I have a house there and this year they've all decided to
spend Christmas and New Year in it.'

'I don't know why we're having this silly conversation,'

Jamie interrupted crisply. 'Ryan already has his own plans for Christmas.' She rose to her feet and pulled open the dishwasher, which was her way of announcing that it was time for the impromptu evening to come to an end. But Jessica was in full flow, quizzing Ryan about his house in the Caribbean, asking him what it looked like, while he answered with just the sort of indulgent amusement that she was accustomed to getting. It had never mattered what boundaries Jessica had over-stepped; the world had always smiled and allowed her to get away with it. Whoever said that beautiful people didn't lead charmed lives?

'I'm open to persuasion,' Ryan finished, leaning back and watching Jamie bang pans into cupboards, frustration stamped on her face, her mouth downturned and scowling. 'What were *you* going to do, Jamie? Bit boring if you had been planning to stay in on your own.'

'I would rather call it peaceful,' she snapped. 'And, besides, I had plans to go out for drinks on Christmas morning with some friends and I would probably have hung around for their alternative Christmas lunch.'

'I want traditional,' Jessica stated flatly.

'What's Greg going to do?' Jamie spun round to look at her sister. 'Does he know that you're planning on abandoning him for Christmas day?'

'He won't mind. He's on call, and anyway, his parents can't wait to have him all to themselves so that they can tell him what a rotten wife I am. So...' That technicality concluded, Jessica turned her attention back to Ryan, who looked as comfortable and settled in the kitchen as though he had been there a million times. 'Will you come? Jamie's never been into Christmas, but I'll make her stick up a tree, and it'll be festive with a turkey and all the trimmings!'

'I'm sure he'll think about it. Just stop nagging him, Jess!' Jamie was pretty sure that she could convince Ryan to ignore her sister's rantings. He was a guy who was in great demand. The last thing he would want to do would be to sit around a small pine table in a kitchen and dine on a turkey reluctantly cooked by his secretary. Just the thought of it made her shiver in nervous apprehension.

'It's wonderful the way you can answer on my behalf.' Ryan grinned at Jamie, who scowled back at him. 'It's probably why we work so well together. You know just when to read my mind.'

'Ha-ha. Very funny.'

'But she's right.' He stood up and glanced at Jessica. 'I'll think about it and let Jamie know.'

'Or you could let me know. I'll give you my mobile number and you can get in touch any time at all. No need to go through Jamie.'

He left five minutes later and Jamie sagged. The peace of having her sister upstairs safely in bed was greatly diminished by the nasty tangle of thoughts playing in her mind.

Not only had Ryan found out more about her in the space of an hour than he had in eighteen months, but she was now facing the alarming prospect that, having wedged his foot through the door, it would be impossible to get him to remove it.

Everything that had always been so straightforward had now been turned on its head.

And what if the man decided to descend on them for Christmas lunch?

Apprehension sizzled in her and, alongside that very natural apprehension, something else, something even more worrying, something that closely resembled...anticipation.

# CHAPTER THREE

CHRISTMAS'S rapid approach brought a temporary lull in the usual relentless work-ethic. Ryan Sheppard made a very good Christmas boss. He entered into the spirit of things by personally supervising the decorations and cracking open champagne at six every evening for whoever happened to be around in the countdown to the big day. Extra-long lunch hours shopping were tactfully overlooked. On Christmas Eve, work was due to stop at twelve and the rest of the day given over to the Secret Santa gift exchanges and an elaborate buffet lunch which would be prepared by Ryan's caterers.

On the home front, Jamie was stoically putting up with a sister who had decided to throw herself into the party season with gay abandon. She tagged along to all the Christmas parties to which Jamie had been invited, flirted outrageously with every halfway decent-looking bachelor, and in the space of a week and a half collected more phone numbers than Jamie had in her address book. There was, ominously, no mention of Greg. If they were in contact, it certainly wasn't via the landline. Jamie had stopped asking because the response of tear-filled eyes, followed by an angry sermon about the valuable space for which she was still searching, was just too much of a headache.

A tree had been erected and Jessica had enthusiastically

begun helping with the lights, but like a child, had become bored after fifteen minutes, leaving Jamie to complete the task. Clothes were left strewn in unlikely places and were retrieved with an air of self-sacrifice whenever Jamie happened to mention the state of the house. The consequence of this was that Jamie's peaceful existence was now a round-the-clock chore of tidying up behind her sister and nagging.

Of course, Jamie knew that she would have to sit her sister down and insist on knowing when she intended to return to Scotland, but like a coward she hid behind the Christmas chaos and decided to shelve all delicate discussions until Boxing Day at the very least.

There was also the hurdle of Christmas day to get through. Ryan had, totally unexpectedly, accepted Jessica's foolish invitation to lunch and, with the prospect of three people cutting into a turkey that would be way too big, Jamie had invited several other members of staff to come along if they weren't doing anything.

Three guys from the software department had taken her up on the invitation, as well as a couple of her girlfriends whom she had met at the gym when she had first arrived in London.

Jamie anticipated an awkward lunch, but when she mentioned that to her sister, Jessica had smiled brightly and assured her that there was no need to worry.

'I'm a party animal!' she had announced. 'I can make any gathering go with a bang, and I've got loads of party hats and crackers and stuff. It'll be a blast! So much better than last year, which was a deadly meal round at the in-laws'. I can't wait to fill Greg in when the last guest leaves.'

'I'm surprised you even care what he thinks,' Jamie had said and was vaguely reassured when her sister had gone bright red.

Not that she had dwelled on that for any length of time.

Most of her mind for the past week had been taken up with the prospect of Ryan descending on her house for Christmas lunch.

And now the day had finally arrived. It came with dark, leaden skies and a general feeling of anticlimax; although some snow had been forecast, it appeared to be in the process of falling everywhere else but in London.

From downstairs came the thud of music, a compilation of songs which Jessica had prepared during her spare time. Peace seemed a distant dream. At eight-thirty, Jamie had thoroughly cleaned the bathroom, which had been taken over by her sister in a series of undercover assaults, so that each day slightly more appeared on the shelf and in the cabinet.

Now, sitting and staring at her reflection in the mirror, Jamie wondered how much longer she would be able to cope with a very hyper Jessica.

Then she thought about her outfit: a long-sleeved black dress that, she knew, would look drab against the peacock-blue of Jessica's mini skirt and her high wedges that would escalate her height to six feet.

By the time the first guest arrived, Jamie was already settling into her role of background assistant to her life-and-soul-of-the-party sister.

Every nerve in her body was tuned to the sound of the doorbell, but when Ryan eventually appeared, she was in the kitchen, as it happened, doing various things with the meal. Outside alcohol was steadily being consumed and Jessica was flirting, dancing and enjoying the limelight, even though the guys concerned were the sort of highly intelligent eccentrics she would ordinarily have dismissed as complete nerds.

The sound of his voice behind her, lazy and amused, zapped her like a bolt of live electricity and she leapt to her feet and spun around, having been peering worriedly into the oven.

'Well,' he drawled, walking into the kitchen and peering underneath lids at the food sitting on the counter, 'looks like the party's going with a swing.'

'You're here.'

'Did you think that I wasn't going to turn up?' Since the last time he had seen her in jeans and a tee-shirt, he had found himself doing quite a bit of thinking about her. As expected, she had mentioned nothing about her sister when she had been at work, which didn't mean that their working relationship had remained the same. It hadn't. Something subtle had altered, although he had a feeling that that just applied to him. She had been as efficient, as distant and as perfectly polite as ever.

'I'm nothing if not one-hundred-percent reliable.' He held out a carrier bag. 'Champagne.'

Flustered, she kept her eyes firmly on his face, deliberately avoiding the muscular legs encased in pair of black trousers and the way those top two undone buttons of his cream shirt exposed the shadow of fine, dark hair.

'Thanks.' She reached out for the carrier bag and was startled when from behind his back he produced a small gift-wrapped box. 'What's this?'

'A present.'

'I'm still working my way through the bottle of perfume you gave me last year.' She wiped her hands and then began opening the present.

Her mouth went dry. She had been privy to quite a few of his gifts to women. They ranged from extravagant bouquets of flowers to jewellery to trips to health spas. This, however, was nothing like that. In the small box was an antique butterfly brooch and she picked it up, held it up to the light and then set it back down in its bed of tissue paper before raising her eyes to his.

'You bought me a butterfly,' she whispered.

'I noticed that you had a few on your mantelpiece in the sitting room. I guessed you collect them. I found this one at an antique shop in Spitalfields.'

'It's beautiful, but I can't accept it.' She thrust it at him and turned away, her face burning.

'Why not?'

'Because…because…'

'Because you don't collect them?'

'I do, but…'

'But it's yet another of those secrets of yours that you'd rather I knew nothing about?'

'It just isn't appropriate,' Jamie told him stiffly. In her head, she pictured him roaming through a market, chancing upon the one thing he knew would appeal to her, handing over not a great deal of cash for it, but it never took much to win someone over. Except, she wasn't on the market to be won over. Nor was he on the market for doing anything but what came naturally to him—thinking outside the box. It was why he was such a tremendous success in his field.

'Okay, but you know that it's an insult to return a gift.' Ryan shrugged. 'I'm in your house. Consider it a small token of gratitude for rescuing a lonely soul from wandering the streets of London on Christmas day.'

'Oh, please.' Her breathing was shallow and she was painfully conscious of the fact that whilst outside the music was blaring, probably getting on the neighbours' nerves, inside the kitchen it was just the two of them locked in a strange intimacy that terrified her.

This was not what she wanted. She urgently reminded herself of Greg and her foolish love-sick infatuation with him before Jessica had arrived on the scene and stolen his heart.

But to insist on returning the brooch would risk making just too big a deal of it. It would alert him to the fact that for some reason his gesture bothered her.

'I haven't got anything for you,' she said uncomfortably.

'I'll live with that. Why butterflies?'

'My father was keen on them,' Jamie said awkwardly as another piece of information left her and travelled across to him. 'Mum told us a lot about him. He loved to travel. He particularly loved to travel to study insects, and out of all the insects butterflies interested him most. He liked the fact that there were so many different varieties of them and they came in so many different colours and shapes and sizes. Mum said that he figured they were a lot more interesting than the human species.'

Her voice and expression had softened as she lost herself in a memory that hadn't surfaced for years. 'So I started collecting them when I was a kid. I just keep the better ones on show, but I have a box upstairs full of silly plastic ones I had when I was growing up.' A sudden blast of music hit her as the kitchen door was pushed open and the moment of crazy reminiscing was lost with the appearance of Jessica, now wearing a shiny party hat and with her arm around one of the computer geeks, who looked thrilled to death with the leggy blonde clinging to him.

'Enjoy the attention, buddy.' Ryan grinned at his top software-specialist. 'But bear in mind the lady's married.'

Outside, the party of six guests had swelled to ten. Jessica had asked a couple of others 'to liven things up'. Bottles of wine were ranged on the sideboard in the living room and the chairs had been cleared away to create a dance floor of sorts.

Walking into the room was like walking into a disco, but

one where the decor was comprised of a Christmas tree in the corner and random decorations strung along the walls. In the centre of it all, Jessica was living up to her reputation as a party animal.

Swaying to the music with a drink in one hand and her eyes half-closed, she was the peacock, proud of her stupendous figure, which outranked even those of the gym queens at the side, and the cynosure of all male eyes.

When the beat went from fast to slow, Jamie looked away as Jessica draped herself over Ryan.

So what else had she expected? That he would actually be able to resist the allure of an available woman? A dull ache began in her head. She mingled and chatted and even half-heartedly danced with her colleague Robbie who charmed her with an enthusiastic conversation about something he was working on at the moment, something guaranteed to be bigger and better than anything else on the market.

While Ryan danced on with Jessica.

Several of the neighbours began popping in, drawn by the music. On either side, they were young, professional couples whom Jamie had glimpsed in passing. Now, she realised that they were people with whom she could easily become friendly, and the distraction was a blessing. It took her out of the living room and into the kitchen, where they congregated and compared notes on the neighbourhood.

She wasn't too sure how the matter of eating was going to be achieved. As expected, the bulk of the preparations had been left to her while her sister had stalked ineffectively around the kitchen with a glass of wine in her hand, sighing and making useless suggestions about what could be done to speed up the whole process. 'Dump the lot and order in a Chinese', had been one of her more ridiculous offerings, especially considering she had been the one to insist on the full turkey extravaganza.

Flushed from the heat in the kitchen, and nursing enough low-level resentment to sink a small ship, Jamie was fetching the wretched turkey out of the oven when Ryan's voice behind her nearly made her drop the hapless bird.

'You need a hand.'

Jamie carefully deposited the aluminium baking dish on the counter and glanced across to him.

'I'm fine. Thank you.'

'Just stating the obvious here, but martyrs aren't known to be the happiest people on the face of the earth.'

'I'm not being a martyr!' She turned to look at him, hacked off and grim. 'I was coerced into doing...*this*.' A sweeping gesture encompassed the kitchen, which looked as though it had been the target of a small explosion. 'So I'm doing it.'

'Exactly—you're being a martyr. If you didn't want to do all...*this*—' he mirrored her sweeping gesture '—then you shouldn't have.'

'Do you have any idea what my sister's like when she doesn't manage to get her own way?' Jamie cried with a hint of hysteria in her voice. 'Oh, no, of course you don't, because *you* haven't had years of her! Because *you* are only being shown the smiling, sexy side that leaves men breathless and panting.'

'My breathing's perfectly normal.' He rescued the potatoes and began searching around for other dishes, into which he began piling the food. 'Look, why don't you go and drag your sister in here and force her to give you a helping hand?'

Jamie opened her mouth to tell him just how silly his suggestion was—because Jessica never, but *never*, did anything she didn't want to do—and instead sighed wryly.

'That would come under the heading of "mission impossible".'

'In that case, I'm helping, whether you like it or not.'

'You're my boss. You're not supposed to be in here helping.'

'You're right, I am your boss—you are therefore obliged to do whatever I ask.'

Jamie couldn't help it. She went bright red at the unintended innuendo and was mortified when Ryan burst out laughing.

'Within reason, of course...' He raised his eyebrows in amusement. 'Although I gather from your sister that there wouldn't be any outraged boyfriend threatening to break my kneecaps if I decided to push the point...'

He was still grinning. *Laughing* at her. She turned away abruptly, knowing that the back of her neck was giveaway-red and that her hands were shaking as she poured gravy into the gravy boat and busied herself with the roast potatoes.

'Jessica shouldn't be talking about my private life!' she managed, on the verge of tears. Tears of pure frustration.

'She said that you didn't have a boyfriend,' Ryan said mildly. 'What's the big deal?'

'The *big deal* is that it's none of your business!'

'You know, it's dangerous to be so secretive. Makes other people even more intrigued.'

'There's nothing intriguing about my private life,' Jamie snapped. 'It's not nearly as glamorous or adventurous as *yours*.'

'If you really thought that my life was glamorous, exciting and adventurous, then you wouldn't be so disapproving—and don't deny that you disapprove. You admitted it yourself—you think I'm an unscrupulous womaniser with no morals.'

'I never said that!' She met his amused grin with a reluctant smile of her own. 'Okay, maybe I implied that you... Why are you being difficult, Ryan Sheppard?'

'What an outrageous accusation, Jamie Powell,' Ryan said piously. 'No one likes being accused of being exciting and adventurous.'

'I never said that. You're twisting my words.'

'You know, you may not be obvious in the way that your sister is, but when it comes to getting a man—and believe me, I know what I'm talking about—you have…'

'Stop! I don't want to hear what you're going to say.'

'Somehow, over the years, your sister has managed to destroy your self-confidence.'

'I have plenty of self-confidence. I work with you. You should know that.'

'Yes, you certainly do when it comes to the work front, but on an emotional level let's just say that I'm beginning to see you for the first time.' *And liking what I see*, he could have added.

Jamie didn't like the sound of that. She also didn't like the way his throwaway remarks were making her question herself. *Was* she lacking in self-confidence? Was he implying that she was emotionally stunted?

'You *were* going to help, or at least that's what you said. You never mentioned that you were going to play amateur psychologist. So can you get the plastic cups from the cupboard over here, and stop giving me lots of homespun advice? And I don't,' she burst out, unable to contain herself, 'have a boyfriend because I've never seen the need to grab anything that's available because it's better than nothing at all!'

She found that they were suddenly staring at each other with the music outside—a dull, steady throb—and the aromatic smells in the hot kitchen swirling around them like a seductive, heady incense.

'Good policy,' Ryan murmured, taking in the patches of heightened colour in her cheeks and the way her eyes glittered—nothing like the cool, composed woman he was so accustomed to working alongside.

'And if I *did* have a man in my life,' she heard herself continue, with horror, 'he certainly wouldn't be the sort of person who runs around breaking other people's kneecaps.'

'Because you can take care of yourself.'

'Exactly!'

'And you definitely wouldn't be drawn to a caveman.'

'No, I wouldn't.'

'So what *would* you be drawn to?'

'Thoughtful. Sensitive. Caring.' With sudden alarm, she realised that somewhere along the line she had breached her own defences and allowed emotion to take control over her careful reserve.

But she had just been so mad. After the nightmare challenge of having to cope with her sister landing on her doorstep with her uninvited emotional baggage, and the chaos of having to deal with a Christmas lunch that had been foisted upon her, the thought of Jessica getting drunk and gossiping about her behind her back to her boss had been too much.

'I'm sorry,' she apologised stiffly, turning away and gathering herself.

*Not so fast*, Ryan wanted to say, *not when you've set my mind whirring.*

'For what?' As in the office, they seemed to work well together in the kitchen, with Jamie dealing with the food while Ryan efficiently piled the dirty dishes into the sink. 'For happening to have feelings?'

'There's a time and a place for everything.' Her voice was definitely back in full working order; frankly, if he chose to snigger at her behind her back at her woefully single state, then that was his prerogative. 'My kitchen on Christmas day definitely isn't either.'

'We could always alter the time and the venue. Like I

said, it's important for a boss to know what's going on in his secretary's life.'

'No. It isn't.' But of course he was teasing her and she half smiled, pleased that the normal order was restored.

Watching her, Ryan felt a sudden kick of annoyance. Would he have taken her out, maybe for dinner, in an attempt to prise beneath that smooth exterior? He didn't know, but he did realise that she was quietly and efficiently re-erecting her barriers.

Oozing sympathy, he turned her to face him, his hands resting lightly on her shoulders. 'People tell me that I'm a terrific listener,' he murmured persuasively. 'And I pride myself on being able to read other people.'

Jamie opened her mouth to utter something polite but sarcastic, and instead found herself dry-mouthed and blinking owl-like as he stared down at her. He really was sinfully, shamefully beautiful, she thought, dazed.

'And I didn't mean to offend you by suggesting that your outgoing, in-your-face sister might have been ruinous on your levels of self-confidence. I'm just guessing that you've been messed up in the past.'

'What are you talking about?' she whispered.

'Some loser broke your heart and you haven't been able to move on.'

Jamie drew her breath in sharply and pulled away from him, breaking the mesmeric spell he had temporarily cast over her. She pressed herself against the kitchen counter, hands behind her back.

'What did my sister say to you?'

Ryan had been fishing in the dark. He had been curious—understandably curious, he thought. In his world, women were an open book. It was refreshing to be challenged with one who wasn't. Now, he felt like the angler who, against all odds, has managed to land a fish.

She was as white as a sheet, and although she was trying hard to maintain a semblance of composure he knew that it was a struggle.

So who the hell was the guy who had broken her heart?

'This is ridiculous!' Abruptly, Jamie turned away and began gathering a stack of plates in her hands. They were all disposable paper plates because there was no way that she would be left standing by the sink after the last guest had departed, washing dishes while her sister retired to bed for some well-deserved sleep after copious alcohol consumption.

'Trust me, he wasn't worth it.' Ryan was enraged on her behalf.

'I really don't want to talk about this.'

'Sometimes those caring, sharing types can prove to be the biggest bastards on the face of the earth.'

'How would *you* know?' She spun round to look at him with flashing eyes. 'For your information, the caring, sharing guy in question was the nicest man I've ever met.'

'Not that nice, if he trampled over you. What was it? Was he married? Stringing you along by pretending he was single and unattached? Or maybe promising to dump his wife who didn't understand him? Or was he seeing other women on the side? Underneath that caring, sharing exterior, was he living it up behind your back—was that it? Word of advice here—men who get a tear in their eye during sad movies and insist on cooking for you because they get home at five every evening don't necessarily have the monopoly on the moral high-ground. You've got to let it go, Jamie.'

'Let it go and start doing *what*?' she heard herself asking as she gripped the paper plates in her hand.

'Join the dating scene.'

'So that I can...?'

'Finish what you were going to say.' Ryan moved to block

her exit. 'Like I said, there's never any need for you to think that you can't speak freely to me. We're not in a work environment here. Say whatever you want to say.'

'Okay, here's what I want to say—whatever hang-ups I have, there's no way I would join any dating scene if there was a possibility of bumping into men like you, Ryan Sheppard!'

Ryan's lips thinned. She was skating dangerously close to thin ice but hadn't he invited her to be frank and open with him? Hadn't he insisted? On the other hand, he hadn't expected her to throw his kindness back in his face. He was giving her the benefit of his experience, warning her of the perils of the sort of smiley, happy jerk she claimed to like, providing her with a shoulder to cry on—and in return...?

'Men *like me*?' he enquired coldly.

'Sorry, but you did ask me to be honest.'

Ryan forced himself to offer her a smile. 'I don't lead women up the garden path and break their hearts,' he gritted.

'No one led me up a garden path!' But she had said too much. She was hot, bothered and flustered and regretting every mis-spoken word. 'We should get this food out there before it all goes stone cold,' she carried on.

'In other words, you want this conversation terminated.'

Jamie avoided his eyes and maintained a mute silence. 'I apologise if I said certain things that you might construe as insulting,' she eventually offered in a stilted voice, and he scowled. 'And I'd appreciate it if we could just leave it here and not mention this conversation again.'

'And what if I don't agree to that?'

Jamie looked at him calmly, composure regained, but at a very high cost to her treasured peace of mind. 'I don't think I could work happily alongside you otherwise. I'm a very private person and it would be impossible for me to function if I feared that you might start...' *Finding my life a subject for conjecture*.

'Start what?'

'Trying to get under my skin because you find it amusing.'

Her eyes weren't quite brown, Ryan caught himself thinking. There were flecks of green and gold there that he had never noticed before. But then again, why would he have noticed, when she kept her eyes studiously averted from his face most of the time?

He stood aside with ill humour and pushed open the door for her and immediately they were assailed with the sound of raised voices and laughter. While they had been in the kitchen, a cabaret had obviously been going on and, sure enough, Jessica had pulled one of the tables to the side of the room and was doing her best to hang some mistletoe from the light on the ceiling in the middle of the room, while surrounded by a circle of guests who were clearly enjoying the spectacle.

Food was greeted with clapping and cheering. The neighbours made a half-hearted attempt to head back to their houses, but were easily persuaded to stay. All hands hit the deck and more drink surfaced while, to one side, Jamie watched proceedings. And Ryan watched Jamie, out of the corner of his eye. Watched as she pretended to join in, although her smile was strained whenever she looked across to her flamboyant sister. Surrounded by an audience, Jessica was like one of the glittering baubles on the Christmas tree.

It was nearly five-thirty by the time the food had been depleted and Jamie began the laborious process of clearing.

Exhaustion felt like lead weights around her ankles and she knew that her tiredness had nothing to do with the task of making Christmas lunch. It was of the mental variety and that was a much more difficult prospect to shake off.

Talking to Ryan in the kitchen, exploding in front of him like an unpredictable hand grenade, had drained her and she knew why.

For the first time in her life, she had allowed herself to let go. The result had been terrifying and if she could only have taken it all back then she would have.

Sneaking a glance to her right, she looked at him. He had dutifully helped clear away dishes, along with everyone else minus her sister, and now he was laughing and joking with the guys from his office. Doubtless he had completely forgotten their conversation, while she…

She watched as, giggling and swaying her hips to the rhythm of the music, Jessica began beckoning him across to where she had positioned herself neatly underneath the precariously hanging bunch of mistletoe.

Ryan looked far from thrilled at the situation and for once Jamie was not going to rush in and try and save her sister from herself. If Jessica wanted to fool around in her quest to find herself, then so be it. Jamie had spent a lifetime standing behind her, desperately attempting to rescue her from her own waywardness.

Lord, in the process she had even forgotten how to take care of her own emotional needs! She had bottled everything up; how pathetic was it that the one time she actually managed to release the cork on that bottle it was with her boss, the least appropriate or suitable person when it came to shoulder-lending! He went through women like water and had probably never had a decent conversation of any depth with any of the bimbos who clung to him like superglue. Yet she had directed all her angst at him—in an unstoppable stream of admissions that she knew she would eternally live to regret.

She was turning away, heading for the sanctuary of the kitchen, when she happened to glance through the window.

No one had bothered to draw the curtains and there, stepping out of his car—the same old battered Land Rover which he had had ever since she had first started working for him— was her brother-in-law.

For a few seconds, Jamie could scarcely believe her eyes. She hadn't seen Greg for absolutely ages. She had fled with her pride and dignity intact, determined to keep her love for him firmly under wraps while he got on with the business of showering Jessica with his devotion. Since then, she hadn't trusted herself to be anywhere near him, because she would rather have died than to let her secret leap out of its box.

The years hadn't changed him. He was turning now to slot his key into the lock; everything about him was surprisingly the same. His fair hair still flopped over his eyes and he still carried himself with the same lanky awkwardness that Jamie had once found so incredibly endearing. She could make all that out even under the unsatisfactory street lighting.

She peeled her eyes away for a fraction of a second to see Jessica reaching out to put her hands on Ryan's shoulders. In a second, Jamie thought with a surge of panic two things would happen: Greg would turn around and look straight through the window, and Jessica would close her eyes and plant a very public kiss on Ryan's mouth.

Galvanised, she sprinted across the room. If she had had time to think about it, she wasn't sure whether she would have followed through, but as it was she acted purely on instinct, fired by a driving need to make sure that her sister didn't completely blow the one chance she had in life of true happiness—because Greg was as good as it would ever get for Jessica.

She pulled Ryan around and saw his surprise mingled with relief to have been spared the embarrassment of having to gently but firmly turn Jessica away. Janie reached up and curled her hand around his neck, and even at the height of her spontaneity she was stomach clenchingly aware of the muscularity of his body.

'Wha…?'

'Mistletoe!' Jamie stated. 'We're under it. So we'd better do what tradition demands.'

Ryan laughed softly under his breath and curved his hand around her waist.

As far as days went, this one was turning out to be full of unexpected twists and turns; he couldn't remember enjoying himself so much for a very long time indeed.

He didn't know what had brought about this change in Jamie but he liked it. He especially liked the feel of her body as it softened against his. He felt her breasts push against his chest. She smelled of something clean and slightly floral and her full mouth was parted, her eyes half-closed. It was the most seductive thing he had ever experienced in his life.

Who was he to resist? He gathered her to him and kissed her, a long, deep kiss that started soft and slow and increased tempo until he was losing himself in it, not caring if they were spectator sport.

He surfaced when she twisted out of his arms and turned around. Reluctantly, Ryan followed her gaze, as did everyone else in the room, to the blond-haired man standing in the doorway with an overnight bag in one hand and a bunch of straggling flowers in the other.

# CHAPTER FOUR

RYAN looked at his watch and scowled. The offices were pretty bare of staff, just the skeleton lot who got more of a kick at work at their computers, creating programmes and testing games, than they did in their own homes.

Not the point.

The point was that it was now ten fifteen and Jamie should have been in one hour and fifteen minutes ago. Christmas day had come and gone. Boxing Day had come and gone. She hadn't booked any holiday time beyond that.

He swung his jean-clad legs off his desk, sending a pile of paperwork to the ground in the process, and stalked across the floor-to-ceiling window so that he could look outside and, bad-tempered, survey the grey, bleak London streets which were eerily quiet in this part of the city.

He was still reeling from the events of Christmas day, much to his enduring annoyance. He had gone to satisfy a simple and one-hundred-percent understandable curiosity and had got the equivalent of a full round in a boxing ring—starting with that little conversation in the kitchen with Jamie, followed by her kissing him and culminating in the appearance of the man at the door.

It had been a comedy in three acts, except Ryan couldn't be further from laughing.

He could still feel the warmth of her mouth against his.

The memory of it had eaten into his Boxing Day, turning him into an ill-tempered guest at the party given by his god-child's parents, a party which had become a tradition of sorts over the years and which he had always enjoyed.

Glancing at his watch again, he was beginning to wonder whether Jamie had decided to jettison work altogether. A week ago such an act of rebellion bordering on mutiny would have been unthinkable, but in the space of a heartbeat all preconceived ideas about his quiet, efficient, scrupulously reserved secretary had been blown to smithereens.

He was in the process of debating whether to call her when his office door was pushed open and there she was, unbuttoning her sensible black coat and tugging at the scarf around her neck.

'This is getting to be a habit,' Ryan grated, striding back to his desk and resuming his position with the chair pushed back and his long legs extended to the side. 'And don't bother to try and tell me stories about delays on the Underground.'

'Okay. I won't.'

Things had irreparably changed. Over a fraught day and a half, Jamie had resigned herself to that and come to the conclusion that the only way she could continue working for Ryan was if she put every single unfortunate personal conversation they had had behind her. Lock them away in a place from where they couldn't affect her working life. And the kiss…

The horror of that moment and the fact that it still clawed away in her mind was something that would have to be locked away as well.

All the same, she was having a hard time meeting his eyes as she relieved herself of her coat, gloves and scarf and deposited the bundle of post on his desk, along with her laptop computer, which she switched on in an increasingly tense silence.

'Look, I'm sorry I'm late,' she eventually said when it seemed like the silence would stretch to infinity. 'It's not going to be a habit, and you know that I'm more than happy to work late tonight to make up for the lost time.'

'I can't have unreliability in my employees—beside the point, whether you're happy to work late or not.'

'Yes, well, I hoped that you might understand given the fact that half the country is still on holiday.' She couldn't prevent the edge of rebelliousness from creeping into her voice, but the past day and a half had been beyond the pale and nothing seemed to be changing. Greg had appeared on the doorstep, putting a swift end to proceedings on Christmas day. Who on earth had been willing to listen to Jessica's histrionics—because her sister had had absolutely no qualms about letting the rest of the world into her problems. Apparently no one. There had been a half-hearted attempt on the part of some to try and clear the sitting room but within forty-five minutes they had all dispersed—including Ryan, although in his case Jamie had had to push him out of the door. In true intrusive style, he had been sharply curious and more than happy to stick around. Jamie was having none of it.

And since then her house, the bastion of her peace of mind, had become the arena for warfare.

Jamie now knew far too much about the state of her sister's marriage for her liking.

With nowhere else to stay, and determined to put things right, Greg had now taken up residence in the sitting room, much to Jessica's disgust. Everything was chaotic and, although Jamie had sat them both down and gently advised them that perhaps sorting out their marriage problems was something that could be better done in their own home, there seemed to be no glimmer of light on the horizon.

Jessica was standing firm about needing her space and

Greg was quietly persistent that he wasn't going to give up on them because she was having a temporary blip.

And now Ryan was sitting stony-faced in front of her and she wasn't sure that she could bear much more.

'Can we get on with some work?' she half pleaded. 'There are a few contracts that you need to look at. I've emailed them to you, and I think Bob Dill has finally completed that software package he's been working on.'

Ryan discovered that he had been waiting to see how things would play out when she showed up for work. Now, it dawned on him that she intended to bury the whole Christmas episode, pretend none of it had ever happened.

He steepled his fingers under his chin and looked at her thoughtfully. 'Yes,' he agreed, tilting his head to one side. 'We certainly could have a look at those contracts, but that's not imperative. Like you said, half the country's still recovering from Christmas.' It was interesting to see the way she flushed at the mention of Christmas. 'Which brings me to the subject of Christmas day.'

'I'd rather we didn't talk about that,' Jamie told him quickly.

'Why not?'

'Because...'

'You find it uncomfortable?'

'Because...' Flustered, Jamie raised her eyes to his and found herself consumed with embarrassing, graphic recall of that kiss they had shared. She had never, in the end, even shared a kiss with Greg. All through that time she had dreamed about him, the closest she had come to actually touching him was on the odd occasion when his hand had accidentally brushed hers or when he had given her a brotherly peck on the cheek.

So why had she spent her every waking hour thinking about Ryan Sheppard, when she had happily worked alongside him for ages and always managed to keep him at a healthy distance? Was she so emotionally stunted that she had just switched infatuation? Did she have some kind of insane inclination to fancy the men she worked for? *No!* Jamie refused to concede any such thing. 'Because we have a perfectly good working relationship and I don't want my private life to start intruding on that.'

'Too bad. It already has.'

He abruptly leaned forward and Jamie automatically pressed herself back into her chair.

'And,' he continued remorselessly, 'it's already affecting your working life. That guy who appeared on your door-step…'

'Greg,' Jamie conceded with reluctance. 'Jessica's hus-band.'

'Right. Greg. He's staying with you, is he?'

Jamie flushed and nodded. She looked wistfully at her computer.

'And you have no objections to having your house turned into a marriage counselling centre?'

'Of course I object to it! It's an absolute nightmare.'

'But they're still under your roof.'

'I don't see the point of discussing any of this.'

'The point is it's affecting your life and you can't sepa-rate the strands of your private life from your working life. You look exhausted.'

'Thank you very much.'

'So what are you going to do about it?'

Jamie sighed with frustration and shot him a simmer-ing, mutinous look from under her lashes. Ryan Sheppard had a restless, curious mind. He could see things and ap-proach them from different angles with a tenacity that al-ways seemed to pay dividends. Where one person might look at a failing company and walk away, he looked and then looked a bit harder, and mentally began picking it apart until he could work out how to put it back together in a way that benefited him. Right now he was curious and, whilst she could hardly blame him, she had no intention of becoming his pet project.

But she grudgingly had to concede that he had a point when he said that the strands of her life were interwoven. She had shown up late for work because she had slept through her alarm, and she had slept through her alarm because Greg and Jessica had been engaged in one of their furious, long-winded arguments until the early hours of the morning. The muffled sound of their voices had wafted up the stairs and into her bedroom and she just hadn't been able to get to sleep.

Something in her stirred. She had never been a person to share her problems. Deep ingrained into her psyche was the notion that her problems belonged to her and no one else. It seemed suddenly tempting to offload a little.

'What *can* I do about it?' she muttered, fiddling with her pen.

'I can immediately think of one solution—kick them both out.'

'That's not an option. I'm not about to kick my sister out when she's come to me for help and support. Believe me, I know all of Jessica's failings. She can be childish and badly behaved and irresponsible, but in times of crisis she needs to know that she can turn to me.'

'She's a grown adult. She's fully capable of helping and supporting herself.' He was beating his head against a brick wall; he could see that. Lazily, he allowed his eyes to rove over her body, finally coming to rest of that full, downturned mouth. Out of the blue, he felt himself begin to harden and he abruptly looked away. Good God. It was as though his body was suddenly possessed of a mind of its own.

'You've met my sister. You can't really believe that.' Jamie smiled to lighten the mood, but Ryan's eyes remained grimly serious on her.

'Because you took her on as your responsibility at a young age doesn't mean that you're condemned to stick to the program till the day you die, Jamie.'

'My mother made me promise that I'd be there for her. I... You don't understand. I think of my mother asking me to make sure that I looked after Jessica, and my hands are tied. I couldn't let her down. And I couldn't let Greg down.'

Ryan stared at her and noticed the way she glanced away from him, offering him her delicate profile, noticed the way her skin coloured.

He thought back to that kiss, the way she had pulled him towards her and curved her small, supple body against his, offering her lips to him. And then Greg's appearance at the door, like an apparition stepping out of the wintry depths. His brain was mentally doing the maths.

'Why would that be?' he asked casually. Her eyes weren't on him as he strolled towards the coffee machine, which was just one of the many appliances he kept in his vast office to make life a bit easier when he was working through the night. He handed her a mug of coffee and Jamie absent-mindedly took it. It was her first cup of coffee of the morning and it tasted delicious.

'It's pretty hard on him,' she confessed, watching as Ryan rolled his chair towards her and took up position uncomfortably close. In fact, their knees were almost touching.

'Explain.'

'He's doing his best with my sister. She isn't the easiest person in the world. He's very calm and gentle but she more than makes up for it.'

'Calm and gentle,' Ryan mused thoughtfully.

'He's a vet. He has to be.'

'You worked for him, didn't you?'

Jamie shrugged and said defensively, 'I did, a million years ago. The point is, he likes talking to me. I think it helps.'

'He likes talking to you because you're a trained marriage counsellor?' Ryan found himself stiffening with instant dislike for the man. He had known types like him—the kind, caring, calm, gentle types who thought nothing of taking advantage of any poor sap with a tendency to mother.

'No, Ryan. I'm not a *trained marriage counsellor*, but I listen to what he says and I try to be constructive.'

'And yet you haven't constructively told the pair of them to clear off because they're wrecking your life. My guess is that your mother wouldn't like to think that you're sacrificing the quality of your life for the sake of your sister.'

'Not all of us are selfish!'

'I'd call it practical. Why did you leave?'

'I beg your pardon?'

'Why did you leave your job working for the gentle vet?'

'Oh.' Jamie could feel herself going bright red as she fished around for a suitable reply.

'Was it the weather?' Ryan asked helpfully as he drew his own conclusions.

'I... Um, I guess the weather did have something to do with my decision. And also...' Coherent thought returned to her at long last. 'Jessica was old enough to stand on her own two feet and I thought it was a good time to start exploring pastures new, so to speak...'

'And, I guess, with your sister marrying the caring, sharing vet.'

'Yes. There was someone to look after her.'

'But I suppose you must have built up some sort of empathetic relationship with our knight in shining armour who rescued you from your sister,' Ryan encouraged speculatively. His eyes were sharp and focused, noting every change of expression on her face. She had a remarkably expressive face. He wondered how he could ever have missed that, but then again this was new territory for both of them.

'Could you please stop being derogatory about Greg?'

Ryan glanced down. There was no need for him to ask her why. He already knew. Had she actually been in love with the guy? Of course she had. It was written all over her face. And that, naturally, would have been why she had fled the scene of the crime, so to speak. Had they slept together?

Ryan found that that was a thought he didn't like, not at all. Nor did he care for the fact that his conclusions were leading him inexorably in one direction.

That kiss she had given him, the kiss that had been playing on his mind for the past two days, had had its roots in something a lot more unsavoury than just a woman with a little too much wine in her system behaving out of character for the first time in her life.

She had seen Greg, and Greg had seen her, and she had succumbed to the oldest need in the world. The need to make another man jealous.

Had she been reminding Mr Vet of what he had missed? The sour taste of being used rose in Ryan's throat. It was a sensation he had never experienced. She had wanted to bury the incident between them. As far as he was concerned, he would fetch the shovels and help her.

'He doesn't have anyone else to talk to,' Jamie was saying now. 'He's an only child and I don't think his parents really ever approved of the marriage. At least, not from what Jessica's told me over the years. So he can't go to them for advice, and I suppose I'm the obvious choice to confide in because she's my sister and I know her.'

'And what pearls of wisdom have you thrown his way?' Ryan couldn't help the heavy sarcasm in his voice but Jamie barely seemed to notice. She was, he thought, too wrapped up in thoughts of her erstwhile lover.

She might complain about her house being invaded but chances were that she was loving every second of it.

'I've told him that he's just got to persevere.' She smiled drily. 'Who else is going to take Jessica off my hands?'

'Who else indeed?' Ryan murmured. 'So there's no end to this in sight?'

'Not at the moment. Not unless I change the locks on the front door.' Making light of the situation was about the only way Jamie felt she could deal with it, but her smile was strained. 'Things will sort themselves out when Christmas is done and dusted. I mean, Greg will have to return to work. He said that he's got cover at the moment but I think his animals will start missing him!'

Ryan stood up and began prowling through the office. Usually as easy-going and as liberal minded as the next man, he was outraged at the nagging, persistent notion that he had been manipulated to make another man jealous. He was also infuriatingly niggled at the thought that Jamie might have slept with the vet. Naturally, people were entitled to live their lives the way they saw fit, but nevertheless...

Could he have been that mistaken about her?

'And what if things don't sort themselves out over Christmas?'

'I prefer to be optimistic.'

'Maybe,' Ryan said slowly, 'what they both need is time on their own.'

'Do you think I haven't suggested that?' Jamie asked him sharply. 'Jessica has dug her heels in. She doesn't want to return to Scotland and Greg doesn't want to leave without her.'

'Wise man.' Ryan's voice was shrewd. 'She's an unexploded time bomb.'

'I don't see how this is helping anything,' Jamie inserted briskly. 'Course it's nice to talk, and thank you very much for listening, but…'

'Maybe they need time on their own away from Scotland. Being in the home environment might just pollute the situation.' He had absolutely zero knowledge when it came to psychoanalysis but he was more than happy to make it up as he went along.

A plan of action was coming to him and he liked it. More to the point, it was a plan that would benefit them both. He sat on the edge of his desk and looked at her.

'Pollute the situation?'

'You know what I'm getting at.'

'Where else are they going to go? I can't think that Greg has enough money to move them into a hotel indefinitely. Besides, that would only make things worse, being cooped up in a room twenty-four-seven. There would be a double homicide. Actually, it wouldn't get that far. Jessica would refuse to go along with the plan.'

Ryan made an indistinct but sympathetic noise and gave her time to consider the horror of housing a bickering couple for the indefinite future, because the caring vet might just prioritise his marriage over the animals pining for him in his absence.

'What a hellish prospect for you.' He egged the mixture as he scooted his chair back to his desk. 'I'll bet your sister doesn't exercise a lot of restraint when it comes to airing her opinions either.'

'That's why I was late,' Jamie glumly confessed. 'They were arguing into the early hours of the morning and I could hear them from my bedroom so I couldn't fall asleep. I was so tired this morning that I slept through the alarm.'

'I'm going to be joining my family in the Caribbean day

after tomorrow. Stunning house in the Bahamas, if I say so myself,' he murmured and Jamie nodded.

'Yes. I know—I booked the tickets, remember? Lucky you. I know what I should be covering while you're away but there are a couple of things you'll need to look at before you go. I'll make sure that I bring them in for you by the end of the day. Also, if your visit over runs, shall I get Graham to chair the shareholders' meeting on the eighth?'

Ryan had no intention of becoming bogged down in point-less detail. He frowned pensively up at the ceiling, his hands linked behind his head, then startled her by sitting forward suddenly and placing his hands squarely on his desk.

'Just an idea, but I think you should accompany me on my trip.'

For a few seconds Jamie wasn't sure that she had heard him correctly. Her mind was still half taken up with the technicalities of rearranging his schedule should he remain out of the country for longer than anticipated. There were a number of prickly clients who liked to deal with Ryan and Ryan alone, as the mover and shaker of the company. They would have to be coaxed into a replacement.

'Jamie!' Like a magician summoning someone out of a trance, Ryan snapped his fingers and she started and sur-faced to slowly consider the suggestion he had posed.

'Accompany you?' she repeated in confusion.

'Why not? From where I'm sitting it sure beats the hell out of having to duck for cover from verbal missiles in your own house.' He stood up, began pacing through his office. He peered down at the stack of papers he had inadvertently sent flying to the ground earlier, decided to tidy it all up later and stepped over them to make his way to his coffee machine so that he could help himself to another mug of coffee.

'Also,' he offered, 'your sister and the vet might benefit from not having you around. I know you probably feel obliged to offer free advice, but sometimes the last thing people need in a time of crisis is a do-gooder trying to sort things out on their behalf.'

'I am not a *do-gooder* trying to sort anything out!' Jamie denied heatedly and Ryan shrugged.

'Okay, maybe the vet would be better off fighting his own battles without relying on his trusty ex-assistant to join in the fray.'

Looked at from every angle, that was an insulting observation, but before Jamie could splutter into more heated defence he was continuing in a thoughtful voice,

'And if they both prefer to hang out their dirty laundry in neutral territory, and a hotel room is out of the equation, then your place is as good as any—without you in it. You'd be doing them a favour and you'd be doing yourself a favour. No more sleepless nights. No more war zones to be avoided. No more playing piggy-in-the-middle. Chances are that by the time you get back they will have resolved their differences and cleared off and your life can return to normal.'

The promise of normality dangled in front of Jamie's eyes like a pot of gold at the end of a rainbow. She was in danger of forgetting what it was like.

'I couldn't possibly intrude on your family holiday.' She turned him down politely. 'But,' she said slowly, 'it *might* be a good idea if I weren't around. Perhaps—and I know this is very last-minute—I could book a few days' holiday?'

'Out of the question.' Ryan swallowed a mouthful of coffee and eyed her over the rim of the mug.

'But if I can leave here to go to the Caribbean, then surely I could leave to go somewhere else?' The weather was immaterial. It was the prospect of putting distance between Jessica, Greg and herself that was so tantalising. The Far East sounded just about right, never mind the jet lag.

'You can come to the Caribbean because I could use you over there. As you know, I'm combining my holiday with the business trip to Florida to give that series of presentations on trying to get our computer technology into greener cars.'

He glanced at the papers lying on the ground and strolled over to roughly gather them up and dump them on his desk. 'Still, sadly, in a state of semi-preparation.' He indicated the papers with a sweeping gesture while Jamie looked at him, unconvinced. Ryan rarely gave speeches that were fully prepared. He was clever enough and confident enough to earn a standing ovation by simply thinking on his feet. His grasp of the minutest details to do with the very latest cutting-edge technology was legendary.

'You could consider it something of a working holiday. I could get up to speed with these presentations before I fly to Florida. And,' he added for good measure, 'it's not as though you haven't travelled with me on business before...'

Which was a very valid reason for having her there— business. Of course, he was the first to acknowledge that it wasn't *exactly* the only reason for having her there. He genuinely thought that her presence in the house with her warring, uninvited guests was doing her no good whatsoever and there was also the small question of his curiosity; that was a little less easy to justify. But those recent revealing glimpses of her had roused his interest; why not combine his concern for her welfare with his semi-pressing need to get his presentations done and wrap them both up in a neat solution? Made sense.

He uneasily registered that there was a third reason. His mother and his sisters were relentlessly concerned with his moral welfare. His sisters had an annoying habit of bustling around him, trying to impose their opinions, and his mother specialised in meaningful chats about people who worked too hard.

Jamie would be a very useful buffer. There would be considerably less chance of being cornered if he made sure that she was floating somewhere in the vicinity whenever the going looked as though it might get dicey. Were he to be on his own, any attempt to excuse himself on the pretext of having to work would be thoroughly disregarded. With Jamie around, however, even his sisters would reluctantly be forced to keep a low profile in the name of simple courtesy.

'It's not the same.'

'Huh? What's not the same?'

'You're going to be with your family,' Jamie said patiently. 'Doing family stuff.' She wasn't entirely sure what that entailed. Family stuff, for her, had long meant stretches of tension and uncomfortable confrontations simmering just below the surface.

'Oh, they will already have done the family stuff over their turkey on Christmas day. They'll be desperate to see a new face and my mother won't stop thanking you for showing up. When my sisters get together, they revert to childhood. They giggle and swap clothes and waste hours applying make-up on each other while their men take over babysitting duties and countdown to when they can start on the rum cocktails. My mother says that it's impossible to get a serious word out of them when they're together. She'll love you.'

'Because I'm serious and boring?'

'Serious? Boring?' His dark eyes lingered on her and Jamie flushed and looked away. 'Hardly. In fact, having seen you over—'

'Who would cover for me in my absence?' she interrupted hastily just in case he decided to travel down

Memory Lane and dredge up her un-secretary-like behaviour on Christmas day.

Ryan dismissed that concern with a casual wave of his hand before giving her a satisfied smile.

'I haven't agreed to anything,' Jamie informed him. 'If you really think that you might need me there to help with the presentations...'

'Absolutely. You would be vital. You know I can't manage without you.'

'I don't want you to think that I'm in need of rescuing.' Sometimes that dark, velvety voice literally sent a shiver through her, even though she knew that it was in his nature to flirt. 'I don't. I might be in an awkward position just at the moment, but it's nothing that I wouldn't be able to handle.'

'I don't doubt that for a second,' Ryan dutifully agreed. 'You'd be doing *me* a favour.'

'Won't your family think it a bit strange for you to be dragging a perfect stranger along to their family celebrations?'

'Nothing fazes my family, believe me. Besides, what's one more to the tally?' He lowered his eyes. 'You have no excuse for refusing unless, of course, you can't bear to lose your role of personal adviser to the vet.'

'His name is Greg.' It was weird but Greg's effect on her was not what she had expected. She had always imagined that seeing him again would catapult her back to that time when she had been firmly in his power and used to weave innocent fantasies about him. She always thought that she would be reduced to blushing, stammering and possibly making a fool of herself but she hadn't. His allure had disappeared over the years. Now she just felt sorry for him and the situation in which her sister had placed him.

Watching her, Ryan felt a spurt of irritation that she had ignored the better part of his remark.

'Well?' he prodded. 'Do you think that you're too invaluable as unpaid counsellor to take a few days away from them? We'll be there for roughly five days. My sisters and their various other halves and children will leave at the beginning of the New Year. We will stay for a further three days until my conferences are due to begin and you can fly back to London when I fly to Florida. It's a lot to pass on, for the sake of being the vet's sounding board. Are you worried that he might not be able to survive this crisis without your input?'

'Of course I'm not!'

'Then why the hesitation?'

'I told you, I don't want to intrude.'

'And *I* told *you* you won't be intruding.'

'And I don't,' she belatedly pointed out, 'think that I'm invaluable to Greg. Like I said, I'm the only one he feels comfortable discussing all of this with.' Once upon a time, she might have been flattered, but now she was just impatient. 'But you're right—you're my boss. If I'm needed in a work capacity, then I'm more than happy to oblige. I'm very committed to my job, as you know.'

'I'm not a slave driver, Jamie. I won't be standing over you wielding a whip and making sure that I get my money's worth. Yes, we will do some work, but you'll have ample time to relax and de-stress. It'll be worth it to have you back in one piece when we resume work in January.'

Jamie nodded briskly. Whichever way it was wrapped up, Ryan was doing this for his own benefit. She had been inconsistent recently and he didn't like that. She was his efficient, well-run, well-oiled secretary and that was what he wanted back. It was why she was paid so handsomely. He could easily do whatever work he needed to do without her, but he had decided that her home life was interfering with her work life and, since her work life was the only thing that mattered to him, he was prepared to take her with him, away from the chaotic environment in which she now found herself.

'I'll see to the ticket, shall I?'

'First-class, with me. And sort out your replacement for while you're away. It's a quiet time. There shouldn't be anything that can't be handled by someone else for a short while.'

'Is there anything in particular you'd like me to read up on before we get out there? I wouldn't want to come unprepared.'

Ryan narrowed his eyes but her face was bland, helpful and utterly unreadable.

But that, he thought with a kick of satisfaction, was just an illusion, wasn't it? Strip away the mask and she was a hotbed of undiscovered fire.

'Nope. No reading to be done. But you might want to think about packing a few swimsuits. I'm going to insist that you enjoy yourself, like a good boss, and the house comes with an amazing pool. And don't look so appalled. When this is over, you're going to thank me.'

# CHAPTER FIVE

So far she *had* thanked him; on at least four separate occasions she had thanked him. She had thanked him variously for giving her the opportunity to enjoy 'such a wonderful place', for allowing her to relax in 'such amazing surroundings', it was a 'guilty pleasure'. She had thanked him the day before when he had shooed her off to explore the tiny nearby town with his sisters. She had thanked him when he had insisted that there was no need for her to wake at the crack of dawn with her laptop at the ready, just because he happened to need very little sleep and enjoyed working first thing in the mornings.

Her copious gratitude was getting on his nerves. He had been hoping to reacquaint himself with the intriguing new face he had glimpsed behind her polite, efficient mask but so far nothing. Although, to be fair, his plans for her to be a buffer between himself and any awkward conversations with his family members had been spectacularly successful and he was rarely in her company without some member of the troupe tagging along, unless they were specifically working.

They had established one of the downstairs rooms as a makeshift office but its air-conditioned splendour, whilst practical, felt sterile when through the windows they could see the stretching gardens, fragrant and colourful with tropical flowers which spilled their vibrancy under the palm trees. So they had migrated to one of the many shady areas of the wide veranda that circled the house. Which, in turn, meant that they were open to interruption, sometimes from one of the four kids belonging to two of his sisters who used outside as their playground. Sometimes from one of his sisters or—and he would have to fling his arms up and concede defeat when this happened—all three. And sometimes from his mother, who would appear with a tray of cold drinks and proceed to embark on a meandering conversation with Jamie to whom she seemed to have taken a keen liking. This was partly because Jamie was such a good listener and partly because his mother was, by nature, a sociable woman.

But when they were alone together, Jamie was not to be distracted from what she considered the primary purpose of her all-expenses-paid winter break. The very second they were together, their conversation focused entirely on work and on progressing a series of elaborate flip charts in which Ryan had no interest and probably wouldn't use anyway. She asked him innumerable questions about various technicalities to do with car manufacture, displaying an admirable breadth of knowledge, but, the minute he attempted to manoeuvre the conversation to something a little more interesting and a little more personal, she smiled, clammed up and he was obliged to return to the subject in hand.

Right now, the evening meal was finished. Two of his sisters were settling their children, who ranged in ages from three to six. They would be chivvying their husbands, Tom and Patrick, into performing a variety of duties and neither would be released until those duties were satisfactorily completed. His sisters were nothing if not bossy. Susie—older than him by two years, and seven months pregnant—had disappeared back to England with her husband. The house was at least becoming quieter. It would be quieter still in a day's time when his other sisters headed back to their various homes.

Enjoying the peace of the gardens and lost in his thoughts, Ryan was only aware of Jamie's presence nearby by the low murmur of her voice.

His ears instantly pricked up. He had assumed that she had retreated to the conservatory with a cup of coffee.

Naturally, he knew that it was beyond rude not to announce his presence by making some obvious noise—rustling a few leaves or launching into a coughing fit, perhaps.

Instead, he endeavoured to make as little noise as possible. Of course, if she looked around carefully, she would be able to spot him, although it was dark and this part of the extensive gardens was a lattice-work of trees and shrubbery leading to the infinity pool, which overlooked the sea from the cliff on which the house was majestically perched.

The breeze was warm and salty and ruffled the fronds of the palm trees, leaves and flowers like a very gentle caress. In the distance the sea stretched, flat and black, towards the horizon.

And down the small flight of stone steps Ryan spotted her, sitting by the pool in darkness, talking softly into her mobile phone.

If she needed to make a call, she could have used the landline; he had told her this at the very start. Instead, she had chosen to sneak off to the pool so that she could...*what*? Conduct a clandestine conversation? And with whom? The vet, of course.

His lips thinned and he sprinted down the steps, appearing in front of her so suddenly that she gave a little shriek and dropped the phone.

'Oh, dear. Did I startle you?' He bent to retrieve the mobile which lay in various pieces on the ground.

Jamie, half standing, scrabbled to get the phone from

him as he clicked various bits back together, put it to his ear, shook it and then shrugged. 'You got cut off. Sorry. And I think the phone might be broken.'

'What are you doing here?' Over the past three days she had contrived not to be alone in his presence at all. Away from the safety net of the office, she had felt vulnerable and threatened in this island paradise. There was just too much of him for her liking. Too much of him wearing shorts, going barefoot, bare chested, getting slowly bronzed. Too much of him lazing around, teasing his sisters, letting them boss him around and then rolling his eyes heavenwards so that one of them laughed and playfully smacked him. Too much of him being silly with the children who clearly adored him. Too much of him being a *man* instead of being her boss. It unnerved her.

'What are *you* doing here?' He threw the question back at her, then sat down on one of the wooden deck chairs and patted the one next to him so that she reluctantly joined him. 'If you needed to make a call, you know that you could have used the landline. I did tell you that.'

'Yes, well…' She could barely make him out. He was all shadows and angles, and rakish in his low-slung khaki shorts and an old tee-shirt. To see him, no one would have guessed that he was a multi-millionaire.

'Personal call, was it?' Ryan prompted, undeterred by her reluctance to talk. 'How are they back home? Still alive and kicking, or has you sister put the vet out of his misery? I'm thinking that if they had sorted out their differences and returned to Scotland in the throes of rekindled love you would have reported it back to me.'

The darkness enfolding them in its embrace lent an air of intimacy that Jamie found disturbing. In fact, her heart was beating like a hammer inside her and her mouth felt horribly, treacherously dry. She physically longed for it to be daylight, with Claire, Hannah and Susie lurking nearby, and a flip chart behind which she could conveniently hide.

'Nothing's been sorted as yet,' Jamie conceded grudgingly. She felt very visible in her shorts and small striped vest, but it had been the first thing to hand after she had had a shower half an hour earlier. She hadn't expected to run into Ryan lurking like an intruder in the shadows.

'Oh, dear,' Ryan murmured sympathetically. 'Was that the vet on the phone?'

'Will you *please* stop calling him the vet?'

'Sorry, but I thought that's what he did for a living— tended to all those wounded animals who pined for him in his absence.'

Jamie glanced across at him but he was a picture of innocence. The light breeze ruffled his hair and he looked perfectly relaxed, a man at home in his surroundings.

'Yes, it was Greg, as a matter of fact.'

'Making a secretive call behind his wife's back? Hmm…'

'It wasn't a secretive call!'

'Then what was it? Obviously not a call you felt comfortable taking in front of the family.'

'You're impossible!'

'So what did the vet have to say?'

Jamie gritted her teeth together. Ryan was provocative by nature; it was nothing personal. They had both also strayed so far from their boundaries that the lines between them were getting blurred. She had met his family, seen him relaxed in his own home territory. She, in turn, had confided things she wouldn't have dreamt possible. But he was accustomed to breaking down boundaries and getting into the heads of other people; it was part and parcel of what made him a success. And if *she* found it impossible to deal with then it was a reflection on her, and to start huffing and puffing now and trying to evade his natural curiosity would seem strange. Strange was the one thing she knew was dangerous. It was an instinctive realisation. So what was the big deal in telling him what was going on with Greg and Jessica? It wasn't as though he was out of the loop. He was firmly embedded in it, thanks to a sequence of circumstances which she might not have invited but which had happened nevertheless.

'Jessica told me that the reason she felt that she needed more space was because she felt bored and isolated where they live. It's at least forty minutes into Edinburgh, and Jessica has always liked to be in the thick of things.'

'Odd match, in that case.'

'What do you mean?'

'I mean that the vet didn't strike me as the sort of man who prides himself on having a wild social life. I can't see him being the life and soul of any party.'

'You met him for five minutes! You don't know him at all.'

'Oh, yes, I'm forgetting that you two shared a special bond.'

'We didn't share a *special bond*.' But she could feel herself flushing, thinking about her youthful, romantic dreams.

Ryan ignored her heated protest. He didn't have to see her face to be able to take stock of the fact that she was flustered by what he had said—but then she would be, he thought edgily. He was beginning to loathe the caring vet with his menagerie of loyal animals.

'So what did your flamboyant sister see in him?' he persisted.

'He's absolutely one-hundred-percent devoted to her.'

'Ah, but is it mutual? One-way devotion could become trying after a while, I should imagine.'

'Won't your family be wondering where we are?'

'We're adults. I don't suppose they'll be worried in case

we miss our footing and fall in the pool by accident. Besides, Claire and Hannah are doing their nightly battle with the children, and my mother was feeling tired and took herself off to bed with a book and a cup of hot chocolate. So you can put that concern of yours to rest!'

'You have a fantastic family.' Jamie sighed wistfully, and for a moment Ryan was sufficiently distracted to silently wait until she expanded. Women always enjoyed talking about themselves. In fact, from his experience, they would hold court until the break of dawn given half a chance, but generally speaking their conversations were usually targeted to sexually attract. They flirted and pouted and always portrayed themselves in the best possible light. In the case of the women he dated—supermodels and actresses—their anecdotes were usually fond recollections of their achievements on stage or on the runway, often involving getting the better of their competition.

'A bit different from yours, I expect,' he murmured encouragingly when his lengthy silence didn't appear to be working.

'Totally different. You never talk about them.'

'And you've only now started talking about yours.'

'Yes, well, my situation is nothing like yours. When I think of Jessica, I start getting stressed. But *your* sisters… they're very easy-going.'

Ryan grinned. 'I have vague recollections of the three of them trying out their make-up on me when I was younger. Not so easy-going for me, I can tell you.'

Jamie laughed. She couldn't help herself.

'Still, it was tougher on you, raising a teenager when you weren't even out of your teens yourself.'

Lost in her thoughts, she was seduced by the warm interest in his voice, by the soft, warm breeze and the gentle, rhythmic sound of waves breaking against the cliff face.

She felt inclined to share, especially after her conversation with Greg.

'Even before Mum died, Jessica was a handful. I just did my own thing, but she was always demanding, even as a child. She was just so beautiful and she could twist Mum round her little finger. When I look at your sisters and see the way they share everything... Anyway.' She pulled herself together. 'I always think that there's no point weeping and wailing over stuff you can't change.'

'Quite. You were telling me about your conversation with the vet. You thought that your sister was bored because she was a party animal and the vet only enjoyed the company of his sick animals.'

'I never said any such thing!'

'I'm reading between the lines. Have you got an update on the real situation?'

Of course, Jamie thought, brought down to earth, he was keen to find out whether matters were being sorted. He needed her back and functioning in one piece, and the sooner Greg and Jessica sorted themselves out and cleared off the better for him. She would do well to remind herself that his interest was mostly self-motivated. She would also do well to realise that allowing herself to slip into a state of familiarity with him just because he happened to know a little bit more about her private life than he ever had would be madness. There was no chance that she could ever be interested in him in the way that she had been interested in Greg, because Greg represented just the sort of gentle, caring person she found attractive. But still...

'I think we might be seeing the true cause of everything that's been happening between Greg and my sister,' she told him crisply. 'Apparently Greg wants children and he thinks that it's a good time for them to start trying. That seems to have caused everything to explode.'

'Your sister isn't interested?'

'She hasn't mentioned a word of it to me,' Jamie said with a shrug. 'I'm guessing that she might have been feeling a bit bored, but the minute Greg mentioned kids she took fright and started feeling trapped. The only thing she could think of doing was to escape, hence her appearance on my doorstep. At least there's something tangible now to deal with, so you can relax. I'm sure they'll both get to the bottom of their problems by the time I return to England, and once they've disappeared back to Scotland everything will return to normal. I won't be arriving late to work and I'll be as focused as I've always been.'

She stood up and brushed the backs of her thighs where tiny specks of sand had stuck from the chair. She did her best to ignore his dark eyes thoughtfully watching her.

'So what are our plans for tomorrow? I know that your sisters leave with Tom and Patrick and the kids. I have no objection to working in the evening. You've been more than kind in letting me take so much time off to relax.'

'Let's not get back on that gratitude bandwagon,' Ryan said irritably. His eyes skimmed over her, taking in her slender legs, slim waist and pert breasts barely contained underneath the vest. Her work suits did nothing to flatter her figure. The memory of her full mouth pressed against his flashed through his head and ignited a series of images that made him catch his breath sharply. 'I haven't seen you at the pool,' he continued, standing up and swamping her with his potently masculine presence. Jamie instinctively took a small step backwards.

'I… I've sat there with my book a bit.'

'But not been tempted to get in the water. Don't you swim?'

'Yes.' She *had* stuck on her black bikini on one occasion, but the thought of parading in a pool in a bikini with

Ryan—her boss—splashing around, having fun with the family, had been too much. She had promptly taken it off and replaced it with her summer shift. Much safer.

'Then why the reticence? Did you feel shy with my noisy family all around?'

'No. Of course not!'

'Well, they'll be gone by tomorrow evening, and things will be a lot quieter here. You can start enjoying the pool in peace and quiet.'

'Maybe. I really should be getting in now.'

'Wild imagination here, but I get the feeling you don't like being alone with me. A guy could get offended.'

Jamie tensed. His lazy teasing was dangerously unsettling.

'Correct me if I'm wrong, but I spent three hours alone with you today.'

'Ah, but in the company of a flip chart, two computers and a range of stationery.'

'I'm just doing my job! It's what I'm paid to do and I'm going to head back now.'

Up the stone steps leading down to the pool, the path skirted the house, taking them across the sprawling gardens where palm trees fringed the edges, leaning towards the sea. Underneath, a huge variety of plants and shrubs were landscaped to provide a wild, untamed feel to the garden.

Jamie's feet seemed to have wings. She was acutely conscious of Ryan behind her. She had never been very self-confident about her body. With Jessica as a sister, she had been too aware growing up of the physical differences between them. She was shorter, her figure so much less eye-catching. And she was wearing shorts!

Of their own accord, her thoughts flew back to the parade of models who had flitted in and out of Ryan's life: blondes with legs to their armpits and hair to their waists.

Unconscious comparisons sprang to mind, addling her, and maybe that was why she stumbled over the root of a tree projecting above-ground, walking so quickly, rigid as a plank of wood, arms protectively folded and her mind all over the place. It was a recipe for disaster on a dark night in unfamiliar surroundings.

She gave a soft gasp as her body made painful contact with the ground but before she could stagger to her feet she was being lifted up as though she weighed nothing.

Jamie shrieked. 'Put me down! What are you doing?'

'Calm down.'

The feel of his muscular arms around her and the touch of his hard chest set up a series of tingling reactions in her body that made her writhe in his arms until she realised that her writhing was having just the opposite effect; he tightened his hold, pulling her more firmly against him. Instantly, she fell limp and allowed herself to be carried up to the veranda where he gently deposited her on one of the wicker chairs which were strewn at various intervals around the house.

'I'm absolutely fine,' she muttered through gritted teeth and was ignored as Ryan stooped down and removed her espadrilles.

His long fingers gently felt her foot and her ankle, which he ordered her to try and move.

'I haven't twisted anything!' she exclaimed, trying to pull her foot out of his grasp while her treacherous body was tempted to go with the flow and succumb to the wonderful sensation of what his hands were doing.

'No. If you had, you wouldn't be able to move it.'

'Exactly. So if you don't mind…'

'But you're bruised.' He was peering at her knee and then doing it again, sweeping her up and informing her that it was just as well to put no strain on it but that she needed cleaning up.

'That's something I can do myself.' Her breasts were pushing against his chest and, good lord, her nipples were hardening as they scraped against the fabric of her bra, and between her legs felt damp. Every bit of her body was responding to him and she hated it. It terrified the life out of her. She just wanted him to put her down so that she could scuttle back to the safety of her bedroom, but instead he was carrying her through the house, up the short staircase that led to the wing of the house where he was staying and then—when it couldn't get any worse as far as she was concerned—into his bedroom. Jamie closed her eyes and stifled a weak groan of despair.

She hadn't been here yet. His room was huge and dominated by an impressive bed fashioned out of bamboo. The linen was a colourful medley of bold reds and blacks and looked positively threatening.

Beneath the window was a long sofa and he took her to it and sat her down.

'Don't move a muscle. I have a first-aid kit in the bathroom—hangover from my Boy Scout days.'

'This is ridiculous—and you were never a Boy Scout!'

'Of course I was!' He disappeared into the adjoining bathroom and through the open door Jamie glimpsed him rifling through a cupboard, searching out the first-aid kit. 'I may even have earned a few badges.' He reappeared with a small tin and knelt at her feet. 'If you ever need a tent erecting, or a fire to be lit using only two pieces of wood, then I'm your man. Tsk, tsk—do you see those bruises on your knees? If you hadn't been rushing off like a bat out of hell this would never have happened.'

Jamie clamped her teeth together and refrained from telling him that if he hadn't appeared in front of her, broken her phone and then insisted on having a long, personal conversation with her she wouldn't have felt inclined to rush off and wouldn't be sitting here now in his bedroom while he...

She squeezed her eyes tightly shut, intending to block out the image of his down-bent head as he tended to her bruises, applying alcohol wipes to the surfaces, then antiseptic cream which he gently rubbed into her skin.

'No good applying any plasters,' he informed her. 'You want the sun to dry out these cuts and scratches.'

'Yep, okay. Thank you. I'll leave now, if you don't mind.'

'Shall I carry you?'

Her eyes flew open and she saw that he was grinning at her.

'Don't be ridiculous!'

'And to continue our conversation...'

'To continue our conversation about *what*?'

'About tomorrow, of course.'

She caught his eyes. He looked as innocent as the pure driven snow.

'What about tomorrow?' she stammered, walking towards the door.

'Well, you were telling me about what you wanted to do. Work wise.'

Had she? She couldn't think. Every nerve ending in her body was on fire. She was tingling all over and it was ludicrous. Having an insane crush on Greg had been bad enough but at least she could see the sense there. With Ryan Sheppard? She didn't even respect the sort of guy who dated a string of models, who never seemed to see beyond the long legs and the perfect figure! Ergo, she couldn't possibly have a crush on him. The soaring tropical heat was getting to her. She wasn't used to it.

'Yes!' The place was going to be empty, aside from his mother. Suddenly, the thought of even a tiny window when they would be together without the possibility of interruption was scary beyond belief. 'There are still loads of things to do and I have lots of ideas about your presentations—like, you really need to give a strong argument for implementing your system in their cars. New technology can do so much for the environment.'

She had reached the door without even realizing. Now her back was against the door frame and he was looking at her with his head to one side, the picture-perfect image of someone one-hundred-percent interested in what she had to say.

So why the heck was she feeling so nervous?

She quailed when he took a few steps towards her.

'Are you entirely sure that you're all right?'

He loomed over her, a darkly, wickedly sexy guy who was sending her mind into crazy disarray.

'Because you've gone pale.' He leant against the door frame and looked at her with concern. 'Nothing broken, but you could still be in a bit of shock at losing your footing like that. Happens, you know—you have a minor accident and you think you're fine but really...'

'I don't *think* I'm fine. I *am* fine.'

'I think we can afford to give work a miss tomorrow. Those harridans known as my sisters will be leaving, and as soon as they've gone the house is going to feel very empty. It might be an idea to do something with my mother, occupy her...'

'I'm more than happy to do that.'

'I think I might like to be included in the exercise,' Ryan murmured drily, looking down at her. She noticed the fine lines around his eyes that spoke of a man who lived life to the full, the thick sweep of his dark lashes, the deep bitter-chocolate of his irises flecked with tinges of gold. He was beautiful but not in a detached, frozen way. He was beautiful in a devastatingly sexy way and her pulses raced in easy, treacherous recognition of that.

'Of course! Actually, I think it might be a good idea if you and your mother had some, um, time together. You've hardly had a one to one with her since we got here.'

'Oh, there's no need for a one to one. Can I let you in on a little secret?' he murmured huskily, leaning towards her.

Jamie nodded because quite honestly she didn't trust herself to speak. She didn't think her voice would sound normal because her tongue appeared to be glued to the roof of her mouth.

'One to ones with my mother can sometimes be a little dangerous.'

'What are you talking about?' Locked into this intimate atmosphere, she found it impossible to tear herself away from his mesmeric dark gaze.

'She's developed an unnerving habit of cornering me about my private life.' In actual fact, Ryan hadn't meant to mention this at all. Underneath the confident, self-assured charm he was a lot more watchful and contained than people suspected, but he wanted to get under her skin. With each passing day, the desire had grown more urgent. He was frustrated by the way she blocked him, and frustrated with himself for a curiosity he couldn't understand. On a basic level, he realised that the confidences she had shared with him—which would hardly be termed earth shattering by most people's standards—were hugely significant for her. Possibly she regretted them. Scratch that—she *did* regret them but she was now unable to retreat.

However, that didn't mean that she was now on a new, no-holds-barred, sharing level with him. And he wanted her there. He actively wanted her to invite him into her thoughts—which would entail some confidence sharing of his own.

So, when she looked at him in silent curiosity, he heard himself say with utmost seriousness, 'I'm not sure that my mother is a firm believer in the virtues of playing the field. Nor, for that matter, are the harridans.'

'I don't think that there's any mother who would be thrilled to have a son who takes the fastest exit the second there's the threat of commitment with a woman.'

'Is that what you think I do?'

'Isn't it?' The silence that greeted her question was thick and heavy with a peculiar, thrilling undercurrent. Jamie desperately wanted to repeat her mantra about going to bed, but a weird and powerful sense of anticipation held her to the spot. When after a few seconds he didn't answer, she shrugged lightly and began turning away.

'Well, it's none of my business anyway. Although I resent the fact that you feel it permissible to ask whatever questions you like about my private life, even though you know that I don't want to answer them, and yet you can't be bothered to answer any that are directed at you. Not,' she added for good measure, her hand on the door frame, 'that I care one way or another.'

'I could be hurt by that,' Ryan murmured softly. 'You're my irreplaceable secretary. You're supposed to care.' It wasn't his imagination; when it came to women, he had the instincts of a born predator. He knew when they were reacting to him and Jamie was reacting to him right now. It was there in the slight flare of her nostrils, the faint flush that spread across her cheeks and the way her pupils dilated. Her mouth was half-open, as though she was on the verge of saying something, and her full, parted lips allowed a glimpse of her pearl-white teeth.

The urge to press her against the door frame and kiss her senseless was as overpowering as a blow to the stomach. He wanted to slide his hand underneath that tiny vest of hers and feel the weight of her breast against the palm of his hand. He wanted to taste her, right here, right now on his bed.

Interest and curiosity were one thing, being torn apart by inexplicable sexual desire was another. Jamie Powell might have suddenly become dangerously intriguing but it would be lunacy to follow it through simply to see where it led. For a start, she was the best secretary he had ever had. For another, she was no bimbo ready and willing for a romp in the hay, no strings attached.

'You're right. It's none of your business.'

'Good night, Ryan. Thanks for taking care of my cuts and bruises.'

He reached out and his long fingers circled her arm. 'My father took his eye off the ball,' Ryan told her softly. 'He got married, had four children… Like I said, he took his eye off the ball. While he was busy being domesticated, his finance director was helping himself to company funds. By the time my father noticed, the company was virtually on its knees. In my view, he worked himself into an early grave trying to get it back in order but by then it was too late. I inherited a mess, and I got it where it should be, and I have no intention of taking my own eye off the ball. Thanks to my efforts, my mother has the lifestyle she deserves and my sisters have the financial security they deserve. So, you see, I have no time for the demands of a committed relationship. I don't need the distraction.'

Jamie found that she was holding her breath.

'So you're never going to get married? Have kids? Become a grandfather?'

'If I do, it will be on my terms to someone who is willing to take second place to the fact that my primary concern is being one-hundred-and-ten-percent hands-on with my company. There's nothing that goes on at RS Enterprises that I don't know about. That situation exists because I make sure that I never let my attention slip.'

'Lucky lady, whoever snaps you up,' Jamie murmured with sarcasm and Ryan released her and laughed softly and appreciatively.

'I date women who understand where I'm coming from.'

'Was Leanne the exception?'

'Leanne knew the score the minute she became involved with me. I'm honest to a fault.' He couldn't read a thing in the cool, brown eyes assessing him. He continued, irritated by what he took to be silent criticism from Jamie. 'I never make promises I can't fulfil and I never encourage a woman to think that she's got her feet in the door. I don't ask them to share my space. I discourage items of clothing from being left overnight at my apartment. I warn them that I'm unpredictable with my time.'

Jamie marvelled that he could still think that just because he laid down ground rules hearts would never be broken.

'Maybe you should tell your mother that.' Jamie snapped out of her trance and broke eye contact with him. 'Then perhaps she would stop cornering you with awkward questions.'

The shutters were back down. Ryan wondered whether he had imagined that response he had seen in her. Had he? Disconcerted, he frowned and half turned away.

'Maybe I'll do that.' He smiled at her with equal politeness. 'Honesty, after all, is always the best policy...'

# CHAPTER SIX

CLAIRE and Hannah, their husbands and children left in a flurry of forgotten stuffed toys that needed to be fetched, a thousand things that had to be ticked off their check list and lots of hugs and kisses and promises to meet up just as soon as life returned to normal. And then they were gone and the house felt suddenly very quiet and very empty.

In two days' time, Ryan would take one plane to Florida while she took another back to England and Vivian, his mother, would stay on for a further week, joined by several of her friends for their annual bridge holiday.

With Vivian excusing herself for an afternoon nap and Ryan announcing that he intended to work, waving her down when she immediately started to talk about what they would be doing, Jamie found herself at a loose end. For the first time, she realised that it was a relief to have been deprived of her mobile phone. Normally, she would have been following the crisis between Greg and her sister in a state of barely suppressed stress, but without the means of contacting them unless she used the landline, which she didn't intend to, she felt guiltily liberated from the problem—at least temporarily.

For the first time since she had arrived, she decided to take advantage of the empty swimming pool, and was there in her bikini with her towel, her sun block and a book within forty minutes.

It felt like a holiday. The pool offered spectacular views of the sea and was surrounded by palm trees and foliage, ripe with butterflies and the sound of birds. Jamie lay down on her sun lounger and let her mind wander, and every one of its meanderings returned to Ryan. His image seemed to have been stamped on her brain and she wasn't sure whether that had always been the case or whether it was something that had occurred ever since some of the barriers between them had been eroded. Had she been sucked into his charming, witty, intelligent personality without even realising? Or had all that charm, wit and intelligence only begun working on her once he had uncovered some of those private details that she had striven so hard to keep from him?

She had been determined never to repeat the folly of getting personally involved with the boss. Falling for Greg had been a youthful indiscretion and she could now look back on that younger self with a certain amount of wry amusement, because her crush had been so *harmless.*

This situation with Ryan was altogether more dangerous because Ryan was just a more dangerous man. There were times when she physically reacted to him with something that was unconscious and almost primitive in its intensity, and when she thought about that she wanted to close her eyes and faint with the horror of it.

In comparison, her silly infatuation with Greg was exposed for what it had really been: something harmless that had occurred at just the time she had needed it. An innocent distraction from the stress and trauma of her home life. She had taken refuge in her pleasant daydreams, and her working life, which had involved spending hours in Greg's company, had been a soothing panacea against the harsh reality that had been waiting to greet her the second she had walked back through the front door at the end of the evening.

Greg had been kind, thoughtful and gentle and he had been a buffer between herself and the disappointment of having to give up on her dreams of going to university.

Ryan, however...

Yes, he was kind and thoughtful and gentle. She had seen it in a thousand ways in his interaction with his sisters, his mother, his nephews and nieces. But he was no Greg. There was a core of steel running through him that made her shiver with a kind of dangerous excitement that enthralled and scared her at the same time. When his dark eyes rested on her, she didn't feel a pleasurable flutter, she felt a wild rush of adrenalin that left her breathless and exposed.

It would be a relief to return to England. She hoped that Greg and Jessica would have sorted out their differences by then, but even if they hadn't she would still be returning to the protection of the office, her colleagues and the self-imposed distance between boss and secretary. Out here, a million miles away from her home territory, it was too easy for the lines between them to be eroded.

She flipped over onto her stomach, but even after half an hour, and with her sun protection liberally applied, Jamie was beginning to feel burnt. The sun out here was like nothing she had felt before. It was fierce and unrelenting, especially at this hour of the day. When she tried to read her book, her eyes felt tired from the white glare and after a while she dragged the wooden lounger under the partial shade afforded by an overhanging tree.

Then, when she began feeling uncomfortable even in the shade, she dived into the pool. Pure bliss: the water was like cool silk around her. She began swimming, revisiting a pleasurable activity which she had indulged only occasionally in London, because her working hours were long and she just never seemed to find the time.

Like a fish, she ducked below the surface of the water, mentally challenging herself to swim the length of the pool without surfacing for air.

Uncomfortable thoughts began to gel in her head as she swam, reaching one end, gulping in air and then setting off again.

She had given up going to the swimming baths because of her work. She had given up going to the gym three times a week because of her work. She made arrangements to see friends in the evening but had often cancelled at a moment's notice because Ryan had needed her to do overtime. She had thought nothing of it.

She had assumed herself to be a goal-focused person. She had patted herself on the back for being someone who was prepared to go the distance because she was ambitious and worth every penny of the three pay rises she had been given in the space of eighteen months. She had never thought that maybe she had gone that extra mile because she had enjoyed the opportunity of being with Ryan. Had she been the ever-obliging secretary because, without even realising it, she had wanted to feed a secret craving? Had she been smugly pleased with herself for having learnt a lesson from her experience with Greg, only to be ambushed by repeating her mistake without even realising it?

That thought was so disturbing that she was unaware of the wall of the pool rushing towards her as she skimmed underneath the water. She bumped her head and was instantly shocked into spluttering up to the surface.

When she opened her eyes, blinking the water out of them, it was to find Ryan leaning over the side of the pool like a vision conjured up from her feverish imagination, larger than life.

He was in his swimming trunks, some loose khaki-coloured shorts with a drawstring, and his short-sleeved shirt was unbuttoned.

Jamie was confronted with a view of his muscled, bronzed torso, which was even more disconcerting than the bump on her forehead.

'What are *you* doing here?' she gasped, in the flimsy hope that her fuddled brain was playing tricks on her.

'Rescuing you again. I had no idea that you were so accident prone.' He reached out his hands to help her out. Jamie ignored him, choosing to swim to the steps in the shallow end and sit there, half immersed in the water.

'What were you thinking, swimming like greased lightning and not bothering to judge how far away the wall was?' Ryan shrugged off his shirt and settled into the water next to her. 'Here, let me have a look at that bump.'

'Let's not do this again,' Jamie snapped, touching the tender spot on her head and wincing. 'My head is fine, just as my feet were fine when I fell yesterday.'

'Bumps to the head can be far more serious. Tell me how many fingers I'm holding up.'

'I thought you were working,' she responded in an accusing voice, watching out of the corner of her eye as Ryan lounged back against the step behind him, resting on his elbows. His eyes were closed, his face tilted up to the sun and, like an addict, Jamie found herself watching him, taking in his powerful, masculine beauty. When he opened his eyes suddenly and glanced at her, she flushed and looked away.

'I *was* working, but I couldn't resist the thought of coming out here and having a dip. I didn't realise that you were such a strong swimmer.'

'Were you *watching* me?'

'Guilty as charged.' But he wouldn't let on for just how long. Nor would he let on that he had felt compelled to follow her out to the pool. For once in his life, he hadn't been able to concentrate on work. Watching her from above as she had whipped like a fish through the water had mesmerised him. Her bikini was a modest affair in black, the least obviously sexy swimsuit he had ever seen on a woman, and yet on her it was an erotic work of art. Sliding his eyes across, he took in the generous cleavage and the full swell of her ripe breasts—more than a generous, *very generous*, handful.

Just looking at her like this, with sexual hunger, was playing with fire. Ryan was getting dangerously close to the point of no longer caring whether she was his perfect secretary or not or whether going to bed with her would be crazy or not.

'Have you been in touch with your sister?'

'Have you forgotten that you broke my phone?'

'You'll be amply compensated for that the very second I get back to England. In fact, you're authorised to use company funds to get yourself the best mobile phone on the market as soon as *you* get back to England. No stinting!'

'That's very generous of you.'

'Well, it was my fault that you dropped your phone and broke it, although strictly speaking you should have listened to me in the first place and used the landline.'

'Funny the way you cause me to drop my phone and break it and yet it's still my fault.'

Ryan gave a rich chuckle. 'My mother says that you're the only woman she's ever met who can keep me in line. I think it was the way you accused me of cheating at Scrabble last night and insisted I remove my word and take a hefty penalty. And, hearing that acerbic tone of voice now, I'm inclined to agree.'

'And *I'm* sure that all those other women you dated would be inclined to disagree!'

'Have I ruffled your feathers? It was meant as a compliment. And just for the record, all those other women I dated were perfectly happy to let me take the lead. I can't think of any of them keeping me in line.'

'You haven't *ruffled my feathers*! And if any of them had worked for you...'

'Worked *with* me. We're a team, Jamie.'

'Well, whatever. If any of them had worked *with* you, then they'd find out soon enough that the only way to survive would be to try and...'

'Take control? I never thought that I would enjoy a woman who took control, bearing in mind my own disposition, but spending time with you here is certainly—'

'Useful!' Jamie interrupted hurriedly. 'I really hope that you're managing to accomplish all the work you set out to do.'

'It gets on my nerves when you do that.'

'When I do what?'

'And don't try that butter-wouldn't-melt-in-your-mouth routine. You know exactly what I'm talking about. The second the conversation veers off work, you frantically start trying to change the subject.'

'That's not true! I've chatted about all sorts of things with your family.'

'But not with me.'

'I'm not paid to chat about all sorts of things with you.' Jamie desperately tried to shove the genie back into the bottle.

'Are you scared of me? Is that it? Do I make you nervous?'

Jamie suddenly bristled. 'No, you don't make me nervous. But I know what's going on here—you're not accustomed to lazing around for days on end. I haven't known you take more than a weekend off work in all the time I've known you.'

'You've actually noticed?'

'Stop grinning! You're out here and maybe a little bored, so you're indulging yourself by…by confusing me.'

'Am I? I thought I was trying to get to know you.'

'You *already* know me.'

'Yes. I do, don't I?' Ryan murmured softly for, thinking about it, he did. Not the details; he had only just discovered that she had a sister. But he knew *her* in a weird sort of way. Working so closely with her, he had somehow tuned in to her personality. He knew how she responded to certain things, her mannerisms, her thoughts on a whole range of subjects from remarks she had made and which he had clearly absorbed over time. All this had built a picture lacking only in the detail. Like an itch he couldn't scratch, the thought of the vet being the privileged recipient of those details niggled at the back of his mind like a nasty irritant.

'As much as you must know me, my conscientious little secretary, which means that you must know that I don't want you holding off on contacting your sister because you feel awkward using the telephone here. Unless, of course, you don't want your conversations with the vet overheard by anyone. Or maybe you're embarrassed to be caught playing long-distance counsellor with a married man.'

'That's totally uncalled for!'

'Every time I mention the guy, you look guilty and embarrassed. Why is that?'

'You don't know what you're talking about.'

'I have eyes in my head. I'm telling you what I see.'

'You have absolutely no right to make suggestions like that!'

'I take it that's the guilt talking, because you sure as hell aren't answering my question. Was there something between the two of you? *Is* there still something between the two of you?'

'That's an insult!' Jamie pushed off from the step and began swimming furiously towards the other end of the pool, her one instinct just to get away from him.

She knew that he was right behind her when she reached the other end and heard the sound of him slicing through the water, but she refused to look around.

'Greg is married to my sister!' She fixed angry eyes on him as soon as he was next to her. 'There is *nothing* going on between us.'

'But he wasn't always married to your sister, was he? In fact, *you* knew him before your sister did. I saw the way you looked at him when he came through your front door on Christmas day...'

'That's ridiculous. I didn't look at him in any way.' Had she? Yes, of course she had. She had seen him for the first time in ages and at that point she hadn't even been sure that she had put her silly infatuation to rest. Slow colour crept into her face.

'Out of sight,' Ryan murmured, 'doesn't necessarily mean out of mind.'

Flustered, Jamie looked away but she could feel a nervous pulse racing at the base of her neck just as she was aware of his watchful eyes taking in every shadow of emotion she was desperately trying to conceal.

'Is that why you rushed down to London?'

'I came to London because...because I knew that it would be easier to find a job down here. Also, when Jessica got married, I sold our childhood home and split the proceeds with her. It gave me enough to put aside some savings for a place of my own, and sufficient for me to find somewhere to rent while I looked for work. It was just a...a matter of timing.'

'Why am I not buying that?'

'Because you have a suspicious mind.'

'Did you sleep with him?'

'That's outrageous!'

'Good.' So she hadn't. He gave her a slow, satisfied smile. 'Although I sense that any competition in that area wouldn't be worth worrying about.'

'What are you saying?'

'Read between the lines. What do you think I'm saying?' Ryan didn't know when he had made the decision to overstep the mark. He just knew that he wanted her. The control that he had always been able to access when it came to women had disappeared under the force of a craving that seemed to have crept up on him only to pounce, taking him by surprise and demolishing every scrap of common sense in its voracious path.

He didn't give himself time to think. He also didn't give *her* time to think. In one smooth motion, he circled her, trapping her to the side of the pool by the effective measure of placing his hands on either side of her. He leant into her, felt her breath against his face, read the panic in her eyes that couldn't quite extinguish the simmering excitement. He had been right all along when he had sensed her forbidden interest in him and the knowledge gave him a rock-hard erection even before his lips touched hers.

Nothing had ever felt this good. That brief, public kiss they had shared at Christmas had been just a taster. Her mouth parted on a moan and, while her hands scrabbled against his chest in protest, the feel of her tongue against his was telling a different story.

He pushed her back against the wall so that his big body was pressed firmly against hers. The bottom of the pool sloped slightly upwards at this end and, standing at a little over six-two, Ryan was steady and balanced on his feet. For Jamie to keep her balance, however, she had to hook both her arms up on the wooden planks, which threw her breasts into tempting prominence. She attempted to say something and he killed the words forming on her tongue by deepening his kiss. Her eyes were half-closed. When she broke free to tilt her head back, he trailed his tongue against the slender column of her neck and Jamie shuddered in instant reaction.

More than anything else, she wanted to push him away but her will power had self-imploded and her body was as limp as a rag doll's as she soaked up the amazing feelings zipping through her as if a million shooting stars had been released inside her body.

She was dimly aware of him reaching down to hook her legs around his waist, and the nudge of his erection between her spread legs brought her close to swooning.

Water sloshed over the side of the pool as they moved frantically against each other. When he pulled down the straps of her bikini, she was self-conscious but only for a brief moment, then that, like her inhibitions, disappeared completely. With her body arched back and angled half out of the water, the touch of his mouth on her nipple was exquisite as the hot sun blazed down on them.

She could have stayed like this for ever, with him suckling on her breasts, massaging them with his big hands, rolling her nipples between his fingers and then teasing them with his tongue into hard, sensitised peaks.

It was only when he began to tug down her bikini bottom so that he could slide his fingers into her that Jamie's eyes flew open and she took horrified stock of the reality of what she was doing.

How on earth had this happened?

Of course, she knew. Why kid herself? She had been lusting after him for months—indeed, it felt like for ever. This was nothing at all like what she had felt for Greg. Not only had Ryan ignited something in her that had never been ignited before, but it was all the more powerful because it was wrapped up in a package that was more than just physical attraction. The whole complex, three-dimensional person had swept her off her feet. She hadn't even known that she had been carried away until now.

She wriggled, pushing him away from her, and then ducked under his hands so that she could swim away with frantic, urgent speed towards the far end of the pool.

Ryan easily caught up with her.

'What the hell is the matter?'

Jamie couldn't meet his eyes but she had to when she felt his fingers on her chin and was roughly made to look at him.

'I...I don't know what happened,' she whispered.

'That's fine because *I* know what happened and I'm more than happy to explain it to you. We're attracted to one another. I touched you and you went up in flames.'

'I didn't!'

'Stop pretending, Jamie. Why did you stop?'

'Because it's...it's wrong.'

She wasn't saying anything that took him by surprise. Only twenty-four hours ago he had thought about her and dismissed any notion of getting her into his bed as flat-out crazy. Yet here he was, and it didn't feel crazy.

'We're adults,' he growled. 'We're permitted to be turned on by each other.'

'You're my boss. I work for you!'

'I want more than your diligence. I want you in my bed where I can touch you wherever I want. I'm betting that that's what you want too, whether you think it's right or wrong. In fact, I'm betting that if I touch you right now, right here...' Ryan trailed his finger along her cleavage and watched as she fought to catch her breath '...you're not going to be able to tell me that you don't want me too.'

'I don't want you.'

'Liar!' He kissed her again and her lies were revealed in

the way she clutched at him, not wanting to but utterly unable to resist.

Jamie felt her weakness tearing her apart. Her mouth blindly responded and she missed his lips when he pulled back to look at her.

'*Now* tell me that you just don't know what came over you.'

'Okay. Okay. Maybe I'm attracted to you, but I'm not proud of it.' The words felt agonisingly painful and she twisted away from his piercing gaze. 'I... You're right, okay? I felt things for Greg. That's why it was important to leave, to live somewhere else, somewhere far away.' This felt like the final confession. She was now waving goodbye to her privacy for ever, but what was her option? She had to dig deep and find the strength to turn away from him with a good excuse because if she didn't he would devour her. She knew that.

Ryan had stilled. For a minute, his stomach twisted into a sickening knot. So she might not have slept with the vet, but she had felt something for him, maybe even loved him. He was shaken by the impact that her admission had on him.

'I made a mistake with Greg and I've learnt from it. I haven't come this far to make a second mistake. I won't climb into bed with you just for the hell of it. I'm going to go and I want you to promise me that you'll never mention this again.'

'What a lot of things I'm now under orders never to mention,' Ryan rasped in a savage undertone. 'And who ever said that sex between us would be a mistake?'

'I did.' This time she met his eyes squarely. 'I'm not like you. I'm not willing to fall in and out with bed with someone just because I fancy them. If you don't think that you can put this behind us, then I'm telling you right now that

I'll have my resignation waiting for you on your desk when you return to England from Florida.'

This wasn't a veiled threat, she meant every word of it; Ryan mentally cursed to himself. He had always accepted his ability to win women over. Jamie felt like the first woman he had ever really wanted and she was turning him down. Frustration ripped through him and he clenched his fists but there was nothing to say.

She was waiting for confirmation and he nodded curtly and in silence.

'Good.' Her body was still burning, but she had rescued what she could of her dignity. It felt like a very small victory. 'I'll head inside now.' She stepped out of the water and tried not to think of his hands all over her and his mouth lingering on her breasts. It had happened and it wasn't going to happen again. Just for good measure, and to show him that she meant business, she shot him one final look over her shoulder. 'Is there anything you'd like me to be getting on with?'

'Why don't you use your initiative?' Ryan said coolly. 'I would suggest something suitably engrossing that can help you forget this sordid little business of sexual attraction.'

On the tip of his tongue was the temptation to tell her that perhaps the vet *had* ended up with the wrong sister. Jamie didn't want a real man. She didn't want to be sexually challenged. No wonder she had fallen in love with a guy whose top priority was his sick animals with everything else taking second place. How demanding would a relationship with him be? Not very. Which would have suited his prim, efficient secretary right down to the ground.

And that closing thought should have made him feel a lot better as he watched her walk away with her towel firmly secured around her waist, but it didn't.

In fact, he felt a distinct urge to bash something very hard.

Instead, he made do with the pool. He swam with intensity, not looking up, until the muscles in his arms began to burn and the sun began its descent. He had no idea how long he did it. He was a prodigiously strong swimmer but even for him over two hours without rest began to take its toll.

Nevertheless, he might have continued swimming, slackening his pace, if he wasn't distracted by the sound of footsteps—running footsteps.

In the tropics, night fell quickly, preceded only by a window of blazing orange when the sun dipped below the horizon. The sky was orange now. Soon, it would be replaced by deep, velvety charcoal-black, but in the fading light he made out Jamie's slight figure as she paused at the top of the steps and then began running down them.

No wonder the woman had so many accidents!

Ryan heaved himself out of the water and without bothering to dry himself slung on the shirt which he had earlier discarded.

'Urgent work problem?' he asked sarcastically, and then paused when his eyes focused on her face and he took in her expression. She was panicked and her panic was contagious. He felt a sudden cold chill of apprehension. 'What is it? What's the matter?'

'It's your mother, Ryan. Something's wrong with her.'

'What are you talking about?' But he was already heading away from the pool, half running and half turning so that Jamie could talk to him.

'I had a shower, and when I couldn't find her anywhere I thought I'd check her bedroom to find out whether she wanted a cup of tea. When I went in, she was lying on the bed, white as a sheet. She said that she's had some tingling in her arms, Ryan, and her breathing's erratic. I rushed down here as fast as I could…'

They were at the house and Ryan was taking the stairs

two at a time, while Jamie raced behind him, out of breath in her haste to keep up. She must have been gone all of five minutes, if that, and she hoped, as she nearly catapulted Ryan in the doorway to the bedroom, that his mother had had a miraculous recovery. That all those little signs were no more than a bout of extreme exhaustion.

Vivian Sheppard was awake but obviously unwell and extremely frightened.

Within seconds, Ryan was on the phone to the hospital. The strings he was capable of pulling were not limited to his homeland; Jamie listened as he urgently asked for a specific consultant, watched as he nodded, satisfied with whatever reply he received.

'The ambulance will be here in five minutes.' He knelt by the bed and took his mother's hand in his own. Vivian, usually sprightly and full of laughter, was drawn but still managing to smile weakly at her son.

'I'm sure there's nothing to worry about,' she murmured and tut-tutted when he told her not to speak.

Behind him, Jamie hovered uncertainly, feeling like an intruder at a very private moment. She longed to see his face and desperately wanted to comfort him, but she kept her hands stiffly behind her back. As soon as she picked up the sound of the approaching ambulance, she ran downstairs and directed them to Vivian's bedroom.

To remain behind or to accompany them in the ambulance? Rather than impose an awkward situation on Ryan, who was grey with worry, she quietly informed him that she would stay at the house but would remain up until he returned.

'I can't tell you when that will be,' Ryan said, barely looking at her as he shoved on a tee-shirt and stuck his feet in his loafers.

'It's okay.'

'Thank God you went in to check in on her.'

Jamie placed her hand on his arm and felt the heat of his body through the dry tee-shirt. It took a lot to keep her hand there and not whip it away as though it had been burnt.

'I know you must be worried sick, but try not to be. Worry is contagious. You don't want your mother thinking the worst.'

'You're right,' Ryan agreed heavily. 'Look, I have to go. I'll phone the landline as soon as I can. Or better still...' he flicked out his mobile phone and handed it to her '...take this. I'll use my mother's phone to call you.'

Then he was gone, and in a heartbeat the sound of the ambulance siren was fading in the distance until the only sounds she could hear, once again, were the crickets and other night-time insects and the soft breeze sifting through the trees and shrubs.

Over the next three hours, she sat on the sofa in the living room with the windows open and a gentle breeze blowing back the white muslin curtains. His mobile was right there, on the small rattan table next to her, but it didn't ring. She must have dozed off; she was awakened by the sound of the front door slamming, then the sound of footsteps, and then Ryan was standing at the door to the room before she had much of a chance to gather herself.

'I thought you were going to call,' she said sleepily, shoving herself into an upright position on the sofa. 'I was worried. How is your mother doing? Is she going to be all right? What is the prognosis?'

Ryan walked towards her and sat on the sofa, depressing it with his weight and bringing her fractionally closer to him in the process.

'A minor stroke. The consultant says that there's nothing to worry about.'

'But you're still looking worried.'

'Can you blame me?' He leant forward and rested his head in his hands for a few moments, letting the silence settle between them. Then he looked at her and her heartbeat quickened because every instinct in her wanted to reach out and draw him to her so that she could smooth away the lines of worry on his face.

'Anyway, they did a number of tests on her, and they're going to keep her in for a couple of days so that they can do some more, but it's all very reassuring.'

'Did they say what caused it?'

'One of those things.' That was what had been said to him. Personally, he put it down to stress, and here things got a little difficult because what was there for his mother to stress about? She lived a relaxed and comfortable life. The only thing she had ever been known to worry about had been her children, and with Claire, Hannah and Susie all settled and happy with their respective broods *he* was the only one left for her to be concerned about.

Over the past few hours, while he had sat on a hard chair in the hospital waiting for doctors to return with results of tests, Ryan had had time to think.

His mother had been worrying more and more over the past couple of years about his singleton status, the women he dated and the hours he worked. Had she been more anxious about it than she had let on? While he had been travelling the world, working all the hours God made and fitting in his no-strings attached relationships with sexy airheads, had she been fretting to the point that her health had suffered? He was assailed by guilt.

'Have you been in touch with your sisters?' He didn't want to talk. His silence was leaden and he was obviously a million miles away in his head. For some reason, that was painfully disappointing. Jamie wanted him to turn to her and she had to mentally slap herself on the wrist for her foolish weakness. It was as if a door in her mind had been unlocked and flung open and now that it had been she was besieged by frightening and unwelcome revelations about herself and the way she felt about him.

When she was beginning to think that she should go to bed, because she was clearly an inconvenience when he just wanted to be by himself, he looked up at her.

'I phoned Hannah and explained the situation. Of course she wanted to get straight back on a plane over, but I managed to persuade her that there would be no point. I will stay here until my mother is fit to travel and then I will return to the UK with her.' He hesitated and for the first time he focused fully on the woman sitting next to him.

'You'll have to cancel my trip to Florida. Get in touch with the office. Either Evans or George Law can handle it. Email them whatever information they need.'

Jamie nodded. He was still looking at her as though there was more to be said but he wasn't quite sure how to say it. Maybe, she thought, he was embarrassed to have her there when this family crisis was happening. Maybe he wanted her to leave immediately but was uncertain how to frame the request, considering it had been his idea to have her tag along with him in the first place.

'Of-of course,' she stammered, chewing on her lower lip. 'And…just to tell you that you shouldn't be, you know, embarrassed because you want me to leave. I absolutely and fully understand. What's happened is completely unexpected and the last thing you need is for me to be here. This isn't a time for your secretary to be hanging around getting in the way.' She tried a reassuring smile on for size. 'I'd probably feel exactly the same if the roles were reversed and you were *my* secretary.'

Her attempt to lighten the strained atmosphere fell flatter than a lead balloon but after a few seconds he did manage to give her a crooked smile.

'I think you've got hold of the wrong end of the stick,' he said eventually. 'I'm not sure how to tell you this...'

'Tell me what?' For the first time, Jamie felt a stab of real apprehension. The incident by the pool resurfaced in her mind and she cringed at the memory: that was the reason for his hesitation. He had had the chance to reflect on their inappropriate behaviour and now had come the moment of reckoning. Tears of bitter regret pushed their way to the back of her eyes as she envisaged her wonderful, well paid, satisfying job disappearing like a puff of smoke in the air.

# CHAPTER SEVEN

RYAN continued to look at her. She had obviously fallen asleep on the chair; her cheeks were flushed and her hair was tousled. She looked young and innocent and nothing at all like the businesslike, crisp, efficient secretary he had become accustomed to. But then hadn't he seen the living, breathing, exciting woman behind the professional persona?

He reined back his imagination which would break free and gallop away. Right now, he needed to focus, because the conversation that lay ahead was probably going to be difficult.

'I honestly don't know how to say this...'

'I can't imagine you're ever stuck for words.' This was sounding worse by the second.

'My mother saw us. By the pool. Earlier today.'

'Oh, no.' Jamie put her hand to her mouth in dismay. Hot colour spread across her cheeks. 'How do you know? Did she tell you?'

'Of course she told me. I didn't use my imagination to work out a possible scenario. She decided to go for a little stroll around the gardens to see if some fresh air would give her more energy and she heard us. She followed the sound of our voices and I think she got a bit more than she bargained for.'

'I'm sorry. This is all my fault!' Suddenly there was no

part of her that could keep still and Jamie stood up to wander agitatedly around the room. She had to clasp her hands together to stop them from trembling and the wave of shameful discomfort was like a thousand painful burrs underneath her skin.

'I'll leave immediately.' She went to stand in front of him and drew in her breath to fortify herself against the mortification of meeting his eyes. 'It'll take me half an hour to pack.'

'Oh, for God's sake, don't be absurd!'

'I can't stay here. I don't think I'd be able to look your mother in the face. What we did was terrible. A mistake. She must have been appalled. Is that why…? Did we cause…?'

'No! Now sit *down*!' He waited until she was seated, although she still looked as though she would have liked to flee through the open door. 'What she saw didn't cause her to go into some kind of meltdown. My mother is pretty liberated when it comes to her children and what they get up to, believe me. In fact…'

'In fact *what*? I wish you'd just say what you have to say, Ryan. I'm a big girl. I can take bad news.'

'In fact, my mother was overjoyed at what she witnessed before she walked back to the house, no doubt with a smile on her face.'

'I'm sorry, but I don't know what you're saying.'

'I'm saying, Jamie, that my mother, as I've told you, has been, shall we say, anxious about my lifestyle for quite some time. I have no idea why, but there you go. The harridans have assured me that it's because I'm her only son and the baby of the family. At any rate, she saw us and she's jumped to certain conclusions.'

'What conclusions?' Jamie asked, totally bewildered by this point.

'That we're somehow involved.'

'We are. I work for you.'

'Strangely, seeing me all over you at the side of the pool didn't point to that particular conclusion. I've always maintained a healthy distance from the women who have worked for me in the past.'

'Involved?' Jamie squeaked, horrified.

'As in, an item. As in, romantically connected. As in...'

'I get the picture!'

'I'm not sure that you do, actually. My mother is under the impression that I've been too sheepish to say anything because I've always made a big deal of keeping my work life separate from my private life. In her wild and inventive imagination, we've only managed to keep our hands off one another while my sisters and their brood were around, but the second they all left we just couldn't help ourselves, it would seem.'

Jamie put her hands to her cheeks, which were burning hot. 'And did you tell her the truth?'

'Well, now here comes the tricky part...'

Ryan allowed a few moments of silence, during which he hoped she would join the dots and read what he was trying to say without him having to spell it out in black and white, but for once it seemed like her fine mind had deserted her.

'I couldn't,' he finally said bluntly.

'What do you mean *you couldn't*?'

'My mother has taken a shine to you. She's met a few of my girlfriends in the past and they haven't come up to her exacting standards.'

Distracted, Jamie couldn't resist the temptation to mutter under her breath that some of the girlfriends *she* had met would have fallen short of most mothers' standards, even if the standards weren't particularly exacting.

'She seems to think that we're involved in a serious relationship. I couldn't disillusion her because she's just had a stroke, albeit a mild one, and the last thing I want is for her to be subjected to any unnecessary stress. Not to put too fine a point on it, her last words before they wheeled her off for the first series of tests were that she was overjoyed that I had finally come to my senses and found myself a woman who could keep up with me.'

'This is awful!' Suddenly Jamie was really, really angry. Not only had she made a horrendous mistake—thrown away her precious privacy, engaged in wildly inappropriate behaviour and, worse, allowed herself feelings for a man who had no feelings for her—but now she was effectively being told that she wouldn't be able to put the whole sorry episode behind her because his mother had jumped to all the wrong conclusions and Ryan had made no effort to enlighten her.

'I appreciate that your mother doesn't need additional stress, Ryan, but it's going to be even more stressful for her if you deceive her over this and then have to tell her the truth when she's back on her feet. She'll never trust you again!'

'So you think that I should take the risk of damaging her health to be honest, do you? Do you imagine that you're the only person with a sense of family responsibility? My father died and my mother became the lynchpin of the family. She's been through a hell of a lot! She's had to cope with the shock of realising that the family finances had become a joke. She's had to suffer through tough times when so-called friends dropped by the wayside because she was no longer living in a big house and driving a big car.'

'And you had to witness all of that. How awful for you. I'm so sorry, Ryan. Truly I am.'

'We all have our stories to tell. Jamie! I was there to pick up the pieces, and when it comes to my mother's health and her peace of mind I'm not going anywhere. I'm still going to be here to pick up the pieces.'

It was shocking to see the lines of pain and worry etched

on his face. The Ryan who could take on the world and win was letting down his guard. Behind the dominant, powerful male, she had a glimpse of the confused boy who was forced to grow up fast. As she had.

'So I let my mother have the luxury of believing what she wanted to believe.'

'I...'

'You know what, Jamie? Perhaps you're right. Perhaps it would be better for you to leave. I'm sure I'll be able to explain your absence to my mother.'

In possession of what she thought she had wanted, Jamie found that she was now reluctant to leave. Ryan adored his family; he didn't have to verbalise it. Right now, he looked drained and so unlike the vibrant man she knew that her heart felt as though it was tearing in two. She knew that he wouldn't try to stop her if she decided to take him up on his offer and walk away, but their relationship would be irrevocably changed for ever. Would she even be able to continue working for him?

And why was she so angry at the thought of giving in to what he wanted? His mother was ill, and if a piece of harmless fiction would allow her to recover more quickly then where was the crime in that? They would return to London and in due course Ryan would gently break the news that they had broken up, amicably of course, and his mother would probably be sorry to hear it but her health certainly wouldn't suffer. Whereas now, still vulnerable, what if she *did* react badly? She was old and old people could be strangely fragile when it came to certain things, when it came to the well-being of their loved ones.

With a sickening jolt of self-awareness, Jamie knew why she was angry. Her anger stemmed from fear, whatever excuse she chose to hide behind, and her fear stemmed from the fact that Ryan had become far more than a boss to her.

She had feelings for him, and she might just as well have dug a hole for herself, jumped in and begun shovelling the earth over her head. She didn't want the pretence of being involved with Ryan because she was scared that the lines between fact and fiction might become blurred, scared that she would be left damaged, that the fiction would not be harmless after all, at least not to her.

Stuck between a rock and a hard place, Jamie navigated her way through a series of grim scenarios and, like a drowning person finally breaking the surface of the water, found the one and only way she could justify going along with his crazy idea and breathed a sigh of heady relief. She would treat it as a business proposition. He wanted her to play a pretend game, having no idea how dangerous for her the game could be, and she would box the pretence into a neat, controllable package and coolly look at it as just another part of her job.

'What exactly would this pretence entail?'

'Are you saying that you're willing to go along with me? It's a big ask, Jamie. I know that and, believe me, I would be very grateful indeed. But if you decide to jump in feet first then you can't decide halfway through that you'd really prefer the moral high-ground.'

'I'm taking it that this charade would only be appropriate while we're out here with your mother?'

'Naturally.'

'Which would be how long, exactly?'

'At least another week. I'm pretty confident that she will be able to travel back to the UK by then. She might even be able to travel back before, but I'm not into taking risks when it comes to my family.' He gave her a crooked smile, and Jamie tried to maintain a professional distance by not smiling back at him, although she could feel the hairs on the back of her neck stand on end. 'I've always saved my risk taking for the work arena.'

'Another week.' Jamie stared off into the distance and tried to break down the week into smaller, more manageable segments. Seven days during which there would be long periods of time in which there would be no need to pretend anything because his mother would probably be asleep or resting. 'Right,' she said crisply. 'I'll agree, on the condition that we get one thing perfectly straight.'

'And what might that be?'

'What happened out there by the pool was a terrible mistake.' Jamie looked at him squarely and directly. 'The sun, these exotic surroundings... Well, it was a moment of madness in unfamiliar surroundings and, yes, of course you're an attractive man. Things happened that shouldn't have happened. But I need your word that, if we're to pretend to be something we aren't for the sake of your mother, nothing physical must happen again. In other words, there must be very clear boundaries between us.'

A lull of silence greeted this remark, as thick and as heavy as treacle. Ryan's dark, inscrutable eyes resting lazily on her face made it difficult to hold on to her composure and she could feel tension coiling inside her, trickling through every part of her nerve-wracked body. Only a lifetime's habit of keeping her emotions to herself allowed her to maintain his gaze without flinching.

'Is that speech directed at yourself as well?'

'What do you mean?'

'I'm not some kind of arch seducer, lurking behind walls, waiting to pounce on an innocent victim. Sexual attraction is a funny thing in my experience. It hardly ever responds to the calm voice of reason.'

'Perhaps in your case, but certainly not in mine.'

'Maybe,' Ryan murmured, 'if you had ditched the virtue

and flung yourself at the vet he might have married a different sister.'

And just like that, he had changed the tenor of the conversation. With a single flick of the finger, he had overturned the pedestal on which she had valiantly sought to place herself, safely out of reach. Jamie's skin burned as she contemplated the awkward question that he had dragged out into the open.

How was it that she had never, not once, been really tempted to put her attraction to Greg to the test? How had it been so easy to restrain herself around him when with Ryan, a far more unsuitable and inappropriate candidate for her affections, she had gone up in flames, had found it impossible to rein back her frantic, screaming urge to touch him and to let him touch her? Was he now wondering the same thing? Would she be condemned now to always play the role of the woman who couldn't resist him? When they returned to England, and he resumed his life with the blonde bimbos and the airhead catwalk queens, would he still be smirking to himself that his quiet little secretary was lusting after him as she ducked behind her computer? Galling thought!

'Maybe I respond to you,' Jamie returned sharply. 'But I was thinking of Greg! Maybe it was all just a piece of weird, delayed emotional transference.'

'You used me as a substitute, in other words? Is that what you're saying?'

'I'm saying that there's no point analysing anything. What happened happened, but it's not going to happen again, and I need your word on that or else I won't agree to any charade. You needn't worry about me and those ideas you have about sexual attraction. I can handle myself.'

So, Ryan thought with slow-building murderous rage the likes of which he had never felt before, when she had arched back and succumbed to the sensation of his tongue gently caressing her nipple while the water lapped warmly around them had she actually been seeing the vet's face in her mind's eye? Ryan had never had much time for psychobabble but he could grudgingly see that the sudden appearance of the vet might have kick started something in her that had culminated in the temporary breaking down of her inhibitions with him. And he didn't like it.

'You have my word.' He smiled grimly and stood up. 'We should both get some sleep now. It's late. I'll be leaving for the hospital first thing in the morning.'

'Would…would it be okay if I came along with you? I've grown very fond of your mother in the short time I've known her. I'd like to see how she's doing for myself.'

Ryan began heading for the door. There was no point dwelling on the unsavoury possibility that he had been used as a substitute for someone else, that he had been the wrong boss, in the wrong place at the wrong time. He resisted the unnatural urge to worry the remark to death until he succeeded in extracting some alternative, more favourable explanation for the way she had responded to him. Instead, he locked the door on those unsettling thoughts and half-turned to find her right behind him.

Switching off the light, the room was suddenly plunged into semi-darkness but he could still make out the anxious glitter in her eyes. Whatever murky water happened to be flowing underneath their respective bridges at the moment, there was no doubt that she cared about his mother.

'There's no point, really. I'll tell her that you wanted to visit, but she'll be back here within a day or so and you can tell her for yourself. Your time would be better spent here, seeing to all the rearrangements that will have to be put in motion for the meetings in Florida. You'll need to make sure that all the relevant information gets emailed to George

Law. He would be a better bet to cover for me than Evans, I think. He might even find all those graphs and flip charts you prepared a handy tool.'

Jamie felt tears prick the corners of her eyes. She had to look away quickly and was grateful for the relative darkness. This was the Ryan she found so sweetly irresistible—the teasing, laid-back Ryan—and when that side of him went into retreat it was as if a dark cloud had settled over her world.

'You were never going to use any of them, were you?' she queried lightly, knowing that they were both attempting to find some of the familiar ground they had lost.

'I would have taken them all with me. As for using them, well, my speeches tend to be of the "winging it" variety, although that chart with all the different colours was very appealing.'

'I'll make sure that everything is sorted out,' Jamie promised, stepping into the hall and closing the door behind her.

'I'm sure you will. I have every faith in you.'

There was no need to dwell any longer on the dos and dont's of the strange game upon which she had agreed to embark.

As it turned out, she had less time to worry over it because Vivian was released the following day.

Jamie, having put through the final call to one of the senior conference organisers in Florida, was leaving the office at a little after five in the afternoon when she heard the sound of Ryan's car drawing up on the drive outside.

He had been out of the house since eight-thirty, calling only to tell her that he intended to stay in the town and use his time meeting with one of the head honchos of the tourist board so that he could throw around a few ideas he had had about the possibility of opening a boutique hotel on the island. Jamie knew that he had been playing around with the notion of extending the boundaries of his empire over the past few months, and she wasn't surprised that he would choose the island which he knew intimately.

She had no idea how the rest of the evening would evolve, and her stomach clenched into nervous knots as she headed towards the front door. But when it was pushed open she saw Vivian, pale but looking much healthier than before, preceding her son into the airy, flagstone open area.

'Darling girl, I'm so pleased to see you.'

Jamie walked into a warm embrace and managed to catch Ryan's eye over his mother's shoulder.

'How are you feeling, Vivian?'

'Like an old woman.' She dismissed it with a smile, linking her arm through Jamie's and walking towards the sitting room, which was one of the coolest rooms in the house thanks to the expanse of French doors which could be flung open to admit the balmy breezes, and the overhead ceiling fan. 'I thought that I was as healthy as a horse,' she confided, settling herself on the striped sofa where she suddenly looked much more frail. 'But don't we all, until something comes along to remind us that we aren't? Thankfully, my stroke was very, very mild. A warning, the doctor told me. I need to start slowing down.' She closed her eyes briefly and then opened them to smile at her son who had taken up position behind Jamie.

His hand was curved lightly on the nape of her neck and she was acutely conscious of the gentle stroking of his thumb on her skin. So this was what the charade felt like—a casual intimacy which his mother would expect of two people who were an item, and which was devastating on her senses.

Vivian was a smaller, softer, rounder version of her son. The same dark hair, the same dark eyes. These dark eyes were now happily taking them both in.

'My darling,' she said warmly. 'I can't tell you how thrilled I was when Ryan explained the situation.'

Jamie edged away from those disturbing fingers to sit on one of the upright chairs, leaving Ryan to sink onto the sofa next to his mother, conveniently no longer within touching distance. She tentatively touched the back of her neck where it still tingled, and pinned an engaging smile on her face.

'He's been a naughty boy. There was no need for the cloak-and-dagger routine. Of course, we all know how firm he's always been about keeping his love life—'

'Mother! I'm right here!'

Vivian patted his knee fondly but her eyes remained on Jamie. 'I know, and that's why I refrained from saying your *sex* life.'

Ryan groaned and flushed darkly. It was a pinprick of the comic in an awkward situation, if only Vivian knew.

'Away from the office, but I couldn't be more delighted. He must have told you that I've been worrying for some time now that he needs to find himself a good woman and settle down.'

'It's been mentioned,' Jamie murmured when she realised that an answer was expected of her, and Vivian greeted that acknowledgement with a beam of satisfied approval.

'Knowing that he has has made all the difference. I'm certain I'm back on my feet so quickly simply because I'm just so happy!'

Over the course of the next hour and a half, Vivian swatted aside enquiries about her nutrition regime, exercise plan and plans for when she returned to England in favour of the more absorbing topic of her son's good fortune in finding Jamie. She asked questions which brought a rush of embarrassed colour and tongue-tied silence to Jamie but which Ryan, Oscar-winning actor that he seemed to be, answered with aplomb.

She wondered aloud at her amazing ability to read a situation, exclaiming that she had just guessed from the *very start* that something was up by the way her son looked at Jamie. She blushed delicately when she referred to that moment when her suspicions had been confirmed, having accidentally spied them kissing at the side of the pool. She hastened to add that she had not lingered and so had witnessed nothing beyond 'a passionate kiss that said it all', while Jamie wished for the ground to open and swallow her up, hopefully to disgorge her into a world where the events of the past few weeks had never happened.

Vivian retired to bed with a light supper of tea and toast, leaving Jamie to glumly contemplate the mess into which they had both managed to get themselves.

'This,' she announced, as soon as Ryan was back in the sitting room, 'is a nightmare.'

'We'll discuss this outside. I no longer trust my mother not to pop up in unexpected places, and she doesn't need to have her high hopes dashed by a few careless words from you.'

He turned on his heel and she dashed behind him out onto the veranda, and then away completely from the house as they manoeuvred down the hill via a series of twisting wooden steps until they emerged onto the white, sandy beach below.

It was dark, but out here, under a full moon, the sea glinted and glittered like a placid lake of slick, black oil.

It was only the third time Jamie had actually been on the beach, and the first time at night, and she marvelled at its spectacular isolation. The house was very cleverly situated atop a natural, protected cove which could only be accessed by boat or via the grounds of the house, which were private property. Thus, it was perfectly peaceful. Bits of driftwood were scattered here and there, and the husks of fallen coconuts had been a never-ending source of fun and play for the little ones when they had been at the house. Ryan stooped to pick one up now and absently threw it out to sea in a long, wide arc before moving to sit on the sand, out of the reach of the sea gently lapping on the shore.

'I had no idea your mother was so…'

'Taken with the idea of you and I?'

'I was going to say desperate to see you settled down.'

'Are you saying that only a desperate man would choose you to settle down with?' He lay back on the sand with his hands folded behind his head and Jamie flounced down next to him, although sitting up so that she could glare at his face.

'That's not what I'm saying,' she denied in frustration. 'What on earth are we going to do?'

'We've already been over this.'

'I hadn't thought it through. I hadn't realised that we would have to build a great detailed story of how we…we…'

'Fell into each other's arms? Were drawn to one another over the coffee machine and the filing cabinets?'

'How can you think that it's funny? Your mother really believes that we're on the verge of announcing our engagement!'

'Now you're beginning to realise the position I was in when I found myself having to humour her. In her fragile condition, the last thing I could have done would have been to announce that we were involved in a little light-hearted hanky panky. I'm afraid she sees you as someone far too decent and moral and responsible to get carried away by lust, which would have left her thinking that I had seduced you for a bit of passing fun, only to toss you aside the second I was through with you.'

'You mean the way you usually treat the women you've been out with?'

'I refuse to be baited into an argument. This is the reality we're dealing with. I explained the situation to you and you signed up to the deal.'

'Yes, but I didn't sign up to any physical contact. You know that.'

He continued staring up, and to get his attention before her frustration ran away with her Jamie gathered some sand in her fist and slapped it down on his chest.

Quick as a flash, and before she could even think of taking avoidance tactics, his hand was curled round her wrist and he half sat up, propping himself up by his elbow.

'We're lovers, remember? My mother might be old but she's not away with the fairies. Keeping a healthy distance and smiling politely is going to set the alarm bells going in her head.'

'Yes, but—'

'But *what*? I touched you for three seconds on the nape of your neck. I wasn't plunging my hands down your tee-shirt!'

Jamie squirmed. His fingers were like a steel vice around her wrist, burning a hole in her skin.

'Why don't you pretend that I'm the vet?' he gritted savagely. 'Then you might start enjoying the occasional passing touch.'

She squeezed her eyes shut. She should never have implied that she had used him, should never have implied that she had been fired up by thoughts of Greg when Ryan had been touching her in the pool. That had been an outright lie, and afterwards she had felt like a coward who was happy to shunt the blame for her behaviour onto someone else because it was easier than having to accept responsibility for her own actions—misguided, stupid or otherwise.

She would not have liked it if a man had touched her intimately and she had responded to his touch, only to be told that she had been nothing but a fill-in for the woman he really wanted but couldn't have.

'That wouldn't work,' she confessed in a tight voice. 'Now, please let me go.'

Ryan released her immediately. He didn't know what the hell had prompted him to drag the vet into the conversation. He had determined to put that unpleasant conversation of earlier behind him and move on. Evidently, it had continued to prey on his mind.

'What's that supposed to mean?' He sat up and watched her narrowly as she massaged her wrist.

'I shouldn't have said what I said about... Sorry, I shouldn't have implied that you were a substitute for Greg. I've discovered that I put Greg behind me a lot longer ago than I thought.'

'Go on.'

'To what? There's nothing else to say. If I gave the wrong impression to you, then I apologise.'

'Let me get this straight.' Ryan only became aware of his black mood now that it was in the process of vanishing. 'You don't get turned on at the thought of the vet?'

'It would seem not.'

'So by the pool, that hot response really *was* all for me?'

'That still doesn't mean that it was right! What we did...'

'And you don't want any physical contact because I turn you on and you don't like that.'

'Something along those lines,' Jamie muttered, hot all over and agonisingly conscious of his glittering dark eyes fixed like laser beams on her face. 'I should tell you what I managed to sort out on the work front. I haven't had a chance, what with everything this evening.'

But, while her head was telling her that that was the best route away from this uncomfortable topic, her addled brain was refusing to go along for the ride.

Ryan tilted his head obligingly to one side. God, he suddenly felt on top of the world. He must have an ego as tough as an egg shell, he thought wryly, if a few insinuations and ill-chosen words from a woman who wasn't even his lover could reduce him to an ill-tempered bore. And if a retraction could reverse the effect in a heartbeat.

'You spoke to Law?' he prompted.

'And emailed all the info over. And…um…' Jamie licked her lips. 'I also contacted all the relevant people in, um, Florida.'

'And? Um? Ah, um…'

'You're making fun of me!'

'I'm intrigued by your sudden attack of nerves.'

'Can you blame me?'

Ryan didn't pretend to misunderstand her. 'No. No, I can't. You owned up to something you found difficult and I admire you for that. It was a brave thing to do. I'll keep all physical contact to the minimum, of course. If that's what you want.'

'It is.' Even to her own ears, she could hear the telltale waver in her voice.

'Okay, I won't touch you, but feel free to touch *me*,' he said in a husky undertone. 'Any time you like and anywhere you like because I'm happy to admit that you make me feel like a randy teenager. In fact, right now I'm hot for you, and I won't run screaming like an outraged virgin if you decide to touch me and feel for yourself.'

He hadn't just thrown down the challenge, he had hurled it like a javelin, and it lay between them now, waiting for her to decide what to do with it.

'Why do you have to make me laugh? It's not fair.' Jamie's breathing was shallow and painful and she leaned forward, resting on her outstretched hands, already knowing what she would do with that hurled challenge.

'Life seldom is. If you want me, you have to reach out and touch me.'

'Just while we're here,' she said on a soft moan. Of its own accord, her hand reached out to curl into the opening of his shirt, between two buttons, so that her knuckles were brushing his chest. 'Just for this week. If we can pretend to be something we're not for the sake of your mother, let's just pretend to be different people to one another. I won't be your secretary. You won't be my boss. Just for a few days, can we simply be two people, strangers who happened to meet on a very beautiful island in the Caribbean? Can we?'

'We'll pretend whatever you want,' Ryan growled. 'Now, take off your tee-shirt. Very, very slowly. And then your bra, also very slowly. I want to look at every intimate inch of your glorious body before I begin to touch it.'

A shiver of wicked, exquisite anticipation ripped through her. She should have been back-pedalling; she wasn't. Being here was a step out of time and why shouldn't she just give in to this thing? She had always lived a life of responsibility. She had always toed the line, trundling along in the slow lane, while her sister had lived life to the full in the fast lane. She had spent so much time picking up the pieces of Jessica's misadventures that she was in serious danger of forgetting what being young and carefree was all about.

So why shouldn't she spend a few days out here remembering? She had a sudden craving for some misspent time before it was too late.

With a smile and then a gurgle of laughter, she hooked her fingers under her tee-shirt and did as he asked. She pulled it over her head very, very slowly. Then she reached back to unclasp her bra, which she also removed very, very slowly.

Then she gave Ryan a gentle push back and when he was lying on the sand she straddled him, her breasts like ripe fruit waiting to be handled.

Between her legs, his erection was a rod of steel pushing against her.

And the look in his eyes! The hunger and the appreciation.

'What else,' she asked wickedly, 'would you like me to do?'

# CHAPTER EIGHT

RAMPANT appreciation flared in Jamie's eyes. She couldn't help it and, after days of blissfully throwing caution to the wind she no longer bothered trying to keep her guard up. Why should she? Ryan was nakedly, enthrallingly turned on by her. In their moments of wild passion, he would whisper how much into her ear, and every husky syllable represented yet another wrecking ball aimed at her defences.

And it wasn't just about the sex. They took time out, shooed out of the house by Vivian who claimed she needed peace and insisted that the only way she could get it was if they weren't making a racket in the house. Not that they did, but Ryan was happy to go with the flow. The island was stunningly beautiful and he had seen precious little of it. He hadn't realised how much of his work he took with him wherever he went, and for the first time he sidelined it in favour of showing Jamie around.

He took her to the Blue Hole where they swam in crystal clear waters. They took boats to the various islands. She forced him to traipse through bush so that they could experience some of the wildlife and laughed when he confessed to a fear of all things creepy-crawly.

'I think you'll find that *real* men, like me, are proud to admit to things like that,' he informed her haughtily, keeping a healthy distance as she allowed a praying mantis to scramble over her hand.

She had never had overseas holidays as a child. Losing her dad at such a young age had imposed financial restrictions on their lives. In the still, dark hours with just the sound of the sea lapping on the beach below the house, it seemed easy to shed her natural reserve and observe her childhood from a distance, with Ryan sitting next to her, an encouraging listener.

And of course they still worked together. Their mornings were still spent in the office in the house, but working had taken on a whole new perspective. They never touched one another, but sometimes he would lean over her, reading something over her shoulder on her computer, and his proximity was tantalising and electric. She would look at him and their eyes would tangle with full-blown lust even though they would be conversing perfectly normally about something mundane and technical.

Right now, Jamie was primly logging off her computer, but under her tee-shirt she was bra-less and under the small stretchy skirt the dampness between her legs announced the urgency her body felt at the prospect of being touched there.

Ryan was on the telephone, sprawled back in the leather swivel chair, his eyes broodingly following her movements as she stood up, smoothed down her skirt, caught his eyes and held them in a bold, inviting gaze.

'We got the contract.' He pushed back the chair, stuck his feet on the desk in a manner that was so typically him that it brought a half smile to her lips and beckoned her to him with his finger. 'George was eternally grateful for your exquisite attention to detail in the reports you emailed to him before the meetings began.'

'Good.' Jamie allowed herself a smile of professional satisfaction.

'Is that all you have to say by way of congratulations?'
Ryan murmured, his eyes darkening as he took in the gentle
sway of her breasts under the tight tee-shirt.

He was finding that he could barely look at her without his body slamming into immediate response. Where
was the man with the formidable control when it came to
women? He seemed to have been hijacked by a guy with a
semi-permanent erection and a head full of erotic images
that only went away when he was in deep sleep. Even then
he had woken up on a couple of occasions to find himself
thinking of her, needing an immediate cold shower, because
despite his attempts at persuasion she had refused to share
his bed for the duration of the night.

'What else would you like me to say?'

'I'm someone who believes that actions speak louder than
words.'

'How would you like me to act?' Jamie blushed when he
raised his eyebrows fractionally and let his eyes travel with
slow, lazy insolence over the length of her body. 'We can't.'
Her voice was breathless. 'Your mother will be waiting on
the veranda for us to join her for lunch.'

'Forgot to tell you. She got Junior to drive her into town
for a check-up with the consultant and she said that she's
going to meet one of her friends for a bite out while she's
there. I have yet, to see someone recover more quickly from
a health scare,' he continued drily. 'In fact, I haven't seen
her so relaxed in a long time.' Now that he and Jamie were
open in their relationship, whatever that relationship might
be, his mother was as chipper as a cricket, lapping it all up,
planning who only knew what in that head of hers.

Ryan closed his mind to what lay round an otherwise
unexplored corner in the future. Instead, he focused on the
sexy, sexy woman standing inches away from him in a skirt

that revealed newly brown, slender legs and a top that was begging to be ripped off.

'So you have all the time in the world to demonstrate how thrilled you are that we've managed to hook this new, lucrative contract. On second thoughts, I think that *I* should be the one to show *you* how impressed I am for your invaluable contribution to us closing the deal.'

He sat forward and ran his hands along the sides of her thighs, stroking their soft, silky length until he felt her begin to melt. Then he slid his hands higher, hooked his fingers over the lacy elastic of her underwear and tugged. Jamie trembled. She propped herself against the edge of his desk and closed her eyes, losing herself in the glorious sensation of skirt and panties both being pulled down. She was burning up even though the air-conditioning was on, circulating cold air through the room.

Their love-making was usually at night, after his mother had retired for the evening. The stars and the moon had borne witness countless times to them on the beach, lying on a giant rug on the sand, lost in each other. Twice they had cooled off in the sea only to fall right back into each other's arms the second they were out. They had made love in his bedroom. In her bedroom. Once, memorably, in the kitchen, late at night and with the kitchen door shut just in case, which had involved certain mouth-watering delights that Ryan had enjoyed licking off her.

But the office had been a designated work area so that now there was something deliciously wicked about being in it half-undressed.

'We should go upstairs,' she whispered. Her fingers sifted through his thick, dark hair. She looked down as he stared up at her for a few seconds.

'Oh, I don't know,' Ryan drawled. 'It seems only appropriate that I should show my deep and undying gratitude for your hard work in a working environment.'

'What if one of the gardeners sees us through the window?'

'Good point. I'll dip the shutters while you stay right where you are and don't move a muscle.'

She did and when he resumed his position on the chair she yielded to his devastating fingers and tongue until she was on the point of collapse. He tasted her until she thought that her whole body was going to explode, until she was begging him to take her. Her breasts ached under the tee-shirt and she was driven to roll her fingers over her sore, tender nipples in a bid to assuage their painful sensitivity. Every time she glanced down to that dark head buried between her thighs, she felt weaker than a rag doll. There was something intensely erotic about the fact that he was still fully clothed while she was dishevelled and half-dressed.

'I can't stand this any longer,' she groaned shakily, and she knew that he was smiling as he continued to tease her throbbing clitoris with his tongue.

'I love it when you say that.' Ryan finally released her screaming body from the onslaught of his attention and carried her, cave-man style, to the long sofa where she lay and watched as he stripped off his clothes. She never tired of feasting on the hard muscularity of his body.

Of course, he worked out. In London, he was a member of a gym, where twice a week he treated himself to gruelling games of squash with a couple of guys from the office. He also seemed to play every other sport imaginable. Here, he ran—at five in the morning, he had told her a few days ago. She hadn't believed him until this morning, on the way to the bathroom, she had glanced out of her window to see him disappearing down the drive. They had only gone their separate ways a few hours before. He was a man who needed next to no sleep.

When he lightly touched himself, an involuntary groan escaped her lips and he grinned. Her arm was resting lightly across her forehead and she looked like a very beautiful Victorian maiden caught in the act of swooning. Which, now that he thought about it, was an image that was intensely appealing.

'I'm glad you're satisfied with my level of appreciation, milady,' he told her huskily.

He positioned himself directly over her, her legs between his, and he pulled her tee-shirt over her head. She was already arching back, inviting his mouth to her breasts, offering the twin peaks of her nipples for his pleasure. Irresistible. Making love to her was a constant struggle to keep himself under control. The challenge of breathing in the dampness between her legs had been struggle enough when it came to self-restraint, and it was no easier as he dipped his head so that he could suckle on her nipples, one at a time, loving the way they engorged in his mouth.

He entered her with one single thrust when they could no longer bear to go so far but not far enough. Her body shuddered as within seconds she was climbing that peak, tumbling into an orgasm that rocked her body, taking him with her, their slick, slippery bodies fused as if one.

It was bliss to lie with him, squashed on the sofa, as they gradually came back down to earth. It was just as well that his mother was out, Jamie thought, because she knew that there was no way she could have sauntered out onto the veranda for lunch without betraying the tell-tale signs of a woman who has been branded thoroughly by her man.

She stretched, settled down more comfortably against his body. He cupped her breast absently, as though it was impossible for him to be this close to her without him touching her intimately. She loved it. She loved that feeling of possession. Sometimes he would cup between her legs or else just distractedly stroke her nipple with his finger, circling its outline and then teasing her as he waited for her to react to his feathery touch.

Jamie could have stayed like this for ever.

She said, reluctantly raising the subject, 'Now that the deal is done and dusted and your mother is pretty much back on her feet...'

Ryan stilled because he knew that this was a conversation they had to have. He was needed back in London. He could delegate, but only to a certain extent. Decisions had to be taken about crucial deals and those decisions could not be made out here where the tropical sun and gratifying, relaxing sex on tap—not to mention their daily jaunts out where thoughts of work disappeared—were combining to erode his appetite for ferocious concentration.

Jamie waited for him to pick up the threads of the conversation, but he didn't and she stifled a sigh.

'We should be thinking of returning to the UK.'

'Yes,' Ryan said slowly. 'We need to.' Until this moment, he had really not considered the matter in a truly concrete way. He did now. It took seconds. The truth, laid bare in front of him, was that he couldn't walk away from what they had begun. Had he envisaged this outcome when he had casually enrolled her in his clever plan to placate his mother's nervous concerns?

'I'll need to make reservations.'

'You know how to ruin an atmosphere, Jamie.'

'I'm not trying to. I'm just...being realistic.'

'We'll leave on the weekend. That's the day after tomorrow.' He rolled onto his back and stared up at the ceiling where the sun filtering through the half-open shutters played on the woodwork in an ever-changing kaleidoscopic pattern.

'And then we go back to being the people we were before we came here.'

'How easy is that going to be?' He inclined his head to look at her, but her face was giving nothing away. 'Do you really imagine that we're going to be able to return to the soulless working relationship we had before all of this?'

'It wasn't a soulless relationship!'

'You know exactly what I mean. We can't tell the past to go away because it's inconvenient.'

'What are you trying to say?'

'I'm saying that this stopped being a game of charades the second we climbed into bed, and if you think that we can pretend that none of it ever happened, then you're living in cloud cuckoo land. It happened, and it will still happen even when we're back in London and you're sitting at your desk and I'm at mine. When we look at one another, we're going to remember, and you can't wish that simple fact away.'

'We should never have started this.' There was always a price to be paid at the end of the day, and for so much pleasure the price was going to be steep. Jamie was now realising that she had got far more than she had bargained for. She had thrown off her old, careful, cautious self and let in a sentiment she now knew had been hovering on the sidelines, barely kept at bay, waiting to devour her. She had fallen in love with him and now she was drowning.

'Tell me I'm not going to get a long sermon loosely based on the notion of regret,' Ryan said curtly. 'I really thought that we had moved past all of that.'

'To what? Moved past it to what, exactly? You're right. It's going to be impossible to look at one another and pretend that none of this ever happened.'

'So we do the logical thing.' He smiled slowly and relaxed.

'Which is?'

'We continue seeing one another when we get back to London. What we have isn't going to go away because we tell it to, so why bother to try? If anyone had told me two months ago—less—that we would end up in bed together, and loving every second of the experience, I would have thought they were crazy. But here we are and I'm not willing to put this thing to sleep, not yet, not when I still burn for you and you're on my mind every second of the day.'

*Not yet.* Those two words stuck in Jamie's head and in between the glorious temptation to greedily take what was on offer the reality of its inevitable ending dripped through the fantasy like poison.

This was a moment in time, a moment which he wanted to extend because he was enjoying himself. He had broken through his self-imposed taboo of sleeping with someone he worked with, and now that he had done that it was all systems go as far as he was concerned.

He wouldn't be lying there, getting himself twisted into little knots, as he mentally journeyed into the future and found all the flaws in his plan. He wouldn't be stressing because at some indeterminate time their relationship would end and he would be left hurt and ripped to shreds. None of that would occur to him, because for him she was a casual fling, something that had defied belief in taking shape and, having taken shape, had further defied belief by being enjoyable. And Ryan Sheppard was a man with a very healthy capacity for enjoyment.

Looking at him now, he was the picture of a man satisfied with what he saw as a perfectly reasonable solution to a situation.

'I can't believe I'm saying this,' he confided, 'but you're the sexiest woman I've ever taken to my bed.' He folded her in his arms and covered her leg with his thigh. 'And, as an added bonus, you make me laugh.'

Jamie would have given anything to just close her eyes and carry on living for the moment, just as she had spent the past days doing. She had slept with him and loved every minute of it, but now they were about to head back to London, and she could no longer pretend that she was the kind of girl who could live indefinitely in the present without a thought of the future. She was cursed with the burden of responsibility and too well-trained in the many ways of dumping it on her shoulders.

'When I touch you,' he admitted roughly, 'I forget what the concept of stress is. I've never played truant until now—all those trips when the thought of work never crossed my mind. And my mother is overjoyed with this situation.' He kissed her eyelids, which fluttered shut. 'Let's not put a spanner in the works by talking about regret. We agreed to put on an act. We didn't have to, as it turns out. Let's see where this thing takes us, Jamie, and when it's over I won't have to concoct a lie to my mother.'

*When it's over.* She wondered how he could build so many negatives into something he was trying to persuade her was a positive step forward, but of course he wouldn't even be aware of that. He was so accustomed to the short-term nature of his relationships that he wasn't even capable of thinking of them in any other way. Every adjective he used reminded her that, for him, this was a sexually satisfying but temporary situation. How long would it take, once they had returned to London, before the sexiest woman he had ever taken to his bed became yesterday's news?

Here, on the island, there was no competition. In London, there would be competition lurking round every corner, waiting to ambush him from behind every door, phoning him and texting him and emailing him. Where would *she* stand then? He would no longer be playing truant and she wouldn't be the person making him laugh.

She pushed herself up into a sitting position, feeling suddenly very exposed without a stitch of clothing on.

'We should get up. Get dressed. I'm hungry, and your mother will be back soon. I'm sure she won't want to stay out for too long in this sun, not after what she's been through.'

'I doubt she would turn a hair if she discovered that we were doing more than filing reports in here.'

'That's not the point,' Jamie told him sharply. She began levering herself off the sofa, only to be pulled back down so that she half fell on top of him, her breasts squashing against his chest.

'This conversation isn't over,' he grated. 'You opened it, and neither of us is going anywhere until it's been closed.'

'I don't know what you want me to say.'

'You damn well do, Jamie.'

'Okay. You want me to tell you that I'll continue sleeping with you until you decide that you're sick of me and chuck me over for your usual blonde-haired, legs-up-to-armpits bimbo!'

'Where did *that* come from?' He pinned her to the sofa and stared at her fiercely, although underneath his bristling brows she could see his bewilderment. He hadn't a clue what had prompted that outburst and that, in itself, was hurtful. She had a brief, searing fantasy in which he soothed away her fears and insecurities by telling her that there would never be another blonde-haired, legs-up-to-armpits bimbo, that she was the only woman for him, that he worshipped the ground she walked on and loved her to death. The fantasy vanished virtually as soon as it materialised.

'I've really...enjoyed *this*, but when we get back to London, things between us are going to get back to what they were. I know it's going to be difficult, but it won't be impossible. You'll be busy and distracted with other deals in the pipeline. I'll be busy trying to get rid of my sister who is still at my house. Your mother will probably want to see you a bit more often than she has in the past. In no time at all, we'll both look back on this as if it was a dream, something that never really happened.'

Ryan couldn't quite believe that she was effectively dumping him. He knew that she had been a reluctant bed-partner. He knew that she had principles which, once upon a time, he would have derided as positively archaic but which he had come to respect. But once she had slept with him, he had assumed a straightforward path leading towards a mutually agreed-upon outcome. Hell, people embarked upon marriage with fewer scruples and less psychoanalysis! The thought of no longer being able to touch her—or, worse, of seeing her on a daily basis and no longer being able to touch her—made his blood run cold, but Ryan suddenly felt as though he had gone the extra mile in the seduction stakes. He wasn't going to beg.

'Besides, it would be awkward. Sooner or later, people would find out. You know how that office buzzes with gossip. Both of us would lose respect.'

'Do yourself a favour and don't worry on my behalf. Gossip has never bothered me.'

'Well, it would bother *me*,' Jamie told him coolly. 'I've never liked the thought of people talking about me behind my back. Anyway, let's be honest, this isn't a relationship that's going anywhere.' She was disgusted with herself for the tiny thread of hope that continued to blossom inside her, the hope that he would leap into instant denial or at least pretend to give the matter some serious thought.

But he just said with an impatient shrug, 'Why does a relationship have to go somewhere? We're happy with this. That's all that matters.'

'Not to me!'

'Are you telling me that you want me to ask you to marry

me?' Ryan said slowly, fixing her with those fabulous eyes that gave the illusion of being able to see right down deep into her innermost soul.

'No! Of course not!' Jamie gave a shaky laugh. In her head, she could imagine his incredulity at such a preposterous idea: the secretary who after a few days romping in the sack suddenly got thoughts above her station, encouraged by his mother. 'But I don't want to spend time with someone in a relationship that's not going anywhere. I guess I've learnt some lessons from Greg.' Within reason, she was determined to be as truthful as possible.

'Right.' Ryan stood up and strolled towards the bundles of discarded clothes on the floor, his back to her, offering her a rejection that made her eyes sting. 'So it's back to business as usual,' he remarked, pulling on his clothes while she continued to watch him helplessly. He found himself thinking of creative ways he could use to get her to change her mind and scowled at his own weakness. He had had the rug pulled from under his feet and that, he decided, was why he now felt like hitting something very hard.

She had managed to scuttle back into her tee-shirt and knickers by the time he eventually turned around.

'We could continue to enjoy ourselves for the little time here we have left...' Jamie was ashamed of the desperation behind this suggestion.

The fact that she was as cool as a cucumber enraged Ryan even more. She had been nothing if not a star pupil, he thought savagely. From shrinking violet, she was now brazen enough to offer her body to him for a day and a half, with their cut-off point doubtless to be when Junior was carrying their cases to the car.

'A few more sex sessions for the road?' he asked with thick sarcasm and Jamie flinched. 'How many do you think we can fit in before the car is revving in the drive to take us to the airport?' This was supposed to have been fun. Once they returned to London, they would be working alongside one another and there would be no room for misplaced emotion.

Ryan shook his head, frustrated at his own inability to put things into perspective. Had it been a mistake to start this in the first place? Jamie was nothing like the women he had slept with in the past. At her core, she was intensely serious. She wasn't into the clubs, the parties and the expensive trinkets, and he had been challenged and seduced by the novelty of someone so different from what he was accustomed to. Add to the mixture the fact that she was intelligent and humorous, and then throw in the ease with which she had engaged his notoriously picky family members—was it any surprise that he had chosen to overlook the simple reality that she would not be satisfied with the sort of relationship he preferred?

'Get dressed.' He couldn't have a conversation with her when her body was still on tempting display.

Jamie went bright red and gathered up the rest of her clothing, taking his command for what it was. Now that they were over, he was already relegating her to his past. He was a guy who specialised in moving on when it came to women and he was already moving on, no longer interested in her body, possibly even turned off by the physical reminder of what they had shared.

She would take her cue from him. It had been a mistake to suggest that they enjoy themselves for the brief time they had left on the island, and she knew that that sign of weakness would return to haunt her at a later date.

'We'll have to maintain this fiction while we're still here,' Ryan told her with a shuttered expression and Jamie nodded, thankful for her hair swinging across her face as she looked down, hiding her giddy confusion.

She composed herself before raising her eyes to meet his. 'Of course.'

Her calm smile got on his nerves. He gritted his teeth together and shoved his hands into his pockets, where they bunched into fists.

'Look, I'm really sorry,' Jamie said awkwardly, trying to elicit a response, but the Ryan she had known over the past few days had disappeared from view. In his place was a cold-eyed stranger that chilled her to the bone and made her wonder whether they would ever be able to rescue their working relationship and return it to the uncomplicated place it had once inhabited.

'Sorry? For what?' He shrugged casually, walked towards the door and held it open for her to precede him out of the office, straight into the balmy tropical air that suddenly made him feel as though he was trapped in a greenhouse. 'I asked you to come here. You were quite happy to remain in London and play nursemaid to your sister.'

Jamie bit her lip and stifled the urge to argue with him on that point. He was now her boss once again and she seemed to have lost the right to speak her mind. Besides, he was barely aware of her presence, walking briskly towards the French doors and out onto the breezy veranda. She lagged behind and chose to hover by the door with her arms folded.

Ryan sprawled on one of the wicker chairs and stretched out his legs. 'I also persuaded you to play a role because it suited me, so I have no idea what you're sorry for, unless it's for climbing into bed with me—but, hell, we're both adults. We knew what we were signing up for.' He glanced over his shoulder to where she was dithering slightly behind him. 'Why don't you go and see to the arrangements for our flights back? And then you might as well use the rest of the day to get your things together.'

Jamie left him staring out at the distance. Effectively dis-

missed, she miserably obeyed orders. She managed to get
them flights for the following day, which was a relief. In
front of his mother, they made a passable show of togetherness but she retired very early for bed.

Landing in London was like reconnecting with a place she
no longer recognised. After the sharp, bright technicolor
of the island, and the slow, tranquil pace of life, the hustle
and bustle of the grey streets and even greyer skies was a
mournful reminder of what she had lost.

She felt like a different person—the person who had lived
life in the slow lane, imagining herself to still have feelings
for Greg, had disappeared. Ryan had awakened her and, for
better or worse, she was no longer going to be the careful
person in the background she had spent years cultivating.

For that, she was thankful. On every other score, the
bright smile she kept pinned to her face bore no relation to
the misery and confusion she was feeling inside—especially
when, as they delivered Vivian to Claire and Hannah, both
of whom had made the trip to the airport to collect their
mother, she saw Ryan pick up a mobile on his cell phone.

She knew him so well that when he turned away, lowered his voice, gave that throaty chuckle, she realised that
he was on the phone to a woman.

'Please tell me that I won't start back tomorrow with the
usual delivery of flowers for the new woman in your life?'
Her voice threatened to break when she said this, but it
didn't, and in fact she was rather proud of her composure.
The sun had turned him into a bronzed god and her breath
caught in her throat as memories flooded her head, making her feel a little dizzy, but she kept smiling and smiling,
even when he raised his eyebrows in a question.

'No idea what you're talking about.'

'Okay!' she said brightly, sticking out one hand to hail a cab.

'But if it did,' Ryan drawled, 'would it bother you?'

Jamie tugged her coat protectively around her. 'Honestly?'

Ryan felt an uninvited leap of interest. After the dance they had been doing around one another for the past day and a half, the thought of cutting through the facade was irresistible. A little honesty? Who could resist? He tilted his head to one side in a semi-nod.

'It wouldn't feel good.' Jamie kept her voice low, even and well-modulated. 'But I would do it, so please don't think that you would have to tiptoe around me. The working relationship we have is much more important to me than a brief fling. In fact...' She paused and glanced around her to where Ryan's driver was patiently waiting. He would be going straight to the office. She, on the other hand, would be returning to see what damage her sister had inflicted on her house in her absence.

'In fact...?' Ryan prompted.

'In fact, all said and done, you've done me a huge favour.'

'What are you talking about?'

'You've taken me out of cold storage. I think I had spent far too long kidding myself that I still had feelings for Greg. You made me see what a big mistake it was to bury myself in the past.' There was a strong element of truth in that but, more importantly, Jamie liked the control she could impose on her fractured life by rationalising her behaviour. She could almost kid herself that everything had happened for the best and, if she could convince herself of that, then she would be able to cope with Ryan whispering sweet nothings down the end of a phone to another woman. It made sense, and Jamie had to be sensible again. Her life depended on it.

'I'm a different person now. I'm going to really start enjoying London. I can see that I wasted a long time hibernating. Not consciously, of course, but I took a back seat and I shouldn't have. So, that's all I wanted to say. Except, well, your mother still thinks that we're about to tie the knot any second now... Can I ask you when you intend to tell her the truth?'

'Does it matter? After all, you're out of the equation now,' Ryan told her politely.

'Yes, but *what* will you tell her? I'm very fond of Vivian and the more I've got to know her the less I've liked what we did.'

'Don't worry. I won't blacken your name, Jamie.'

'Thank you, because I would quite like to see your family. Some time.'

'That won't be appropriate.'

'Right. I understand.' She felt a lump in her throat and looked away quickly.

'My mother is given to fond flights of fancy,' Ryan continued. 'And I don't want her to be encouraged into thinking that we're still an item. It won't work. As soon as she's settled back, I'll break the news to her that we've parted company, on perfectly amicable terms that allow us to carry on working harmoniously together. Rest assured that if my mother apportions blame to anyone, it'll be to me.'

'She'll be upset.' Jamie knew what it was like to live in a bubble and how painful it could be when that bubble burst.

'In which case, I shall have to make sure that I give her something else to think about and look forward to,' Ryan murmured, leaning down so that Jamie felt his warm breath against her ear, tickling her and doing all sorts of familiar things to her body.

'What do you mean?'

'Well.' He straightened up and shot her a devilish grin that made her toes curl. 'Maybe this has been a learning curve for both of us!'

'Really?'

'Of course! You haven't got the monopoly on life lessons, Jamie. Whilst you're busy getting out there and discovering London, let's just say that *I* might finally start my search for the perfect partner. My mother wants me to settle down. The harridans keep nagging me. Yes, maybe it's time for me to think about tying the knot!'

# CHAPTER NINE

RYAN looked at the blonde perched on the sofa in his office and she looked expectantly back at him. She was in search of an evening of fun, involving a very expensive meal, a very expensive club and possibly a very expensive trinket to wear around that slender, white neck of hers, something that would complement the tumble of vanilla curls that fell to her waist in artful disarray.

It was Friday night and he couldn't think of a single reason why he shouldn't shove the work to one side and look forward to the prospect of what was prominently an offer.

Instead, he found himself thinking of excuses to back out of his evening of fun and he scowled at his own idiocy.

Where was Jamie? Ever since they had returned to London two weeks ago, she had turned into an annoying clock watcher. Only now did he realise how accustomed he had become to her willingness to work long hours at his beck and call, and only now did he realise how much of his time had been spent in her company. A Friday evening had often seen them brainstorming something, occasionally with some of his computer whizz-kids who could be relied upon to sacrifice entire weekends in the pursuit of tweaking computer programs, very often on their own, calling in a takeaway and enjoying it with files and papers spread between them on his desk.

Gone; all of it. She was still the super-efficient secretary, always polite and unfailingly professional, but now she left when she should leave and didn't arrive a second before she was due.

Clearly she was pursuing that fabulous single life she had mentioned when they had parted company at the airport. He wouldn't know. She never mentioned a word of it and there was no way that he was going to play the loser and actually show an interest.

Abigail, whom he had now seen a couple of times and of whom he was already beginning to tire, leaned forward, flashed him a coy smile and stood up.

'Are we actually going to go out, Ryan, baby? Please don't tell me that we're going to spend Friday night in this office!'

'I've spent many an enjoyable Friday night here,' Ryan grated, but standing up and moving to help her with her coat.

'Well.' She pouted and then stretched up to briefly peck him on the lips. 'That's not *my* sort of thing. And good luck finding any woman who would enjoy that!'

Which brought him right back to Jamie. Pretty much everything seemed to bring him right back to Jamie these days. He didn't want to feel driven to watch her, but he did. He absorbed the way she moved, the way she leaned forward when she was studying something in front of her, tucking her hair behind her ear and frowning. He absorbed the way she nestled the telephone against her shoulder when she spoke so that she could do something else at the same time and then the way she lightly massaged her neck afterwards. He noticed how she shifted her eyes away from him when he spoke to her, and the faint colour that stole into her cheeks, which was the only giveaway that under the polite surface all was not as evenly balanced as she would have him believe.

Or was it?

Ryan didn't know and he hated that. Having always found it easy to walk away from relationships once they had begun to out-stay their welcome, he was finding it impossible to do the same with this one. Why? He could only think that it was because what they had had been terminated before it had had time to run its course. It was unfinished business. How could he be expected to treat it with a sanguine shrug of the shoulders?

Also, *he* hadn't generated the break-up. Ryan knew that that was nothing but wounded male pride, but it went into the mix, didn't it? And the whole mix, for him, was adding up to a very unpleasant fixation which he was finding hellishly difficult to shift.

It would help if he could generate more of an interest in her replacement.

It was after ten by the time they entered the exclusive club in Knightsbridge. They had dined in one of the most expensive restaurants in London, where Abigail had made gentle digs about his choice of dress. He had ordered more wine to get him over his growing irritation. She had spent far too long trying to engage his attention on various titbits of gossip concerning friends he didn't know and could not care less about. She bored him with anecdotes about the world of acting, which made him recognise the folly of dating yet another woman who thought that everyone was interested in a bunch of people egotistic enough to imagine that what they did for a living really was of immense interest to the rest of the human race. Abigail tittered, trilled, pouted and flaunted a body that he considered far too thin, really.

The trip to the club would probably mark the death knell of the relationship, if relationship it could be called, and that was the only reason he entered with something approaching a spring in his step.

It took him a few seconds for his eyes to adjust to the dim lighting. The club was intimate, with a number of tables for anyone wanting to dine or just sit and enjoy the spectacle of people on the dance floor. The bar area, sleek and very modern, was busy and waiters were doing the rounds, taking orders and pocketing the very generous tips given by the patrons. A live jazz band ensured that the atmosphere remained up market and sophisticated.

Ryan had been to this club a number of times before but this time he was less than impressed by the subdued lighting and eye candy. Maybe he was getting too old for this sort of thing. He was in his thirties now and there was a fine line between trendy and sad. He hadn't seriously intended to start hunting for the perfect marriage partner, as he had nonchalantly told Jamie two weeks previously, but now he wondered whether the time really had come to settle down. After all, he didn't want still to be coming to this place in five years' time, with another Abigail clone hanging on to his arm.

On the verge of telling his date that if she wanted to stay she would be staying on her own, he spotted Jamie, and the shock of seeing his secretary in a *club* was almost enough to make him think that his eyes were playing tricks on him.

Since when did Jamie frequent clubs? Ryan was rocked by the upsurge of rage that filled him. Was this what she had been busily doing on all those evenings since they had returned to London, when she had tripped over herself to join the throng of people leaving the building on the dot of five-thirty? Was this her bid to throw herself into living life in the fast lane?

Abigail had spotted some of her friends and he absently nodded as she disappeared into the crowd by the bar. He was keen to see who Jamie had come with. Her sister, maybe? She hadn't told him the outcome of Jessica's situation. Obviously, that had been just too personal a conversation for her to endure, and pride had stopped him from asking.

However, Jessica must still be on the scene, perhaps having ditched the caring, sharing vet, and was now introducing Jamie to what she had been missing: a sleazy, over-priced night club in the heart of Knightsbridge.

Ryan almost laughed out loud. Had she come to him for advice on where to go, he would willingly have told her, and would have steered her away from the dubious pleasures of seedy joints where middle-aged men tried to pick up young girls.

He had three bottles of the finest champagne sent over to Abigail and her crowd of giggling friends and received a beaming smile of appreciation in return. Then he got himself a whisky and edged over to wait for Jamie. She had disappeared in the direction of the cloakroom, on her own. Several heads—he noticed grimly, several *male* heads—had followed her progress across the crowded room and he could understand why. Gone were the flat shoes, the hair neatly tied up, the sober suit. In fact, gone was everything he associated with his secretary. She had been at pains over the past couple of weeks to revert to projecting the hands-off image, a daily reminder of her position within his company and in his life. She worked for him. She obeyed orders. She carried out her duties. And she locked him out of everything else.

Ryan swallowed a generous slug of whisky and scowled. She had vanished temporarily but her image was still seared into his head: the high stilettos, the tight, outrageously short red dress, the poker-straight hair parted to one side so that it swept across her face, giving her a come-hither look that frankly set his teeth on edge.

He couldn't spot Jessica anywhere or else he would have been tempted to personally congratulate her on the miraculous transformation of her sister.

He had worked his way towards the door through which Jamie would return and was on his second whisky by the time she emerged. He was in just the right position to reach out and grab her by the arm.

It gave her the fright of her life.

Jamie was bitterly regretting the crazy impulse that had brought her to the club with Richard, one of Greg's friends to whom she had been introduced just three days previously. Clubs just weren't her thing. The music seemed very loud, too loud to permit any sort of decent conversation, and it was really dark—especially when wearing very high heels. One wrong move and she would embarrass herself by crashing to the floor, so she had spent the past two hours taking very small steps and only reluctantly allowing herself to be dragged to the dance floor for a couple of upbeat tunes that she recognised.

And Richard… Well, he was a nice enough guy, fashioned in the same mould as Greg. Both of them had been to university together and both had studied to be vets, with Richard opting to work in London while Greg had moved north. He should have made the ideal date and Jamie was sure that, had she met Richard a year before, she would have warmed to his gentle personality and perhaps even embarked on a relationship that might have gone somewhere.

But she had been ruined by Ryan. Her ideal man no longer seemed to be the kind, placid sort. Compared to Ryan, with his vibrant, explosive, overpowering personality, Richard was a shadow of a man and they had established early on that there was no attraction. Which made this excursion to the club slightly more bearable; at least she didn't have to ward off unwanted attention from her date.

But she had dressed to kill and she knew that other men had been looking at her.

She was half-expecting one of them to sidle over and really throw her into a tizzy by asking her to dance, and the sudden tug on her arm as she emerged from the cloakroom where she had been taking cover for as long as had been humanly possible made her jackknife in startled horror.

Jamie turned, mouth open, to give whoever had had the nerve to grab her a piece of her mind. She was also poised to run. The club seemed full of lecherous old men with suspiciously young and beautiful girls dangling like trophies on their arms.

She was so taken aback at seeing Ryan that her mouth literally fell open in startled shock.

'What are *you* doing here?'

'Snap! I was about to ask *you* the same thing. Are you here with your sister? Painting the town red?'

'No, I'm not. And, in fact, I'd better get back to my table. My date will be wondering where I am.'

'Date? Date? What date? Are you telling me that you're here with a *man*?'

Jamie bristled at the tone of his voice. Did he imagine that she was incapable of having a life outside work? She had made it perfectly clear that she did. She had been at pains over the past fortnight to make sure that she left on time and arrived on time, the implication being that she had lots of other exciting things to do with her life aside from devoting all her time to him.

'That would be most people's definition of a date!'

'You came here with him or did you pick him up here? Because if you picked him up here then I would have to warn you to lower your expectations. Most of these guys come here to scout and see what they can pick up.'

Jamie started moving away and Ryan followed her. She had come here with a man. He was outraged at the thought of that. It felt suddenly imperative that he meet this guy. How had she managed to achieve that in the space of two weeks? Of course, he knew how. She had the body of a siren and she had obviously been determined to flaunt it.

His jaw tightened, and he was further disgruntled to discover that the man rising to greet her looked like a decent sort of guy: short brown hair, pleasant smile, wire-rimmed spectacles. Just the sort of man she had once professed to go for. Ryan tried not to scowl as introductions were grudgingly made. She hadn't been aware of him following her but, having turned around to see him towering behind her, she had had no option but to introduce the men to each other.

Next to Ryan, Richard looked flimsy and insubstantial, which further annoyed her.

'Can I be terribly rude, old man—' Ryan stepped in before she could dismiss him, which was what she clearly had in mind '—and ask your date for a dance? She left work ridiculously early today.'

'I left on time!'

'And there were one or two things I needed to discuss with her. I don't normally drag my work out with me, but...'

'Aren't you here with someone?' Jamie asked tartly, then she lowered her voice to hiss into his hear. 'Or are you one of those men who come here scouting to see what they can pick up?'

'Not my style.' He slipped his arm around her waist, already taking it as a given that the neat little guy she had come with would give his permission to have his date whipped away for a few minutes. He didn't look like the sort to put up much of a fight. Indeed, the man was happy to let his hot, sexy date get on the dance floor with someone else's arms wrapped around her, even though the hot, sexy date was making all sorts of noises about feeling tired and needing to sit it out.

'Tired?' Ryan murmured in a low, velvety drawl that had her skin breaking out in goose bumps. 'Surely not? How are you going to paint any town red if you're yawning at eleven on a Friday evening?'

The music had obligingly shifted from fast to slow, and Jamie stiffened as he pulled her towards him in a clinch that was far too intimate for her liking. She tried to pull back and he tugged her closer, resting his hand on the small of her back, reminding her of what it felt like to be touched by him. It was not a memory she wanted to linger over.

'I'm sure your date wouldn't approve of us dancing,' she said primly, following his lead and trying to hold herself as rigidly as possible. 'Where is she, anyway?'

'Behind you—a quarter to ten. Bright blue dress. Blue shoes.' He swung her around so that Jamie had a perfect view of a tall blonde with lots of long, tousled blonde hair and long, long legs. The pull of jealousy was so overpowering that she felt momentarily giddy.

Ryan had kept this one quiet. There had been no emails popping up on his computer, the password for which Jamie had, no breathy phone calls, no mention of anything having to be rearranged so that he could fit in his latest woman.

She didn't want to think about it, but she did. Was this one the serious one?

'She's very pretty,' Jamie said crisply. 'Have you introduced her to your mother as yet?'

'My mother,' he said into her ear, dipping her which made her feel very exposed in her too revealing dress, 'has yet to learn that you and I have broken up.'

'You mean you haven't told her?'

'No opportunity. Who's the guy, Jamie? Now that you've quizzed me about my date.'

'I haven't quizzed you!'

'Are you trying to avoid my question?' Her breasts against his chest were turning him on and he drew back slightly rather than risk having her feel his erection pushing against his zip.

'I don't see that it's any of your business.'

'I'm concerned about you. We *were* almost married, don't forget.'

'We were *never* almost married!'

'My mother would probably disagree. So I don't feel it's out of place to tell you that it's a big, bad world out there and you don't have much experience of it. In the space of a couple of weeks, you've managed to get yourself a man. He could be anybody.'

'How dare you?' Jamie gritted. 'I don't believe I'm hearing this!'

'You should be flattered that I continue to take an interest in your welfare. That guy may have a neat haircut and wear deodorant but it doesn't necessarily make him one of the good guys.'

Jamie almost snorted in disgust. Did Ryan Sheppard consider *himself* one of the good guys? Good guys didn't string women along! She bit back the temptation to ask him whether his date for the night—the one who had been abandoned in favour of his secretary for no other reason than he was incurably *nosy*—would categorise him as a 'good guy' when she was probably after love, marriage and the whole fairy-tale story. Chances were slim that he would deliver.

In fact, she wanted to ask him just how serious he was about the blonde. But there was no way that she was going to do that. The past two weeks had been agonising. Every day had been a challenge to not look at him, not react to him, desperately try to pretend that she was over whatever passing fling they had enjoyed. She wasn't going to encourage any kind of personal conversation now, and it infuriated her that just being here with him, seething at everything he had just said, still made her feel more alive than she had felt ever since she had returned to London.

'You read the papers. You watch the news. Low lifes are everywhere and some of them do a good job of passing for normal.'

'Well, thank you very much for you concern and your wise words, Ryan, but you can relax. Richard comes with personal recommendations.'

'Really? Spill the beans.'

'Greg introduced me to him, if you must know. He and Greg went to university together and Richard works in London.'

'Another vet? Didn't you get your fill of guys who miss their sickly animals whenever they're away from them for too long?'

'I'm not going to stand here and listen to this.'

'You're not standing. You're dancing.' He twirled her around and watched as the colour mounted in her cheeks and her hair became tangled and dishevelled. 'And is vet-number-one here with his erstwhile wife?'

The music stopped but when Jamie would have walked off he kept her firmly anchored by virtue of his fingers curled around her wrist. Out of the corner of his eye, he could see Abigail looking at them with scowling displeasure, and he knew that he should go across to her, at least make a show of wanting to spend some time in her company.

Without releasing Jamie, he beckoned across a waiter, who magically materialised, and whispered something into his ear. A few more bottles of champagne, he reasoned, to be delivered to the tall blonde in the blue dress—and his most sincere apologies, but he had business to discuss with his secretary. The thought of abandoning his conversation with Jamie was out of the question.

'I'm sure your date won't mind if we trip the light fantastic for a bit longer. And you were going to tell me about Vet One and your sister.'

Jamie gave an exasperated sigh. She didn't want this. She didn't want to be dancing with him, to feel his hand resting on her waist and the heat from his body scorching her. She was aware of the guilty thrill spreading through her body and she didn't want that either. She reasoned that it would do no good to storm off in a petulant strop. She was only dancing with him, for heaven's sake! And, besides, Ryan could be as tenacious as a dog with a bone. Did she really want him following her to her table? Joining them? Calling across his girlfriend to share the fun and laughter? No! One more dance and he would be gone and she would be able to breathe properly, she told herself fiercely.

'They've patched things up,' she said reluctantly and Ryan held her back so that he could look at her with interest.

'Why haven't you told me this before?'

'I didn't think that you would be that interested.'

'I'm cut to the quick, Jamie.' His voice was light, but he was surprised to discover that he didn't like being kept out of the loop with this information. Hell, she had retreated back into her impenetrable fortress and slammed the door firmly in his face. 'What happened?'

'Long story.'

'I'm happy to keep dancing until you've got it off your chest.'

'I had a heart-to-heart with Jessica when I got back to London.' Jamie was distracted enough not to notice the way he had pulled her closer to him. She thought back to that fateful conversation with her sister. It had been the best thing she had ever done and for that, she knew, she owed a great deal of thanks to Ryan and his family. She had seen, first hand, how relationships between family members should operate. She had witnessed how important it was to be open and honest.

She had also not been in the best of moods, back in her house, when she had been confronted with a sister who had not budged in her stance that marriage was a bore and she was due a life of fun and excitement. Greg was still there trying to play the persuasive card and so, it seemed, were all the ensuing arguments.

For the first time in both their lives, Jamie had sat her sister down and really given her a piece of her mind.

'I told her that it wasn't acceptable for her to descend on me and not really give a hoot whether she was disrupting my life or not. I told her that she was thoughtless and inconsiderate and that she was old enough to sort out her problems. I also said that she was being an utter fool, that Greg was crazy about her, that he was a treasure, and that if she decided to end the relationship then she should do it and stop dithering. Most of all I told her that she would have to sort things out somewhere else because I was fed up with both of them in the house.'

'A red-letter day for you, in other words,' Ryan murmured. Wisps of her hair brushed his lips and he stifled a shudder of pure craving. When she looked up at him with an open, genuine smile, the first he had glimpsed since they had returned to London, he was overwhelmed with the crazy sensation of just not feeling right in his own skin.

'It all came out then. Jessica told me that she was terrified of getting pregnant and losing her figure. I suppose I always envied her. She did what she wanted to do, and she always pulled it off because she was so beautiful, while I stayed in the slow lane, always being responsible, always there to pick up the pieces.'

Talking to him, Jamie realised how much she had missed it. It was unbelievable that in such a short period of time she had become accustomed to sharing her thoughts with him and appreciating his always humorous, always intelligent take on whatever she had had to say.

She felt a suspicious lump at the back of her throat and looked away quickly. It was very important not to give in to all those waves of nostalgia and regret that had a nasty habit of sneaking up on her when she wasn't looking. She had to remember that they had moved on from that place of lovers. He had a new girlfriend—probably a model or an actress, by the looks of her—thereby proving that he would always run true to form, that *she* had been nothing but a novelty to be enjoyed on the run. And she, in turn, had been making a huge effort to get out there. Well, she had accepted a date, which was a promising start.

'So there you have it!' she told him brightly. 'Not a particularly interesting story.'

'Let me be the judge of that. So where was hubby when all this soul-searching was taking place?'

'Out meeting Richard for a drink.'

'How very thoughtful of him to introduce the two of you.'

Jamie was finding it hard to recall exactly what Richard looked like. As usual, Ryan's image superimposed itself on everything and she felt angry and helpless at the same time at his way of just taking over her thoughts.

'Yes. We hit if off instantly.'

'Did you, now?' Ryan said through gritted teeth.

'Maybe I have a thing for vets!' she trilled gaily. 'Just like you have a thing for actresses and models.' Jamie hadn't wanted to say that, but the words popped out of her mouth, and her heart sank a little when he didn't utter a blanket denial to her sweeping generalisation.

'Maybe you do. Well, make sure that you give me ample warning if you decide to get married and start having a brood of children.'

'I don't think that marriage is something to be rushed into. Besides, I've only been out with Richard...' *once* '...a couple of times.' She smiled politely and drew away from him as the song came to an end. 'And, yes, I'll make sure that I tell you well in advance if and when I decide to tie the knot.'

'Hell, Jamie, have you ever heard of playing the field?' Ryan raked his fingers through his hair and glowered at her. A couple of dates and she wasn't denying the possibility that this might be the real thing! He wanted to root her to the spot, involve her in another dance, take the opportunity to tell her that throwing herself into the first relationship that came her way so shortly after they had broken up wasn't the right thing to do, but she was already walking away, threading a path through the crowds.

'You know that's not the way I am!' she told him over her shoulder, her voice bright and casual. 'And please don't follow me back to the table or I shall begin to feel really guilty about your poor girlfriend having to amuse herself.'

'Abigail's perfectly fine.'

'Really? Because she seems to be seething.'

'Question.'

Jamie stopped and looked at him. Even in this crowded place, he dominated his surroundings. His physical beauty leapt out and made a nonsense of all the other men in the cavernous room. No wonder his girlfriend looked put out. The competition in the club was stiff, lots of airhead blondes with long legs and short skirts, and a fair amount of them were openly sizing up the biggest fish in their midst.

'What is it?'

'Have you slept with him yet?'

His light-hearted, bantering tone said it all and an angry flush spread across her cheeks. Was he laughing at her? Was he thinking that she cut a ridiculous figure here, out of her comfort zone, dressed like a bird of paradise but without the streaming long hair and the endless legs? She wanted to hit him, and she balled her hands into fists and narrowed her eyes coldly.

'I really think it's time we ended this conversation, Ryan. I'll see you at work on Monday. Have a good weekend.' She turned away abruptly and walked with quickened strides towards the table, where Richard was waiting for her.

Why, she agonised, couldn't she have fallen for a man like Richard Dent? On paper, he was everything she had always reckoned she would want in a prospective partner. He was pleasant to look at, he was friendly, considerate and thoughtful. He had brought her flowers and had ruefully but manfully accepted it when she had told him that she liked him as a friend but that she wasn't interested in promoting a relationship with him. They had talked and, when she might have expected him to make his excuses and leave as soon as he could, he had insisted that they go out to the club, because why shouldn't friends have fun together?

She tried very hard to focus on what he was saying but her eyes kept straying, searching out Ryan, watching his body language with his girlfriend, torturing herself with thoughts of what they would be getting up to later.

Jamie spotted them leaving when Richard dragged her up to the dance floor for one last dance. Ryan's girlfriend seemed to be doing a great deal of excited gesticulating. He appeared to be ignoring her. Before she could look away, he caught her gaze, held it and then gave a slight inclination of his head. To her it seemed like a mocking salute, and in response she unconsciously and defensively allowed herself to relax in Richard's arms.

Of course it was a foolish, hollow gesture. Whilst he would be heading back to his place to fall into bed with yet another pouting blonde, she would be giving Richard a light embrace, exchanging mobile numbers and promising to meet up for a drink when their diaries permitted.

Her house, when she returned an hour later, seemed eerily empty. Jessica had taken everything with her and once Jamie had cleaned the place it was as though her sister had never been there. They had parted on good terms, and for the first time she wished she had her sister with her, someone to talk to instead of wandering alone into the kitchen where she made herself a cup of coffee and settled down to consider her options.

The reality of seeing Ryan with another woman had come as a brutal shock. Ahead of her stretched an endless future of seeing him with other women, waiting for him to fall in love with one of them. Out there, there would surely be a leggy blonde who had the personality to suck him in. How would she feel when that happened? Would she still be able to plaster a professional smile on her face and pretend that everything was all right? And, if she honestly couldn't see that happening, then surely the only course of action left would be to hand in her resignation?

It seemed like the next step forward and she was doodling on a piece of paper, working out what she would write, how she would explain her defection from a highly paid job which she had always loved, when the doorbell rang.

Jamie could only think that it might be Richard, at nearly one-thirty in the morning.

Still in her small red dress, but with her shoes kicked off in favour of some fluffy bedroom slippers, she wearily pulled open the door to find Ryan lounging outside, hands in his pockets.

'Do you usually open your door at this hour of the morning to anyone who comes calling?' He looked past her, compelled to see whether there was evidence of her date lurking around. 'It's dangerous.' He placed the flat of his hand on the door. 'You're going to ask me what I'm doing here and then you're going to tell me to leave. I'm not leaving. I want to talk to you. No—I *need* to talk to you. Where is your date?'

'He dropped me home and then left.' She hesitated, then took a deep breath. 'Which is just as well, because I need to talk to you too.' In that moment, Jamie made her mind up. She would have to hand in her resignation. She couldn't have Ryan taking time out from his hectic love life to deliver unwanted, uninvited advice to her. She didn't want him preaching to her about things she should or shouldn't do because they had been lovers and therefore he felt a misplaced sense of obligation. She certainly didn't want him thinking that he had a right to show up at her house whenever he felt like it to sermonise about her choices.

She led the way towards the kitchen and made him a mug of black coffee. Then she swivelled the draft copy of her resignation letter towards him.

Ryan stared down at it for a few seconds, during which his brain seemed to grind to a standstill. He picked up the piece of paper and reread her few polite lines but nothing appeared to be sinking in. 'What's this?'

'What does it look like, Ryan? It's my letter of resignation.' She wrapped her hands around the mug and stared at him, her heart racing like someone caught up in a panic attack. 'It's just a draft. I intend to type it out properly and it'll be on your desk first thing on Monday morning.'

'Over my dead body.' He crumpled the letter and tossed it on the table. 'Resignation not accepted!' He stood up, walked across to her, leaned down and shot her a look of savage fury. 'You're not resigning, and you're definitely not going to waste your time with that loser you're dating.'

# CHAPTER TEN

'Don't you dare tell me what to do, Ryan Sheppard!' Jamie cringed back in the chair.

'Somebody's got to. For your own good.'

'Is that why you dashed over here? To give me a long lecture on being careful, because I'm obviously too naive and simple-minded to actually know how to live my own life?'

'You can't be serious about that guy after a couple of dates.' He pushed himself away from her and prowled angrily through the small kitchen, his movements jerky and restless. 'Did you tell him about us? Did he ask you to leave your job because of it? Because if that's the case then I'm warning you that the man is no good for you. Can you really see yourself in a position of subservience for the rest of your life?'

Jamie looked at him in complete bewilderment.

'Have you been drinking?' she asked eventually, which earned her a glowering look.

'You would drive any sane man to drink,' Ryan muttered under his breath. 'You told me that marriage wasn't on the cards!'

'Are you *jealous*?'

'Should I be?'

The silence stretched between them. 'Have you done anything that I should be jealous about?' Ryan shook his head and dealt her an accusing look. 'I don't do jealousy. I never have.' Suddenly those standard words which had once been true were exposed for the lie that they were. He was jealous as hell. Wasn't that why he had rushed over to her house? The thought of her being touched by anyone else had galvanised him into frantic action. She was still in her clubbing clothes. Had her date touched her underneath the skimpy little red dress?

Had he just missed the man by a whisker? Suddenly Ryan felt as though he needed something a lot stronger than a mug of black coffee.

'You can't resign,' he said finally. 'I won't let you.'

'Is that because I'm so indispensable? No one's indispensable. I think I'm quoting you when I say that. I can work out my month's notice and I'll make sure that I find someone equally dedicated to replace me.'

'You're irreplaceable.'

Jamie ignored the flush of pleasure those words gave her. Of course, Ryan would think her irreplaceable. Not only was he accustomed to the way she worked, but now that he had slept with her he must truly have entered his comfort zone. The physical side of their relationship might be over, but at the back of his mind he would always have how submissive and responsive she had been with him. It would have been easy for him to assume that that responsiveness would have been lasting, that she would have been even more obliging when it came to working overtime and putting herself out to suit him. Hence his horror now, faced with her resignation.

'Oh, please,' Jamie retorted with biting sarcasm.

'I didn't like seeing you with that guy.'

Jamie was so busy stoking herself into self-righteous anger, that Ryan had had the nerve to invade her privacy so that he could lecture her, that it took a few seconds for those words to sink in.

'What do you mean?'

'It seems that I do get jealous after all,' Ryan muttered in such a low voice that Jamie had to strain her ears to hear what he had said.

He returned to sit at the kitchen table, where he proceeded to frown at the floor before leaning forward, elbows on his thighs, rubbing his eyes with his fingers then looking up at her.

'You're jealous…' Jamie's heart sang.

'You've disappeared every evening on the dot of five-thirty ever since we got back to London.' Ryan glared at her accusingly. 'And then suddenly I discover the reason why. You've been going to clubs and seeing men behind my back.'

'I haven't been *seeing men*, and anyway you've been seeing women as well,' Jamie countered, without letting on that she had been torn apart with her own little green monsters. And had he told her anything about his latest blonde? No, he had been spectacularly silent on that matter, so how dare he start criticising her for trying to have a life?

'Abigail was a mistake. I have no idea what I was thinking.'

'Did you…did you sleep with her? Not that I care. I'm just curious.'

'You *should* care. You should care about everything I say and do and think because that's how I feel about you. And, no, I didn't sleep with her. I wasn't even tempted.'

Jamie breathed in sharply, almost not wanting to exhale just in case she broke the spell. Had he just said what she thought he had, or was she just imagining it?

'You didn't even tell me about your sister.'

'I…I was scared to carry on confiding in you, Ryan. I felt that we had been down that road and that if we were to continue working together then things would have to go back to where they had once been. I would have to start learning how to keep my private life to myself.'

'I was cut out of the loop and I didn't like it,' Ryan told her heavily.

Jamie felt giddy when their eyes met. Her mouth was dry and suddenly the kitchen just wasn't the right place to be having this kind of conversation. Her thoughts were in a muddle and she was beginning to ache from the hard kitchen chair. She needed to sink into something soft and yielding that would mould her trembling body.

'Perhaps we should go into the sitting room,' she suggested in a shaky voice. 'And if you're finished with that coffee I can make you another.'

'Because you think I need to sober up? I've had a bit to drink, but I'm by no means drunk.'

Jamie didn't say anything. She walked into the sitting room, very conscious of him following behind her. She had no idea what to make of what he had said to her. He was jealous; he *cared* about what she thought. He stridently, aggressively and possessively wanted her to care about what he thought. And he hadn't slept with the blonde bombshell.

Every instinct in her was nourishing the fragile shoot of hope that had begun to grow, but experience was still holding fast. She had made mistakes in the past. She forced herself to remember Greg. In retrospect, he had been nothing, but at the time she had happily built castles in the air and started hoping.

And then, with Ryan, she had fallen for him and had kidded herself that hopping into bed with him had been a moment of complete recklessness that she had long deserved. She had blinded herself to the obvious, which was that she had more than wanted him. She had needed him, was dependent and addicted to him. Then, once they had slept together, she had immersed herself in the pretence of being involved for Vivian's benefit, and those important lines between reality and fantasy had become blurred. She had started hoping for things. She seemed to make a habit of it.

So now, although she was badly tempted to take everything he said at face value and put the best possible interpretation on it, she resisted. Where would it get her? Was he just after a few more weeks or months with her because the leggy blondes were not quite doing it for him at this point in time? Or was he interested in having her around because he had chickened out of telling his mother the truth and he wanted to buy a little more time before he broke the news to her?

'I don't understand why you're telling me all of this now,' she said as soon as she was on the sofa. 'If you cared so much about being out of the loop, then it's funny that you didn't show any interest for the past couple of weeks.' She looked at him levelly. He had taken up position on one of the squashy chairs. It allowed her important breathing space. Still, she knew that her body was alive with emotion. Like an illness, the symptoms of which were branded in her brain, she could recognise all the familiar responses he evoked in her.

'You dumped me, Jamie.'

'I had to.' She looked away quickly, her face colouring. 'I'm not casual enough for a prolonged fling. I told you that at the time and I meant it.'

'Which brings us back to the date. Has he made you promises you think he'll keep?'

Jamie sighed and shook her head. 'It was nothing serious,' she confessed. 'Richard is a really nice guy, but...' *But he's not you.* 'But maybe I don't go for vets after all.'

'And I don't go for leggy blondes, now that we're on the confession bandwagon. It doesn't matter what glossy magazine they've stepped out of.'

Jamie held her breath, then exhaled slowly. 'What do you mean?' She watched cautiously as he stood up and walked towards her, hesitating before sitting down on the sofa.

'I used to, once. A hundred years ago. I thought it was what I wanted—a rich, rewarding work life and fun on the side with women who didn't make demands. I don't know when things started to change,' Ryan admitted with painful honesty. 'You came to work for me, Jamie, and you spoilt everything I had always taken for granted.'

'What do you mean?' But the open vulnerability on his face made her heart swell. When he reached out to stroke her wrist, she didn't pull her hand away.

'I got accustomed to having a relationship with a woman on my own level.'

'We didn't *have* a relationship.'

'I'm not talking about a sexual relationship. I'm talking about an emotional and intellectual relationship. Those are the strongest building blocks on the face of the earth, only I didn't realise it at the time. I just knew that I was increasingly frustrated with the women I dated. They were empty and shallow and they bored me. And then we went away, and we didn't just sleep together. We...we talked.

'For the first time this week, it finally dawned on me just how much time we spent together, how much I enjoyed that and just how far down the road I'd gone when it came to really having a conversation with a woman. When it was gone, it was like something I should have appreciated and valued had disappeared from my life and I didn't know how to reclaim it. We got back to London and you were never around. I missed you. I miss you.'

'You miss me?' Jamie stretched those three words out for as long as she could, so that she could savour every syllable.

'When you kissed me at that Christmas party, it was as if a light had suddenly started shining from nowhere. I told myself that you had only kissed me to make the vet jealous. I figured that you were still emotionally wrapped up with him.'

'I stopped being wrapped up with Greg a long time ago. He started going out with my sister, and I can't even remember being terribly upset about it, although I thought that I *should* be.' That episode was like a dream she had had a million years ago. It was something that was no longer relevant in her life at all. 'I kissed you because my sister was going to. She'd had too much to drink. I wasn't about to let Greg see his wife kissing some other guy under a sprig of mistletoe. That would have been the end of their marriage and there was no way I was going to allow that to happen.'

'And that's the only reason why?'

Jamie went bright red.

'I've bared my soul,' Ryan murmured. 'Are you going to shoot me down in flames now by not being truthful with me? I can take it.'

'I kissed you because I wanted to.' She met his eyes, held them. 'I didn't think so at the time but, looking back on it afterwards, yes, I wanted to kiss you because I'd been attracted to you practically from the first time I set eyes on you, Ryan Sheppard.'

'But you once told me that attraction wasn't enough.'

Her breath caught in her throat. They had both said a lot to each other, but the word 'love' had never entered the conversation. She had never allowed herself to wear her heart on her sleeve and even now it floated unspoken around them, challenging either one to pluck it out of the silence and give it a name. When Jamie thought about doing that, her throat went dry and she felt as though she suddenly had cotton wool stuffed in her mouth.

'I remember,' she croaked shakily.

'You were right.' He fiddled with her fingers but Jamie

could hardly concentrate on that. 'I fell in love with you and I don't even know when it happened. When we finally made love, I never stopped to ask myself why it just felt so damned *right*.'

'You fell in love with me?'

'You look shocked,' he said wryly. 'I'm surprised you haven't put two and two together already. I said goodbye to Abigail and couldn't wait to get over here. I was going mad wondering what you were getting up to with your date. He looked like the kind of sensitive, tree-hugging guy who wouldn't hesitate to pour out his feelings after five seconds. I felt like I'd left things too late.'

'I can't believe you love me.' Jamie reached out one tremulous hand to stroke his cheek. 'I love you too. I feel like I've waited all my life for you. When we made love and got involved in that pretend relationship for your mother, I knew that I couldn't carry on with it when we got back here because I would want much more. I knew you were into flings, and I knew that if you tossed me aside I would never recover. I thought that I had to be proactive.'

Ryan pulled her into him. After two weeks, the feel of her body against his was like a taste of coming home.

They fell back onto the sofa and she wriggled on top of him. It was unbelievably good. When he began kissing her, she was completely lost.

Later, she struggled to remember how they had made it up to her bedroom. She had a fuzzy recollection of clothes being discarded along the way.

She gave herself to him with a blissful sense of completion. There was no other way of describing it—Ryan Sheppard *completed* her. Without him, she was lacking.

Afterwards, with his arms around her, he murmured softly into her hair, 'Now, my darling, I never want to go through the torture I've been through over the past few weeks. I'm afraid your brief taste of clubbing is at an end, unless I'm there, keeping a watchful eye on you. And the only way I can think of doing that is to marry you. So...will you marry me, Jamie?'

'Yes!'

'As soon as possible?'

'Absolutely!'

'I'm a happy man.' He lay back, one arm flung over the side of the bed, and smiled with contentment as Jamie covered him with little kisses.

Left to his own devices, Ryan would have married Jamie within the week. His mother, however, was having nothing of the sort. She wanted a full-blown affair, and in spite of his low-level grumbling—for he couldn't understand why on earth she hadn't already had her fill of full-blown weddings with his three sisters—Jamie was thrilled to accommodate her.

She was even more thrilled when Jessica offered to come down to London for a week so that they could go bridal shopping together.

'But no clubs and drinking,' Jamie felt compelled to warn her sister the week before she was due to arrive, and her warning was met with a burst of laughter.

'You have my word,' Jessica readily agreed. 'I'm pregnant! I was going to wait and surprise you with a picture of the scan, but I might just as well tell you over the phone. So when we're not looking for the perfect ivory wedding dress you might find yourself checking out prams and cots.'

Jessica had changed in more ways than one. Having confessed to feelings of deep insecurity at the thought of losing her figure should she get pregnant, she had finally surfaced to realise that Greg loved her for the person she was and not for the perfect figure she happened to have had imprinted in her genetic code.

And, as Jessica always did, she was now throwing herself into her pregnancy, even travelling with her baby books which she insisted Jamie read.

'Because you'll be next...'

It proved to be an accurate prediction.

One year and two months later, Jamie would sit in Ryan's apartment with a dark-haired, gloriously chubby-faced Isobella gurgling in her basket next to her and with details of country properties spread out on the table.

'London,' Ryan had announced, 'is no place to bring up a baby. At least, not central London.'

So they were moving out to Richmond. Not too far, but far enough from the traffic and chaos. As was Ryan's style, once the decision had been made he moved into immediate action, sourcing houses and submerging himself so well into the role of the domesticated man that Jamie could only sit back and smile.

Loving her, he had told her, had changed him. The birth of his first child had changed him even more. Gone was the workaholic and in its place was a man who enjoyed immersing himself in all the small things that made life go round.

Now Jamie joined him in the kitchen, where he was pouring them both a glass of wine, and she dangled a brochure in front of her.

'Not too big,' she said, 'not too small and in the perfect location...'

'I knew that one would get to you.' He dropped a kiss on her head and grinned. 'Clambering roses, beams, view of the park... We'll have to wait and see, though. As we both know, size matters.'

Jamie giggled and warmed at the teasing hunger in his eyes.

'But…' he murmured, stepping towards her so that she could feel the size and girth of his erection. 'I actually wasn't talking about that. I was talking about the house. It has to be big enough for, let's just say, all future additions.'

Ryan couldn't imagine greater contentment. He cupped her head with his hand and kissed her tenderly on her lips. 'And,' he said, moving to hold her tighter and deepening his kiss, 'the sooner we get started on those additions, the better.…'

* * * * *

# CHRISTMAS AT THE TYCOON'S COMMAND

## JENNIFER HAYWARD

For my editor, Nic. I couldn't have written this without your guidance and inspiration. You are amazing and I look forward to working on many great books together.

# CHAPTER ONE

SHE WAS NOT losing this one.

Chloe Russo fixed her gaze on the bright yellow taxi that had appeared like an apparition from heaven in the ferociously snarled First Avenue traffic, its lit number her only chance at salvation in the monsoon that had descended over Manhattan.

Shielding her eyes from the driving rain, she stepped a foot deeper into the layers of honking, snarling traffic and jammed her hand high in the air. The driver of a Bentley sounded his horn furiously as he swerved to avoid her, but Chloe, heart pounding, kept her eyes glued to the taxi driver's face, willing him to stop.

The taxi slid to a halt in front of her in a cacophony of screeching horns and spraying water. Heart soaring, she waded through the giant puddle that stood between her and victory, flung the door of the taxi open and slid inside, reeling off Evolution's Fifth Avenue address with a request to step on it that made the cabbie roll his eyes.

"Lady," he muttered caustically, "have you *looked* outside?"

She'd been *standing* in it for half an hour, she wanted to scream. While thirty-five of his coworkers had passed her by—she knew because she'd counted every one of them.

But picking a fight with the last remaining cab driver in Manhattan seemed unwise, given her present situation.

She was late for her first board meeting as the director of Evolution's fragrance division. An inauspicious start.

Her teeth chattered amid a chill that seemed to reach bone-deep. She pushed off the hood of her raincoat and mopped her face with a tissue, thankful for her waterproof mascara. Let out a defeated sigh. She should have left earlier. Had forgotten taxis on a rainy day in Manhattan were akin to spotting a western lowland gorilla in the wild. But in truth, she'd been dreading today and everything about it.

Her cell phone vibrated in her bag. She rooted around to find it as a loud pop song joined the symphony of honking horns. Fingers curling around the sleek metal, she pulled it out and answered it before her grumpy driver deposited her back into the downpour.

"I just landed," her sister, Mireille, announced. "How are you? How was your flight? Did you get settled in okay? It's *so* amazing to have you back in New York."

The verbal torrent pulled a smile from her lips. "Good, good and yes. Although it just took me half an hour to get a taxi. I'm soaked to the bone."

"You've been living in Europe too long." Her sister's voice lowered to a conspiratorial whisper. "Of course, I'm really calling to see how your dinner with Nico went. I've been dying to know. Uncle Giorgio has himself all in a dither with this campaign of his to unseat him."

Chloe bit her lip. Nico Di Fiore, the new CEO of Evolution, her family cosmetic company, was a loaded subject of late. Her late father's godson, Nico had been appointed CEO upon her parents' deaths last spring according to the terms of her father's will, assuming a position that should have been her uncle Giorgio's. He had also been appointed financial regent for Chloe and Mireille until they reached the age of thirty, an unexpected and unacceptable development that had been the last straw for Chloe, because it meant four years of *him* in her life.

"I didn't have dinner with him." Her offhand tone hid the apprehension dampening her palms. "I wanted to keep things professional. I suggested we meet tomorrow instead—on my first day back."

Mireille drew in a breath. "You *blew* Nico off for dinner?"

"It wasn't like that." Except it had been exactly like that.

There was a pregnant pause on the other end of the line. "That really wasn't wise, Chloe."

"He *summoned* me to have dinner with him," she came back defensively. Just like he'd *summoned* her home from Paris, where she'd been perfectly happy. "This is *our* company, not his. Isn't it driving you crazy having him in charge?"

"It was what Father wanted." Mireille sighed. "I know Evolution's your baby—far more than it is mine. That Uncle Giorgio has you all wound up, but you need to face reality. Nico is leading the company. I don't know what's going on between you two, but you're going to have to come to terms with it."

"There's nothing going on between us." Hadn't been since Nico had broken her heart far too many years ago to remember now. And she *had* been attempting to do exactly that—to process this new reality that had seen Nico take over Evolution when her parents had been killed in a car crash in Tuscany six months ago, turning her life upside down in the process. But she couldn't quite seem to get there.

Evolution's stately, soaring, gold-tinted headquarters rose majestically in front of her as the taxi turned onto

Fifth Avenue. A fist formed in her chest, making it hard to breathe.

"I have to go," she murmured. "It's the board meeting tonight."

*"Right."* A wealth of meaning in her sister's tone. "Better you than me." As a junior executive in Evolution's PR department, Chloe's younger sister was not a member of the board. "Promise me you won't fight with him, Chloe."

"That," she said grimly, "is impossible. I love you and I'll see you tomorrow."

She handed the taxi driver the fare as he pulled to a halt in front of the building. Slid out of the car and stepped onto the sidewalk, teeming with its usual wall-to-wall pedestrian traffic huddled under brightly colored umbrellas.

A frozen feeling descended over her as she stood staring up at the giant gold letters that spelled out *Evolution* on the front of the building. Her parents—Martino and Juliette Russo—had spent two decades building Evolution into a legendary cosmetics brand. They had been the heart and soul of the company. *Of her.*

She hadn't been in the building since she'd lost them, buried in work in the Paris lab. The thought of going in there now without them present seemed like the final admission they were gone, and she couldn't quite seem to do it.

The crowd parted like a river around her as she stood there, heart in her mouth, feet glued to the concrete. A woman in a Gucci raincoat finally jolted her out of her suspended state, crankily advising her to "move on." Her fingers clutched tight around her bag, she made her way through the glass doors, presented the security guard with her credentials and rode the elevator to the fiftieth floor, where Evolution's executive offices overlooked Central Park.

A slim, blond-haired woman with trendy glasses pounced on her as she emerged into the elegant cream marble reception area. "Clara Jones, your new PA," the blonde introduced herself, relieving Chloe of her dripping raincoat in the same breath. "You're the last to arrive. Nico is—well, you know..." she said, giving Chloe a meaningful look. "He likes to start on time."

Her heart crawled into her throat. "I couldn't get a cab."

"It *is* awful out there."

Clara led Chloe down the hall toward the large, plush conference room with its expansive view of a wintry, lamp-lit Central Park. "Nico gave me your presentation. It's ready to go."

Now if only she was. Memories deluged her as she stood surveying the crowded, warmly lit room full of Evolution board members and directors enjoying a glass of wine and hors d'oeuvres before the meeting began. Of her father manning the seat at the head of the table that Nico now would as the chairman of the board. Of her mother swanning around, captivating the executives with her sparkling wit and charm.

Her stomach swam with nerves. She was a *scientist*. Her mother had been a self-made genius with a larger-than-life personality who'd created a multibillion-dollar empire out of a tiny bath products company she'd founded to serve her husband's financial clientele. Chloe was far more comfortable in the lab creating beautiful things than presenting to a stiff-suited board like her mother had been. But this was her job now. A necessary evil.

Any nerves about her presentation, however, faded to the background as Nico spotted her. Clad in a sleek, dark gray Tom Ford suit, the white shirt and silver tie he wore beneath it making the most of his dark good looks and olive skin, he was faultlessly elegant. It was when she lifted her gaze to his that she realized just how much trouble she was in.

His lips set in a flat line, jaw locked, smoky gray gaze full of thunderclouds, he was *furious*. Fingers of ice crept up her spine as he murmured something to the board member he was speaking with, then set his tall, impressive frame into motion, eating up the distance between them. Clara took one look at his face, muttered something about checking the AV equipment and disappeared.

Chloe's heart ricocheted in a hard drumbeat against her ribs as Nico came to a halt in front of her. She tipped her head back to look up at him, refusing to reveal how much he intimidated her. With his leonine dark head, cold, slate blue eyes and cheekbones at forty-five degrees, he couldn't quite be called handsome in the traditional sense because he was far too hard for that.

His wide, full mouth made up for that lack of softness, however—lush and almost pouty when he wanted to seduce a response out of the person in question. Which was not now.

Her heart battered up against her chest in another wave of nerves at the dark fire in his eyes. At the realization that any hope she'd had that she'd developed an immunity to him after seven years in Europe had been utter self-delusion. That the man she'd once thought had been *the one* had hardened into a ruthless, sapphire-edged version of himself she couldn't hope to know.

She might hate him, she *did* hate him for teaching her the cruel lesson he had, but he was still the most potently gorgeous male she'd ever encountered.

"I'm sorry," she murmured, forcing the words past a constricted throat. "I forgot it's impossible to get a cab in Manhattan on a rainy day."

His stormy gaze darkened. "We'll discuss it afterward,"

he said quietly, so quietly it sent her pulse skittering into a dead run. "Take ten minutes to say hello and we'll start."

She nodded. Forced herself through the round of small talk, latching gratefully on to her uncle Giorgio, Evolution's flamboyant director of marketing, before Nico called the meeting to order.

An undeniably compelling speaker, he outlined the big picture as Evolution headed into its first Christmas season without its cofounders. Investor confidence was shaky, he observed candidly—the company's stock price in trouble—with the world worried the loss of Juliette Russo, the creative force of the company, would strike a death knell for Evolution.

Chloe's heart sank as he went on to detail the keys for a successful path forward. It wasn't true that Evolution was a fading star. Her parents had built a company rich with talent. Vivre, the line of fragrances Chloe had spent three years developing with one of the most brilliant French perfumers, *would* be the hit Christmas product the company needed. But, she reminded herself, the world didn't know that yet.

Nico called her up last in the parade of directors presenting their holiday season highlights, after the head of the skincare division had made a big splash with his luxurious, all-natural skincare line. She suspected Nico did it on purpose.

She rose on legs the consistency of jelly, smoothed the pencil skirt of her still-damp suit and moved to the front of the room. Hands clammy, mouth full of sawdust, she clicked the remote to begin the presentation. Focusing on her passion for her work, she began. Too fast and clunky in her delivery at first, she gradually relaxed as she explained her vision for Vivre and the aspirational campaign that would accompany it. It will, she told those assembled, redefine how beauty is framed in a world that badly needs inspiration.

Instead of salivating over her exciting launch plan that featured celebrities who would spread the inspirational message, the board members peppered her with questions.

*"Isn't the perfume market oversaturated?"*

*"Your mother could have sold this, but can you?"*

*"What about all the workplaces that are going scent-free?"*

*"Wouldn't it be better to focus on the all-natural products that are dominating the market?"*

She took a deep breath and answered the questions the best she could. She had been working with her mother in the lab ever since she was a little girl, she told them. She knew where the magic was. She already had her own signature fragrances to back her up. And the celebrity endorsement she had planned for the Vivre campaign would help her create the buzz she needed.

When she ran out of answers and needed big-picture help, she looked to Nico because she didn't have that backup in her head. But instead of coming to her rescue, he sat back in his chair, arms crossed over his chest, and focused that glittering gray gaze of his on her.

Her stomach swooped. He was punishing her. The bastard. She looked at the director of the skincare division, who stared blankly back at her, clearly not about to help either and diminish his own product line. A trickle of perspiration ran down her back.

Finally, her uncle stepped in with a passionate rebuttal, reminding the board of the founding tenants Evolution was built on—luxury perfumes like Vivre that had taken the world by storm. But by then, her credibility was in tatters.

Answering the final question, she sat down red-faced.

\* \* \*

Nico held on to his temper by the threads it had been hanging from all evening as the last board member disappeared toward the elevators and home.

"My office," he murmured in Chloe's ear. *"Now."*

Head tossed back, she stalked out of the room in front of him and down the hall toward his office. It would be difficult, he surmised, eyeing her curvaceous backside, for her to find it when she had no idea where it was.

She came to a sliding halt in front of the sophisticated lounge that was a new addition to the executive floor, her gaze moving over the photos of the company's cofounders gracing the walls.

"What happened to my father's office?" she demanded, spinning on her heel, dark eyes flashing. "Or couldn't you even leave that alone?"

"I didn't think it was appropriate for me to assume it," he murmured, directing her down the hall toward his office with a hand at her back. Something in him hadn't been able to simply wipe his mentor from existence by redecorating a space that had always been quintessentially Martino's. But he didn't feel the need to explain his actions to Chloe at this particular moment. He was barely resisting the urge to strangle her for the ever-present recalcitrance that had pushed him one step too far this time.

He closed the door to his office with a decisive click. Strode to the window and counted to ten because that was what Chloe did to him. Pushed buttons he didn't even know he had. Elicited emotions he had always had to exert the most extreme self-control to silence. Because Chloe was the chink in his armor. The one weakness he couldn't seem to kick. And wanting her had always been a swift trip to hell.

"You were punishing me, weren't you?" Her voice drifted over his shoulder, trembling with rage.

He turned around and leaned against the sill. Studied the fury on her beautiful face. The way her delicate features had settled into an intriguing beauty that was impossible to ignore. The arms she had crossed over her firm, high breasts, the feet defiantly planted apart in her haute couture Parisian suit.

She was a study in rebellion. It was insane the fire that rose up inside him, the desire to crush those lush lips into submission under his own, to shock her out of the self-protective state she'd descended into since her parents' passing. To unearth *some* sign the passionate Chloe he knew still existed.

But having her had never been an option for him. He had conditioned it out of himself a long time ago because he'd had to. Just like he'd eliminated every other undesirable need he'd had in a life that had never had any room for self-indulgence.

He pointed at the chair in front of his desk. "Sit."

She crossed her arms tighter over her chest. "I'd prefer to stand."

*"Bene."* He took a seat on the corner of his desk, eyes on her. "I hung you out to dry in there because you needed to learn a lesson."

"That you are the king of the castle," she challenged, eyes flashing.

"Yes," he said evenly. "I am. And the sooner you realize it, the easier this is going to be on both of us. It was your father's wish, Chloe, that I run this company. And while I don't intend for one minute to deny you your place at the center of it—in fact, my intention is the opposite—you need to get that particular fact straight in your head."

Her mouth curled. "Giorgio should be the head of this company, not you."

"That's why your father made me second in command a year ago?" he rebutted coolly. "Think rationally."

She flicked a wrist at him, ebony eyes snapping with heat. "Because you somehow *brainwashed* him into it. How else would his will have been so *perfectly* in order when he died? Because it was your master plan, of course."

A low curl of heat unfurled inside him. "Watch it," he said softly. "You're starting to sound like your very bitter, very deluded uncle. Martino put me in control of Evolution in the event something happened to him and Juliette because he knew Giorgio would drive the company into the ground with his big spending ways. Your uncle has neither the business brain nor the common sense to run Evolution."

"That's a lie," she breathed. "He is widely reputed to be one of the most brilliant marketers there is. And don't forget," she added, eyes darkening with old wounds, "I have firsthand knowledge of how ambitious you are, Nico. Success is the only thing that matters to you."

"And *that*," he said, emphasizing the word, "is the problem between us, Chloe. I am grieving, too. We are *all* grieving. And yet you are fixated on ancient history when it has no place here. You need to grow up and move on."

Her eyes widened. "I am *not* bringing the personal into this."

"Aren't you?" He slid his gaze over her fire-soaked cheeks. "That's why you've spent the last six months hiding away in Paris instead of taking your place in this company? So I finally had to *order* you back? Because there's nothing personal here?"

A muscle pulled tight at the corner of her mouth. "You have *such* an overinflated ego. Vivre wasn't ready."

"So you said," he responded quietly. "My contacts in the lab say it was ready six months ago. That you have been stalling, perfecting imperfections that don't exist."

He fixed his gaze on hers. "Hide from the world or hide from me, Chloe, both of them are ending now."

She glared at him. "I *hate you*."

"I know." He'd decided a long time ago that was preferable in this relationship of theirs.

She drew a visible breath that rippled through her slim body as she collected her composure. "Have you reviewed my launch plan, then? Since Vivre is so clearly *ready*?"

"Yes," he murmured, picking it up off his desk. "*This* is what I think of it."

Her eyes went as big as saucers as he tossed the sheaf of papers into the wastebasket. "What *are* you doing?"

"Putting it where it belongs." He shook his head, his hands coming to rest on the edge of the desk. "You have no business case in that plan. All you have is fluffy, over-inflated, feel-good market research that relies on your legacy to sell it. A *fifty-million-dollar* launch plan in which the linchpin for success turns on a celebrity endorsement program you don't have a hope in hell of attaining."

Her chin lifted. "That is a *brilliant* launch plan, Nico. I have a *master's* degree, in case you had forgotten. Maybe I should have been more detailed with the numbers—and I *can* be because I was focusing on the big picture—but the consumer testing has been off the charts for Vivre. One of the most important French perfumers in the industry thinks it's inspired—as brilliant as anything my mother has done. *This* is the product that is going to prove Evolution is back this Christmas, not some generic all-natural skincare line you couldn't distinguish from any of its competitors."

He surveyed her flushed, determined face. The passion that had been missing for months. "I am backing Emilio's skincare line for the holiday push. I agree with the board."

Her jaw slackened. "That's *insane*. This company was

built on our signature perfumes. People are looking for an inspirational campaign from us. That's what we do—*we inspire.*"

"And you," he pointed out, "delivered the product late. Even if I did approve the campaign, it's the beginning of October. You'd never get it into market in time."

She faltered for the first time. Because he was right and she knew it. He was not, however, oblivious to the fact that Chloe was a genius. That she had her mother's touch. That the success of Evolution rested on her shoulders as Juliette, her mother, had known it would. But sinking fifty million dollars into an impossible-to-execute holiday campaign would be foolhardy when the company desperately needed a Christmas hit.

"Work with the sales and marketing team," he said. "Show me the numbers. Lay the timeline out for me so I know it can work. And," he qualified, "and this is a big *but*, the only way I'd ever green-light a launch plan like this is if you can supply the big-name celebrities you've earmarked up front. Which is very unlikely given the hit the brand has taken. So, consider a plan B."

"There is no plan B," she said flatly. "I chose those celebrities because of their personal history. Because they embody the spirit of the perfumes. I created them with them in mind. If I can talk to them, if they can experience the fragrances, *understand* the message I'm trying to tell, I know I can convince them to do it."

He absorbed the energy that surrounded her. The unshakable belief in what she had created. And wondered if she realized the campaign was about *her.* About the battle she had always fought within herself to shine in the shadow of her charismatic mother and stunning sister.

"Prove me wrong, then," he challenged. "Give me what I'm asking for. But know this, Chloe. Your flashy degree is worth nothing in the real world until you prove you know how to use it. *I* can help you do that. Your father *asked* me to provide that mentorship to you. But I have better things to do than babysit you if you're not willing to learn."

*"Babysit?"* The word dripped with scorn. "You're not satisfied with ruling me financially? Now you need to master me professionally?"

His mouth tightened. "That is exactly the kind of attitude I'm talking about. Every time I try to forge a working relationship between us, you shut me down. You're mysteriously lost in the lab. You're too busy to talk. That ends now."

"I don't do that," she rejected. "I've been extremely busy."

"Unfortunate for you tonight." He rubbed a palm over his jaw. "Here's how it's going to work from here on out. I'll give you the rest of the week to get settled in. To iron out your launch plan. You come back to me with the details and we decide how to move forward.

"Second, we'll start having regular morning meetings beginning next week. I can teach you the business end of things and we can check in with each other as needed. That's what your father did with me. And," he added, pausing for emphasis, "you *will* attempt to listen rather than fight with me at every turn."

A stony look back.

"Finally," he concluded, "we will begin building your profile with the press. The PR department is going to schedule a training session for you."

Her chin dipped. "I'm terrible with the media. I either clam up or say things I shouldn't. Let Giorgio do it."

"Giorgio is not the future of this company. *You* are. You'll learn to do better."

Resistance wrote itself in every line of her delicate

body, her dark eyes shimmering with fire. "Are you done, then? With all your ground rules? Because I'm exhausted and I'd like to go home. The time difference is catching up with me."

"One more," he said softly, eyes on hers. "I am your boss, Chloe. Hate me all you want in private, but in public you *will* show me the respect I'm due."

# CHAPTER TWO

CHLOE WAS STILL fuming over her encounter with Nico the next morning as she woke up to brilliant sunshine in her cozy townhouse on the Upper East Side. It was almost as if last night's monsoon had never happened. Everything looking sparkly and brand-new on a crisp fall day that was perfection in Manhattan.

A grimace twisted her mouth. Now if only she could say the same for her combative showdown with Nico.

She slid out of bed, threw on a robe and made herself some coffee in an attempt to regain her equilibrium. Java in hand, she wandered to the French doors that looked out over the street and drank in the sleepy little neighborhood she now called home.

A splendor of gold and rust, the vivid splash of color from the changing leaves of the stately old trees was the perfect contrast to the cream stuccoed townhouses that lined the street. She and Mireille had fallen in love with the neighborhood one Sunday afternoon on a walk through the village. Her father had bought them each a townhouse side by side, Chloe's in anticipation of her return home to New York to take her place at Evolution, Mireille, while she studied public relations at school.

*We know you're too independent to come home and live with us*, her father had teased. *But we want you close.*

A wave of bitter loneliness settled over her. She wrapped her arms around herself, coffee cup cradled against her chest. Usually she managed to keep the hollow emptiness at bay—burying herself in her lab until she crawled into bed at night. But this morning it seemed to throb from the inside out, scraping her raw.

She missed her parents. So desperately much she had no idea how to even verbalize it. How to release the emotion that had been stuck inside her so long lest it swamp her so completely when she did, she would never emerge whole. Because her parents had been her glue, her innocence, the force that had shielded her from the world. And now that they were gone, she didn't know how to restore the status quo. Didn't know how to reset herself. Didn't know how to *feel* anymore.

She was *scared* to feel.

Her mother had been her best friend. A bright, vivid star that bathed you in its warmth—their shared passion bonding them from their earliest days. Her father, the wisest, smartest man she'd ever known, with a heart so big it had seemed limitless. He would be furious if he saw her like this, because Nico was right—she had been hiding, from the world and from herself.

She hugged her arms tighter around her chest as she watched the neighborhood stir to life. She needed to move on. Nico had also been right in that. Paris was no longer her life. New York was now. Assuming the role her mother had groomed her for, even if the thought of doing so without her was one she couldn't even contemplate.

Jagged glass lined her throat. *Baby steps*, she told herself, swallowing hard. She could do this. She just needed to take baby steps. And guard against her feelings for Nico while she did it because her instinctive response to him last night had revealed too much.

She wasn't a teenager anymore in the throes of a wicked crush, overwhelmed by a sexual attraction she'd had no hope of fighting. The connection she and Nico had shared hadn't been special as she'd thought it had been. He'd killed any romantic illusions she'd had about him dead the night he'd slept with another woman and made it clear they were over.

That she still found him compelling was an indication of her weakness when it came to him, one she needed to stamp out dead now that she was back in New York.

Because like it or not, he *was* her boss. The man who could green-light or kill her dream. Either she could keep fighting that fact, fighting *him* as she had been for the past six months, or she could prove him wrong. And since launching Vivre in time for Christmas, preserving her legacy, was all that mattered, her decision was clear.

Her first step was to dust herself off after her disastrous performance last night and make her first day back in New York a success.

A determined fire lighting her blood, she dressed in her most stylish cherry-colored suit, walked to work amid the crisp autumn glory and spent the morning meeting with Giorgio about Vivre.

She was excited to discover the splashy Christmas launch in Times Square she had planned was doable, but the tight deadlines to complete the advertising campaign made her head spin. It meant she would have to have her celebrities secured within the next week, their advertising spots filmed shortly thereafter, which might actually be impossible given how slow those things worked.

But it was doable. She focused on that as she spent the rest of the day nailing down the details Nico had requested so he would have nothing to question when she presented him with the revised plan. Then she took Mireille out for dinner at Tempesta Di Fuoco, Stefan Bianco's hot spot in Chelsea, as she turned her attention to her most pressing issue.

Celebrities were her sister's world. Socially connected in a way Chloe had never been with her sparkling, extroverted personality and undeniable beauty that mirrored their mother's icy blonde looks, there were few people Mireille didn't know in Manhattan.

Her sister refused to talk business until they had exotic martinis sitting in front of them. "All right," she said, sitting back with her drink in hand. "Tell me about the campaign."

Chloe cradled her glass between her fingers. "It's about an authentic beauty, as you know. About expressing your true colors. But we're approaching it from a different point of view with each perfume. One, for example, is about moving past your physical limitations. Another about incorporating a difficult past as part of what makes you unique. *Irreplaceable.*"

"I love it," said Mireille, looking intrigued. "It's brilliant. Give me your list."

Chloe took a deep breath. "Number one. Carrie Taylor." The supermodel had made it big as a plus-size model and was gracing the cover of every magazine on the newsstands.

Mireille cocked a brow. "You aren't reaching high, are you?"

"I told you I was. Second is Lashaunta." A pop singer who had recently had a string of chart-topping records, she had forged a successful career despite a prominent scar on her face. Or perhaps *because* of it, as it gave her such a distinctive look.

"Next?"

"Desdemona Parker." A world-class athlete, she'd made

it to the top of her sport despite the inherited disease that had nearly ended her career. "And finally," Chloe concluded, "Eddie Carello for our men's fragrance."

Mireille blinked. "You're kidding."

"He's a survivor," Chloe said quietly. "He grew up in the projects. He perfectly embodies the spirit of Soar."

Mireille let out a husky laugh. "I can see why Nico cut you down to size. He's not wrong about the brand taking a hit. It isn't going to be an easy sell. Do you have backups?"

Chloe listed them. "But I need my A list. It's Nico's nonnegotiable."

Her sister pursed her lips. "I can help with Lashaunta and Carrie. You're out of luck with Desdemona and Eddie, however. Eddie is near untouchable, he's too hot right now. Desdemona, I have no connections to, and neither does anyone in our PR department. We're not big in sports."

Chloe's face fell.

"Lazzero, however," her sister mused, "might be able to help. I read in the paper this morning Eddie is attending the launch party for Blaze, Lazzero's new running shoe, at Di Fiore's tomorrow night. Desdemona has an endorsement deal with Supersonic. She might be there, too."

Chloe chewed on her lip. Her father had been godfather to all the Di Fiore brothers when his good friend Leone had died, including Nico's middle brother, Lazzero, and youngest, Santo. But only Nico had ended up at Evolution after her father had taken him on as his protégé. Lazzero and Santo had put themselves through school on sports scholarships, going on to found one of the hottest sportswear companies on the planet in Supersonic, with an investment from Martino to help them along.

Chloe's lashes lowered. "I wanted to do this by myself. To prove to Nico I can."

"Lazzero is not cheating. Lazzero is being *resourceful*."

Chloe tapped her fingernails on the table. "Do you think he'd let us attend the party?"

"There's only one way to find out." Mireille picked up her phone and made the call.

"Lazzero, darling," she purred. "I need you."

Whatever was said on the other end of the phone made her laugh. "I do so call you just to chat. But right now, Chloe and I need a favor. We need an invite to your party tomorrow night to chat up Eddie Carello and Desdemona Parker for an influencer deal."

Mireille frowned at Lazzero's response. "Oh, she isn't? That's too bad. Eddie is, though, right?"

Chloe's stomach dropped. *No Desdemona.*

Mireille nodded at whatever Lazzero said in response. "It won't be me, I have plans. It will be Chloe. And I will pass the message on. You are, as usual, a doll."

Chloe eyed her as she signed off. "What did he say?"

"Desdemona is out of town, but he's emailing me and her agent and making the introduction. As for the party, it's a yes. He'll leave your name at the door." A wicked smile curved her sister's lips. "He said to wear a short dress. Eddie likes legs."

And so that was how Chloe found herself the following night passing her credentials to the big lug in a dark suit at the door of Di Fiore's, the upscale bar in midtown Manhattan Lazzero and Santo ran as part of their sports conglomerate.

Clad in the very short, rose-gold dress Mireille had lent her and surrounded by the trendy crowd, Chloe felt hopelessly out of place.

"You can come this way," said the lug, plucking Chloe out of the lineup and ushering her through a side door and into the party that was already in full swing. There he handed her over to a hostess who led her through a crush of people to where Lazzero held court at the bar. He was supremely sophisticated all in black. Chloe had always found his hawk-like profile and dark eyes highly intimidating. Unlike Nico, who had intrigued her from the very beginning with his quiet, serious demeanor—as if the weight of the world had been placed on his shoulders.

Lazzero, however, made an effort to put her at ease, handing her a glass of wine and chatting idly with her about what she and Mireille were up to. Having not had time to eat, Chloe felt the wine go straight to her head, making the crowd seem much less unapproachable.

After a few minutes, Lazzero nodded toward the end of the bar. "Eddie at three o'clock."

Her pulse gave a flutter as she turned to find the famous bad-boy actor lounging his lean, rangy, jean-clad body against the bar while a group of rather exquisite women attempted to capture his attention. Her stomach fell. How was she supposed to compete with that?

She turned back to Lazzero. Ran a self-conscious hand over her hair. She wasn't going to get another opportunity like this. She just had to *do* it. "Do I look okay?"

His dark eyes glittered with amusement. "Affirmative. Ten minutes, Chloe. That's all you've got. I have a rule at my parties—no one hassles you. It makes them want to come back."

She moistened her lips. "Got it."

He eyed her. "Are you sure you want to do this? He's a bit of a piece of work."

"Yes."

He pressed another glass of wine into her hand. "Go."

Chloe took a sip of the wine, sucked in a deep breath and started walking, forcing herself to trace a straight line toward the actor before she chickened out. The girls around him looked down their noses at her as she approached. Used to this treatment when she was with Mireille, Chloe ignored them, walked right up to Eddie and stuck out her hand. "Eddie, I'm Chloe Russo. My family and I own Evolution. I'd like to talk to you about a fragrance I've developed with you in mind."

The actor swept his gaze over her dismissively, before he got to her legs, where he lingered. "Who did you say you are?" he queried absentmindedly.

Chloe repeated her spiel, refusing to give in to the knots tying themselves in her stomach.

Eddie lifted his slumberous dark gaze to hers. Flicked the girl off the stool beside him. "Have a seat."

Nico pointed his car home, a brutally hard day of meetings behind him. A beer and the hot tub at his penthouse beckoned, but so did a phone call with his brothers at the end of the day. Old habits died hard, and checking in with Lazzero and Santo to make sure their world was upright was one of them.

It had been that way ever since their father's company had imploded when Nico was a teenager, his father and his marriage along with it, leaving Nico as the last line of defense between his family and the street when his mother had walked out. When life as you'd known it had dissolved once beneath your feet, you made sure it never happened again.

He punched Lazzero's cell into his hands-free. It rang five times before his brother picked up, the sound of music pulsing in the background.

"Sorry." The music faded as Lazzero moved to a quieter spot. "It's our Blaze launch tonight."

Nico rubbed a palm against his temple. "*Mi dispiace.* I just walked out of my last meeting minutes ago."

"No worries." An amused note flavored his brother's lazy drawl. "You didn't tell me you were sending your little bird my way."

"My little bird?"

"Chloe. She's here chatting up Eddie Carello for some sponsorship deal."

Nico blinked at the bright headlights of an oncoming car. "*Chloe* is there chatting up Eddie Carello?"

"And doing a pretty good job of it I might say. Must be the dress. I told her he likes legs."

Nico brought his back teeth together. "Shut it down, Lazzero. You know better than that. She's no match for him."

More of that patented male amusement in his brother's voice. "She looks like a match for him to me. She has his *undivided* attention at the moment."

"Lazzero," Nico growled. "Shut it down."

"Gotta go," his brother apologized. "A client just arrived. You should drop by."

Nico swore a blue streak, yanked the steering wheel around and did an overtly illegal U-turn. Approaching celebrities was the PR department's job. He was already feeling guilty about the board meeting and the necessarily harsh lesson he'd administered to Chloe. She was so vulnerable despite that sharp mouth of hers. But it had seemed to do the trick of jolting her out of that frozen state she'd been in, and for that, he'd considered it a success.

She did, however, need to be treated with kid gloves at the moment. She was the key to Evolution's success. She had to *believe* she could take her mother's place. But the question mark with Chloe had always been her confidence. Her belief in herself.

It didn't seem to be lacking, however, as Nico strode into Di Fiore's to find Lazzero romancing a tall blonde at the bar and Chloe doing the same with the most notorious womanizer in Hollywood.

Her dark hair shone loose around her lovely face, the champagne-colored dress she wore as she sat perched on the high stool highlighting every dip and curve of her slim, perfect figure. Her legs—and there was a lot of them— were a jaw-dropping, toned work of art. They made his mouth go dry.

And that was before he got to those gorgeous eyes of hers—dark rippling pools framed by the longest, most luxurious lashes he'd ever seen. Eyes that had once made him lose his common sense. He thought maybe she'd put about ten coats of mascara on.

Carello had one hand on his jean-clad thigh, the other around his drink, talking in an animated fashion while Chloe listened, her clear, bright laughter cutting through the din of the crowd. Nico's mouth tightened as the actor slid his arm to the back of her stool and moved in closer.

Resisting the urge to walk over there and pluck her off the stool, he lifted his hand and signaled the bartender instead. The young hipster called out a greeting to him and slid his favorite dark ale across the bar.

"You thought that was a good idea?" he growled as Lazzero lost the blonde and ambled over.

His brother hiked a shoulder. "I'm not her babysitter. You are. How you found yourself in that role is beyond me."

"You know full well how I did. Martino made it impossible to say no."

Lazzero took a sip of his beer. Eyed him. "When are you going to tell her about his cancer? It would make your life easier, you know."

It would. But Martino had made him promise not to tell his girls about the rare form of cancer that would have eventually claimed his life. He'd asked Nico to take care of them instead by taking his place at the helm of the company and ensuring it prospered. Telling Chloe now would only add to the emotional upheaval she was going through. And quite frankly, he needed her head on the job.

He threw back a swig of his beer. Wiped his mouth. "I have no idea why Martino even thought this was a good idea."

"Maybe because you did such a good job with Santo and me," Lazzero goaded. "We are such model citizens."

"I am questioning that right now." Nico slid his attention back to Carello. Watched him put a palm on Chloe's bare thigh. She didn't flinch, throwing her hair back over her shoulder and laughing at whatever he said.

Heat seared his belly. "How much has she had to drink?"

"Enough to boost her confidence." Lazzero leaned a hip against the bar. Slid an assessing gaze over him. "Tough day?"

"Evolution's stock is in the toilet, we desperately need a hit product and Giorgio has been executing an internal smear campaign against me. It's been a joy."

Lazzero's mouth curled. "He is a nuisance. He's not a serious threat."

But he was distracting him at a time he couldn't afford to be distracted. When Evolution was teetering on the edge of a defining moment. And that, he couldn't have.

A tall, lanky male with razed blond hair pushed through the crowd to the bar, leaning over to say something to Eddie. The actor gave Chloe a regretful look, then said something that made her face fall, then brighten as Carello took something out of his wallet and slid it onto the bar.

Nico's fingers tightened around his beer bottle as the actor bent and pressed a kiss to each of Chloe's cheeks, staining her skin with two twin spots of pink. Then he and his entourage headed off through the crowd.

\* \* \*

A surge of triumph filled Chloe as she sat holding Eddie Carello's agent's business card, his parting words ringing in her ears. *Call my agent. Give him the details. Tell him I gave this the green light if he's good with it.*

She shook her head bemusedly. Slid off the bar stool, a half-finished glass of champagne in her hand. The world rocked ever so slightly beneath her feet. She'd never had much of a head for alcohol, but Eddie had insisted on that glass of champagne, and OMG, he'd just said yes. Never in her wildest dreams had she imagined he would.

*Untouchable, my foot.*

She turned and headed for Lazzero to thank him. Pulled up short. Nico was standing beside his brother at the bar, the jacket of his dark suit discarded, a drink in his hand.

Her pulse went haywire. Why did that happen every time? And why did he look so good in a shirt and tie? The tie loosened, his hair ruffled, he looked younger, like he had when they'd first met. *Devastating.*

But *that* Nico didn't exist, she reminded herself, heart thumping against her chest like a bass drum. And she'd do well to remember it.

She straightened her shoulders and walked the length of the bar to where the two men stood. Lazzero waved off her thanks and melted into the crowd to greet someone. Nico set that penetrating gray gaze of his on her.

"I told you to *secure* him. Meaning use the PR department. Not take on Hollywood yourself."

She lifted a shoulder. "The PR department didn't have access to him. Mireille said he was untouchable. So we asked Lazzero for help."

He leaned back against the bar, his free hand crossed in the crook of his folded elbow. "What did he say?"

A victorious smile played at the corners of her mouth. It might have been her best moment ever. "He said yes."

His eyes widened. "He did?"

"Yes. But," she qualified, "it's contingent on his agent's approval."

Nico's gaze warmed with a glimmer of something that might have been admiration. "I'm impressed. How did you convince him?"

"I explained the campaign to him. Why he was the inspiration for Soar. He was flattered—said he liked the idea of having a fragrance created for him. It turns out," she concluded thoughtfully, "that men are true to their biology. They like to have their egos stroked. It's their Achilles' heel."

A hint of a smile played at his mouth. "That may be true," he acknowledged. "But Carello is not to be played with. His reputation precedes him. Get his agent to sign off, then leave him the hell alone."

"I *know* that." Irritation burrowed a bumpy red path beneath her skin. "That's why I told him I had a boyfriend. Honestly, Nico, do you think I'm a total neophyte?"

"Sometimes I do, yes."

She made a sound at the back of her throat. "Well, you can go home now. The show's over. Your babysitting duties are officially done for the night."

He nodded toward her glass. "Finish that and I'll drive you home."

*Oh, no.* She was not having him shepherd her home like some stray sheep who'd wandered into the wrong field. She had conquered tonight, and she was leaving under her own steam. Because, truthfully, all she wanted was a hot shower and her bed now that the world had blissfully right-sided itself.

She lifted her chin. "I'm not ready to leave. It was so

nice of Lazzero to invite me. It's a great party. There's dancing and everything. I think I'll stay."

He set his silvery gaze on hers. "Let's go dance, then."

Her heart tripped over itself. She knew how good it felt to be that close to all that muscle and masculinity. How *exciting* it was, because he'd subjected her to its full effects before he'd cast her aside and chosen another.

"I didn't say I wanted to dance right *now*." She held up her half-finished glass of champagne. "I still have this."

"I think you've had enough." He plucked the glass out of her fingers, captured her wrist in his hand and was leading her through the crowd toward the packed dance floor before she could voice an objection. She knew it for the bad idea it was before they'd even gotten there. Eddie had touched her bare thigh and hadn't even caused a ripple. Nico's fingers wrapped around her wrist were like a surge of electricity through her entire body. She felt it right to the tips of her toes.

But then they'd reached the mosaic-tiled dance floor with its elegant chandelier. With a smooth flick of his wrist, Nico tugged her to him. A little more pressure and she was firmly within the circle of his arms, shielded from the other dancers by his height and breadth.

One of her hands in his, the other resting on his waist, it wasn't a close hold. But this was Nico. Every inch of her skin heated as it came into whisper-soft contact with his tall, powerful body. And then the scent of him kicked in, filling her head and electrifying her senses.

Smoky and elusive, it was pure, understated sensuality. Vetiver, the warm Indian grass known for its earthy, hedonistic appeal her mother had highlighted in Voluttuoso, her final fragrance. Chloe had always thought it was sexy. On Nico, with his overt virility and intensely masculine scent, it was knee weakening.

*One dance.* She kept her gaze riveted to the knot of his elegant silver tie. Unfortunately for her, the song was a jazzy, sexy tune, in keeping with the über-cool vibe of the party. A smooth, instinctive dancer, Nico was an excellent lead, guiding her steps easily in the small space they had carved out with a light pressure on her palm.

It should have been simple to exercise the mind control her yoga instructor was always preaching. Instead, her thoughts flew back to that sultry Fourth of July night that changed everything.

Her in Nico's arms...the illicit, forbidden passion that had burst into flames between them...how for the first time in her life, she'd felt truly, completely alive.

She lifted her gaze to his, searched for some indication that everything they'd shared hadn't been the imaginings of her eighteen-year-old mind. That she'd *meant* something to him like she'd thought she had. But his cool gray gaze was focused on her with a calculating intensity that sent that irrational, naive hope plunging to the bottom of her heart.

"We started off on the wrong foot the other night," he murmured. "We need to work as a team, Chloe, *together*, not apart, if we have any hope of preserving what your parents built. Full-out warfare is not going to work."

She arched a brow at him. "Is that an apology?"

"If you like," he said evenly. "Like it or not, we are in this together. We succeed or fail together. You decide which it is."

Her lashes lowered. "I agree we need a better working relationship. But this is my company, Nico. You need to listen to me, too. You can't just run roughshod over me with that insatiable need for control of yours. I *know* what's going to make Evolution a success. There's no doubt in my mind it's Vivre."

"Put the rest of the pieces of the plan in place and I might agree. And," he said, inclining his head, "I promise to listen more. *If* you stop trying to bait me at every turn."

Her mouth twisted. "A truce, then?"

A mocking glint filled his gaze. "A truce. We can celebrate by attending the Palm Beach fund-raiser together. It will present a very public united front."

Her parents' favorite fund-raiser. A glittering, star-studded musical event in Palm Beach every year in support of breast cancer—a disease her mother's best friend had succumbed to. Her stomach did a nervous dip at the thought of attending it with Nico.

She tipped her head back to look up at him. "You mean you don't have one of your hot dates lined up for it?"

Hot in the sense they never lasted with Nico. She wasn't sure she'd ever seen him photographed with the same woman twice.

"I haven't had a hot date in six months," he drawled. "It will have to wait until Evolution isn't in danger of falling through the cracks."

A calculated insult intended to remind her of her irresponsibility and his immutable focus. "However will you survive?" she goaded, skin stinging.

"I will *manage*," he murmured, eyes on hers. "Careful, Chloe, we've barely gotten this cease-fire of ours under way."

She sank her teeth into her lip. At the erotic image that one word inserted into her head. It took very little of her imagination to wonder what he would look like in the shower satisfying that physical need, his beautiful body primed for release.

She closed her eyes. She *hated* him. This was insanity.

The song finished. She stepped hastily out of his arms,

smoothing her dress down over her hips. Nico gave her a pointed look. "Ready to leave?"

The concrete set of his jaw said there was no point arguing. He wasn't leaving her here. He would wait all night if he had to because this was Nico—relentless in everything he did. Patient like the most tenacious predator in achieving what he wanted.

"Yes," she agreed with a helpless sigh.

He placed a palm to her back as they wound their way through the crowd to say good-night to Lazzero. The heat of it fizzled over her skin, warming her layers deep, a real-life chemical reaction she'd never been able to defuse.

It rendered her silent on the trip home, the warm, luxurious interior of the car wrapping her in a sleek, dark cocoon as they slipped through quiet streets. She was so tired as Nico walked her to her door, she stumbled with the key as she tried to push it into the lock.

His fingers brushed against hers as he collected the keys from her hand and unlocked the door. Little pinpricks of heat exploded across her skin, a surge of warmth staining her cheeks as she looked up at him to thank him. Found herself all caught up in his smoky gaze that suddenly seemed to have a charge in it that stalled the breath in her throat.

"Go inside and go to bed, Chloe," he said huskily. "And lock the door."

His intention ever since he'd walked into that bar tonight, she reminded herself, past her spinning head. To prevent her from slipping into Eddie Carello's hands.

She slicked her tongue across suddenly dry lips. Cocked her chin at a defiant angle. "Mission accomplished. I'll be in bed by midnight. But then again, you always get what you want, don't you, Nico?"

His gray gaze was heavy-lidded as it focused on her mouth for an infinitesimal pause. "Not always," he said quietly.

Then he disappeared into the night.

# CHAPTER THREE

IT HAD BEEN the champagne talking. Chloe convinced herself of that version of events as she walked to work the next morning. That cryptic comment from Nico on her doorstep, the chemistry that had seemed so palpable between them. Because not once in all the years since their summer flirtation had he ever looked at her like that.

She'd merely been a blip on his radar. A casual diversion he'd regretted when more sophisticated choices had come along. Thinking it had been any more than that would make her a fool where he was concerned and she'd stopped being that a long time ago.

Whatever misguided sense of duty he was displaying toward her, this *power trip* he was on, Nico's ambition was the only thing he cared about, a fact she would do well to remember. She'd agreed to this truce of theirs only for the greater good of the company. Because saving Evolution was all that mattered.

She perfected her spiel for Eddie's agent as she rode the elevator to her office, said good-morning to Clara, whom she'd decided was not only witty but astonishingly efficient, and took the messages her assistant handed her into her office.

Done in antiques, with a Louis XVI writing desk and chairs, ultra-feminine lace-edged, silk curtains and warm lamp lighting, the office that had once been her mother's wrapped itself around her like a whisper-soft memory. But her mind was all business as she picked up the phone and called Eddie's agent. A good thing, too, because when she reached him, he told her he was on his way out of town but could have lunch that day before he left.

Apprehensive Eddie would change his mind if it waited, Chloe jumped on the invitation. Unfortunately, his agent wasn't immediately sold on the endorsement, but in the end he relented, only because Eddie seemed so keen on the project and the actor had a movie coming out at Christmas, just as the massive campaign for Soar would appear.

Chloe floated back to the office and announced her victory to Mireille, who was just as excited as she.

"*I*," she informed Chloe, "have good news and bad news for you. The good news is that Lashaunta is interested. She loves the campaign. It really resonated with her."

Chloe's heart soared. Lashaunta was a megastar. "That's *amazing*."

"The bad news is that Carrie Taylor is a no. She's about to represent a competing fragrance. Desdemona," she concluded, "I'm still working on."

Which meant they needed to secure their plan B supermodel, Estelle Markov, for Nico to give them the green light. He might approve the plan with only three of their four celebrities in place, but any less than that and Chloe knew she'd be out of luck.

While Mireille worked on Estelle, Chloe went off to put the final piece of her buzz campaign into effect, personally delivering samples of the Vivre fragrances to each and every Evolution employee's desk, explaining the story behind the perfumes. A streak of the devil possessing her, she also had Clara courier samples of the fragrances to the board members, making sure she also sent one for their significant other.

She *would* win them over.

Hurricane Chloe had entered the building.

A wry smile tugged at Nico's lips as he waved Chloe into his office late on Friday afternoon and motioned for her to take a seat as he finished up a conference call.

She walked to the window instead, vibrating with the perpetual energy she'd been displaying all week in her very effective campaign to prove him wrong. Her slender body encased in a soft, off-white sweater, dark jeans tucked into knee-high boots and a fawn-colored jacket topping it off, she wore her hair in a high ponytail, her flawless skin bare of makeup.

The hard kick she administered to his solar plexus wasn't unexpected. He'd been fighting his attraction to Chloe ever since the first moment he'd set foot in the Russo household and eyes on Martino and Juliette's eldest daughter.

Twenty to Chloe's sixteen, he'd been hard and bitter from his experiences. But something about the quiet, passionate Chloe had penetrated his close-packed outer shell. Perhaps he had recognized a piece of himself in her—the need they had both had to bury themselves behind their layers to protect themselves against the world. Perhaps it had been how she had sold her subtle beauty short when he'd always found her far more attractive than her stunning sister.

He'd told himself he couldn't have her. That he would never put his position as Martino's protégé in jeopardy—the career that had meant everything to him as he'd finally built a solid footing under his feet. Until unintended and explosive, the attraction between him and Chloe had slipped his reins at the Russo's annual Fourth of July party.

Martino, who'd witnessed the kiss, had brought him up short, asking his intentions when it came to his daughter. Pursue Chloe seriously or leave her alone, he had said, knowing what Nico *was*—a man who would never trust, never commit to a woman because of the scars his early life had left behind.

So he'd walked away. Done it the hard way so it would be a clean break. So he wouldn't be tempted with what he couldn't have. Because Martino had been right—he would have broken Chloe's heart far worse than he had in the end.

Martino might not be alive, he conceded, studying the delicate length of her spine, and Chloe wasn't a teenager anymore, but he had a new responsibility now. To protect her, not bed her. To nurture her as Martino had asked of him. It was a promise he would not break.

His call with the West Coast team over, he pushed out of his chair and walked to where she stood at the window. She turned, her face expectant. "Did you look at the plan?"

"Yes." He glanced at his watch. "I have time to go through it before my dinner plans if you'd like."

When she answered in the affirmative, he strode out to reception, sent his PA, Simone, home, then returned to pour himself a Scotch. When Chloe refused his offer of a drink, he joined her in the lounge, where she stood at the windows, enjoying the view.

Designed to work and entertain with its Italian glass chandeliers, dining room for ten and magnificent vista of a night-lit Central Park, the view was Nico's favorite thing about the space he spent far too much time in.

Chloe turned around. "So what did you think?"

"I think you've made a very persuasive case for Vivre being the Christmas focus. The plan is excellent." A wry smile touched his mouth. "It was also impossible," he conceded drily, "to miss your blitz campaign. Very clever. I couldn't walk the halls without hearing about it. Simone can't stop raving about Be. Jerry Schumacher called me this morning to beg for an early production bottle for his wife."

A tiny smile curved her mouth at the mention of Evolution's most senior board member. "I did say I would win them over. But more important," she added, excitement filling her voice, "the media is raving about Vivre, Nico. The editor of the most influential fashion magazine in America is crazy about Soar. She wants to feature it as her must-have product for Christmas. I think it's going to be a huge hit."

He held up a hand before she got too carried away. "I saw that. I do, however, still have real concerns about the timing. It seems inordinately tight. I want more than Giorgio's rose-colored glasses making this decision."

"It is a tight timeline," she admitted. "I may not sleep. But we can do it. The advertising space is booked, and all four of our celebrities have the time in their schedule to film the spots."

He addressed the one glaring hole in the plan. "I don't see Carrie Taylor in there. What happened to her?"

She sank her teeth into her lip. "She's representing a competing fragrance. But Mireille has a verbal commitment from Estelle Markov, who's making it big in Europe. I think she'll be perfect to target that audience."

"I've never heard of her." He frowned. "She doesn't have Carrie Taylor's cachet, Chloe. Nor is the European market anywhere near the size of the North American one."

"But she's amazing." Her eyes shimmered with fire. "When was the last time you were a twentysomething fashionista with breasts?"

A dry look back. "Point taken."

"Not to mention the fact that Eddie and Lashaunta could carry this campaign on their own if they had to," she plunged on. "Carrie is not a make-or-break for us."

He took a sip of his Scotch. Considered his options. The skincare line he had favored was, in truth, not going to set the world on fire. It would, however, provide very solid profits. Vivre might be that superstar product line Evolution so desperately needed, but was he insane to bet the company on it?

"This is a *fifty-million-dollar* campaign," he said, fixing his gaze on Chloe's. "We've never done anything of this magnitude before. It needs to be executed flawlessly—right down to the last detail. Needs to put Evolution on everyone's lips again. Are you *sure* you can get it into market in time?"

"Yes." Her head bobbed up and down. "Trust me, Nico. I can do this."

He gave her a long look. "Okay," he said finally, pointing his glass at her. "Let's do it, then."

The world tilted beneath Chloe's feet. "Did you just say yes?"

He smiled. *"Si."*

"Why?"

"Because I believe in you," he said quietly. "You're a brilliant scientist, Chloe. Juliette said you have even better instincts than she had at this age. That you have the *magic* in you. I just wasn't sure you or Vivre was ready."

Hot tears prickled beneath her eyelids. A knot she hadn't been conscious of unraveled in her chest. Three years of blood, sweat and tears. Six months of praying she had created something that would do her mother proud. To be so close to watching her dream reach fruition almost undid her.

But there was also *fear*. Her stomach clenched hard at the responsibility that now lay on her shoulders, icy tentacles of apprehension sinking into her skin. What if she failed? What if she'd been overly optimistic and couldn't get the campaign into market in time? What if she was wrong about Vivre? What if it wasn't going to be the smash hit she thought it would be?

She inhaled a deep breath. Steadied herself. She wasn't wrong. She knew it in her heart. She just wished her mother was here to tell her that. To be the second half of her she had always been. Instead, she had to do this herself.

"I know this is the right path for Evolution," she said huskily. "I can feel it in my bones."

Nico nodded. "Then let me give you a few additional thoughts I have."

They sat at the table in the dining room and worked through the plan. Released one by one in limited-edition launches in the weeks leading up to Christmas, the campaign for Vivre was all about buzz building and creating a sense of exclusivity for the perfumes.

Vivre's four celebrity ambassadors would do exclusive appearances at the Times Square pop-up retail location in conjunction with the massive promotional campaign that would blanket the globe, intensifying the buzz.

Nico frowned as he looked at the timeline. "When does Eddie's movie come out?"

"The second week of December." Chloe pointed to the date on the timeline. "That's why we're launching Soar that week."

"What are you doing on his side of things to cross-promote?"

She pursed her lips. "I hadn't gotten that far yet."

"You should do something with the theaters. Hand samples out. Put the fragrance in the gift bags at the premieres. Run the campaign on theater screens."

*So smart.* She tapped her coffee mug against her chin. "I don't know if we have time."

He lifted a brow.

"We'll make it happen," she corrected hastily. "No problem."

He offered a half dozen more brilliant ideas before they were done, Chloe frantically scribbling notes. She had to reluctantly admit by the time they were finished that while she and her uncle had created an inspired plan, Nico had taken it to a whole other level with his innate sense of timing and brilliant business instincts.

Which had never been in question, she brooded as he got up from the table to shrug on an elegant black dinner jacket. Her father would never have taken him on as his protégé if he hadn't possessed Leone Di Fiore's uncanny sense of financial wizardry. What she couldn't forgive was how Nico had taken advantage of the trust her father had placed in him with what Giorgio had described as a systematic campaign to gain power.

She had always believed Nico operated by a rigid code of honor instilled in him by the adversity he'd faced in his younger years. Until he'd slept with Angelique Dubois to seal a deal and she'd seen how far his ambition could drive him.

A painful wound echoed down low. Unfortunately, it didn't diminish her physical awareness of him one bit. He did formal better than any man she'd ever known—the exquisitely cut black dinner jacket accentuating his broad shoulders, the dark pants molding his powerful thighs, the white shirt and black bow tie casting his startling good looks into harsh relief. He was so intensely virile he made her stomach flip.

Clearly he had much more exciting plans than she for tonight. In his life that didn't include hot dates.

"There is," he murmured, returning to lounge against the table, "a condition to my saying yes to the plan."

Her stomach fell. *Not another hoop to jump through.*

She pushed out of the chair and stood to meet him on even ground. "Which is?" she prompted, tipping her head back to look up at him, prepared to do whatever she needed to do to make this happen.

"The company is suffering without a visible creative force. Everyone responsible for the future of the company is looking for a sign the magic is still there—that it didn't disappear along with your mother." He pointed his Scotch at her. "You and I both know it didn't, but that's not good enough."

Her stomach dropped right to the floor this time. "What are you asking me to do?"

"The company needs a face, Chloe. Vivre, with its massive promotional campaign, is the perfect opportunity to position you as the creative force behind the company. The heir apparent. To tell your story. But we can't do that if you're holed up in the lab."

The knot that had begun to unravel twisted itself back into place. "No, Nico. Don't ask me to do this. Not now."

"It has to be now." He lifted a shoulder, a sympathetic gleam in his eyes. "I wanted to put it off. To give you more time to find your feet, but I can't do that if I'm betting the bank on you. On Vivre. It would be irresponsible of me. But I promise you, I will be there by your side every step of the way."

Old demons mixed with the apprehension climbing her throat. With the pressure, too much pressure, that had been heaped on her for months. *Forever.* It rose up inside her, pushing at the edges of the tightly held composure she'd been clinging to for weeks.

"I am not my mother," she said, a raw edge to her voice. "She was larger than life, Nico. She had incredible charisma. I don't have that kind of a story to tell."

"I'm not asking you to be her," he countered. "I'm asking you to be *you*, Chloe. You created your own signature fragrance at *seventeen* that sold like wildfire. How is that not a great story to tell?"

"It's not the same thing."

"How is it different?" He shook his head, mouth flattening into a straight line. "This is your Achilles' heel, I get that. You've never been comfortable in the spotlight. You don't think you can live up to this image you have of your mother and Mireille, so you hide yourself away in the lab, when what you really need to be is comfortable in your own skin."

The oh-so-accurate assessment hit her square in the chest. She *knew* her weaknesses. This, however, was not one she had the bandwidth to deal with right now.

"You would regret it," she told him. "I am a loose cannon with the press. They start firing questions at me and I freeze. Put a camera in front of me and I'm worse. I can't answer a question, let alone articulate a vision."

"You will improve. You'll have the best training available."

She bit her lip. "I can't do it."

"You *won't* do it," he corrected harshly. "This isn't about you anymore, Chloe. It's about a company we're trying to save together."

"No, I can't." She clenched her hands into fists, the band around her chest tightening until she felt like she couldn't breathe. "I know what I'm supposed to be, Nico. I've spent my life trying to live up to that. I have given you Vivre, what I know will be a smash hit. But what you're asking of me now is too much."

"Why?" Harsh, implacable.

Because if she stepped into her mother's shoes, she would have to admit she was gone. She would have to acknowledge a pain so deep it might shatter her into pieces and she might never be able to put herself back together again. Because she was barely hanging on as it was.

Heat lashed the backs of her eyes, swift and unrelenting. She walked unsteadily to the window, where she stood staring out at a glorious amber-and-yellow-painted Central Park.

"Chloe," Nico said huskily, closing his hands around her shoulders. She shrugged, attempted to jerk out of his hold, but he sank his fingers deeper into her flesh and turned her around to face him.

"I know you can do this," he murmured, fixing his gaze on hers. "You just have to *believe* you can do it."

The dark, sensual scent of him wrapped itself around her. An irresistible wall of heat that drew her in a way she didn't want to acknowledge, he was overwhelmingly solid in a world that seemed to have dissolved around the edges. She knew she should look away, put some distance between them, because he was the last man on earth she should be drawn to in that way. But she couldn't seem to do it.

His eyes darkened. Electric currents vibrated the air between them as he lifted a hand to stroke his thumb along the line of her jaw. The tension coiling her insides snaked tighter, caging her breath in her lungs.

*Walk away, Chloe.* It was the smart thing to do. Why, then, would her feet not seem to move?

A discreet cough cut across the charge in the air. Her pulse beat a jagged edge at her throat as she stepped back, inordinately grateful for the distraction. Pivoting, she took in the elegant blonde standing in the doorway.

Nico's date, she assumed. Who was one of the most beautiful women Chloe had ever laid eyes on. Shoulder-length blond hair cut into a sleek bob, curvaceous figure clad in a sapphire-blue beaded dress she wore with sky-high heels, she was undeniably his type.

Turning on that effortless charm of his, Nico asked *Helene* to give them a minute. Chloe turned back to face him as the blonde retreated to reception. "Your *nonhot* date?"

"The president of Germany's largest department store chain," Nico corrected. "She has a thing for Mario Conti. He's doing *Tosca* at the Met tonight."

"And you are solidifying that relationship." She lifted her chin as an ancient hurt lashed her insides. "A specialty of yours."

His gaze narrowed, razor-sharp, as it rested on hers. "The Source Minerale deal was signed a month before my relationship with Angelique began, Chloe. So whatever your list of my faults, you can take sleeping my way to the top off it."

A rush of color stained her cheeks. She tugged her lip between her teeth, caught utterly flat-footed. "It was everywhere in the papers, Nico."

"The announcement was strategically timed to coincide with a key anniversary for Source Minerale. The deal, however, was done way before then." His mouth curved in a mocking smile as he crossed the room to his desk. "Don't lose any sleep over it. I'm sure you'll find at least half a dozen of my other failings to cling to."

Her skin stung from the rebuke. She watched as he dumped a sheaf of papers into his briefcase. Considered this new piece of information. If Nico had not slept with Angelique to seal the Source Minerale deal just days after they had shared that passionate encounter at the Fourth of July party, it could only mean his preference for the beautiful Angelique had dictated his actions.

A low throb pulsed inside her where his betrayal still lived. Clearly what they'd shared had always meant far more to her than it had to him, and she needed, once and for all, to realize that, instead of thinking he was something he wasn't. Instead of imagining *moments* between them like that one just now that weren't real.

Nico snapped his briefcase shut. Set a level gaze on her. "We have a deal, then?"

She lifted her chin. "You're leaving me no choice. But I guess you know that." She scooped up her things and stalked to the door. "Enjoy your evening. Apparently, Mario Conti brings down the house."

Mario Conti did bring down the house in the first half of *Tosca* at the stately, always magnificent Metropolitan Opera House. Puccini's dramatic story of love, lust and murder against a backdrop of the politics of soon-to-be Napoleon's Rome was spectacular, with Conti playing the opera's protagonist, the doomed Angelotti, to perfection.

But Nico's mind was on Chloe instead of the moving performance, and her high emotion as she'd stormed out of his office. Had he pushed her off the edge of the cliff with his demand she be the face of Evolution? Was it too much pressure for her to handle?

He was also, he acknowledged, as Conti took an extended bow, annoyed with her and with himself for letting her goad him into dredging up ancient history in Angelique. Because he'd hurt her again. He'd seen it in her face. And perhaps, in hindsight, ending things like that between them might not have been the right way to go about it. But he'd been young, his emotional IQ not yet fully developed.

His honor, however, he fumed inwardly, had never been in question. And that was what annoyed him most of all. If it hadn't been for his *honor*, he would have taken everything Chloe had been offering that night. Which would have been a disaster for them both.

The standing ovation complete, he escorted Helene to the bar for a drink. While she went to the powder room, he installed himself at the bar. Attempted to right-side his mood. But the bar was jam-packed, which left him cooling his heels with ancient memories of that night with Chloe imprinted in his head.

A kiss in the garden as fireworks had exploded over their heads. Chloe's silky-soft curves beneath his hands. The raging hunger of his youthful hormones as she'd returned the favor with an innocence that had nearly brought him to his knees. He'd put a stop to that soon enough, because that would have been true insanity, but he'd touched her plenty, her short, cherry-colored dress an irresistible temptation, with even softer skin to be found beneath.

His throat went so dry he almost crawled across the bar and poured the drink himself. If he lived to be a hundred, he would never forget the sound of her cries in his ear as he'd brought her untutored body to the peak of pleasure. It had nearly unmanned him.

He threw some bills at the bartender as he arrived with his drink. Took a sustaining gulp of the Scotch, welcoming its smooth, hot burn.

"I didn't figure Puccini as your thing."

A smile touched his mouth as Santo, his youngest brother, slid into place beside him at the bar. Dressed in a sharp black tux, he had their mother's coloring, as light as he and Lazzero were dark. Electing to scruff up his impossibly perfect golden good looks tonight with some dangerous-looking stubble, it did nothing to make him look any less angelic.

"Not so much," Nico commented drily. The arts were Santo's thing. "Who's the lucky female? I'm assuming you brought one."

"Kathleen O'Keefe, a business reporter for one of the dailies." Santo caught the bartender's attention and ordered two glasses of wine before he leaned back against the bar, arms crossed over his pristine Armani. "We're sitting two boxes over from you. I tried to get your attention, but you were someplace else. Who's the hot blonde, by the way? She would have distracted me, too."

"Helene Schmidt, the president of Stil 049."

"Gorgeous and successful," Santo murmured. "Tell me this is ending up horizontal."

"I don't date clients."

Santo fixed him with an assessing look. "*Santo* Nico," he drawled. "Mamma had the names all wrong."

Nico took a pull of his Scotch in response.

"I saw your little bird the other night," Santo said idly. "She looked...*fantastic*. When are you going to admit she is a problem for you, *fratello*? Or should we saint you now and get it over with?"

Nico swirled the amber liquid in his glass. "She isn't my *little bird*. And I took care of that problem a long time ago."

"You think so?" Amusement dripped from his brother's voice. "The first step in addressing a problem is admitting you have one. Chloe is all grown up, Nico. She doesn't need your brand of protection anymore."

She sure as hell did. She'd been as delicate as a wisp of wind in his office tonight. And what had he done? He'd piled more pressure on her.

"Anyway," Santo said with a dramatic sweep of his

palm, "Kathleen gave me a piece of intel last night in bed. I wanted to pass it along."

"Save that for yourself," Nico deadpanned. "I've never had any complaints in that area."

Santo's mouth quirked. "Very funny. Kathleen is a *business* reporter. Her editor had lunch with Giorgio Russo last week. Giorgio spent the whole lunch giving him the background scoop on the 'political unrest' at Evolution. He said he has half the board in his pocket."

Red blazed in his head. His hand tightening around the crystal tumbler he held, he absorbed a burn of pure fury. He'd been content to watch Giorgio spin his wheels with his fruitless internal campaign to discredit him, but taking it public was crossing the line. He wasn't worried about the board being solid behind him because he knew that they were. But if Giorgio was shooting his mouth off to journalists, it could *create* an aura of political instability around Evolution with the very forces that determined its future—the analysts, the market, the shareholders—worried the company would implode from the inside out. And that he couldn't have.

*"Grazie,"* he murmured to Santo. "That is good information to have."

Santo lifted a brow. "What are you going to do?"

"Shut him down."

# CHAPTER FOUR

THERE WERE PRIMA DONNAS and then there was Lashaunta. The pop singer took the concept to a whole other level.

Chloe buried her head in her hands as the diva walked off the set for the fifth time to take a phone call from her boyfriend, with whom she shared some strange kind of bizarre pseudo-addiction. From the high-end champagne she'd demanded for her dressing room to the red roses that needed to cover every surface because they put her in a good "mental place" to the incessant phone calls with Romeo, they hadn't captured even one decent piece of footage all day.

Given the singer went on tour for a month tomorrow, it was a problem. Chloe rubbed her palms against her temples, massaged the dull ache beginning to penetrate her skull. She must have been crazy to think she could do this. The timeline was insanely tight, with absolutely no room for miscues. If she went down in flames with this launch, so did Evolution.

*You are only as good as your supporting team*, Nico had counseled in their morning meetings in which she'd done her best to behave and listen. *Trust them to execute this for you.* Which she did. Now if only her pop sensation would save her torrid romance for the midnight hour so she could wrap this spot up before she and Nico left for

Palm Beach on Friday. Which was key because Lashaunta kicked off the campaign in the middle of November, with Desdemona following her—a one-two punch that would hopefully put her perfumes on everyone's lips.

Lashaunta sauntered back onto the set. Chloe took a deep breath. Walked down onto the set and took the pop singer through the concept for Be. *Again.* Lashaunta stared at her blank-faced. *OMG.*

"Can you think of a moment in your life," Chloe said patiently, "when you realized you had become what you were destined to be? When you let yourself be stripped down, naked, *raw*, to hell with what anyone else thought, because this was *you*, and you couldn't be anything else but what you are?"

The pop singer's exotic eyes brightened. "Sure. When I met Donnie," she said dreamily. "I mean, we are *real* with each other."

Chloe almost cried. "I was hoping for something a little more impactful than that. Not that Donnie isn't that," she hastily backtracked when Lashaunta eyed her, "but you know what I mean."

The diva pressed red-tipped fingers to her wide, passionate mouth. *"Yes,"* she finally said. "When I was standing on the stage at the Billboard Awards last year. I'd just sung 'Butterfly.' It was the craziest moment—the applause went on forever. I just stood there and drank it all in. In wonder, really, because this was just me—the girl from a tiny Caribbean island no one's ever heard of. I knew then," she said huskily, "that finally I'd arrived. It was full-on, girl."

Chloe remembered it. It had held her and the rest of the world transfixed—the moment almost religious in its intensity. "Can you please," she said evenly, "say that on camera?"

"No problem."

Chloe was an hour late for her media training session by the time she flew upstairs to her office. Her headache had, unfortunately, elected to go south, but at least Lashaunta's spot was in the can. Which faded to a pleasant memory as her media trainer, whom she liked to refer to as her military drill instructor, pushed her through two hours of brutal interviews. Which didn't go well because she hadn't had time to read the prep notes and was flying by the seat of her pants.

"Better," said the drill instructor when she'd finished her latest effort. "But can we do it again? I'm not really *feeling* the passion when it comes to what you do."

She gritted her teeth. Felt huge sympathy for Lashaunta. She knew what she was *feeling*, and it was an almost uncontrollable urge to strangle her instructor to a slow and painful death.

Head throbbing, she pulled off her mic. "No," she said, getting to her feet. "I'm done. We can pick this up tomorrow."

The trainer's mouth fell open. "We have two hours left. And you have your big interview on Friday."

"Then we'd better hope I improve by then."

She snatched up her lab coat and stormed out of her office, the crew staring after her. And walked straight into a brick wall in Nico.

It hadn't been that bad, Chloe told herself a couple of hours later as she pulled herself out of the pool in the rooftop executive spa, a perk that put working at Evolution on top of every Manhattanite's dream job list.

Nico *had* been furious with her for ditching the media training session, but thankfully he'd been on his way into a meeting. And she *had* explained what her day had been like to her stony-faced boss.

And who cared, really? She grabbed a thick towel and blotted the water from her skin. She still had work to do in the lab after the break she'd decided was mandatory. She was doing her best, and if he didn't want to see that, well, *tough*.

A glass of cucumber water beckoned, along with the steam room to ease a few of the knots in her shoulders. Slinging the towel over her shoulder, she hummed a tune as she pushed open the glass doors to the luxurious cream marble space. The sight of Nico in low-slung graphite swim trunks lounging on a bench stopped her in her tracks.

*She couldn't be this unlucky.* Her pulse bounded beneath her skin as she took him in. She definitely wasn't staying—that was for sure. But first, she needed to stop drooling over the jaw-dropping washboard abs, which seemed as if they might be a gift from heaven as the sweat poured down them. The muscles that bunched thick in his shoulders. The *thighs* that were so powerful they took her thoughts to places they most definitely shouldn't go.

He was dead to her. He had smashed her heart into little pieces and left her like roadkill by the side of the highway. She kept that thought top of mind as she lifted her gaze to his. Not his normal calm, steely gray, she registered, noting the heated flame that burned there.

A thread of unease tightened around her chest, then unraveled so fast her heart began to whirl. So he hadn't cooled off.

"Enjoy," she murmured, pivoting on her heel. "I've changed my mind. I think I'll shower instead."

He set an even gaze on hers. "Sit down, Chloe. I think we can share the same space without taking each other apart."

She wasn't actually so sure that was true.

* * *

Nico could have cursed Santo. Because all he could think of beyond his extreme aggravation with the woman opposite him was how amazing she looked in that swimsuit.

You couldn't even say it was provocative. There was too much material to the fuchsia-colored bikini for that. Which made it all the more enticing because it left so much of her slim, curvaceous figure unexposed.

Where she'd been all long, slim limbs at eighteen, she had filled out in all the right places since. *Not a teenager anymore.* A beautiful, desirable woman he was sure some man had already discovered. *If* he'd been able to get past her mile-high walls. Why he hated that idea was frankly irrational.

Irritated at his own weakness, he swept a towel across his face. Focused his anger on her instead as she wrapped a towel sarong-style around herself and sat opposite him on the marble bench.

"You cost the company a thousand dollars today. You can't just decide you've had enough and walk out. We made a deal, one you are going to stick to, or I swear I'll pull the plug on your campaign."

She lifted her chin, eyes shimmering, dark pools of light. "I'm only one person, Nico. I'm spreading myself too thin. Something's got to give."

"Stop micromanaging your team, then, and let them do their job."

"We wouldn't have gotten Lashaunta's spot filmed today without me." She shifted on the bench, drawing his eye to a creamy stretch of undeniably luscious thigh.

"I'm terrible at the media stuff," she announced flatly. "I told you I would be. What's the point?"

He tore his gaze away from those delectable thighs. "You would be better at it if you knew your key messages. Have you even looked at them?"

She stared at him, affronted. "Have they been giving you *reports* on me?"

"I asked for one."

Hot color shaded her cheeks. "I fell asleep reading them last night."

"Because you were in the lab until ten o'clock." He shook his head. "You are *banned* from the lab until you master this, Chloe. Not one step past that door."

A slight widening of her big brown eyes was her only reaction. She leaned her head back against the tile and eyed him. "John Chisolm told me this morning my father took a step back last year. That, in essence, you have been running Evolution ever since. What was he talking about?"

Nico kept his face bland. "Your father decided it was time to enjoy life a bit more. He had me, so he could afford to do so."

"My father didn't know the meaning of downtime," Chloe countered. "Evolution was his passion. He always said he'd run it until either his mind or his body gave out."

*Dannazione.* He hated this. "Later life tends to give you perspective," he murmured.

Her gaze sharpened on him. "What is it you aren't telling me?"

"You're reading too much into it," he said flatly. He wiped another rivulet of sweat from his eyes. "What you *might* expend your energy on is convincing your uncle to put a muzzle on himself. All his smear campaign is doing is making him look like a fool while everyone who plays a role in the future of this company worries the internal politics will make us implode."

She was silent for a long moment. "Give me a reason to trust you," she said quietly. "Because right now I feel like I am missing a piece of the puzzle and I don't know what it is. If my father had you running the company, why didn't he tell Giorgio that? Why not make it clear what the succession plan was? Why let it fester like this?"

The thought that he should just *tell* her flashed through his head. Because what did it matter now? Martino was dead. Was keeping Chloe in the dark doing more harm than good? Except, he acknowledged, he'd given Martino his word not to say anything, and his word was his word. As for Giorgio? He'd soon hang himself on his own insurrection.

He set his gaze on Chloe's. "You know you can trust me. Have I ever broken a promise to you?"

"Yes," she whipped back, fire in her eyes. "The one where you promised *to be there* for me and then you weren't."

*Oh, hell.* Chloe bumped her head against the wall as if to knock some sense into herself. She'd sworn she wasn't going there. Had *promised* herself she wasn't going there. And then she had.

Nico closed his eyes. Exhaled. "I have *always* been there for you," he said finally, opening them again. "I started something I shouldn't have that summer with you, Chloe. I was your father's protégé, four years older than you, a *lifetime* at that age. We both knew it wasn't going to end well. It was far too...*complicated* and you were far too vulnerable. You were looking for something I couldn't give."

She blinked. Attempted to take in everything he'd just said. Everything she'd never been privy to because he'd never explained it to her.

"I—I never asked you for anything," she stammered. "I was eighteen, Nico. I just thought we had something good."

"You were infatuated with me," he said matter-of-factly. "For me it was hormones. I wanted you, but I didn't want the entanglements that came with it. You wanted every-thing—the moonlight, the candles, the romance. I couldn't give you that. Better you go off and find a nice French boyfriend who could."

Instead, he'd kissed her to within an inch of her life, branded her with his touch as he'd made her come apart in his arms and then walked away, leaving that compari-son to haunt her every time she'd kissed a man since. Be-cause kissing Nico, experiencing the passion she had felt in his arms, had felt like a revelation.

Her stomach twisted into a tight, hot knot. "So," she said, eyes on his, "you slept with Angelique—why? Be-cause you simply moved on?"

"Because I thought it was the easiest way to drive home the point we were done." He rubbed a palm against the stubble on his jaw. "Perhaps it wasn't the right way to han-dle it, but I'm not sure anything else would have worked."

Because she'd pursued him afterward. Refused to take no for an answer.

Humiliation flared through her, hot and deep. "You could have just explained it to me, Nico. I would have *gotten it*, I assure you. Because honestly," she said with a shoulder shrug, pride driving her on, "I was simply look-ing to sample what you offer so freely to other women. That legendary *expertise* you're known for. It would have been an excellent base to work from."

"You think so?" The low rumble in his voice should have been her first clue she'd crossed a line. Some invisible marker that tumbled them straight from a safe, combat-ive place into entirely unknown territory. The incendiary glimmer in his eyes, glowing like the last banked em-bers of a fire, cemented it. "I think you have no idea what happens when you play with fire. Someone always gets burned, I can assure you. Which is why I walked away ten years ago. Because *this* is never happening between us."

Her heart felt as if it had fallen into a deep, dark pit with no bottom. Swallowing hard, she searched for air. Half of her wanted to know what it was like to walk into the fire—to *get* burned, because she'd never felt as alive as she'd felt in his arms that night. The other half wanted to run for safety—to retreat into the sheltered, familiar world she had always existed in.

She felt shaky, unsure of everything in that moment. *Nothing* felt concrete anymore. Everything seemed to be mired in a gray haze she had no idea how to navigate.

Not messing up this chance to prove herself Nico had given her seemed to be the only coherent thought she had.

"Maybe your lesson in all this," she said, fixing her gaze on his, "is that you don't need to make decisions for me, Nico. I'm perfectly capable of making them myself. In fact," she said quietly, "I wish I had."

She left then. Because it seemed the only rational thing to do.

# CHAPTER FIVE

WHY HAD SHE agreed to this?

Chloe paced her office twenty-four hours after her confrontation with Nico, the key messages she'd been attempting to inhale for her big interview circling her head like puzzle pieces that refused to form themselves into a coherent picture.

The interview was tomorrow morning, looming like her worst nightmare. *D-day.* She *knew* how important it was. The feature piece for the fashion section of the most distinguished paper in the nation was an amazing opportunity to gain profile for Evolution at a time when the company desperately needed it. But if one more person attempted to imprint that fact into her head, she was going to scream.

She collapsed on her mother's Louis XVI sofa and took a deep breath. She was being ridiculous. Of course she could do this. She just needed to get over the block in her head. She thought it might have something to do with the million things she *wasn't* doing at the moment that needed to be done.

Another thing she didn't *need* appeared in the doorway of her office. Dressed in a dark gray suit, a lilac shirt and an eggplant tie that enhanced his swarthy coloring, Nico looked disgustingly energized at seven o'clock in the evening. As if he could take on another full day with one hand tied behind his back. A bit *dazzling*.

She cursed her ever-present awareness of him. She'd been doing so well keeping their relationship on a business footing, but that confrontation in the spa had ignited something between them she couldn't seem to turn off.

"I'm studying," she grumbled, waving the papers in front of her at him. "No need to lecture."

"You look exhausted," he said bluntly. "I heard the session today didn't go great."

"Nope. No surprises there." She sat back against the sofa and exhaled a long sigh. "I have no idea why I'm so blocked. I can't seem to articulate myself the way I want to."

He crossed his arms over his chest. "Then we'll work through it together."

She sat up straight. Eyed him warily. Nico and his overbearing tactics were the *last* thing she needed right now.

"I can handle this myself."

"You could," he conceded. "But I can help. I've done a million of these interviews."

With effortless, supreme confidence, she assumed, watching helplessly as he shrugged off his jacket, slung it over the back of a chair and walked to the bar, where he pulled a bottle of wine from the rack and set out two glasses.

"*That* is not going to help."

He ignored her and opened the wine. "You need to relax. You're so far in your head right now you can't see the forest from the trees."

Likely true. Although she wished she could attain some kind of clarity when it came to *him*. Figure out what he was keeping from her. She'd talked to Mireille about their father's supposed step back. It might have been true, Mireille had conceded, that their father had taken a bit of a foot off the gas over the past year, but he had been sixty-two. Would it really have been so unexpected for him to want to take a break?

No, but why, then, wouldn't he have simply communicated that to Giorgio? She'd spoken to her uncle, who'd insisted his version of events was true. When she'd voiced her apprehension his campaign to discredit Nico would destabilize Evolution, it had been like talking to a brick wall. Which did worry her. She had no idea what he was up to—and that couldn't be good.

Another issue she couldn't tackle right *now*. Nico carried the wine and glasses over to the sofa and sat down beside her. All of a sudden, the delicate piece of furniture seemed so much smaller with him in it. Long legs sprawled in front of him, wineglass in hand, his shirtsleeves rolled up to reveal corded, muscular forearms, he was impossible to ignore.

She'd tried to convince herself that Gerald, the handsome Frenchman she'd dated for a few months, had been just as attractive. But that had been wishful thinking. Nico had a hint of the street in him beneath that outward elegance he'd cultivated. The *rough set of cards life had dealt him*, according to her father. It made him intimidating, fascinating, *dangerous* in a way Gerald could never hope to emulate.

He eyed her. "So what exactly," he asked, pointing his wineglass at her, "is it that you are struggling with?"

"The big-picture questions. My creative vision… I have no idea how to explain it." She waved a hand at him. "Everyone thinks it's this mystical thing that involves divine inspiration, when in reality, it's like a puzzle I have to solve. A painting I need to layer bit by bit. It's different for each individual scent I develop depending on whom I'm creating it for."

He considered that for a moment. "Maybe you need to use some of your mother's techniques."

"Like what?"

"She would use the interviewer as an example, for instance. Pretend she was creating a scent for him or her. It was a brilliant technique—got the journalist very involved in the process. They were fascinated by it."

"Which is fine if you can think on the spot like my mother could." Chloe pursed her lips. "It takes me months, *years*, to come up with a fragrance."

"But you must have some sense when you meet someone what will suit them. What do you do when you design custom fragrances?"

She thought about it for a moment. "I do an interview of sorts, a history taking if you like, to get a sense of who the person is. Their past, present, what they like, dislike. It would give me an initial idea of what kinds of scents they would prefer, but it wouldn't direct me, if you know what I mean. Someone can say to me they like beachy, breezy fragrances, but that might not be what suits them at all. Or what they're really asking for."

He took a sip of his wine. Swirled the ruby-red liquid in his glass. "Try it with me, then. You've never designed a fragrance for me. I would be the perfect test case."

She gave him a wary look. "Right now?"

"Why not?" His eyes held the spark of a challenge. "It would be the perfect test run. I know you can do this, Chloe. Stop censoring yourself and let your instincts take over."

She thought censoring herself was exactly what she should be doing when it came to him. But she had never been one to back down from a challenge.

"Fine," she agreed. "But I need a prop."

\* \* \*

Nico eyed Chloe as she sat down on the sofa with a testing tray in her hands. He was capable of keeping his hands off her, that he knew, but *her* putting her hands on him? That might be a different story. That had been where all their issues had begun in the first place.

He lifted a brow. "Are you planning on putting those on me?"

"No." She observed the skeptical note in his voice. "That would be counterproductive. Everything would blend into one another. I'll put them on scent strips and have you give your impression. It won't be the full test I'd do if I was creating a perfume for someone, but it will give you an idea of the process."

*"Bene."* He settled back against the sofa, wineglass in hand. She plucked the glass from his fingers and set it on the table.

"The red wine will throw your sense of smell off."

"Right." He studied the focus on her intent, serious face. Found it more than a bit sexy. "Do we start with the interview, then?"

"I'm going to skip it because I know you. We'll start with the scent test instead. I can fill the rest in myself."

He opened his hands wide. "I'm all yours."

A flush stained her olive cheeks at the unintended innuendo. He stared at it, fascinated. When was the last time he'd seen a woman do *that*? Chloe had an innocence, a transparency about her that had always amazed him—as if she had been poured straight from the source, uncontaminated by life. Which, he conceded, was pretty much the case.

Was that what had always drawn him to her? Because it was exotic to him, *compelling*? Because it seemed to rub off on everyone who came into contact with her, reminding them of an innocence, a *goodness*, that still existed in the world? Or was it just because he'd always wanted what he couldn't have?

She dabbed two feather-shaped scent strips with a unique essence from the glass bottles. "Think of it as a blind taste test," she instructed, handing them to him. "Except you're smelling instead. This is you picking your favorite scents in a process of elimination that will help me choose the top, middle and base notes of the fragrance."

"So you're not going to tell me what they are?"

"No. Take one in either hand," she directed. "When you smell the one on your left, it's going to be clean and woodsy, with a hint of warmth to it. When you switch to the other, you will smell something deeper, less clean. Tobacco and spice dominate. Now you come back to the initial scent, it's crisp and clean, airy, not as warm as it was before. Then you go back to the second. There's tobacco and spice, a boldness, a complexity to it. A *sensuality*."

He brought the first scent strip to his nose, fascinated to find the experience exactly as she had described—the first light and less complex, the second rich and seductive.

"Close your eyes," Chloe encouraged. "Give yourself over to it. Let yourself be hedonistic, fully aware of your senses. Scent is *intimate*," she murmured. "Intensely personal. React to it. Let *it* tell you where you want to go."

Nico closed his eyes. Listened to her talk him through each pair. Found himself utterly distracted by the passion with which she approached her calling. How sensual an experience it actually was.

On they went, bouncing back and forth. Him choosing his favorite and giving his gut reaction, Chloe making notes.

The slide of her fingertips against his, the sensual lilt to her voice, the accidental brush of the soft curve of her breast against his arm were the most potent aphrodisiacs he'd ever encountered. It turned him hard as stone.

Not his brightest idea.

"And these two?" she prompted.

"The one on the left," he murmured, "reminds me of the cottage we used to go to in Maine as kids. The ocean."

She nodded. "That's called a scent imprint. A memory associated with a scent. We all have them. They're very specific to us personally. Good. And the other?"

"Warmer. Intense, illusive. It smells like—" *Her.* Like the fragrance she'd always worn. Except on Chloe it was exotic and intoxicating, the way it came off the heat of her skin. "Summer," he finished lamely.

She handed him two more strips. "And these?"

"Tropical," he said of the first one. "Sweet. Rich."

"And the next?"

He inhaled. Found himself in the middle of a smoky, earthy scent that was just a little...*dirty.*

"Sex." He opened his eyes and fixed them on hers. "That one is definitely sex."

Her eyes widened. Shimmered with a heat that snagged his insides. Potent and thick, the air around them suddenly seemed dense—layers deep—all his good intentions evaporating as her gaze dropped to his mouth. Stayed there.

She drifted closer, her floral scent melding with his, the hitched sound of her breathing stirring his senses. It took every ounce of his willpower not to close the last few centimeters between them and cover those lush lips with his, because a decade later, he still remembered how sweet they were...how perfect she'd tasted beneath him. How *forbidden.*

"Chloe," he murmured. "Are we almost done? I feel like we should be done now."

"Yes," she breathed, dragging her gaze back up to his.

"You're very good, by the way. That one has lots of indole in it. It comes from—" She sank her teeth into her full bottom lip. "Well…you know."

He didn't know. Didn't *want* to know. Because the only place his mind wanted to go right now started with an *s* and ended with an *x*. And that couldn't happen with this particular woman. Not now. Not ever.

Chloe cleared her throat, her eyes dark, liquid, so brown they were almost black. "There's two more. But we could probably leave those because I'm sure I know which way I'm going to go."

"Good. Let's do that." He reached for his wine and took a gulp. Ruthlessly pulled his libido back under control.

"So," he prompted, "what is your analysis?"

Chloe wasn't sure how her brain was supposed to function after that look Nico had just given her. As if he wanted to consume her whole. As if *she* was what he wanted to get intimate with. Because that hadn't been her imagination talking, she was sure of it.

Her head spun as she made a show of gathering up her materials and stowing them on the tray. Knowing after all this time the attraction between them wasn't one-sided like she'd thought it had been, that it was clear and *present*, was a bit mind-boggling. Also head-scratching was the fact that for a moment there, she'd felt compelled to play with that fire he'd declared off bounds. Which *was* crazy. For so many reasons.

She closed trembling fingers around the stem of her wineglass, lifted it to her mouth and took a sip. Gathered her brain back into some sort of working order because she wasn't done yet.

"You wear my mother's Voluttuoso," she began, setting her gaze on his, "which is a gorgeous fragrance, one of my favorites. And it does reflect the innate…*sensuality* about you. But I would have gone with something different."

"I like that fragrance," he countered. "I think it suits me. Why not it?"

"Because you're more complex than that," she said quietly. "Vetiver, the warm Indian grass that predominates in Voluttuoso, is sexy, but you have a strength, a *toughness* about you that comes from your past. With Voluttuoso, it's only showing one facet of you. If it were me, I would veer toward something darker and more complex."

"Such as?"

"Something with a base note of the tobacco you were drawn to, for instance. I'd have predicted that. It has depth, like you. Some cedar," she continued thoughtfully, "to reinforce the tobacco and to bring in that scent memory you have of your early years at the cottage. Some other warm notes to give it added complexity," she continued, formulas shifting in her head like puzzle pieces. "Amber or nutmeg, perhaps. And jasmine, definitely jasmine, for that sensual edge."

A smile curved her mouth. "Bold, rich and *haunting*."

He lifted a brow. "Haunting?"

She gave a self-conscious shrug. "A turn of phrase. Evocative words sell perfumes."

"And so do you," he murmured. "I was buying everything you were selling, Chloe. Hook, line and sinker. You had me on the edge of my seat." He pointed his wineglass at her. "You didn't *tell* me about the creative process, you *demonstrated* it. Do that tomorrow and you'll be gold."

Or she could blow it completely and let everyone down.

# CHAPTER SIX

ARMED WITH A strong cup of coffee and as much confidence as she could muster, Chloe played host to the hip, young journalist Carrie Mayer from the nation's most respected daily newspaper at 10:00 a.m. the next morning in her office. The reporter spent the first few minutes raving about the decor, which only reminded Chloe of what a big personality her mother had been and cranked up her nerves yet another notch.

How could she possibly *be* that?

But she refused to retreat back into her head, because this was too important. Luckily, she and Carrie clicked and were soon whizzing through the questions. Chloe wasn't perfect in her answers, knew she'd missed some of her key messages along the way she'd probably get her hand slapped for, but she kept things on track, even when Carrie asked about her mother's death and what she had meant to her.

It was, however, when she went through the scent test with Carrie and offered her personal recommendation that the journalist's eyes lit up. "Brilliant," she murmured, madly scribbling notes. "Can I quote all of that, or are there trade secrets in there I can't use?"

Chloe told her to go ahead and use it. Gave the reporter a bottle of her mother's Cygne Blanc, which would suit her perfectly.

Nico, Chloe admitted as she showed Carrie out, was very smart. She might just tell him that. But first, she had a whirlwind shopping trip with Mireille to accomplish in the lunch hour before her and Nico's flight to Palm Beach, because she had absolutely nothing to wear that was in any way suitable for the black-tie charity fund-raiser that evening that attracted the world's elite.

Luckily, Mireille was miraculous with clothes and knew just where to shop. In the space of an hour, they'd found the perfect gown for the Champagne and Diamonds fund-raiser. They'd also acquired a couple of outfits for the warmer Palm Beach weather while they were at it, given Chloe and Nico would spend the weekend at the Di Fiore brothers' luxurious South Beach estate.

Nico had made golf plans with clients tomorrow, which gave Chloe a chance to enjoy a day in the sun. Which was, she acknowledged, another source of nerves. Keeping her attraction to Nico under wraps from a distance was one thing—doing it while they shared the same roof was another.

It was not helpful, then, when she met Nico at the small private airport in New Jersey they would fly out of, to find him dressed in black jeans and a long-sleeved crew-necked sweater in dove gray that matched his eyes. Draped against an unused check-in desk while he tapped away on his phone, he was so stunning every woman in the tiny lounge was making him the preboarding entertainment.

He gave a pointed look at his watch. "We're up next."

"I had to shop. My slave driver of a boss has me toiling all hours."

A curve of his amazing mouth. "How did the interview go?"

"Well, I think. You were right," she conceded with a tip of her head, "the reporter loved the essence test. She said it was brilliant content for the piece." She shrugged a shoulder. "I'm not sure I got every key message across. I was too nervous with the difficult questions. But I did okay."

His smile deepened into one of those rare lazy ones he offered so infrequently, it made her breath catch in her chest. "Then I'm sure it will be great. Now you can relax and enjoy the weekend."

"Yes." She swallowed past the fluttering feeling inside her. "Thank you," she said quietly. "For helping me. You were right. I was so far inside my head, I couldn't seem to get out."

His gray eyes warmed. "I promised you I would be there for you, Chloe, and I will. You are not in this alone."

And why did she feel so reassured by that? She pondered the answer as an official gave them a nod and they were escorted across the tarmac to the sleek ten-person Evolution jet, where the pilot was ready to go. Why was her guard beginning to come down with Nico?

Because she was starting to wonder if she'd been wrong about him, in more than one way? Because everyone she spoke to at Evolution loved working for him—*appreciated* his leadership?

Because he *had* been there for her—exactly as he'd promised? Or had it been that moment in her office where she'd become shockingly aware that the chemistry between her and Nico wasn't one-sided? Was that messing with her head?

She had no idea *what to do* with that particular piece of information. Knew it wasn't wise to pursue it—that Nico had been right about that—but she couldn't seem to get it out of her head.

She was so exhausted, she slept most of the short flight to Miami. Which was helpful, because by the time they arrived and stepped onto the waiting helicopter that would take them to the Di Fiores' South Beach estate, she'd gotten her second wind.

The ultra-modern villa the Di Fiore brothers had built on the ocean was all sleek, square lines, with a spectacular view from its streamlined, wide-open spaces. She felt herself exhaling, the tension seeping out of her bones, as she breathed in the humid, fragrant, warm air.

Boasting double-height ceilings that led to an oversize infinity-edge pool, a custom Italian kitchen and a hand-carved mahogany wine cellar that made her head spin with its extravagant selection, it was Chloe's idea of heaven. Lazzero, who spent the most time at the house, enjoying the party scene for business purposes, had hired a lovely housekeeper, who showed Chloe to a gorgeous, airy bedroom on the second floor, done in dark woods and stark white, with colorful accents thrown in.

Chloe fell in love with the stunning pink-and-orange bougainvillea that seemed to climb into her ethereal bedroom and wished dearly she could take a dip in the ocean before dinner, but since they were due for sunset cocktails at the Buchanans' nearby estate, it would have to wait.

Energized by the heady aroma of tropical flowers and the salty, fresh sea air, Chloe slipped on the gorgeous coffee-colored lace dress she'd bought with Mireille at lunch. Floor length and glamorous, with pretty cap sleeves and a deep plunging back, it was a daring style she never would have chosen on her own.

Catching her hair up in a loose knot, she spritzed on her favorite perfume and declared herself done.

Nico was leaning against the railing, staring at a view of forever, when Chloe joined him on the terrace that overlooked the ocean. A waft of her unmistakable intoxicating perfume hit him just before she did. Then it was his heart going *kaboom* as he turned around and took in the sight of her dressed in a lacy sophisticated number that echoed the creamy color of the silky expanse of skin it revealed.

If he hadn't been fully in lust by the time he'd covered off the delectable curves, he was when he took in her sexy disheveled hairstyle, which left her silky dark curls half up and half down. There was only one thing a man wanted to do when a woman wore her hair like that, and that was to dismantle it completely.

If she was his. Which she wasn't.

He swallowed hard. Santo might be right. He might have a problem. He'd been so far under Chloe's spell during that perfume-testing routine, he'd fled the room moments after it had mercifully ended. Sharing a villa with her wasn't necessarily a great choice either, but with his place ten minutes away from the Buchanans', it would have been silly not to take advantage of it.

What had Santo said? Admitting you had a problem was the first step toward solving it?

Chloe flashed him an uncertain look from beneath those long, amazing lashes of hers. "Am I not dressed appropriately? Mireille thought this would be perfect for tonight. But maybe it's too much?"

"You look gorgeous," he said quietly. "We should go so we aren't late."

She tipped her head back, luminous brown eyes resting on his. "Are you okay? You seem off."

"I'm good." He placed a hand at the small of her back to direct her toward the stairs, his palm nearly spanning her delicate spine. The satiny softness of her skin beneath his fingers unfurled a curl of heat inside him, one he ruthlessly leashed. He might have a problem, but he knew how to deal with it.

They made the quick, ten-minute drive through Palm

Beach's quiet, exclusive streets, behind whose twelve-foot hedges had once resided some of America's oldest families—the Kennedys, Du Ponts, Posts and Fords had all had homes there. The Buchanans' ornate Palm Beach mansion, however, was the king of them all. An eclectic mix of many of the great European architectures—Venetian, Spanish, Portuguese and Moorish—it sat directly on the ocean, more a palace than a mansion, rising majestically among fifteen acres of manicured, glorious gardens.

The statement property mirrored the big personality of its billionaire owners, Josh and Evelyn Buchanan. Josh, a big, bombastic Brit who'd been a close friend of Martino Russo's, had made his money in electronics and now owned an English football team. He'd fallen in love with his American wife, Evelyn, three decades ago and chosen to stay, building Palacio en el Mar, the "Palace on the Sea," for her.

Josh and Evelyn greeted them warmly, introducing them around the poolside soirée where the crème de la crème of the world's elite were gathered to hear the legendary pop star Rodrigo Carrera in a private concert.

It was a magnificent setting—the sun a ball of fire as it sank into the Atlantic, the lazy jazz band that preceded Carrera excellent, the affluent crowd, decked out in their diamonds and black-tie apparel, supremely elegant.

A glass of champagne in his hand, Nico focused on the valuable networking opportunities, rather than the beautiful woman at his side, ensured he and Chloe made that public, political statement of unanimity so necessary for Evolution's stability right now, which was recorded for posterity's sake by the society photographers in attendance.

Chloe tried hard to exercise the same enviable networking skills Nico possessed throughout the cocktail hour and dinner. She found it wasn't so awful as she'd imagined, easier than it had once been for her to complete the end-less rounds of socializing with the budding confidence she'd developed and Vivre to talk about.

But it didn't come naturally to her—the ability to make casual small talk, to forge connections out of a throw-away comment someone made. She found herself more susceptible than usual, as a result, to the attentions of the Buchanans' handsome son, Oliver, whose attention over dinner had drawn her out of herself.

Tall and blond, with the most piercing blue eyes she'd ever seen, he was gorgeous. Successful. *Nice.* Exactly the kind of man a woman with a healthy sense of self-preser-vation should gravitate toward. Unfortunately, that didn't seem to be her. Never had been.

She accepted his offer of another glass of champagne as dinner broke up and the guests mingled on the terrace, waiting for Carrera to begin. Watched as Nico laughed at something the beautiful redhead he'd been sitting next to at dinner had said.

Tall and statuesque, with the perfect bone structure of a runway model, she was stunning. Everything Chloe wasn't. He wasn't looking at *her* as if she had a garbage sack on as he had Chloe earlier. He was looking at her as if she was utterly his type. It hurt in a way she couldn't even begin to articulate. Didn't want to articulate.

Her skin stung, her heart felt sore in her chest. Why had it always been Nico? Why couldn't she just move on? Would it have been different, she wondered, if he'd bro-ken her heart like he surely would have done those years ago? Would she have had closure when it came to him? Because every man since had been a poor substitute—Nico the benchmark by which she had judged them all.

If they could make her feel her emotions right to the

pit of her stomach…if they could make her heart race as he did.

Nico looked up from his conversation with the redhead. Slid his gaze over her. Over the proprietary hand Oliver had placed at her waist. For a single, heart-stopping moment, a flash of heat blazed in his gray gaze. It scorched through her. Singed her right to her toes.

*He wanted her, but he didn't want to want her.* The very visible slip in his daunting self-control rocked her back on her heels. Stole her breath. Then the redhead said something to Nico and he turned away.

Chloe stood there, heart beating a jagged edge. Oliver bent his head to hers. "Let's dance," he murmured. "Carrera is coming on now."

She forced a smile and followed him to the dance floor. She had promised herself she was going to relax and enjoy herself this weekend. Pining after Nico, thinking thoughts that were inherently *unwise* when it came to him, was not accomplishing that. If she were smart, she'd do exactly what Nico was doing—pretend this thing between them didn't exist.

By the time midnight rolled around, however, and Carrera was done with his intimate, fabulous concert, his voice as rich and amazing as it had been in his heyday, Chloe was officially done. She was sure she didn't have one more word of small talk left in her.

"Ready to go?" she asked Nico hopefully.

He nodded. "Let's find Josh and Evelyn and say goodnight."

They wound their way through the thick crowd toward their hosts. A feminine voice, with a Southern drawl, cut through the din.

*"Nico."*

Chloe turned to see a beautiful blonde approaching them.

Elegant and undeniably striking with her sparkling blue eyes and chic, sleek bob that angled fashionably to her ear, she moved with a grace and fluidity that captured the eye.

Chloe looked up at Nico, wondering who she was. Found his face frozen solid, not one whisper of emotion visible.

A former lover? She quickly discarded the idea as the woman drew upon them. She had to be in her midfifties. As gorgeous up close as she had been from afar, she must have been outrageously beautiful when she was younger. She still was.

The woman stopped in front of them, her gaze trained on Nico. Nico said nothing, an oddity with his impeccable manners. The woman ignored Chloe completely, waving a fluttering, nervous hand at Nico. "Evelyn just told me you were here. I had no idea. We— I arrived late."

Nico's expression hardened. "I hope you caught some of the concert. It was excellent." He nodded toward Josh and Evelyn, who were seeing guests off. "If you'll excuse us, we were on our way out."

The woman flinched. Chloe drew in a breath. Who was she? And why was Nico being so rude to her?

The blonde shifted her attention to Chloe, as if seeking assistance. "I'm sorry." She held out a perfectly manicured hand. "I'm Joelle Davis. Formerly Di Fiore. Nico's—"

"—mother," Nico finished. "In the biological sense, anyway."

Chloe's stomach dropped. *His mother?* All she'd ever known about Joelle Di Fiore was that she and Nico's father had divorced before his death and Nico never, ever talked about her.

"A pleasure," she murmured, taking Joelle's hand, because it seemed impolite not to.

"As I said," Nico repeated curtly, setting a hand on

Chloe's waist, "we were on our way out. You'll have to excuse us."

*"Nico."* There was no mistaking the appeal in his mother's voice, the raw edge that slid across Chloe's skin. "I hate the way we left things in New York. I don't want it to be this way." She shook her head and fixed her too-bright gaze on her son. "I've recognized my mistake. Can't you at least acknowledge that?"

*"Bene,"* he agreed, his voice utterly devoid of emotion. *Fine.* "I recognize you recognize you made a mistake. Can we go now?"

Chloe gasped. Joelle's blue eyes glistened. "Nico—"

A tall, distinguished silver-haired man separated himself from the crowd and headed toward them. A stony look claimed Nico's face. He pressed his palm to Chloe's back. "If you'll excuse us."

They left Joelle Davis standing in the crowd. Said goodnight to the Buchanans. Nico didn't say a word on the drive home, his face so closed Chloe didn't dare open her mouth. She could feel the tension in him, coiled tight in his big body as he drove, his knuckles white as they clenched the steering wheel. It made her insides twist into a cold, hard knot.

When they arrived at the house, Nico threw his car keys on the entrance table and wished her a good night.

Chloe eyed him. "Do you want to talk about it?"

"No." He flicked her a glance. "Go to bed, Chloe. You look exhausted."

But she couldn't sleep. Her beautiful bedroom with its elegant four-poster bed was heavenly, the book she'd brought with her entertaining, but as exhausted as she was, she was too wired to settle.

She was worried about Nico. About the emotion he always held inside, her head spinning with curiosity about what had happened with his mother to evoke that kind of a reaction. Eventually, she slipped out of bed, put on her new white bikini and a cover-up dress and went downstairs. The house was in darkness, as was Nico's office as she padded across the hardwood floors, but the pool area was lit with recessed lighting, tranquil and inviting under a clear, starry night.

Nico must have gone to bed, she surmised, when she found the terrace deserted, too. It was still warm out, the air just the slightest bit cool on her skin as she took off her dress. A slight shiver moved through her as she descended the steps to the infinity pool with its magnificent view of the ocean. Still warm from the sun, the water was divine.

The heady fragrance of a dozen tropical flowers scenting the air, ideas for a new perfume filled her head. She swam twenty lazy laps with only a cavalcade of stars as her witness. When she had tired herself out, her limbs heavy, body rejuvenated, she climbed out of the pool and reached for a towel on the rack. Stopped dead in her tracks at the sight of Nico sprawled in a lounge chair.

Obscured by the shadows cast by the half wall that divided the pool and lounge area, a glass of what she assumed was whiskey dangling from his fingers, he looked disheveled in a way she'd never seen him before. His jacket and tie gone, the top few buttons of his shirt undone, his hair spiky and ruffled, he looked like he'd been there for a while.

Her gaze shifted to the whiskey bottle beside the chair, a good dent taken out of it. Back up to his stormy gray gaze. He raked it down over her still-dripping body in the brief white bikini, a frank, appraising look so raw and uncensored, it rocked her back on her heels.

Heat, wild heat, unraveled beneath her skin. Stained

her cheeks. She'd always wondered what Nico unleashed looked like. *If* he ever unleashed himself. Now she knew.

She wrapped the towel around herself, tucking it against her chest with trembling fingers. "I didn't see you there."

"I figured." Low, intense, his voice was sandpaper rough. "You couldn't sleep?"

"No."

"I'm sure you will now."

She ignored the unsubtle dismissal and walked over to him on legs that felt like jelly, whether from the swim or the intensity of his stare, she wasn't quite sure. Up close, she could read the lust in his eyes, a stomach-curling need that shimmered through her insides. But there was also darker, angrier emotion. A combustibility, a *volatility* that burned there.

"You're angry with her," she said quietly.

He pointed a finger at her. "*Bingo*. You win the prize."

She swallowed hard. "You need to talk about it, Nico. It's not healthy to hold everything inside." When he simply continued to stare at her as if she hadn't even spoken, she sighed and pushed a stray hair out of her face. "We used to talk. We used to be...*friends*."

His mouth twisted. "Can we just get one thing straight? We are not *friends*, Chloe. We were never friends."

She sank her teeth into her lip, the salty tang of blood staining her mouth. "What were we, then?"

He took a contemplative sip of his whiskey. "I don't think," he said decisively, "that should be a point of discussion tonight."

"Fine," she said calmly, more off balance by this barely censored version of Nico than she cared to admit. She sat down on the lounge chair next to him. "How about we talk about what happened tonight, then?"

He lifted a shoulder. "What's there to talk about?"

"The fact that your mother desperately wants a relationship with you and you threw it in her face."

His eyes flashed. "You have no idea what you're talking about."

"Then tell me. This is clearly eating you up inside."

He rested his head back against the chair. Stared at her with those incendiary gray eyes. "She walked out on us when I was fifteen."

Chloe's stomach contracted. Such a tough age to lose a mother. "Why did she leave?"

An entirely unhumorous smile stretched his mouth. "Do you have all night?"

"Yes." She curled up on the chair and tucked her legs beneath her. He gave her a long look, then turned his head to stare out at the ocean. She thought he would shut her down then, but he started talking instead.

"My mother met my father when he was a young stockbroker on Wall Street. She was a dance instructor from Brooklyn. She'd moved to New York from California to make it on Broadway. Then she got pregnant with me. She was bitter about it, had no interest in being a mother, but my father convinced her to have me. He desperately wanted kids. He started making a lot of money, and then she didn't care so much because she loved to spend it."

"My father was best man at their wedding, wasn't he?" Chloe asked, remembering the photos her father had shown her.

Nico nodded. "Those were the good years. Lazzero and Santo came along. We got a big house, had the fancy cars, everything that came with the Wall Street lifestyle. Then Martino decided to leave and start Evolution. My father thought about it, decided he was wasting his talent on his firm and left to start his own company."

"A stock brokerage?"

"No. One of his clients, a brilliant engineer, had developed a technology to block the effects of wireless fields when cell phones became popular—a tiny chip you could put on the back of your phone. It was revolutionary, had limitless potential, but the client didn't have the money to bring it to market on his own. My father went into business with him—sank every dollar he had into it."

Chloe was completely intrigued. "It *sounds* ingenious."

"It was. Unfortunately, it took more time to take off than they had anticipated. A lot of wooing of big companies that move very slowly. My father started borrowing money to keep things afloat. Then a major company ordered thousands of units and they thought they'd made it. They secured another loan, went into large-scale production, only for the company to have second thoughts and the order fall through."

Her stomach dropped. "Oh, no."

His expression was grim. "It was the end. The death knell. They lost everything. We lost the house because my father had remortgaged it. The cars—all of it. My father started drinking, lapsed into a deep depression he never came out of."

"Why didn't he ask my father for help?" she queried, perplexed. "To start over?"

He rubbed a hand over his jaw. "He and Martino were the closest of friends, but they were also wildly competitive with one another. It was always who could execute the biggest deal, who could land the most beautiful woman. The rivalry continued when they started their own businesses. Except," he allowed, "Martino became massively successful, while my father's business failed."

"And he was too proud to ask for help."

He nodded. "He wouldn't speak to Martino or any of the others when they called. Refused to take handouts. My parents' marriage fell apart, and my mother moved back to California, where she's from."

Chloe gave him a horrified look. "She just *left* you with your father like that?"

His mouth twisted. "She said she hadn't signed on for that kind of a life."

She pressed a hand to her cheek, an ache forming deep in her chest. "How did you survive?"

"I left school and got a job. Went to classes at night. We lived in some pretty seedy places, but we made do."

And somehow, in the midst of it all, while he was taking care of his family, *holding it all together*, he had managed to get himself a scholarship to the university where he'd been completing his business degree when his father had died. Her father had reconnected with the boys at Leone's funeral and taken them under his wing.

She swallowed hard. It all made sense to her now. Nico's intense sense of honor. The laser focus with which he'd conducted his life, the *ruthless ambition* she had accused him of. He'd had no *choice*. He'd had two brothers and a father to take care of.

"I'm sorry," she said quietly. "That must have been so difficult, Nico."

He shrugged, the ice in his glass crackling in the still night air. "My brothers and I have always said it made us who we are. That we wouldn't *be* who we are were if not for what happened. So for that, I'm grateful."

*But at what price?* "Did you have any contact with your mother after she left?"

He shook his head. "She said she wanted to start a new life—that she couldn't do that with the baggage of her past along for the ride. She met and married Richard, the man you saw her with tonight, a year later."

Chloe drew in a breath. "I'm sure she didn't mean that."

"She meant it," he said flatly. "My father went to see her—to plead with her to come back. She sent him away. The next time we heard from her was five years ago in New York. She came to apologize—to make amends for her mistakes. None of us wanted anything to do with her."

Her heart hitched. How could a mother just walk out on her children like that? It was inconceivable to her. But if there was anything she knew from her own experience in life, it was that people didn't always express what was deep inside themselves. They hid their hopes and fears. And maybe Nico's mother had been afraid. Maybe she'd simply been unable to cope with the way her life had disintegrated around her.

She wet her lips. "She seems to want to make amends, Nico. Can't you forgive her?"

"No," he rumbled, making her jump with the force of his response. "She walked out on us, Chloe. She *made* her decisions. It is ancient history, and I'm at peace with it."

He looked anything but. There was so much emotion on his face it hurt to look at him. He'd just worked his way through a good portion of a bottle of Scotch—Nico, whom she'd never seen have more than a couple of drinks. And now she knew why.

"Anger is not being at peace with it," she pursued. "Maybe you need to listen to her. To find forgiveness to find that peace in yourself."

He lapsed into silence. Made it clear the conversation was over as he drained his glass. "Go to bed," he said, without looking at her. "You've heard the whole sordid story now. No more to tell here."

"I'm not leaving you like this."

"I don't want to talk, Chloe."

She leaned back on the chair, palms planted in the cushion. "Fine, we won't talk."

He moved his gaze back to her. Hot, *deliberate*, it singed the curves of her breasts where the towel had fallen loose. "I don't want company either. Not when we both know what a bad idea that is."

Her stomach tipped upside down, a tremor moving through her. "Why?" she queried huskily. "We're consenting adults. You wanted to kiss me that night in my office during the perfume testing. I know you did."

He went still. "Which I didn't," he said harshly, eyes on hers, "because I knew the insanity that it was. Which it *is*, Chloe."

She knew he was right. Knew she should keep up her guard when it came to him. But the severe, taut lines of his face held her spellbound. The redoubtable control he prized so greatly. Everything about him that did it for her like no other man ever had.

Did he still kiss the same way? As if he could do it all night? Would he make her turn to flame if he touched her again? Could she bear it if he never did?

She hugged her arms tight around herself. Felt a chill move through her that had nothing to do with the cool night air. She'd been cold for so long, *frozen* for such an eternity, she didn't remember what it felt like to be alive. To live in the moment. And suddenly she knew she couldn't do it one second longer. She wasn't going to leave him alone.

She lifted her chin. Trained her gaze on his. "Maybe I know it's crazy. Maybe I know I'm going to get burned. Maybe I haven't felt alive in so long I don't care."

A muscle jumped in his jaw. "You *should* care. I am not in the right headspace for this, Chloe."

But the heat in his smoky stare said otherwise. She was mesmerized by it as it melted her insides. By the chemical reaction that popped and fizzled between them. When she was in the lab, she manufactured reactions like this. With

Nico, they were *real*. Out of her control. It made her pulse stutter, like she'd ingested some kind of dangerous drug.

"Come over here, then," he murmured, the hard lines of his face pure challenge. "If you're so sure of what you want."

He expected the invitation to frighten her off. She could tell from the look on his face. And for a moment it did, freezing all coherent thought. She sucked in a breath, delivered necessary oxygen to her brain. Knew in that moment this was the only opening she was ever going to get with Nico. She either seized it or wondered "what if" forever.

She shrugged her shoulders and let the towel fall to the chair. Got to her feet and walked over to him. He rested his head against the back of the chair and drank her in. Teeth buried in her lip, heart beating a jagged edge, she sat down on the inch of lounger beside him that was free. He was so gorgeous, so formidable in his disarray, sleeves rolled up to reveal corded, powerful forearms, heavy dark stubble dusting his jaw, her stomach went to dust.

His formidable control held even as his eyes turned to flame. He wasn't going to be the one to cross the line. It was going to be up to her to do it. And so she did, leaning forward and wrapping her fingers around his nape, absorbing the shift of tensile muscle and tendon beneath her fingertips as she brought her mouth down to his.

He didn't resist, but he didn't move to meet the kiss either. She found his lips with hers. Hard, betraying none of that inherent sensuality that was so much a part of him, she thought for a terrifying instant he was going to reject her. Then a soft curse escaped him, his arms clamped around her waist and he lifted her astride him, his hands cupping her bottom in his palms. She had just enough time to take a deep breath before he took her mouth in a hard, demanding kiss that slammed into her senses. *Demanded everything.*

As if it would make her run. As if he *wanted* her to run.

Instead, it made her skin burn. Her insides dissolve into liquid honey. The strong muscles in his neck flexed beneath her fingers as he angled his head to deepen the kiss. *Took*, until he seemed to be everywhere inside her, the taste of him dark and dangerous.

A groan tore itself from his throat. He shifted his hands to cup her jaw and slicked his tongue over the seam of her lips to gain entry. She opened for him, helpless to resist his sensual onslaught. Gasped as he stroked and licked his way inside her mouth, his hands at her jaw holding her in place for his delectation. As if he wanted to taste every centimeter of her. *Devour* her.

As intimate as the sexual act itself, *more*, the kiss made her stomach curl. She spread her palms against his chest, absorbing the latent strength that rested in every honed muscle. He tugged the clip from her hair and sent the heavy weight of it tumbling around her shoulders. Threaded his fingers through it and slowed the kiss down to a hot, languid seduction. The kind she remembered. The kind that went on forever.

His mouth left hers. Chloe murmured a protest, but then his lips were busy on her jaw, and then her neck, inducing those same brain-melting sensations. She shivered as he slid his hands from her hair down to cup her breasts. Tested their weight. Stroked his thumbs over the hard peaks, pushed taut by the night air. The shockingly pleasurable caress through the thin material of her swimsuit sent a wave of heat to her core.

*"Nico,"* she breathed.

The tie of her bikini top gave way to the sharp tug of his fingers, and then there was only the delicious sensation of those strong, provocative hands on her bare flesh. The roll of her nipples between his fingers that made her moan deep in her throat. The heat of his ravenous gaze as he drank her in.

"You're beautiful," he said huskily. *Reverently.* "God, I've wanted to see you like this."

The look in his beautiful eyes made her fall apart inside. The heady male scent of him, the unmistakable musky smell of his desire, the iron-hard strength of his thighs beneath her were like seeing, *feeling*, the world in Technicolor again. She didn't think she could ever get enough of it.

She moved closer, seeking, *needing* more. Encountered hot, aroused male, burning her thighs through the material of his pants.

*Oh. He was phenomenal.* As into this as she was.

She melted into him, liquid with longing. Emboldened by the power she held over him. Whispered his name against his mouth.

"Chloe," he murmured, even as he took more of her weight in the hands he slid to her hips, rocking her against that most impressive part of him. "This is madness."

She bent her head and tugged his sensual bottom lip between her teeth. "I don't care."

His hand at her hips rocked her more firmly against him. Deeper, higher, the inferno raged until she was a slave to it. Until nothing existed except what he was making her feel. She whispered how much she wanted him in his ear. He told her how much he loved to hear her talk to him like that. How passionate, how honest her response had always been.

She gasped as he gripped her bottom tighter and raked her against the hard, aroused length of him, the wet, thin fabric of her swimsuit a delicious friction against the intoxicating steel beneath his pants.

Fire seared through her. She whimpered, moved against him, desperate, *hungry* for him to assuage the sweet ache between her thighs. For him to make her feel the things only he had ever been able to make her feel.

He angled her more intimately against him, giving her what she asked for. Ground himself against the aching center of her again and again until she sobbed her release in his ear.

"God, that is sexy," he murmured, a hand at her buttock holding her there, rotating his body against her until he'd wrung every last bit of pleasure out of her. "Give it all to me, sweetheart," he rasped. "All of it."

She collapsed against him, gasping for air. Shattered by the force of her release, incoherent with pleasure, rocked by the experience they had just shared. He had taken her apart, *dismantled* her. She felt exposed, *bare*, in a way she'd never experienced before.

She laid her head on his chest, listening to the pounding of his heart as he held her. Soothed her. Brought her back down to earth with the smooth stroke of his hand across the bare skin of her back.

Nico wasn't actually sure when he'd lost his mind. It might have been the sight of Chloe climbing out of the pool, dripping wet in the sexy white bikini, all of that flawless, creamy skin on display. Or maybe it had been that first sweet touch of her mouth against his. The palpable vulnerability that clung to her like a second skin. But he hadn't been able to resist her. Or maybe it was himself he hadn't been able to refuse.

His breath a jagged blade in his chest, he clawed back control. Every male urge he had said to finish it, to take what he had always craved. To burn them both to oblivion in what followed, because surely it would be amazing. And completely, utterly *insane*.

He rubbed a palm against his temple, head hazy. What

the hell was he doing? Was he really that weak that one kiss had been enough to dismantle the promises he'd made? To forget he was her boss…in a position of authority over her?

Or maybe it had been the whiskey, something he never should have started on. Another lapse in judgment.

He pulled in a breath, fury at his mother for starting this, disgust with himself, mixing in a potent brew. There was still time to assume control. He hadn't let things go *that* far.

Chloe pulled back to look at him, those devastating brown eyes of hers wide and shell-shocked, luminous with desire. "Nico," she murmured, reading the regret on his face. "Don't. I—"

He pulled her bikini top back into place, his hands fumbling over the ties as he redid them. Stood up, with her in his arms, and carried her inside. He didn't trust himself to talk with her half-dressed, and he sure as hell wasn't continuing what they'd started.

Taking the stairs to the second floor, he strode down the lamp-lit hallway and set her down outside her bedroom door. Leaning a hand against the wall, he pulled in a breath. Searched for something to say. But his lack of control when it came to her was such a lapse of judgment, any coherent thought dissolved in a red tide of fury directed solely at himself.

"That," he said harshly, "should not have happened."

She lifted her chin. "I wanted it to happen," she said evenly. "We have something, Nico. Ignoring it is only making it worse."

He gave her a withering look. "You are too vulnerable to have any idea what you're saying, and I'm too much of a son of a bitch not to have walked away. So *find* a way to get it out of your head, Chloe. For both our sakes."

# CHAPTER SEVEN

NICO WOKE WITH a pounding headache. His alarm clock sounded like a fire engine, the sunshine pouring through the windows threatened to blind him, amplifying every throbbing beat of his head. Swiping at the clock with his hand, he silenced it. Sagged back against the pillows.

The events of the night before infiltrated his head. His mother showing up…that red-hot scene beside the pool with Chloe… *Merda.*

He hauled himself out of bed, showered and drank a gallon of the black coffee his housekeeper brewed for him, apparently not unused to the aftereffects of the whiskey phenomenon with Lazzero's hard-partying nights. The idea of walking for hours in the bright sunshine seemed an abhorrent idea, but as his golf game was with the president of the largest beauty retail chain in America, canceling was not an option.

He left the house with a thermos of coffee tucked under his arm and a prayer of silent thanks Chloe was still in bed, because he could definitely wait until dinner to address *that* giant misstep.

Sliding into Lazzero's Porsche, he gunned the powerful car to life and followed Ocean Boulevard to his destination, a pristine stretch of blue ocean flanking his right.

*You're angry, Nico... Perhaps you need to find forgiveness to find peace.*

Chloe's words from the night before echoed through his head. He tightened his fingers around the steering wheel. Damned right he was angry. His mother had been a selfish, bitter creature who'd beguiled his father with her undeniable beauty, then made him pay every day of his life for getting her pregnant with him, even though, by all accounts, she'd been a dancer of mediocre talent who'd resorted to teaching to pay the bills.

Money had been the currency his mother had been willing to trade in. His father had sold what was left of his soul to give it to her. And when he'd eventually folded under the pressure, his mother had made him pay for failing to provide by walking out on New Year's Day.

*Forgive her?* He took a sip of his coffee. Wiped an infuriated palm across his jaw. *Never.* He was the one who'd had to pick up the pieces after the flashy-suited banker had left the Di Fiores' Greenwich Village home after delivering his instructions to repossess the house and everything in it. He was the one who'd taken one look at his father's grief-stricken face, his father who was *no longer there*, and assured his brothers that everything was going to be okay, when, in actual fact, he wasn't sure it would be at all.

He jammed his foot on the brake as a car cut in front of him. Hell yes, he was angry. *Furious* with his mother for approaching him like that when he'd made it clear he wanted nothing to do with her. He was also, he conceded, furious with himself for his own lack of control. For drowning himself in whiskey, pouring out the whole sordid story to Chloe and allowing himself to fall under the spell of a woman he'd vowed to keep his hands off.

A wave of bitter self-recrimination washed over him. He

should have walked away. Instead, he'd put his hands on her, on everything he'd wanted from the first moment he'd seen her in that dress last night, and crossed the line. Had been so caught up in her uninhibited, innocent responses to his caresses, in the heat they'd generated together, he hadn't *thought*—he'd just taken.

Clearly he needed to find a better solution to his problem than the one he currently had. Luckily, he observed grimly, as he pulled into the perfectly manicured front entrance of one of Palm Beach's most prestigious golf clubs, he had eighteen holes to find it.

*Find a way to get it out of your head.*

Unfortunately, all Chloe *could* think about was last night with Nico as she brooded over a pot of coffee on the terrace in the morning sun. Hot, *erotic*, what they'd shared was indelibly burned into her head, never to be forgotten.

The way he'd *looked* at her...the things he'd said. It had been even more intense, more amazing, than her eighteen-year-old self had remembered.

Her skin burned, a flush spreading from her chest up to her cheeks, singeing them with a fiery heat. Nico had been as caught up in the moment as she had been. As if he'd been giving in to his feelings, too. As if he hadn't been able to help himself. It validated everything she'd thought about them all those years ago. As if that had been the truth of them.

To know she could affect him like that, that she could make him lose control, shook her to her toes.

And then he'd walked away. *Again.*

She sank her teeth into her lip. Stared out at the sparkling, azure sea. She had seduced Nico into kissing her. Pushed him over the edge. With the hopes that what? He would take her to bed? That he would say to hell with the consequences, of which there were many, admit that what they had was special and be so lost in the moment he wouldn't be able to resist her?

Her stomach turned over on a low, antagonized pull. He had *confided* in her. That meant something, because Nico never talked to anyone. Now she knew the experiences that had shaped him—why he never formed lasting attachments with women. Because he didn't *trust* them.

Which should be a giant, blinking yellow caution sign. One she should heed for her own self-preservation. Instead, she felt exhilarated. *Invigorated.* Alive. She'd put herself out there, gone after what she'd wanted for the first time in her life, and it had been *amazing.* And that was where her thought processes began and ended.

She spent the day on the beach, until the sun slanted lower in the sky, Nico's return from his golf game imminent. Then she peeled herself off the lounger and headed up to the house to shower and change for dinner.

Sliding on a short, baby-doll-style dress in moss green silk that hinted at her curves in the subtlest of ways, she caught her hair up in a simple high ponytail, applied a light dusting of makeup, then made her way downstairs, her stomach tight with nerves.

Nico was waiting for her on the terrace. His skin tanned an even darker brown from the day in the sun, muscular body clad in faded jeans that clung to his powerful thighs and a black T-shirt that did the same for his amazing abs, aviator sunglasses on his face, he was drool worthy in a way that stopped her heart in its tracks.

Also vastly intimidating.

"How was your day?" he asked evenly, clearly back in full Nico control.

"Lovely." She could play this game, too. "Yours?"

"It was a good networking day." He tipped his head to the side. "I thought we might have a drink before dinner."

*A good idea.* They could have a mature, honest conversation about last night so her stomach would stop crawling with nerves.

He poured her the glass of white wine she requested. Fixed himself a sparkling water with lime and leaned back against the bar, cradling it between his fingers. Chloe sank her teeth into her lip.

Was he going to take the sunglasses off or was she going to have to guess at what he was feeling?

As if he'd read her mind, he reached up and slid the glasses off. His cool gray gaze met hers. "I think we should talk about last night."

"Agreed." She took a sip of her wine with a hand that trembled ever so slightly. Eyed him.

"It can't happen again." Flat. Definitive.

"Why?"

His gaze narrowed. "Would you like me to list the reasons? Because I am your boss. Because you are my responsibility, Chloe. Because it would be a big, giant mess."

She shook her head. "That's an excuse, and you know it. Yes, we have to work together, but our current situation is already complicating that. As for you being my boss," she said, shrugging, "that's semantics really. I *own* Evolution, Nico. It's my company. So there is no power imbalance between us. Which only," she concluded, "leaves us with the real issue here—that you keep walking away and why."

"I don't sleep with the people I work with," he said matter-of-factly, "regardless of any power imbalance. It's a policy of mine. And you *are* my responsibility, that's a fact. I am your regent."

"And last night?" she prompted, lifting a brow. "What

was that? Because I would say we well and truly crossed the line."

A muscle twitched in his jaw. "It was a...*slip* on my part."

Humiliation fired her cheeks, the clear regret in his voice activating that deep-rooted insecurity she did so well. "Because I threw myself at you again?" she suggested huskily. "A *pity* kiss to get me off your back?"

His lashes lowered in a hooded gaze. "You know that's not true."

"Then what *was* it?" She shook her head, frustration stinging her skin. "I'm going a little crazy here, Nico. I think I'm imagining things one minute, then I'm sure I'm not the next. You're hot, then you're cold. Which is it?"

A flicker of antagonism marred his deadly gray cool. "What would you have me say?" he bit out. "That I wanted to make love to you last night? That I was one step short of carrying you to my bed and taking everything you were offering? Because we both know that I was. And where would that have gotten us?"

Her insides dissolved, the sensory impact behind his words slamming into her brain with visceral effect. How *close* to the edge he'd been with that iron-clad control of his.

"To a place of honesty," she murmured, wrapping her arms around herself. "What you said to me the night of the board meeting. About me hiding from you. Hiding from myself. You were right, Nico. I have been. Because you make me feel things I've never felt with anyone else. Things I want to explore—things I'm *terrified* to explore. But by far, my worse crime has been hiding from myself. Denying what I want and need in life because I'm too afraid to go after it. So last night I did."

His eyes widened imperceptibly, before he schooled his

expression back into one of those inscrutable looks. "You don't want me, Chloe. The relationships I have with women are short and transactional. A few enjoyable nights spent together, a dinner or two thrown in and then I walk away. There are *rules* to it."

"That's right," she murmured, voice dripping with sarcasm. "Your *rules*. Those personal *entanglements* you avoid like the plague. Funny, when I've never asked for that from you. Maybe you should ask yourself what *you* are hiding from."

His jaw hardened. "*Chloe.* Stop pushing."

"Why? Because we might finally get at the truth here?"

He muttered an oath. Strode to the edge of the railing to stand looking out at the ocean, a long silence passing between them. "I made a promise to your father to take care of you. I won't break it."

She blinked. Followed him to the railing. "What promise?"

He turned to face her. "Last spring, your father developed a cough. He thought nothing of it, but when it persisted for a few weeks, he went to see his doctor. He was diagnosed with incurable lung cancer. Told he had two years to live."

Her breath whooshed from her lungs. "*Lung cancer? He didn't smoke.*"

"He did back in his Wall Street days. He said it was a bad habit that had finally caught up with him."

Her brain struggled to process what he was telling her. That step back her father had taken…his pristine will and succession planning. It all made sense now. *He had known he was going to die.* That he would not be around to guide Evolution.

"I don't understand," she said numbly. "Why didn't he tell us?"

His gaze softened. "He didn't want to worry you. He told your mother, of course. Me—because he wanted to get the succession of the company in order—to ensure Juliette and you girls were taken care of before he made the news public. Which he wasn't going to do until he had to because he felt the rumor and speculation would be harmful to the company."

Hot emotion bubbled up inside her, threatening to spill over her carefully contained edges. "You should have told me," she rasped. "I could have come home from Paris. I could have spent that time with them. Time I will never get back."

"Your father didn't want that," he said evenly. "He wanted you to live your life. He wanted to see you fly. It was his *wish*. I couldn't just circumvent it."

*"Yes, you could have."* She threw the words at him, hands tightening into fists by her sides. "How many openings have I given you to tell me this, Nico? I *knew* a piece of the puzzle was missing, I *asked* you, and still you didn't tell me. Where is that trust you were demanding? I'm not seeing it."

He pushed away from the railing. Reached for her. She stepped back, eyes on his.

"I was trying to protect you," he said quietly. "You've had enough blows. I needed you focused on saving Evolution with me."

"And you didn't think I could have *handled* it?" She threw him an infuriated look. "Why does everyone think I need my decisions made for me? Do you think I'm that delicate that I can't handle the truth?" She waved a hand at him. "I'm a grown woman, Nico. You keep telling me to have confidence in who I am—to *believe* in who I am—but you won't trust me enough to make my own decisions."

He regarded her silently for a moment. "You're grieving, Chloe. It makes you vulnerable."

*Vulnerable.* That word she was beginning to hate. "What about my uncle? Does he know?"

He shook his head. "Your father knew how badly Giorgio wanted to run Evolution. That it was going to be a blow that he hadn't chosen him. He was going to tell him at the right time. Position it the right way."

"Instead, he died, leaving Giorgio furious with you and confused about why my father did what he did. A *rogue element.*"

"Yes."

And he, because he was rock-solid Nico, impenetrable in a storm, had taken everything she and Giorgio had thrown at him because he was uncompromising when it came to his sense of honor to those he was indebted to. And he was indebted to her father. He had given Nico a second lease on life, and he would never forget it. Nor would he break his promises when it came to her.

Once again, her choices were being taken away from her.

She pressed her palms to her temples, her brain too full to think. Except for the one thing in her head that *was* crystal clear. "Can we just establish one point?" she murmured, echoing his words from the night before. "I am not too *vulnerable* to handle what happened between us last night. And I don't need you taking care of me, so you can absolve yourself of that responsibility, too, along with your propensity to make decisions for me. I no longer require it."

"Chloe—"

Numb, furious, she turned and headed for the stairs to the beach.

"Where are you going?" he fired after her.

"For a walk. I'm too angry with you right now to be in your presence."

She flew down the stairs. Kicked off her shoes and started walking, the sand still warm beneath her feet, the sun a kaleidoscope of shattered gold on the horizon.

Anger flared inside her, hot and wild, as she walked, toes sinking into the sand. At her father for keeping the truth from her. For taking away her chance to spend that time with him and her mother. For taking away any chance she might have had with Nico. At Nico for not telling her the truth.

Hot tears filled her eyes, blurred her vision. She sank down on the concrete break wall and covered her face with her hands. She wasn't ever going to get a chance to say goodbye…to tell her parents how much they'd meant to her. That phone call in Paris on her way home from work, the one that had seemed far too surreal, far too unfair, far too *sudden*, had been it.

A tear slipped down her cheek. Then another, until they were a steady stream of hot warmth, the salt staining her lips. And once started, she couldn't stop, all of the emotion she'd had locked up inside her escaping on a wave of despair, until her sobs robbed her of her breath, shattered her from the inside out, the pain in her chest nothing compared with the one in her heart.

Nico told himself to leave Chloe alone. That this had been a long time coming. That the wise, *rational* course of action would be for him to give her the space she'd asked for—to allow her to get it all out without complicating things further with an even deeper emotional attachment to a woman he couldn't have. But he couldn't seem to do it, her raw sobs squeezing tight fingers around his heart.

He took a seat beside her on the wall, picked her up and

pulled her onto his lap, cradling her against his chest. She stiffened, as if she might resist, then another sob racked through her and she melted into him, her tears soaking his T-shirt.

He smoothed a hand down her back and murmured words of comfort against her silky hair. Long minutes passed, until finally her sobs turned into hiccuping big breaths and she went quiet against him.

The rhythmic sound of the rolling surf stretched between them, the sun a fiery, yellow ball as it sank into the sea.

"I want them back," she murmured against his chest. "I miss them every day."

A strange ache unearthed itself behind his rib cage. "I know," he said softly, tucking a stray strand of her hair behind her ear. "I do, too. But you have to let them go. And when you do," he promised, pressing a hand against her chest, "you'll find they're *here*."

She looked up at him, eyes twin glimmering mahogany pools. "Is your father there? For you?"

He nodded. "The man he was. Not the man he became."

Her gaze darkened. "I'm glad." She exhaled a long breath. Swiped the tears from her cheeks. "I guess it's just frightening, you know? They were always there for me when life got bumpy. A phone call away. *My safety net.*"

"You don't need it," he said softly, eyes on hers. "You've got this, Chloe. You're proving it."

She caught her bottom lip between her teeth. Something unfurled beneath his skin. A need to comfort, to soothe, to *touch*. To protect her as had always been his urge. To take her amazing mouth with his and make everything better. But a stronger part of him knew it for the mistake it would be. That one more taste of her would be his undoing.

He wasn't *hiding* from his feelings for her—he simply knew his capabilities. He didn't have the capacity to take on another person's happiness, had had enough of that for a lifetime.

"Nico—" She reached up and smoothed her fingers over his jaw, her brown eyes luminous.

He caught her fingers in his. "Dinner's ready," he murmured. "I think we should go up."

Her mouth firmed, eyes cooling. Sliding off his lap, she brushed the sand from her dress. Set off up the stairs to the house, without looking back at him, her spine ramrod straight.

*Bene.* They were back to her hating him. Him knowing it was the better way. At least it was a status quo he knew and understood.

# CHAPTER EIGHT

CHLOE SPENT THE week back at work doing her best to focus on the frantic preparations for the Vivre launch rather than her roller-coaster weekend in Palm Beach with Nico. But she found it almost impossible to do so.

Knowing why her father had done what he had done had made everything seem more confusing rather than less, because that meant Nico *was* the honorable man she'd always thought him to be. It meant she'd been wrong about everything when it came to him, not helpful when he'd taken any chance of *them* happening off the table.

She couldn't change the fact that she'd been wrong about so many things, nor could she do anything about Nico's overinflated sense of honor she loved and hated at the same time. About the fact that he had distanced himself from her ever since Palm Beach. What she could do was make sure Vivre took the world by storm, to *fly* as her father had wanted her to do.

With her campaign set to go live in just a couple of weeks on November 15, everything was falling into dizzying place. She'd travel to Europe to meet with the regional teams next week to put the final pieces in place for the launches in London and Paris. Then she'd come back to New York to launch the campaign at the Evolution Christmas party, with Be on sale to the public the day after, in a splashy launch with Lashaunta.

They were operating on the razor's edge, but they were pulling it off.

She gave her phone a cursory glance as she waited in line for her midmorning latte. Almost dropped her purse at the photo that came up in her news feed.

Juggling her bag and phone in one hand, she scrambled for money with the other, found some dollar bills and shoved them at the barista. Stepping to the side to wait, she scanned the cutline of the photo of Eddie Carello and his current girlfriend emblazoned across the front page of a popular gossip site.

*Eddie Carello Enjoys*
*Wild Night in the Bahamas!*

*Things got a bit out of hand on the weekend at a luxury hotel in Nassau, where Hollywood heart-throb Eddie Carello was enjoying a wild post-concert party.*

*A hotel suite was allegedly trashed during the incident, which apparently caught Carello in flagrante delicto amid a supposed ménage à trois with girl-friend Camille Hayes and a waitress from the hotel.*

*The ruckus began when guests complained about the noise levels in the hotel and staff were dispersed to handle the complaint.*

*When asked about the incident, Carello's spokes-person replied that "the whole thing has been over-blown and people shouldn't believe everything they hear."*

*Meanwhile, Hollywood's hottest star seems to*

*have upped his outrageous antics in advance of his
new movie,* Score, *giving everyone something to talk
about around the water cooler this morning.*

*Nooo.*

Chloe clutched her phone in one hand, latte in the other
and hoofed it back to work. She was out of breath by the
time she reached Mireille's office. Her sister, who was on
the phone, gestured her into the seat opposite her. Chloe
threw her phone on Mireille's desk and collapsed into the
chair, attempting not to panic.

Her sister finished the call. Picked up Chloe's phone
and scanned the story. Started to laugh. "Well, you knew,"
she drawled, "he wasn't lily-white. But that was the attraction, right? He's a rebel—the new James Dean. A perfect
fit for Soar."

"Yes, but—" Chloe gestured at the phone "—isn't this
*bad* PR?"

"PR is rarely bad." Mireille sat back in her chair and
crossed one elegant leg over the other. "If anything, this
is going to make him a hotter property. I wouldn't be surprised if they manufactured this for the buzz. Although,"
she conceded, "he doesn't need it."

"I don't *want* him doing things like this," Chloe said
worriedly. "He was fine the way he was."

Mireille lifted a shoulder. "Not much you can do about
it. If you had a major sponsorship that he was riding on,
you might have something to say about it. But in your
case, he's doing you a favor. Sit tight," she advised, "let
it burn itself out. The news will be on to something else
by the weekend."

Since Mireille was the expert, and she knew nothing
about these things, Chloe took a deep breath and sat back
in her chair. "Okay."

Mireille fixed her with a speculative look. "Any reason Nico bit your head off in the meeting this morning?"

Chloe, who'd planned on keeping her mouth shut about the whole thing, found her cheeks heating. "I kissed him."

Mireille sat up in her chair, eyes wide. "I'm sorry. Can you repeat that?"

She bit her lip. "I kissed Nico…in Palm Beach."

Her sister stared at her. "Forgive me. I'm still stuck at the part where you just said you kissed your boss."

Chloe scowled. "You are not being helpful."

Mireille smiled. "Oh, come on, Chloe, it's about time. In fact, I'm not sure how it hasn't happened sooner. You two have had a thing for each other as long as I can remember. Santo and I always joke about it."

Chloe gave her a horrified look. "You and Santo joke about it?"

Mireille waved a hand at her. "Why the long face, then? What happened?"

Her lashes lowered. "He told me it was a mistake. That it never should have happened."

"Because you are his responsibility. Because he's Nico." Her sister shrugged. "Nico was never going to be a forever kind of guy, you knew that. He's a night-to-remember guy. If you're suicidal enough to want that after everything he did to you, seduce him again and do it right this time. Or find someone else to get over him with."

She didn't want anyone else. That was her problem. She never had.

The passion she and Nico had shared that night flickered through her head—an intoxicating, irresistible memory that refused to be extinguished. A surge of determination coursed through her. Maybe she was done letting everyone else make her decisions for her. Maybe it was time for her to convince Nico this *was* her decision to make.

* * *

Nico waited until he and Jerry Schumacher, the most senior member of Evolution's board, had finished an excellent dinner at Jerry's favorite Manhattan steakhouse, including a superior bottle of amarone, before he broached the subject of the current thorn in his side.

"Giorgio Russo," he said bluntly. "How big of a problem is he?"

Jerry sat back in his leather chair and swirled the dark red wine in his glass. "There are a few board members who have always been sympathetic to him. Maybe he's picked up another couple of late with his campaign. But your support is solid, Nico. Deliver a good Christmas and you'll silence him."

He slid a file across the table to Nico. "The names you asked for."

Nico slid the folder into his briefcase. "*Grazie.* I owe you one." He took a deep sip of his wine. Contemplated Jerry as he set the glass down. "Christmas will be good. We are going big with Vivre—a fifty-million-dollar launch with the A-list celebrities Chloe presented at the meeting. It's going to put Evolution back on the map."

A smile twisted Jerry's mouth. "You never were the faint-hearted type, were you? A chip off the old block."

Nico inclined his head. Refused to reveal how the comparison burrowed under his skin. Jerry had known his father during his Wall Street days when Leone Di Fiore had been known for his big, risky deals—suicidal, some had liked to call them. But he'd always pulled them off. Until he hadn't with the most important one of them all—the one he'd gambled his life savings on.

"The signature fragrances are what the company was built around," Nico pointed out. "They're what's going to bring the company back to life."

A rueful look painted itself across Jerry's face. "My wife sure as hell is a zealot. She's mad about that damn perfume. What is it... Live?"

"Be," Nico corrected.

"Be, right." Jerry frowned, his bushy, white brows drawing together. "Wasn't one of Chloe's celebrities that Eddie character? The Hollywood guy?"

Nico's lips curved. "Yes. He has a big movie coming out in December. Perfect for the launch."

Jerry reached down and scavenged around in his briefcase. Pulled out a newspaper. A tabloid, Nico noted as Jerry handed it to him.

"You buy this stuff?"

The retired CEO gave him a sheepish look. "My wife. She made me promise to bring it home. Apparently, it was all over the radio this morning."

Nico scanned the story on Eddie Carello and his wild threesome in Nassau. He would have been amused by the actor's exploits if he wasn't the cornerstone of his fifty-million-dollar Vivre ad campaign. It was a sensational piece, no doubt about it. Who knew how much of it was true? But he'd seen enough Hollywood stars implode under their own egos that it worried him.

"It will sell lots of perfume," he said to Jerry.

He headed back to the office after he'd dropped Jerry at home. Sought out Giorgio, who was still working. The older man greeted him with his usual lazily satisfied attitude until Nico flipped open the file Jerry had given him and listed off the names of the board members Giorgio had been courting. When Giorgio sputtered and attempted to defend himself, Nico closed the folder and slid it back into his briefcase.

"Food for thought," he told the arrogant, egocentric fool, "while you consider your future within the company.

Because one more errant move on your part and you'll be out of a job."

Leaving him to scramble in a web of his own making, Nico sought out his second, perhaps bigger problem.

Chloe wasn't in the lab when he checked there, the one other person who was telling him she was up in the lounge, screening her promotional spots.

He found her curled up on the sofa in the lounge, watching Eddie's commercial, a pizza box and an assortment of soda cans in front of her. Dressed in black leggings and a figure-hugging sweater, the high boots she'd been wearing kicked off, her hair loose around her shoulders, she looked sexy and takeable.

His inability to forget that hot encounter by the pool appeared to be his third problem.

She eyed him. Sat up straight, picked up the remote control and put the video on pause.

"I just informed your uncle I will fire him if he doesn't cease his smear campaign."

Her eyes widened. "You can't *fire* him. He owns part of the company."

"Your father gave me the green light to do so."

She was silent for a moment, eyes on his. "He loves Evolution, Nico. Tell him the truth."

"He'll find another reason to perpetuate his antics. He has a choice. He can make it." He threw the tabloid he'd purchased on the coffee table. "That discussion is closed. *This* one, however, is a problem."

She glanced at the tabloid. Back at him. "I talked to Mireille. She says there's no reason to panic. That, if anything, this will amplify the buzz around Eddie. Make him even more popular."

"Maybe so," he agreed. "But this is a fifty-million-dollar ad campaign, Chloe. We have staked the future of the company on it. Eddie Carello is a loose cannon...a wild card. What if his behavior amplifies instead of de-escalates?"

"It *will* die down," she insisted. "Mireille thinks it's even possible his handlers manufactured this as movie publicity."

"Not something I want to gamble the Evolution brand on." He blew out a breath. Shoved his hands in his pockets. "I think we should cut him. The other three can carry the campaign."

Chloe gaped at him. Rolled to her feet and came to stand in front of him. "We can't throw Eddie away. He's the anchor of the campaign, Nico—marketing gold. He is going to make the Evolution brand *relevant* again."

"He's too much of a risk," he countered flatly. "Remember when I said not one thing can go wrong with this campaign? I meant *not one thing*, Chloe. This is asking for trouble."

She crossed her arms over her chest. "You're overreacting."

"I am not overreacting. There are no second chances with this. This campaign goes south, so does the company. It's that simple."

"I *know* that." Fire flared in her eyes. "I had the same reaction as you when I walked in today. Then Mireille set me straight. *You* are the one who has been telling me I need to listen to the experts. To lean on my team when I need to. To *learn* from them. Well, I have, and Mireille is telling me it's fine, so it's fine."

He closed his eyes. She pressed the advantage. "The others can't carry Soar. It's a men's fragrance. Eddie needs to. He *is* Soar."

He bit back the response that came to his lips. To *order* her to cut Eddie, because that was what he would have done. He *had* counseled her to consult the experts. Which she had, and Mireille, whom he trusted, had weighed in. So how could he turn around and veto them both?

Perhaps he *was* overreacting. And maybe he didn't know what the hell he was doing anymore. He only knew his head wasn't entirely clear when it came to her.

He had removed a piece of her clothing in Palm Beach. Had been imagining doing it again ever since. Except *all of it* this time.

His mouth thinned, a throb unearthing itself at his temples. He was starting to think *he* had been the naive one to think he could separate the personal from the professional when it came to Chloe because he didn't seem to be doing a very good job of it either.

He brought his back teeth together. Followed his own advice and went with the experts. "Call Eddie's agent. Tell him to tone it down."

She blinked. Nodded. "I will. Thank you."

He gestured toward the TV. "Are you almost finished here? It's late. I can drive you home."

"No, I have more to do. I—" She jammed her teeth into her lip and stared at him.

"What?"

"You're avoiding me and you're snapping at me in meetings."

Caught utterly off guard, he kept his face impassive. "I am not avoiding you."

"You canceled three of our meetings this week, Nico."

"I am busy running the company, in case you hadn't noticed."

She pursed her lips, long dark lashes fanning down over her cheeks. "That's what you said to me about me hiding in Paris. I think you're doing the same with us."

She was right. Absolutely right. He *had* been avoiding her, because his lust was a problem. But he wasn't about to admit it.

"You're imagining it," he said blithely.

"Am I?" Her gaze remained unwavering on his. "Are you punishing me for what happened in Palm Beach?"

*"Yes,"* he agreed, voice heavy with sarcasm, "I am punishing you, Chloe. As we make fifty-million-dollar decisions together."

Her gaze dropped to her stocking-clad feet for a moment before she looked back up at him. "I can't get what happened that night at the pool out of my head. The way it was between us. I don't think either of us can. I think we need to address it."

His gaze narrowed. *"What* exactly are you suggesting?"

"I want to explore what we have. I want to know what that kind of passion feels like. No strings attached."

His jaw dropped. "You're suggesting we have an affair?"

"Yes."

His head pounded, like a grenade ready to go off. Was she really standing there, calmly suggesting they have an affair? The no-strings-attached type he specialized in? She was *insane*.

Except was it really that insane? A part of him knew it hadn't been the whiskey that had made him cross the line that night in Palm Beach. That he'd crossed it because he'd wanted to. Because he wanted *her*. Because it had been a long time in the making. But that didn't mean Chloe's was a sane solution.

"We can't maintain the status quo," she murmured, pressing forward in the silence.

"Perhaps not," he rasped. "But I can assure you that *now* is not the right time for this discussion."

"When do you think might be?"

*"Not now."* He stooped and picked up his briefcase. "Go to Paris, Chloe. Make this launch happen. And keep that damn actor of yours on a leash."

# CHAPTER NINE

PARIS WAS A BLUR.

Nico's warning to execute the launch without a hitch echoing in her head, Chloe threw herself into the final preparations with the regional teams in Europe, visiting Paris first to ensure the pop-up store on the Champs-Élysées was gleaming and ready to go. She stayed at her apartment she'd kept in the sixth arrondissement while she was there, and had dinner with the team and Estelle at one of her favorite cafés to run through the launch event logistics.

Funnily enough, she didn't feel homesick for her adopted home like she'd been sure she would. She found herself at peace instead. She was doing what she was destined to do, there was no longer any question in her mind. And she *knew* she could do it now.

Her meetings with the London team went off seamlessly, as well. She flew back to New York just in time for the Evolution Christmas party. Always scheduled during mid-November, it served as the official kickoff to the holiday season—the most important sales season for Evolution. After the party for the company's employees, customers and partners that evening, Be would be launched to the public the next day with an appearance by Lashaunta in Times Square.

Chloe was running on an adrenaline-induced high by

the time she arrived at her town house to dress for the party with Mireille, a Christmas tradition. It was only when Mireille waved Carrie Mayer's newspaper feature at her that her stomach sank.

What if it was awful? Mireille's deadpan expression wasn't giving anything away.

Heart pounding in her chest, Chloe sank down in an armchair with the paper and took a deep breath.

*Scent of a Woman*
*by Carrie Mayer*

*When I sat down with Chloe Russo, daughter of legendary American perfumer Juliette Russo, I wasn't sure what to expect. A teenage phenomenon who launched her own fragrance at seventeen, she has remained out of the public eye for much of her life.*

*I wondered if she would have her mother's intense charisma...or perhaps she would be the opposite, languishing under the weight of the expectations placed upon her to fill the shoes of a woman who burned as one of the industry's brightest stars.*

*Instead, I found a bit of an enigma. A warm, engaging woman who entranced me from the moment I sat down. Who captivated me with her passion for her calling. A woman whose talent clearly stands on its own.*

*There is, however, clearly a message behind her new perfume line, Vivre, that perhaps echoes the struggle she has waged to forge that identity. And that, according to Russo, is to simply "be." To let your spirit define you. To know the only limitations in life are the ones you place on yourself.*

A tear slipped down her cheek as she read the rest. Then another. They were a steady stream by the time she put down the paper and her sister pulled her to her feet for a hug.

"You've done it, sweetie. Mamma would be so proud. This is your night to shine."

"Oh, no." Chloe pulled out of her arms. "I forgot to buy a dress in all this insanity."

"That's what you have me for." Her sister threw her a satisfied smile as she plucked one off the back of a chair. *"I knew you would. Voilà."*

Chloe tried on the black dress her sister presented. Halter-style, it had straps that crisscrossed around her neck, leaving her shoulders and much of her back bare. Body hugging, it fit her like a glove, highlighting every dip and curve.

It was sophisticated, *daring*. Chloe pursed her lips. "I'm not sure I can pull it off."

"You're the only one who *could* pull it off." Mireille waved a dismissive hand at her. "You wear all those French creations I could never hope to fit into. It's going to make Nico's eyes bug out of his head."

Butterflies swooped low in her stomach. Was that what she wanted? She'd been so busy since she'd left for Europe, she and Nico hadn't broached the subject of *them*. She wondered if she was crazy to have even proposed it. But she knew in her heart it *was* what she wanted, this chance to be with him. So she was letting the chips fall where they may.

Except where were they going to fall? It was almost painful, the waiting.

She slipped on decadently high black heels and the ornate triangular onyx earrings Mireille had given her for Christmas last year, while her sister dressed in a fire-engine-red gown that fit her vibrant personality. And then they were ready for Evolution's big night.

Restored to its original glory in 2008, The Grand Ballroom of the Plaza, which had once played host to Truman Capote's famous Black and White Ball, had retained its glorious neoclassical decor with its grand arches and stunning massive antique chandeliers.

Tonight, as the setting for Evolution's annual Christmas party, the ballroom echoed that classic black-and-white theme, with the invitations, catering and decor all reflecting the elegant color scheme, because it had been Juliette Russo's favorite.

High black vases brimming with white lilies graced the tables scattered around the room, champagne with blackberries as its adornment was the opening cocktail and the massive Christmas tree in the center of the room glittered in cream and ebony.

With the Vivre campaign playing on screens placed discreetly around the room, the stunning, evocative creative adding the perfect touch of Hollywood glamour to the evening, it was simply *magical*. And with Eddie and Lashaunta in attendance tonight, it was also Manhattan's hottest ticket in town.

Chloe and Mireille had arrived before the guests to make sure everything was perfect, as their mother had always done. But the events team had outdone themselves, every festive piece in place. Relaxing with the hotel manager, they chatted about some of the legendary parties that had taken place in the ballroom as they waited for the guests to arrive.

Chloe wasn't exactly sure when she sensed Nico's presence in the room. It was instinctive with her, this awareness of him that seemed to reach soul deep. But when she turned around, he still took her breath away.

Dressed in an elegant black tux, his dark hair slicked back from his face, his fabulous, severe bone structure cast into harsh relief, he looked sleek, lithe and outrageously good. *Dangerous* in a way that sent a convulsive shiver up her spine. Because two weeks away hadn't lessened her attraction to him. It had only intensified it.

Greeting both her and Mireille, he pressed a kiss to Mireille's cheeks first. When her sister discreetly faded away to "check on a piece of missing decor," Nico set his gaze on Chloe. The not-so-subtle heat singed her skin as he moved it down over her body. Lingered at the bare sweep of her shoulders, the length of leg, before he brought his perusal back up to her face.

"You look stunning," he murmured, his husky voice sending another shiver through her as he bent his head and brushed his lips to both of her cheeks. She sucked in a breath at the electric contact, any air she'd managed to consume lodged somewhere in her chest as he straightened and set a silvery gaze on her.

"Did Mireille show you Carrie's piece?"

"Yes." Her chest tightened, as if a fist had wrapped itself around it. He'd been there for her all along. Not just now, but during the hardest months of her life when her parents had died, managing things in the background. *Always there.* She just hadn't seen it.

She wasn't sure she could articulate how much it meant to her. But she tried. "Thank you," she said, eyes on his. "For believing in me. For supporting me. It means everything."

His eyes darkened to a gunmetal gray. "You did it, Chloe, not me. I simply kept you on track."

"But you put your faith in me. It was what I needed."

"I put my faith in your *talent*." A smile flitted across his mouth. "Now we just need to sell some perfume."

And wasn't that the fifty-million-dollar question? "We will," she said, more confidently than she felt.

His smile deepened. "Let's go greet the guests, then. They're starting to arrive."

Santo rested a hand against one of the pillars flanking the ballroom, his eyes on the elegant black-and-white-clad, bejeweled crowd.

"Quite a party," he murmured. "Lashaunta and Eddie Carello in attendance...the mayor, even. This must put even *you* in a festive mood."

Nico ignored the gibe. He hated Christmas. Had ever since their mother had walked out on New Year's Day. It had been all he could do to make it through the elaborate Christmases at the Russos' house in Great Neck without climbing out the window.

"It's a good party," he acknowledged, with a tip of his head. "Your ex was at the bar earlier with her jet-set crew."

"I saw her. She did your print campaign this year, didn't she?"

Nico nodded. Santo's ex—a model scaling the heights of superstardom—was still crazy about his brother. He couldn't figure their relationship out. Neither could his brother, it seemed, the way it went back and forth like a Ping-Pong match.

Nico cocked a brow. "What did she think of you and your reporter date?"

Santo lifted a shoulder. "Not so thrilled. But a relationship can't just be about lust. I'm looking for a soul mate."

Nico's mouth twisted. "Do you actually *believe* the things you say?"

*"Si."* Santo gave him an unconcerned look. "I believe love exists. I simply think it's hard to find."

Santo, Nico mused, was an eternal optimist. How he managed that particular attribute after watching their parents' bitter wreck of a marriage disintegrate was beyond him. At least Lazzero, currently off on business in Brazil, had no interest in Santo's concept of eternal love. Lazzero was even more cynical than he.

"Speaking of beautiful women," Santo said, nodding his head toward Chloe, who was dancing with Eddie in the center of the room, "this is certainly her night. All the big stars repping her perfumes...she must be on top of the world."

"She is." There was a curious tightness in his chest, a pride, he told himself, in everything Chloe had accomplished. She'd become the strong, confident woman he'd always known she could be, taking on her demons with courage and slaying them one at a time. Had demonstrated a core of steel as she'd made an impossible campaign timeline work, refusing to let any setbacks faze her.

He'd be a liar if he said she didn't affect him, because she did. She always had. And perhaps Santo was right. Perhaps she didn't need his brand of protection anymore. Perhaps she was capable of knowing what she wanted when it came to them. Perhaps burning this thing out between them *was* the right answer. But could she handle an affair with him? Or would it make even more of a mess of the situation than it already was?

Eddie bent his head and said something in Chloe's ear that made her laugh. Her bright, vibrant smile kicked Nico right in the chest. He'd missed her these past couple of weeks she'd been in Europe—her quick wit, that razor-sharp brain, the way she challenged him at every turn.

If he were being honest, he'd admit he was fighting a losing battle over something he'd wanted for far too long.

Chloe's head was spinning from all the dancing and conquering she'd done. More than one journalist had pulled her aside to tell her how much they loved her perfumes. Jerry Schumacher's wife had gushed to her about Be and how much she adored it, and the silent auction of her yet-to-become-available complete set of Vivre perfumes was going for thousands.

Eddie and Lashaunta had been a huge hit, Eddie, thankfully, on his best behavior tonight. It couldn't have gone any better. Except, of course, if Nico had danced with her. Which he hadn't. Once again, he'd danced with everyone *but* her.

"It's almost midnight," Mireille murmured. "You need to put the star on the tree."

Chloe's stomach knotted. Putting the star on the Christmas tree had always been her mother's job—the symbolic kickoff to the most exciting, important time of the year for Evolution. She knew it was her job now, she just wasn't sure she could do it.

But Nico, true to his usual, impeccably punctual self, appeared then. The knot in Chloe's stomach grew as they walked toward the center of the room. "I'm not sure I can do this," she murmured.

"Yes, you can," he countered firmly. "I thank everyone for their contributions this year and you stick the star on the tree. Nothing to it."

Except when they got to the center of the room and Nico had quieted the crowd to give his remarks, her heart was beating so loudly it echoed in her ears and her knees felt like jelly.

However was she going to climb that ladder? She could

feel five hundred sets of eyes on her as she toed off her shoes and stepped onto the first rung, Nico spotting her as she went. Climbing to the top, she affixed the beautiful white star to the tree with trembling fingers. Felt something in her heart break. She thought she might have finally said goodbye.

Nico caught her hand in his as she got to the bottom of the ladder. "Put on your shoes," he said. "I haven't danced with you yet."

If she'd thought her heart had been beating fast before, it felt like it might career right out of her chest now at the look of intent on his face. She took a deep breath, slid her feet into her shoes and took the hand he offered.

The band started playing a slow, lazy tune in deference to the late hour. Catching her fingers in his, Nico pulled her to him. One hand laced through his, the other resting on his shoulder, she moved into his arms. Shivered as he slid an arm around her waist and pulled her into an utterly respectable hold that somehow didn't feel so innocent with the undercurrents running between them.

His palm at her back burned like a brand against her bare skin. When she tipped her head back, there was a sexy, smoky heat in his eyes that turned her insides to mush.

"Are you sure you can handle this?" he murmured. "I don't do relationships, Chloe. If we do this, it's to burn this thing between us out. We both walk into it on the same page. Nobody gets hurt."

Her core melted into a pool of fire.

She pulled in a deep breath. Gathered her courage. "I know what I want," she said firmly. "I've always known what I want. If this past year has taught me anything, it's that life is short. You have to seize the moment. And I don't want to spend tonight alone. I want to spend it with you."

He fixed her with an unreadable gaze. Her chest felt tight, hot, as if she could hardly breathe. Finally, after an interminably long moment that seemed to stretch forever, he bent his head to her ear. "You have security access to my penthouse from the night you dropped those papers off. Finish up here and meet me there. I'll leave after you do."

# CHAPTER TEN

NICO'S PENTHOUSE ON Fifth Avenue was dark and masculine, with a stunning cityscape view through floor-to-ceiling windows that left the entire space encased in glass.

Chloe kicked off her shoes in the foyer and walked into the open-concept living room with its jaw-dropping panorama of Manhattan. Oyster suede sofas and tan leather chairs were scattered around the space, gleaming birch floors a perfect foil for the dark architecture of the room. But she was too nervous to sit still, Mireille's analysis of Nico burned into her brain.

*Nico isn't a forever kind of guy. He's a night-to-remember guy.*

Her stomach swooped, like a book dropping off a high shelf. Was she crazy to think she could handle this? What if she couldn't? What if she was a disaster in bed with him—too nervous to enjoy any of it? She'd slept with only one man in her entire life, and that hadn't been a momentous experience.

She stood there, stomach crawling with nerves, until she heard the swish of the elevator arriving. The sound of Nico depositing his keys on the front table. She didn't turn around when he walked into the living room because she was too apprehensive to. The thud of his jacket hitting the sofa made her jump. Sent goose bumps to every inch of her skin as the sound of jazzy, sexy music filled the room.

*Part of his practiced seduction routine?* She almost jumped out of her skin when his hands settled around her waist and he pulled her back against him, his delicious dark, sensual scent wrapping itself around her.

"Maybe we should have a drink," she breathed. "I seem to be a bit jumpy."

"We don't need a drink," he said huskily. "I think we should dance instead. I didn't get a chance to do that with you. Not the way I wanted to."

She sucked in badly needed air. Closed her eyes as he bit down ever so gently on her earlobe, the sensual caress ricocheting through her. "How would that be?" she managed to croak.

He didn't answer. Turned her around and took her in his arms instead. The fingers of one hand laced through hers, he splayed the other across her hip. Possessive, intimate, it made her pulse pound.

His forehead resting against hers, they danced to the sultry tune. Their bodies in perfect sync, as if they'd been molded to fit together, it was, quite simply, the most heart-stoppingly romantic moment of her life.

"Nico," she murmured. And then his mouth was on hers, his thumb stroking her check, the slow, leisurely slide of their lips against each other like the magical prelude to a passionate symphony that would only build and grow.

She stood on tiptoe. Curved her fingers around his neck. Moved deeper into the kiss until she wasn't sure where she began and he ended. His fingers at her jaw, he angled her head to position her the way he wanted her. She opened her mouth to his command, was rewarded by the lazy, sensual slide of his tongue against hers. Deeper, *hotter* the kiss went until every limb in her body melted, utterly supine against his.

He moved the hand he had at her hip down over her bottom. Cupped her in his palm and brought her closer until she felt the thick, hard evidence of his erection against her. Her knees went weak, threatened to give way, but his hand at her buttock held her easily. Kept her pressed against his impressive arousal, his physical strength vastly exciting to her.

So *this* was the kind of dance he'd been talking about. Her blood thundered in her veins, her heart battered up against her ribs, every inch of her skin pulsed to life. It was like she'd spent her entire adult existence waiting for him to touch her like this. She wanted to memorize every second for future reference.

"Tell me what you like," he rasped in her ear. "How you like it. How you *want* it."

"Like that," she gasped as he rotated his hips against her in a sultry movement that turned her insides to molten honey. "You feel so good, Nico."

He took her mouth in a hungry kiss that held no restraint. Raw, erotic, he made love to her mouth with the hot slide of his tongue until she whimpered and pressed closer. He angled her more intimately against him and let her feel every centimeter of the steely length that pressed against his trousers. Gave her more of that pleasure that had driven her crazy that night at the pool.

"Don't stop," she whispered, on a broken plea. But he did, bending to slide his arm beneath her knees to pick her up and carry her to the bedroom. Setting her down beside the bed in the minimalistic airy room with a spectacular view as its only decor, he moved behind her, set his fingers to the zipper of her dress and drew it down. His hands settling around her hips, he pushed the dress up and over her head, cool air caressing her skin as he tossed it in a pool of silk on the floor.

A wave of self-consciousness settled over her as he sat down on the bed and drew her to him. His fingers dealt with the clasp of her bra with an experience and dexterity that made her pulse pound. Off it went into the pile. And then she was naked in front of him except for the black lace panties that clung to her hips.

Standing in front of him, his gaze level with her bare, aching breasts, she took in the hunger in his stormy gray eyes. "You are so gorgeous," he said roughly. "So perfect. I need to have you, Chloe."

Her insides fell apart. He tugged her the last step forward. Cupped her breasts in his hands. Kneaded them, weighed them. Brushed his thumbs over the straining, tender tips until she moaned and pushed closer, his caresses melting her limbs.

With a muttered imprecation, he dropped to his knees in front of her, his hands cupping her buttocks to bring her close. "Nico," she murmured, heart racing as she read his intention. "You can't do that." No man had ever touched her like that.

He looked up at her, eyes hot. "I've waited forever to have you like this. I want to kiss you. Touch you. *Let me.*"

His words took her apart. Annihilated the last of her defenses, what she'd said to Lashaunta that day filling her head.

*When you let yourself be stripped down, naked, raw, because this was you and you couldn't be anything else but who you are.*

It had always been like that with Nico. He had seen every part of her. This would be no different.

She relaxed beneath his hands. Let him part her thighs. He pressed his lips to the trembling skin of her abdomen in a hot, openmouthed kiss. Her muscles tightened as he moved his mouth down to the band of her panties. *Lower.* And then he was caressing her through the damp lace with his mouth, his tongue, his hands at her bottom holding her in place for his delectation.

She dug her fingers into his coarse dark hair. Whispered mindless words of pleasure, her knees jelly beneath her. Begged for more. He sank his fingers into her hips, turned her around and pushed her back on the bed. Sliding his fingers beneath her panties, he stripped them off.

Her heart nearly burst through her chest as he pulled her to the edge of the bed and spread her thighs wide with his big palms. Drank her in. And then he parted her most delicate flesh with his fingers, his gaze reverential.

"You're beautiful here, too," he murmured. "So pink. Wet. *Perfect.*"

She closed her eyes. Curled her fingers in the bedspread. He set his mouth to her, hot and knowing, doing the same wicked things he'd done to her before, only this time there was nothing between her and the searing caress of his mouth, and it was so earth-shatteringly delicious she was lost.

He fluttered his tongue over the tight bundle of nerves at the heart of her. Told her how good she tasted in raw, uncensored words that inflamed her. She begged for more. Holding her hips tighter, he laved her, flicked at her with his tongue, the powerful lash of his caress almost too much to bear.

Her back arched off the bed. "Nico—*please.*"

He slid a palm beneath her hips and lifted her up. Slid a thick, masculine finger inside her in a slow, controlled movement that made her crazy. Gently, insistently, he caressed her with firm, even strokes. It felt so good, so *amaz-*

*ing*, she bit down hard on the inside of her cheek to prevent the cry that rose in her throat.

"You like that?" he murmured huskily, eyes on hers. "It makes you crazy, doesn't it?"

She nodded in helpless surrender. Moved into the sexy, sensual caresses he was administering with a tilt of her hips, because she knew how he could make her come apart with those skillful, amazing hands of his.

The pleasure built. She dug her nails into the bedding, gasping her pleasure, because she couldn't hold it in anymore.

"That's it, sweetheart," he said throatily. "Talk to me. That's so damn sexy."

He filled her with two fingers. Worked them in and out until she was arched like a bow, sobbing for release. Then he pressed a palm to her abdomen, wrapped his lips around the peak of her sex and tugged at her until he sent her flying into a sweet, hot release that radiated from the heart of her outward, until every inch of her was in flames.

Nico felt like someone had drugged him as he pushed to his feet, eyes on Chloe as she lay sprawled across his bed. Exactly as he'd imagined her. But oh, so much more jaw dropping in the flesh.

She was perfection with her taut, high breasts…the slim curve of her waist that flared out to hips that were deliciously feminine…the long legs, toned and magnificent, that he wanted wrapped around him while he took her long and slow and hard.

He swiped a hand over his jaw, heart pounding. He could still taste her in his mouth, how sweet she was. Could still feel how perfect she'd felt beneath his hands—like silk. He craved her so much, his lust so thick in his throat, he wasn't even sure how he wanted to take her. He only knew that now that he'd given in to the insanity, he was going to drown himself in it.

She opened her eyes. Set her shimmering brown gaze on his. He started unbuttoning his shirt. Yanked it off, buttons flying, when it didn't happen quickly enough. Her eyes darkened as he undid his pants, slid the zipper down and pushed them off his hips, his boxers following close behind. The heat of her gaze turned him hard as a rock.

He lifted a brow. "You didn't answer my question."

"About?" Her voice was lazy. Sated.

"How you want it?"

That woke her up. She levered herself up on her elbows. Worried her lip with her teeth. "I don't know."

"What?" he gibed. "There's finally something you would like to defer to me on?"

"Yes." She sank her teeth deeper into the soft flesh he wanted to taste again. It tipped him over the edge.

"You on top," he said evenly. *"Now."*

Her eyes widened. He found a condom in the bedside table. Stretched himself out on the bed and beckoned to her. She crawled over to him, uncertainty and desire glittering in her beautiful eyes.

"You took on the world tonight," he murmured. "Surely you can handle me."

The uncertainty morphed into a look of pure challenge. She straddled him, her gorgeous body a feast for the eye. It was such a turn-on, this confident, spectacular creature she'd turned into, he was transfixed. High color streaking her cheeks, her hair a tumble of silk around her face, she bent to kiss him.

"You were saying?" she murmured, lips parting sweetly against his. He reached up, cupped the back of her head and brought her closer, his mouth melding with warm, honeyed temptation. She tasted exquisite, the subtle stroke of her tongue against his as she kissed him deeply, intimately, offering him all of her in that way she had that made him completely lose his head.

Her hands found his hard length pulsing against his thigh. She caressed him, her smooth, even strokes unpracticed and so much more hot because of it. He cursed as she pushed him close to the edge. "Baby," he murmured, clamping a hand around hers. "Either you do this or I take control."

Her eyes flashed. She didn't like that idea. He handed her the condom. Her hands stumbled over the task. He settled his fingers over hers and rolled it on, the intimate act thickening the air between them to unbearable levels.

Blood pounded his temples as she positioned herself over top of him. Brought the thick crest of his arousal to her slick velvet heat. Cradled against her, he rubbed the length of her. Relished her low groan.

*"Nico."*

It was his turn to groan as she took him just barely inside him. "Slowly," he bit out. *"Dio.* You are so tight."

Her eyes locked on his as she took him deeper, the erotic connection between them so hot it fried his brain. He set his palm low on her belly. Found her center with the pad of his thumb and massaged her in slow, sensual circles. She closed her eyes, full mouth slackening. Her body softened, took him deeper inside, slowly, excruciatingly slowly, until finally she had sheathed him with her hot, silky flesh.

She opened her eyes. Fixed them on his. "I didn't know it could be like this," she breathed. "You feel so good, Nico."

Blood roared in his head. He could have told her it wasn't like this. Not usually. That sex could be good, but it wasn't always this mind-blowing. But that would be admitting things he chose to ignore. That she had always touched a piece of him no one else ever had.

He grasped her hips in his hands. Moved her against him in a slow circle. She was plush, tight, so damn good, he almost lost it right then and there. Gritting his teeth, he counted from ten back to one. Which proved ineffectual when, eyes trained on his, she picked up his rhythm. Drove him insane with the sexy, circular movements of her voluptuous hips.

He curved a hand around her nape. Brought her mouth down to his. Mated his tongue with hers as he possessed her hot, sweet body with insistent, powerful thrusts that made her gasp with every drive. She begged, panted into his mouth. Hands at her hips, he positioned her so she came down at the right angle for him to hit that tender spot inside her.

"Like that," she gasped. "Oh, Nico. Like that."

"Let go," he bit out, fighting a deep, primal need to take. To mark her as his as he'd always wanted to. Then lost the battle as her body contracted around his in a tight fist and she cried out, nails digging into his shoulders. His hands grasping her hips, he thrust up inside her, yanking her down to meet his punishing lunges.

Harder and thicker he swelled inside her, taking his pleasure, until she splintered him apart in a deep, shuddering release and he came harder than he ever had in his life.

The rasp of their breathing the only sound in the room, he held her, sprawled across his chest, stroking a hand over the silky, soft skin of her back until she fell into an exhausted sleep curled against him.

An insidious tendril of unease wound its way through him alongside the powerful, more potent emotions swamping him in the aftermath of the intimacy they'd shared.

It was just good sex, he told himself. Perhaps the best

he'd ever had. He and Chloe shared an intense physical attraction—one he'd been fighting for far too long. What man wouldn't react that way when a woman was so sweet and willing in his arms? So sexy and vulnerable all at the same time?

Curving Chloe's soft, warm body against his, he let sleep take him. They were going to need some *rules*. But tomorrow would be soon enough to have those awkward, line-reinforcing kinds of conversations they needed to have.

# CHAPTER ELEVEN

CHLOE WOKE TO the first, soft yellow light of day making its way into the sky, shrouding the tall skyscrapers in an almost otherworldly glow. It was such a magnificent view, she simply drank it in for a moment.

Her sensory perception expanded beyond the jaw-dropping panorama to the heavy, solid weight draped around her middle. The hot, hard male body pressed against the length of hers. The very *naked* hot, hard male body pressed against hers.

She was in Nico's bed. She'd spent the night with Nico. *OMG.*

Her heart thumped wildly in her chest. She pressed a palm to the hard, staccato beat in an attempt to steady its racing rhythm, but nothing seemed to help. Everything felt utterly off-kilter—like it would never be the same again. Not after *that*.

She sucked in a deep breath. Blew it out slowly. Last night had been indescribable. Romantic. Sensual. *Soul consuming.* Everything she'd dreamed about and more.

She'd always known Nico would be an amazing lover. That unparalleled control of his, the intensity he wore like a glove, the sensuality that was so much a part of him. But nothing could have prepared her for the depth of intimacy they had shared. It made her toes curl to even think about it.

It seemed impossible to imagine that what they had shared was an ordinary connection. It felt *extraordinary*. Nico had taken her apart, exposed every part of her. Made her feel so alive it was *terrifying*. And she could have sworn he'd felt it, too. That it could be the start of something amazing if he let down his walls.

*And maybe that was highly naive, unwise thinking.* She had no experience with a man like Nico. With that kind of passion. Maybe what they'd shared was simply powerful chemistry. The only thing she *was* sure of was that she was completely and utterly out of her depth.

She sank her teeth into her lip. Twisted to face him. His arm fell away to rest above his head, his severe features relaxed, long dark lashes shading his cheeks. He was so gorgeous it made her melt. But it wasn't just the stunning outer packaging that drew her to him. It was the man *inside* the gorgeous facade. Who he was at the heart of him— impregnable in a storm, unyielding in his sense of honor, solid in a way she'd never encountered.

Finding out he was the man she'd always believed him to be had only underscored the feelings she'd always had for him. Made them more inevitable. If she was smart, she knew, she'd guard her heart. Keep her head.

She turned back to look at the bedside clock. *Six thirty. Thank goodness.* Some internal alarm must have woken her. She needed to be downtown at the Times Square store by 8:00 a.m. to prep for Lashaunta's appearance. Given she had no clothes, only the dress she'd worn the night before, that was a problem she needed to rectify. *Fast.*

She slid out of bed. Went searching for her underwear. Another wash of heat claimed her cheeks as she found it scattered around the room. Snatching up her bra and panties, she slid them and her dress on. Pursed her lips as she considered a sleeping Nico. Was she supposed to wake him up and say goodbye? What *was* the proper procedure?

In the end, she let him sleep. Maybe it was the coward in her, because she wasn't sure how to handle this right now. But it seemed the easier way.

Facing Nico's elegant, perfectly pressed doorman while clad in her sparkly dress and high heels wasn't so easy. What did Mireille call it? The *walk of shame*? It certainly felt like it. The doorman, however, greeted her smoothly and whistled for a taxi, as if seeing off women dressed for the night before was all part of a day's work. A good reminder that she was simply *one* of those women for Nico.

She showered and changed at home, then jetted downtown. The crowds outside the store stretched for blocks, Lashaunta every bit the draw she'd hoped she would be. Practically jumping up and down with excitement, Chloe watched as the pop singer sang four songs from her new album for the crowd and the shelves began to empty of the limited-edition Be. Her problem, she soon realized, was going to be keeping up with the demand, because the same thing was happening worldwide.

She was practically floating on air by the time she arrived back at the office. She had just enough time to check in with Clara before she sailed into a meeting. Which was a budget meeting that happened to include Nico. The nerves came back like a fast-moving tornado.

Sitting across from her at the large boardroom table full of executives, he looked ridiculously handsome in a dark, pin-striped suit and a crisp white shirt. Her heart tripped over itself as she took a sip of the coffee Clara had thankfully provided. He had one of those inscrutable looks on his face. All business.

She told herself to play it cool. Wrapped her nerves in a reservoir of calm she wasn't close to feeling. But she couldn't concentrate on the meeting for the life of her. She kept wondering where she and Nico stood after last night.

After an hour of attempting to pretend he didn't exist, she weakened near the end of the meeting and allowed herself a glance at him. Found him staring at her, a flash of something in his gray eyes that made her breath catch in her throat.

"Nico?" the CFO prompted. "You on board with that?"

Nico nodded.

"Chloe?"

She stared blindly at the balding executive. "Ah—yes. Definitely."

"Good. Let's move on."

Nico was in a bit of a mood. He had never, in his life, had a woman walk out on him after a night spent together. There was an etiquette to it—an acknowledgment of how good it had been—a mutual expression of *appreciation* to be communicated.

Instead, he'd woken to an empty bed. Not a text, not a note. He'd known Chloe had her event today, had planned to drive her home *after* he'd had her again this morning. And perhaps that was the problem. He'd woken up hard and hungry for her with a need that hadn't abated, and that was never a good way to start the morning.

He sat back in his chair. Took a slug of his coffee. Considered her across the table. Just to be clear, it *had* been mind-bendingly good sex. *Emotional* sex, even. The most intensely involved experience of his life, if he were to be honest. They had been crazy for each other. So where was the clinginess every woman seemed to display the morning after? It didn't seem to be coming. Instead, Chloe looked cool and aloof. Distant. *Did she regret last night?*

The meeting drew to a close. Chloe headed for the door.

Nico moved fast, stepping into the hallway at the same time she did.

"A minute," he said softly.

Simone, who'd left the room behind them, stopped to ask him something. Her gaze shifted from Nico to Chloe and back again. Registered the charge in the air. She murmured something about asking him the question later and moved off in the direction of his office.

Nico looked at Chloe. "How did the launch go?"

She leaned back against the wall, eyes on his, her lip caught between her teeth. "It went great. We sold out. Had to restock."

"Congratulations." He leaned a palm on the door frame beside her, catching a whiff of her elusive, sexy perfume. "Do you have any idea what budget you just agreed to in there?"

She shook her head. "None."

"You don't think that's a bit irresponsible?"

"I do." A slow nod. "Forgive me. My mind was elsewhere."

"*Where*, exactly?"

"The regions," she murmured. "I have a call with Europe in minutes."

A curl of heat unleashed itself inside him. He didn't believe her for a minute. But he had a meeting, too. "We can talk later, then."

"Of course."

It wasn't until seven o'clock that evening, however, that he had a chance to seek Chloe out, a brutal day of meetings behind him. She was in her office sitting behind her desk, frowning over a report of some kind. Her suit jacket discarded on the back of her chair, she looked gorgeous in a sheer cream silk blouse and a gray pencil skirt that showed off her fabulous legs.

He wanted to unbutton her and consume her whole. But first, he wanted to find out what was wrong with her.

Wary, so wary, were the big brown eyes that landed on his as he shut the door behind him. But there was also a shimmering, dark glitter in her gaze, a sensual awareness that heated his skin.

He walked over to lean against her desk. "What's going on? And don't tell me it's Vivre, because I'm not buying it for a second. I've seen the sales reports. They're astounding."

She put down her pen. "Nothing's going on. What do you mean?"

Frustration fizzled up his spine. "Okay," he murmured, "let's talk about last night, then. How are you feeling about it? Usually women like to talk about it. I thought you might want to, since you walked out this morning without a word."

A guarded look crossed her face. "I had to get to my event. I didn't want to wake you."

"I was going to *drive* you there, had you woken me up. You took a damn taxi home, Chloe. That is not all right."

Her lashes lowered, sweeping her cheeks like miniature black fans. "Last night was amazing, Nico. More than I ever could have imagined. I don't regret a thing, if that's what you're wondering."

Straightforward, matter-of-fact. *Honest.* But then again, this was Chloe, and she didn't play games like other women. She wasn't *like* any other woman he'd ever met. Hadn't he always known that? Wasn't that what had scared him away in the first place? Everything he wanted to know was right there on her face. In those ebony eyes, which looked terribly uncertain at the moment.

"If that's the case," he said quietly, "then why do you look like that?"

"Like what?"

"Like you regret it."

"I don't regret it."

*"Chloe,"* he growled.

She closed her eyes. Was silent for a long moment before she opened them again. "I am out of my depth," she said softly. "You took me apart last night, Nico. Split me wide-open. It *affected* me. *You* affect me. I was trying to get my equilibrium back."

The muscles around his heart contracted. He'd known this was going to happen. Known it was going to be a mess. Chloe had never been able to separate her emotions from her head. But neither could he lie to himself and pretend last night had been just about sex, because it hadn't. What he felt for her had always been more complex than that.

"You don't think I feel something for you?" he rasped, eyes on the naked vulnerability written across her face. "You don't think I was *affected* by last night? You don't think I'm crazy for you, Chloe? Examine my behavior over the past few weeks and it might give you a clue."

She stared at him. The muscles in her throat convulsed. "I want to kiss you again," she whispered. "So badly, I can't stop thinking about it."

His blood fired. Pushing her chair back with a foot, he sank his hands into her waist and lifted her onto the desk in a single, fluid movement that pulled a gasp from her throat. "You should get on that," he said softly, planting his hands on the wood on each side of her thighs. "Although," he murmured, lowering his head to hers so their breath mingled in a warm, intimate caress, "I'm not sure just a kiss is what I'm looking for."

Her breath hitched. He waited, until she curved her fingers around his nape and brought him the rest of the way. It was all he needed to take her mouth in a hot, greedy kiss that blew his brains out. Cupping his jaw in her palms, she kissed him back, opening her mouth for him as he stroked inside with his tongue. Arched her neck back to take him deep.

He abandoned her mouth to explore the delicate line of her jaw. Traced the throbbing line of her pulse with his tongue. His hands dealt with the pearl buttons on her blouse with ruthless efficiency. Exposed her beautiful, rose-tipped breasts cupped in cream lace.

"Nico," she murmured huskily. "We are in the office."

"Everyone's gone home. I checked."

One hand on her hip, the other closed around her breast, he bent and licked the tip of one tightly furled nipple. Absorbed the low moan that raked through her. Played her, teased her, until she pushed into his hand and demanded more. Cupping her firmly, he took her deep into the heat of his mouth. Rolled the straining, taut nub over his tongue. Between his teeth. She was so lush and perfect, so responsive to his touch, she lit his blood on fire.

He transferred his attention to her other nipple. Swirled his tongue around the hard peak as he plumped her other breast in his palm. "I need to have you," he whispered against her ear.

Dragging her closer with the hand he held at her hip, he pushed her skirt up her thighs until he exposed her cream lace panties. They were so sexy against her coffee-colored skin, the blood thundered in his veins.

"Nico," she breathed. "We can't do this here."

"Yes, we can." He stepped between her thighs. Cupped her knee. Gentled her mouth with his. "Let me touch you, please you," he murmured against her mouth. "I need to have you."

Her knees fell apart. She watched him with big, hot eyes as he cupped her damp warmth with his palm. Inhaled the musky smell of her desire. "*Dio*, what you do to me," he breathed. "You make me lose my mind."

Pulling her panties aside, he ran a finger down her desire-swollen folds. Caressed her with leisurely strokes. Her eyes darkened to twin ebony pools.

"Nico," she breathed.

He circled his finger at the slick entrance to her body. Pushed in gentle demand. She was silky and exquisitely tight. He eased inside her, waited while she adjusted to his touch.

"*Please.*" She fixed her gaze on his.

He moved his finger in and out of her in a slow, sweet rhythm that had her moving to meet him with greedy movements of her hips. Pressing a kiss to the ultra-sensitive skin below her ear, he filled her again and again. Felt the tiny tremors that moved through her.

"Nico." She pressed against him in a sinuous movement.

He set his lips to her temple. "You want to come for me, baby?"

"*Please.*"

He rubbed his thumb against her while he filled her with two fingers. Parted them inside her to caress her intimately. To ready her for his possession because he was like steel beneath his pants and she was small and delicate and he wanted her with a craving he'd never felt before—a voracious need that threatened to consume him.

"Nico," she begged, sinking her fingernails into his shoulders.

Wild for her, utterly unhinged, he reached for the button of his trousers, undid it and pushed his zipper down. Pulling her to the edge of the desk, he slid one hand beneath her hip, palmed his hard, hot flesh with the other and slotted himself against her velvet heat. The sensation of her silken flesh cradling him was indescribable.

He let out an oath. Chloe pulled back to look at him.

"A condom," he gritted out.

"I'm protected," she murmured. "It's fine."

He pushed inside, her tissues like liquid fire around him—squeezing him, stroking his length. His mouth at her ear, he told her how much she affected him, how much he wanted her, how much he'd *always* wanted her. She arched her hips, took him deep, until he was buried to the hilt. Seated inside her, sharing the ultimate intimacy, he held her gaze as he withdrew completely, then pushed back in, a mind-blowing, staggering penetration that made his heart beat like a drum.

"Nico." Her passion-filled gaze rested on his, dark, luminous, *irresistible*.

"You make me break all my rules," he rasped. "Every damn one."

He took her mouth in a hot, hungry kiss. Knew in that moment that one more taste of her had been his undoing. That now that he'd let himself have her, he wouldn't be able to stop. But he was too far gone to care.

Grasping her hips tighter, he thrust inside her with a power that made her gasp, until they came together in a release that shook him to his core.

# CHAPTER TWELVE

CHLOE WAS SO EXCITED, she could hardly contain herself.

Checking her appearance in the mirror for what might have been the fifth time, she convinced herself her short fiery-red dress, made of some rich, satiny material that showed a different depth of color every time she moved, was not, in fact, too short, her makeup—subtle but smoky—was unsmudged and the sleek hairstyle she'd chosen to match the sophisticated dress still in place.

She looked the same as she had five minutes ago. But maybe the dress *was* too short.

*Oh, for heaven's sake.* She spun away from the mirror with a disgusted sound and rummaged for her evening bag in the drawer. Perhaps it was the leftover adrenaline from the Soar launch with Eddie today that was making her jumpy. It had been amazing, frenetic, every TV camera in town out for it. Or maybe, she conceded, stomach clenching with nerves, it was the fact that Nico was back from Europe tonight, she hadn't seen him for a week and he was escorting her to Eddie's *Score* movie premiere.

She shoved a lip gloss and her phone into her bag, along with her keys. It could also have been the very sexy phone conversation she and Nico had shared last night when he'd gotten back to his hotel room that had left her skin crawling with anticipation. Or the way they'd gorged on each other for the two weeks before he'd left, Nico seeking her out in the lab or in her office each night, as if he couldn't resist the pull between them any more than she could.

She was falling for him—truly, madly, deeply—an unchecked spiral she knew wasn't wise. If she were *smart*, she acknowledged, pulling high black heels from her closet, she would be keeping her emotions out of this. Sticking to the deal she'd made with Nico, with *herself*, of a no-strings-attached fling. But she was sure he felt something more for her, too. Something deeper. Felt it every time he touched her. She thought he was hiding behind his walls—that it was going to take him time to trust how he felt.

And maybe, she conceded, sliding the heels on, that was simply the rosy view she chose to paint for herself. Maybe it had nothing to do with reality.

And maybe, she concluded, stomach sliding out from beneath her, she needed to get her head together. That appeared to be a top priority.

Snatching up her bag, she went downstairs and pulled a warm wrap from the closet. Was digging through her bag to make sure she'd thrown in the right lip gloss to match the vibrant dress when the doorbell rang.

Her heart beat a jagged rhythm. Setting the bag on the entryway table, she rubbed damp palms against her thighs and pulled in a steadying breath. Attempted to manage some sort of composure as she undid the two dead bolts her father had installed on the door.

All of it, unfortunately, flew out of her head as she swung the door open to find Nico leaning against the brick wall of the entrance in black jeans, a white shirt and a blazer.

God, she loved him in jeans. There wasn't a man on the planet who looked better in denim, all long legs, lean hips and raw masculinity. And then there were the muscles bulging beneath the hip tailored jacket—those powerful, corded arms she'd learned he needed only one of which to hold her in extremely creative positions.

*Good heavens, Chloe.* She dragged her gaze up to his. Registered the amusement glittering in his gray eyes.

"Hold that thought," he murmured. "Unless you'd like to skip the movie. I'm more than up for that."

Her stomach did a flip at that very tempting idea. But she shook her head with a smile. "Not a chance."

She'd never attended a premiere before, and this one was slated to be extremely glamorous with Hollywood's biggest stars set to shine. Not to mention the fact that Soar was going to be everywhere: in the Evolution refreshing stations at the after-party, in the gift bags for attendees, not to mention the fact that Eddie would be wearing it. She didn't plan on missing a minute.

*"Bene."* He walked past her into the hallway and shut the door. She turned to face him, heart thumping like a drum. Snaking an arm around her waist, he tugged her to him, one hand landing on her hip, the other at her jaw. Nudging her up on tiptoes with the hand he held at her bottom, he brought his head down to hers.

"I *like* this," he murmured, sliding a hand over her silk-covered bottom. "It's very sexy. I'm going to enjoy taking it off you."

She couldn't answer because she was pretty much panting for him to kiss her, the brush of his lips against hers igniting a thousand tiny lightning strikes in her blood. Then he did, claiming her mouth in a deep, slow kiss that melted her bones, a sensual tasting that seemed to last a lifetime. Powerless to resist, she wound her arms around his neck and surrendered.

She felt his smile against her mouth as he ended the kiss oh-so-languidly and let her feet slide to the ground.

When she might have slithered right to the floor, he held her up with the hand he had at her bottom.

"That was wholly unfair," she whispered, eyes on his.

"Say the word and we stay in."

She pressed a kiss to the hard line of his mouth. "Hold that thought."

He gave her a look that said he'd rather not. Chloe's mouth curved in a smile as he escorted her to his car and spirited them the short distance to the Museum of Modern Art in midtown Manhattan, where the premiere was being held.

The red carpet shimmered in the spotlight as they arrived at the entrance to the impressive modern building, its entire exterior facade a wall of gleaming glass. The crowd that had gathered to watch the arrival of the stars was dozens deep.

They wouldn't walk the carpet, only the stars would, but Chloe wanted to watch, so they joined Santo and his date in a viewing area for guests off to the side, the atmosphere in the crowd electric. Santo didn't blink an eye at the protective hand Nico had placed at her back, introducing his date instead, a lovely reporter for one of the New York dailies. And then the stars were arriving in long black limousines.

Near the end of the parade of Hollywood glamour came Eddie and his sultry, stunning girlfriend, actress Camille Hayes. Tall and sleek in a plunging silver-and-gold gown, Camille was outrageously beautiful, the perfect dark foil for Eddie's blond good looks. His hand at her back, he escorted her down the red carpet to the appreciative roars of the crowd.

Chloe was so thrilled, she could hardly stand it. Eddie had a megawatt star power that glittered like no other with his saucy smile and entertaining wit as he talked to the press. And with her Soar ad playing on a screen just to the right of the logo-emblazoned step and repeat banner where the stars stopped for photographs, Evolution was front and center tonight.

If she could get any higher, Chloe thought, as they moved inside to watch the action-packed adventure movie *Score*, she wasn't sure how. It was the most exciting night of her life.

The after-party for *Score* was held in a trendy, swish bar close to the museum. A New York institution, the establishment was legendary for its elaborate Christmas decorations, draped in fifty thousand dollars' worth of glitz tonight, according to Santo, who kept track of such useless trivia.

Nico immediately felt his skin tighten at the overabundance of shiny balls, icicles and endless lights hung from every available surface. He would have turned around and walked out the door if it had been any other occasion. But Chloe was having fun, and far be it for him to steal her joy when she'd worked so hard for her achievements. When Evolution was shining tonight and Eddie Carello had taken it upon himself to introduce her around as the creator of his signature fragrance, his massive ego out in full force.

Ignoring the whole unavoidable ambience, he caught up with his brothers at the bar, while Chloe took Mireille and Santo's date off to visit the Vivre refreshment bar, where patrons could touch up their makeup and perfume.

"No date?" Nico observed as Lazzero did his usual aloof, unattainable routine leaning against the bar, which only made half the women in the room turn and stare.

Lazzero lifted a shoulder, his eyes trained on a group of people near the windows. "I felt like flying solo."

Nico followed his brother's perusal to a beautiful brunette who stood at the edge of the group. "Who is she?"

"Who?" His brother took a sip of his bourbon.

"The woman you keep staring at."

"No one important." Lazzero dismissed the subject, clearly unwilling to discuss the fact that she was *something*, because he'd undoubtedly had about twenty women lined up to accompany him this evening and he'd chosen to come alone. But Nico had learned a long time ago Lazzero confided when and how he wanted to.

Santo pointed his glass of bourbon at Nico, clearly coming to the same conclusion. "I see *you're* keeping better company these days."

Nico kept his tone nonchalant. "Chloe and I have agreed on a casual thing."

Santo took a sip of his bourbon. Rolled it around his mouth as he considered him. "You don't just casually see a woman like Chloe. You do it with intent or you don't do it at all."

Nico, who'd been ignoring that very fact for weeks, inclined his head. "And your point is?"

"Nothing," Santo said innocently. "I was just making an observation."

An observation that once in Nico's head, refused to budge as a friend of Santo's came up to greet them and Lazzero set off in the direction of the brunette. His head half in the conversation and half out, he considered Chloe in the very sexy red dress as she chatted up an A-list actress at the perfume bar.

She was glowing, in her glory tonight. It did something strange to his insides to see her like this, rearranged them in a foreign pattern he didn't recognize. She was smart, beautiful, passionate and empathetic. *Transparent.* Everything he'd convinced himself didn't exist in a woman.

He *had* missed her while he'd been in Europe, and not just in a physical sense. He'd missed her *presence*. How alive she made him feel. How she filled him up in places he hadn't even known he'd been empty.

He was crazy about her, if the truth be told.

The admission, after weeks of denial, rocked him back on his heels. But then again, he conceded, taking a sip of his bourbon, hadn't he subconsciously known it was true? He'd broken every one of his rules for her. Was *still* breaking them. And it felt right in a way he couldn't articulate.

"Can you believe it?" Chloe said, bubbling over with excitement as she rejoined him, champagne glass in hand, and they walked outside to the patio to get some fresh air. "Sasha Pierce wants me to design a custom perfume for her. *Sasha Pierce*, Nico. She's *legendary*."

He smiled, drawing her back against his chest as they stood at the railing and enjoyed a view of a light-emblazoned Manhattan. "Of course she wants you to design a perfume for her. Be is the number three fragrance in the world right now. Soar is going to be a huge hit. You're the talk of the town."

She wrinkled her nose. "Not quite."

She was silent for a moment, as if taking it all in, the silence of the high balcony wrapping itself around them. The balcony was deserted, the heaters not quite able to keep up with the chill in the air. And for that Nico was glad because it gave him a chance to clear his head.

Chloe swiveled to look up at him. "Are you having fun, though? You seem quiet."

He shrugged. "It isn't really my thing. But you're having fun—that's what matters."

Something in Nico's voice, a quiet, distant note, made Chloe lean back against the railing to look up at him. Study his face in the diffused, soft lighting the lamps cast across them. "What's wrong?" she murmured. "You've been off since we arrived."

Another of those uncommunicative shrugs. "It's nothing. Jet lag."

"Nico," she said softly, trailing a finger down his cheek. "I know you well enough now to know something's wrong."

"My mother walked out on New Year's Day," he said flatly. "A week later our house was repossessed by the bank. This time of year doesn't hold very good memories for me."

Her throat locked, her skin stretching painfully tight across her body. "I'm so sorry. I didn't know. You never said anything."

"It wasn't exactly dinner-table conversation at the house in Great Neck."

She considered the hard, impenetrable lines of his face. "That must have been awful."

"It was surreal." A shadow whispered across the clarity of his gaze. "My father lost it that day. I mean actually *lost* it. He had been sinking into a depression for some time, but when she walked out, it was the end of him."

A knot formed in her throat. Grew until it was hard to swallow. He'd been only *fifteen.*

"What did you do? Where did you go?"

He balanced his glass on the railing. "I called my basketball coach. He was a mentor to me and my brothers. He knew a guy who owned a corner store in the neighborhood. I went to work for him, and he let us live in the apartment above the store in exchange for the work."

While he'd gone to school at night, refusing to give up on his own future. Her heart gave a painful lurch. "Lazzero and Santo were so young," she murmured. "They must have been devastated."

His mouth flattened. "They were in shock. Lazzero retreated into himself, refused to talk. Typical him. Santo started to cry because he wasn't sure which bike to take with him."

The ache inside her deepened until it hurt to breathe. She bit the inside of her mouth, the salt tang of blood staining her senses. "I think," she said huskily, reaching up to smooth her fingers over the hard line of his jaw, "that you are extraordinary, Nico Di Fiore. That you had the composure and presence of mind to take charge at that age."

He lifted a shoulder. "Who else was going to do it? It wasn't easy—no. I was bitter. Angry at the responsibility I hadn't asked for. Angry at my *life* and the loss of my freedom. But you do what you have to do."

Worse, she imagined, was what it would have been like to watch the man he'd so clearly admired in his father suffer from such a debilitating disease. To become a shadow of himself.

She tipped her head to the side. "You said in Palm Beach you think of your father as the man he was, not the man he became. What was he like—in the early days?"

"Complex." He took a sip of the bourbon. Swirled it around the glass. "He was never home when we were young. The life of an investment banker—always on, always working, always socializing with clients. It made my mother crazy. But to me," he acknowledged with a faint smile, "he was larger than life. He loved us, loved being a father. Whenever he did have time to spend with us, it was the best. He would take us to baseball games, up to the cottage, out fishing. That's when he was his true self. Away from all the pressure."

She frowned. "I remember my father saying he was *the guy* on Wall Street. That everybody wanted to be him. That he was fueled by this ambition that seemed to consume him." She pressed the rim of her glass to her chin. "Where did that come from, do you think?"

He considered the question for a moment before replying. "The estrangement from his own father was a part of it. His father was abusive to his mother. He tried so many times to intercede—to persuade his mother to leave—but she wouldn't. So he left when he couldn't handle it anymore and came to New York to start a life for himself. He had nothing. No money, no one to fall back on. *He* was it.

"It fueled his ambition on Wall Street. He was imminently successful because of it—a risky, brilliant deal maker. But his ambition was also his Achilles' heel. Once he got caught up in the rush, he couldn't turn it off. He constantly needed *more*. The money, the power—it all went to his head. He had affairs, began living on the razor's edge."

Chloe frowned. "So your mother had reasons for being unhappy, other than the loss of her career?"

Antagonism darkened his gaze. "She *drove* him to it. She was never happy, not from the beginning. The affairs weren't right, clearly, but I can see why it happened."

And she could see the whole story was far more complex than it seemed on the surface, even if she understood why Nico wanted to blame his mother for all of it. "There are always two sides to a story," she said, treading carefully. "Perhaps you don't know the whole truth."

His jaw hardened. "Perhaps I don't want to know. Perhaps I don't care. Maybe it's a fact that two people always mess up a relationship one way or another."

"That's not true," she countered quietly. "Look at my parents. How in love they were. What a great team they were. They were *stronger* together."

"What Martino and Juliette had is a rarity, I promise you."

"Perhaps," she agreed. "But it does exist."

"Anything's possible." He shook his head at her. "Don't start spinning romantic illusions around me, Chloe. I've never been a believer in fairy tales. My experiences have taught me differently."

She took a sip of her champagne. Studied the cynicism on his face. He made so much sense to her now—why he was the way he was. He had the same driving ambition his father had had, for exactly the same reasons. Because his once-safe, if tumultuous life had splintered apart and he would never let the same thing happen to him. Would never make the same mistakes his father had.

Instead, he had made himself into a rock in the middle of the storm for his brothers. For *her*. He had given Santo and Lazzero the faith that life could be trusted, people could be trusted, because he had *been there* for them like his parents hadn't been for him.

A hand fisted her insides. She wanted to be that for him. The one who taught Nico he could trust. That he could *believe* in what they had. Because she couldn't lie to herself any longer and say she didn't want all of him, because she did. She always had. And maybe, just maybe, she had enough faith for both of them.

Or perhaps, she acknowledged, her stomach hollowing out, she was setting herself up for a fall.

A dark fire lit his gaze. "Hey," he murmured, his arm sliding around her waist to pull her close. "That's ancient history. We are not letting it kill the mood. And I am in the *mood*. It's been a week since I've had you."

Heat shimmered through her insides. She let him remove her champagne glass from her hand. Framed his face with her hands as she kissed him long and deep. Refused to let fear rule her, that instinctive need to retreat that had always directed her actions, because she was through doing that. She was seeing this thing with Nico through to the end, just like she'd promised herself, because she thought he was worth it. She thought *they* were worth it.

"Are you ready to go?" he murmured, when they came up for air. "I'm done with *holding that thought.*"

Her blood on fire for him, she nodded. They said their goodbyes to Mireille and his brothers, collected the car from the valet and made the drive back to Nico's penthouse in an expectant silence that had every nerve in her body tense with anticipation.

Nico tossed his keys on the entrance table when they walked into the penthouse, shrugged out of his jacket and threw it on a chair in the living room. Sinking his fingers into the knot of his tie, he set his gaze on Chloe as he stripped it off, his body hard and hungry after a week without her.

Lowering himself onto the sofa, he reached for her, pulled her onto his lap.

When her lush lips parted in invitation, her dark eyes full of passion, he didn't hesitate, didn't even try to resist her. Cupping her cheeks with his palms, he settled his mouth over hers in a hot, hungry kiss.

She sighed. He took full advantage, sliding his tongue inside her mouth to tangle with hers, tilting her jaw up to provide him with better access. The taste of her exploded through him, sweet from the champagne she'd consumed. Uniquely her.

He slid his hands beneath the slippery, shimmery material of her dress that had been inflaming him all evening. Found the warmth between her thighs and stroked her through the silky material of her panties with leisurely, teasing caresses. She moaned low in her throat, her soft, breathy sighs making him crazy. But when he would have lifted her to straddle him, desperate to have her, she swept her delicate hand along the hard ridge of him instead, erasing any coherent thought.

"Chloe," he murmured. "I am more than ready."

She ignored him, sliding her fingers up to the button of his jeans to undo it. Every muscle in his body tensed as she lowered his zipper, the rasp of metal against teeth amplifying the pounding of the blood in his head. And then her hands were on him, uncovering him, pulling him out of his boxers.

His heart thundered in his chest as she slid to the floor in front of him. She had been too shy to do that to him up until now, and he hadn't been into pushing her because he'd known with the passion they shared it would happen. He just wasn't sure he could handle it tonight. Didn't know if he had that in him with the need driving him.

He watched, transfixed, as she slid her mouth over the velvet length of him, used her lips and tongue to make him wild for her. Blood pulsing through his body, he arched into her touch, spellbound by her unpracticed seduction.

"Like this," he instructed hoarsely, sliding his hands over hers, showing her how he liked to be touched. How hard. How fast. How to drive him higher.

When he couldn't take it anymore, when he knew he'd finish it that way if he didn't put a stop to it, he reached for her, picked her up and laid her on the sofa like a feast for his consumption.

Red silk dress askew, plunging open to reveal her taut, creamy flesh, her long legs a tangle of olive skin, he had never known such lust. Such need. She was sweetness and innocence, brilliance and fire, an intoxication to his senses he couldn't seem to fight.

He pushed the dress up to her waist. The tiny panties that clung to her hips did little to hide the shadow of her femininity, firing his blood to a fever pitch. He spread his palm over her abdomen, absorbing the shiver that went through her. Trailed his fingers down to the tantalizing piece of silk that covered her. Eyes a deep, dark espresso, she watched him strip it from her.

He got rid of his pants and boxers in one swift move. Came back over her, caging her in with his arms braced on each side of her. "You burn me up," he whispered against her mouth, "until I can't think for wanting you."

She pulled his head down to hers, her fingers sliding into his hair. He slicked his tongue over her lips and gained entry to her sweet mouth. Every stroke, every lick, sensual and earthy, bound him to her in a way he'd never experienced before.

Sliding his palm over her thigh, he found the hollow at the back of her knee. Curved her elegant leg around his waist so that she was open to him. His to take. Settling himself against her moist, welcome heat, he held her gaze as he stroked inside her with a single hard thrust. Claimed her tight, silken flesh with a possession that made her internal muscles spasm in erotic response.

"Fast or slow," he murmured. "Your choice."

"Slow," she breathed, eyes locked on his. "As slow as you can make it."

He regretted asking because he wasn't sure how slow he could take it. His breath coming hard and fast, he possessed her with smooth rhythmic strokes, corralling the fire raging through him as her silken body clenched around his pulsing flesh. Her eyes were liquid fire, the perfection they created together written across them as she curved her leg tighter around his waist and met him thrust for thrust.

It was too intense, *too much*. Burying his mouth in her neck, he tasted her salty skin as he drove harder into her amazing body until they came together in a rush of violent heat that blanked his head.

Emerging from a sex-induced haze what felt like hours later, he took her to bed and made love to her again. When he couldn't sleep, his internal clock messed up from the travel, or perhaps from the intensity of the emotion chasing through him, he left Chloe curled up in bed, went into the living room and poured himself a glass of water.

He carried it into the living room. Sat staring at an always-on Manhattan spread out before him.

He'd told himself he was walking into this thing with Chloe to burn out the attraction between them, when in reality what he'd really wanted was *her*. A no-strings-attached affair had been a convenient excuse to avoid admitting how he really felt about her. That she'd always made him want more. Made him want to *be* more, and he wasn't sure he could be that.

He cared about Chloe—deeply if he were to be honest. But even if he'd always suspected she might be *the one*, offering her the love she needed wasn't a place he was ever going to let himself go. He'd severed that piece of himself the day his life as he'd known it had imploded. Had told himself he needed no one because he'd had to—it was the only way he'd known how to exist.

He took a sip of the water. Tipped his head back as the cool liquid slid down his throat. What would happen when Chloe began to hate him for what he couldn't give her? Because it *would* happen eventually. People changed, emotions changed, and that was when it all fell apart. He knew it as surely as the sun would rise tomorrow.

Martino's voice from that Fourth of July night floated through his head, his raspy Italian lilt as clear as if it had been yesterday.

*You need to make a choice, Nico. Decide whether you can give her what she needs or walk away.*

Hearing the words now, filtered through a decade's

worth of perspective, gave them a different cast. He had assumed Martino had been telling him to walk away, when what he realized now he'd been telling him was that he had a choice—he could decide he could be more, or he could remain the closed-off, hardened man he'd become.

Life was about choices.

How would he even know if he was capable of being what Chloe needed if he didn't try? Would he forgive himself if he didn't and let her go, only for some other man to offer her what he couldn't? He didn't think he would. Not now.

He sat there for a long time, his head too full to think. The only thing he was sure of was that Santo had been right. Either he committed to Chloe or he walked away. There was no in between.

Bright sunlight filtering through a crack in the blinds woke Chloe. She was alone in bed, the sound of water running in the en suite bathroom indicating Nico had risen before her. The man didn't sleep, she marveled, sinking back into the pillows to recall the utterly perfect evening of the night before.

She'd had so much fun showing off Vivre to Hollywood. *A custom perfume for an A-list actress.* It was a coup worthy of her mother. Topped off by an utterly unforgettable, passionate night with Nico.

Her good mood persisted as she slid out of bed, intent on joining him in the shower because that was the way she liked best to wake up. She was almost across the room when her phone rang. *Mireille*, from the distinctive ringtone she reserved exclusively for her sister.

She frowned. Mireille was decidedly *not* a morning person. Maybe she'd seen all the social media coverage from last night and had called to congratulate her on a successful evening. Backtracking, she plucked the phone off the nightstand and took the call. "You're up early."

"Chloe." Her sister's voice was eerily calm. "You and Nico need to meet my team at the office as soon as you can get in."

Her fingers tightened around the phone. "Why?"

"Eddie got into a fight with Camille last night. A big blowup at Gianni's. Club security had to intervene. Also," her sister added, a grim note to her voice, "he said some very derogatory things about women someone caught on video. It's all over the internet."

*Nooo.* Cold fingers clamped down on her spine. The entire Vivre campaign was built around the empowerment of women.

"How bad is it?"

"Bad, Chloe. You need to get in here."

She sucked in air, her breath a sharp blade in her chest. Exhaled. Panic was not going to help. "We'll be there in thirty minutes."

Nico walked out of the bathroom, his brow furrowed. "What was that?"

She pushed a chunk of hair out of her face. Took another deep breath, but it seemed impossible to get the words out of her mouth. Because Nico had warned her about Eddie. He had wanted to cut him. And now, a week before Christmas, the most important sales week of the year, they had a disaster on their hands.

Nico tossed the shirt he was carrying on the bed, walked over to her and tipped her chin up with his fingers. "What's going on?"

She swallowed past the tightness constricting her throat. "It's Eddie. He went off the rails again last night. There was a fight with Camille at Gianni's...club security had to intervene. He also," she added, her gaze falling away from his, "said some awful things about women someone caught on video. It's all over the internet."

Nico uttered a filthy word she'd never heard him use before, his hands falling away from her face. Heart slamming against her ribs, she risked a look up at him, but he wasn't looking at her. He was in full damage-control mode.

"Get dressed," he said curtly. "Was that Mireille on the phone?"

"Yes." Her voice steadied in the face of his fury. "They're waiting for us at the office."

"Good." He ripped the towel off his hips and started to dress. She stood there, frozen.

"Nico, I'm sorry. This is— This *was* my fault."

He spared her a quick glance. "It doesn't matter whose fault it is. We need to fix it."

Mireille and the PR team were waiting in Nico's office when he and Chloe arrived thirty minutes later.

Mireille, always cool and composed, was ashen-faced. "I'm sorry. This was my call."

Nico waved the apology off. "It was a collective decision. I could have cut him." Pouring himself a cup of coffee, he took a seat at the conference table, a move Chloe mimicked. "What's the game plan?"

Cara Cioni, Mireille's boss, who had two decades of experience managing crises for a major auto manufacturer, got up and went to the whiteboard. "First," she said, "we cut Eddie loose. Void the contract using the morality clause. But," she added, a frown pulling at her brow, "we have to be very careful with this. He's the most powerful man in Hollywood. It needs to be finessed."

*"Bene,"* said Nico. "How do we communicate this?"

"A short statement to the press within the next twenty-four hours announcing the split. Reinforcing Evolution's historic commitment to women. I would say today, ide-ally, for the statement, but that may be unrealistic. Legal will want to go through it with a fine-toothed comb. To-morrow morning, latest."

Nico nodded. "What about the ad campaign? We're going to need to pull it."

Giorgio, who looked remarkably unruffled, spoke up. "Online is no problem—we can cut it immediately. TV is the issue. It will take forty-eight hours to get the ad off the air."

During which time Evolution and Eddie would be in-extricably linked in consumers' minds. Tension knotted Nico's stomach as he realized this wasn't going to be as simple as distancing the company from the actor with a quick statement. It was going to be far messier than that.

"Give me the names of the presidents of the networks if you have to," he bit out, fixing the older man with a stare. "I'll call them myself. I want that ad off the air, Giorgio. *Now.*"

"That will distance us from Eddie," Chloe broke in, "which we clearly want to do because the entire Vivre campaign is all about empowerment, and since three of our spokespeople are women, it's more about female em-powerment than anything."

"Yes," said Cara. "Exactly. Soar might be in trouble, but we want to protect the other three fragrances and the investment we've made in them. The *brand.*"

A look of dismay crossed Chloe's face. Nico knew what she was thinking. Soar was her baby. Yet it was now syn-onymous with Eddie because she'd said publicly the actor had been the inspiration for it, a strategy that might cost her the fragrance.

He pushed on because sacrifices would have to be made. "What about Evolution's reputation when it comes to women?" he asked Cara. "How do we reinforce that?"

"We need to make a gesture of some sort. Underscore the commitment we've always had. But it can't be self-serving—it has to be genuine."

Nico raked a hand through his hair. "What about a phil-anthropic program for women? I'd been thinking we should build something off Vivre—use Lashaunta or Desdemona to kick it off."

"That's a great idea," Cara acknowledged, "if they aren't poised to drop us. It's a real possibility they could. Which is our next point of consideration," she said, eyeing Chloe and Mireille. "We need to get on the phone to them now. Reinforce everything we stand for. Make sure they don't jump ship."

They both nodded. "We can run the philanthropic idea past them while we do it," said Chloe.

Cara turned to Nico. "This would not be cheap. We're talking millions. Are you prepared to invest in a program like this on a yearly basis?"

Nico looked grim. "We've staked the future of the company on Vivre. There's no turning back now."

Nico spent the day doing damage control with the PR team to prevent Evolution from being caught up in the public outcry that ensued over Eddie's vitriolic outburst about women that had been carried to every home in America via the amateur video it had been taken on.

Not only had the actor labeled his girlfriend, Camille, *a pointless piece of trash*, he'd dubbed women in gen-eral *an inferior species that are more trouble than they're worth*. Not to mention the punch he had allegedly thrown at his girlfriend, which, thankfully, in his drunken state, had missed.

With Evolution's public statement about the incident in legal review for distribution to the press first thing the next morning, Nico inhaled the key messages the PR team had developed for him in preparation for the press interviews that would come. But by early evening, a Boycott Evolution hashtag had appeared on Twitter, social media was ablaze with ironic amateur videos of Eddie's commercial spot edited to include his inflammatory comments about women and Nico was fighting the biggest crisis of his career.

By the time he made it back to the office after a dinner he'd been scheduled to attend, he was annihilated. Throwing his jacket over the back of a chair, he went to the bar to pour himself a drink. Froze with his fingers on the cap of the bottle of Scotch. Alcohol, thank goodness, had never been a problem for him like it had been for his father. But that had been before he'd drunk a good portion of a bottle of whiskey and given in to his craving for Chloe and put this disaster into motion. Because wasn't that exactly what had happened?

Pulling a bottle of spring water out of the fridge, he grimly poured himself a glass. He had *known* he should cut Eddie. But he had bet the bank on Chloe and her Vivre launch—on a suicidally risky campaign that would either revive the company or sink it, and he'd needed Eddie as the cornerstone of it.

The problem was, he wasn't impartial to Chloe. Never had been. While he'd been making fifty-million-dollar decisions that affected the fate of the company, he'd been imagining what it would be like to bed her. Last night, when all hell had been breaking loose, he'd been buried *inside* her—putting the promises he'd made—Evolution itself—in jeopardy. Because his head hadn't been in the game, it had been on *her*.

He swore under his breath. Braced his palms on the bar. Clearly he *was* his father's son after all, because it was apparent he couldn't juggle his personal and professional life any better than his father had. Over what? Over a relationship he had a questionable ability to fulfill?

He'd seen the look in Chloe's eyes last night. She was in love with him. He had chosen to ignore it because as strongly as he felt about her, he wasn't *there*. He might never be there.

A cold knot tightened in his gut, the pressure that had been building in his head all day throbbing at his temples until he felt as if his head might explode. Had he not watched his father unravel himself over a woman, putting all he'd built into jeopardy? What the hell was he doing playing at something with Chloe he could never follow through on?

A part of him wanted to be that man. To be everything for her. But in reality, he knew how to do only one thing, and that was how to keep the boat afloat. To make this company prosper. And right now, he wasn't even doing a good job of that.

How the hell was he supposed to pull this out of the fire?

Chloe stood in the doorway of Nico's office, her stomach churning. It had been that way ever since she'd gotten the phone call from Mireille, but now it was worse because Nico had been freezing her out every time she'd been in the same room with him, and now she had to deliver more damaging news.

She took a deep breath and crossed to the window where he stood. He turned, as if sensing her presence, the look on his face as remote as it had ever been.

"I have an update on our celebrities."

He inclined his head for her to go on.

"Lashaunta," she said, "thankfully, seems unfazed. Which is a huge relief, because she can carry this for us.

And she loves the philanthropy program. She's in, if it fits with her recording schedule.

"Desdemona," she continued, "worries me. She was very edgy on the phone, but when I explained the women's initiative to her, she said she'd consider it if we get the Eddie situation under control."

"That's positive."

"Yes." She bit her lip. Forced herself to deliver the bad news. "Estelle is out. Her agent wants nothing to do with it."

He looked remarkably calm. "If one jumps ship," he observed, "another could follow suit when they get wind of it. We need to work fast, ensure that doesn't happen."

"I told Lashaunta and Desdemona we'd get them details on the philanthropy program by the end of the week."

He nodded. "You and Cara can spearhead it together. Let me know what I need to know."

She inclined her head. "How was your dinner? Did you get any questions?"

"A few, but Cara had me prepped." His gaze slid over her face. "Have you eaten anything today? You look pale."

"No—I'm not hungry." Needing his reassurance, his *comfort* right now, she lifted a hand to brush her fingers across his jaw. "I know you're angry with me and I understand why, but you can't freeze me out like this."

He caught her hand in his and brought it down to her side. "I'm not angry, Chloe. I'm focused. Go home, get some sleep. I'm going to stay here tonight and monitor things with the team."

Hurt lanced her insides, confusion enveloping her. "Nico, what's going on? Why do you look like that?"

That utterly inscrutable look remained painted across his face. "I don't think now is the right time for us to be having this discussion."

Her stomach turned to stone. "Why not?"

"Because we are in the middle of a *crisis*, Chloe. We need to be focused on fixing it."

That lit a fire inside her. "I *am* focused on fixing it," she bit out. "I've been killing myself all day to that end. We are going to fix this *together*, Nico, because your idea for the philanthropy program is brilliant. Because that's what a partnership is all about. But right *now*, I want to know what's going on with you. Why you're being like this."

"Don't push me," he said quietly. "You know better."

"Why not?" she demanded, ignoring the warning glint in his eyes, because her insecurities were ruling her now.

"Because instead of having my head on my shoulders," he bit out, "I've had it buried between your legs for weeks, that's why. Because I can't *think* when you are in my head, Chloe."

Her jaw dropped. "You cannot possibly be blaming this on us."

"No," he said evenly, "I'm saying it was a mistake. *We* are a mistake. I need to be focused on running this company."

She recoiled as if he'd struck her. "You're *ending* this?"

Not a flicker of emotion in those remote gray eyes. "I'm saying we need to cool it off."

Her heart contracted. He *was* ending it. He didn't have to say it. She could see it in his eyes. "Be honest, Nico."

He shrugged. "I told you from the beginning what my capabilities are. We were both clear on what this is."

Her heart kicked against her ribs. She'd thought it had been *love*. She'd thought he had been falling in love with her. Had been so sure of it, she'd let down every last barrier for him so all he'd had to do was just admit it. Walk right into it. But seeing the impassive expression on his face, how easily he'd delivered that cutting blow, she realized he'd never really given them a chance. That she'd been the one who had been hopelessly deluded—at least when it came to his ability to evolve.

Because hadn't he done this to her *twice*? How many times did she need him to slap her in the face before she got it?

Except she knew where this was coming from. Knew his personal history was at play here. She knew *him* now.

"This is about your need for control," she said quietly. "You aren't in control of this situation. You aren't in control of *us*, so you'd rather choose to walk away than confront what we have. You'd rather use *this* as the perfect excuse to end it, when, in actual fact, we did exactly as you counseled, Nico. We made sound decisions. We listened to the experts, and they made the call. No one," she said, waving a hand at him, "could have predicted Eddie was going to go off the deep end. We all thought it was movie publicity."

"I did," he countered flatly. "And I should have listened to my instincts."

She had no response for that because he was right. He had.

He raked a hand through his hair. Eyed her. "It was always going to end with us, Chloe. It was just a matter of time. You know it and I know it. I am incapable of giving you what you need."

The way he so easily discarded what they had infuriated her. "I think you'd rather *believe* yourself incapable of love than expose yourself to it, Nico. Because then you'd have to allow yourself to *feel* something. Well, I'm not buying it for a minute. I've seen you with your brothers. I know your capabilities. They are miles deep. *Unconditional*. But they aren't on offer to me."

"They aren't on offer to anyone," he said evenly. "We

have a good thing, Chloe. But what's going to happen when you want a man who can love you? Who can give you more? When you start to hate me because I can never give you that?"

It was a fair point. Because the way he was tearing her apart inside right now, she wondered if she was a bit on the masochistic side.

"I love you," she said quietly, before she closed herself off completely. "I have always loved you, Nico, you know that. You are the strongest, most admirable man I know. But if you walk away now, it's the last time, because you're right, not even I'm that much of a glutton for punishment."

His gray eyes glimmered with an emotion she couldn't read. "Better it happen now. Go home, Chloe. Get some sleep."

# CHAPTER THIRTEEN

CHLOE WALKED HOME on a frozen Manhattan night, feeling as numb as the sheet of ice beneath her feet.

She shouldn't have pushed him like that. But if she hadn't, she never would have found out the truth. That, in his mind, Nico had never seen a future for them. That while she'd been spinning those romantic fantasies he'd warned her about, while she'd been offering him everything, he had been preserving those cast-iron walls he had perfected, never intending to let her in.

Letting herself in her front door, she shrugged off her coat and threw it on the bench in the hall. The cozy space felt unfamiliar, *foreign*, because she'd spent the better part of the past couple of weeks at Nico's place, caught up in the fantasy she'd spun for herself. It felt so empty it made her hurt inside.

She couldn't go curl up at Mireille's because she was still at the office working with the team on the statement that would go out in the morning. Numb, utterly unsure of what to do with herself, she made some hot cocoa. Allowed herself a brief look at Twitter, which was a huge mistake. The Boycott Evolution hashtag had caught fire. There were thousands using it.

Her heart crawled into her throat, a feeling of dread twisting her insides. If they didn't contain this tomorrow, if their plan to announce the philanthropy program next week didn't turn the tide, Evolution and everything she'd worked so hard for would be in jeopardy. Everything her parents had entrusted to her.

She raked trembling fingers through her hair. It was all too easy to second-guess everything. Her overly ambitious launch plan, how closely she'd tied her fragrances to the personalities that represented them, how she'd ignored Nico's advice, when if she had listened, they wouldn't be in this situation.

It all ran through her head as she curled up and tried to fall asleep in her four-poster bed. *Alone.*

Hot tears stung her eyes, but there was also anger in that potent brew. Fury that Nico had been such a bastard to her. Fury that he would hide from himself like this, because she knew how he felt. Fury because she needed him now more than ever, his ability to right-side her world something she'd always depended on.

Blinking back the tears, she refused to cry. Refused to let *this* be the thing that felled her. She'd come too far for that. She'd become too much of a fighter. Nico was a *coward*, that was what he was. She would not be that.

She woke at an insanely early hour, just as dawn was creeping into the sky. A determination filled her, steely in its foundation. The massive sales, the overwhelmingly positive response to Vivre could not be wrong. She had not been wrong in her decisions. She could not abandon her vision now or it would all be for naught.

She might have been wrong about Eddie. She *had* been wrong about Eddie. So now she had to fix it. Unfortunately, she had a feeling this was going to get a lot worse before it got better.

It did get worse. By 9:00 a.m., Evolution's already fragile share price had dropped 20 percent and Nico was fielding calls from worried board members in between a seemingly endless number of press interviews, the media's thirst for Hollywood's latest scandal seemingly unquenchable.

Chloe took it upon herself to check in with her uncle to see if he'd made any progress on pulling the television ads before Nico flipped his lid. When Giorgio's PA announced he was on a call, she leaned against the doorway to his office and waited for him to finish. His back to her, his feet on the windowsill, she gathered it was Keith Taylor, one of the Evolution board members, on the other end of the line.

She frowned. Why was Giorgio talking to Keith? She didn't even think they knew each other. The gist of the conversation soon set her spine ramrod straight. *He was pressing his case with Keith as the man who should be running Evolution in the middle of a crisis that could bring the company down.*

Fury singed her blood. She was livid by the time Giorgio set the phone down and swung his chair around. His gaze sliding over Chloe, he had the audacity to wave her into a seat for a coffee with a lazy, self-satisfied expression on his face.

Chloe set her hands on her hips and raked a look over her uncle, the resemblance to her father so strong it hurt sometimes. "You are *courting* the board in the middle of a crisis?" she breathed. "At Nico's expense?"

Her uncle shrugged. "It's the right time to get rid of him. You weren't so happy about him becoming CEO before you started sleeping with him."

She curled her hands into fists by her sides. He was out of control. Utterly out of line. How had she not seen it before? Had she been so deluded about *everything*?

"You're fired," she bit out. "Effective immediately."

Giorgio stared at her, astonished. "You can't do that."

"Father gave Nico the power to do it." She lifted her chin. "And I'm backing him up. This is unacceptable, Giorgio."

She marched out of his office. Absorbed the look of shock on his PA's face. "I will reassign you," she muttered, before she stalked into the hallway.

Her heart broken at her uncle's betrayal, she marched up to Nico's office, told her boss what Giorgio had done and that she'd fired him, then burned a path to her own office, where she focused on the nascent philanthropy program she and the team were creating, keeping in touch with Lashaunta and Desdemona to update them on things and ensure they didn't jump ship. By the end of the week, she and the team had a platform they could brief the two stars on.

Lashaunta and Desdemona both loved the program, which would allocate millions over the next few years to women's causes, and both of them signed on. Helped in part by the fact that things on social media had gradually begun to calm down with Evolution's clear assurance the company had cut ties with Carello.

Lashaunta, with whom Chloe had developed a close relationship over the past few weeks, even agreed to fly to New York for the unveiling of the program, given she was already in America on tour.

By the time Chloe and Nico unveiled the program to hundreds of journalists at a press conference at Evolution, Lashaunta and Desdemona at their sides, Chloe was so exhausted she could barely put one foot in front of the other, investing everything she had left into the emotional remarks she made about why the program was so important to her—how everything she and her mother had ever done had been to empower women with their own particular kind of beauty.

When it was over, she knew she'd done everything she could. Now it was up to the world to decide Evolution's fate. What she could not seem to repair was her broken heart. It was still raw and bruised as Nico and she stepped off the podium and removed their mics.

"You were incredible up there," he said quietly, a warmth in his smoky gray eyes that had been missing for days.

She wrapped a layer of Teflon around her heart. Lifted her chin. "Because I knew we could do this together. Because we are a great team, Nico. That we can weather any storm together. It's you that didn't believe."

Nico stood looking out at a Christmas light extravaganza that was New York in December, nursing a Scotch as he surveyed the view from the floor-to-ceiling windows of his penthouse.

He thought Evolution might finally have turned the corner today. Its stock price had rebounded after its disastrous drop and sales had done the same, with Be flying high again. The one price to pay from all of this might be Soar, of which sales had plummeted. But if that was the only casualty of this mess, he'd take it.

Ads for Be had been everywhere on his way home, plastered across the city, a big flashing reminder of the woman who had shown her steel spine today in that press conference with Lashaunta and Desdemona, passionately and fearlessly handling interviews with the major daily newspapers.

She was light-years from the woman he'd dragged home from Paris—a warrior. *Something to behold.* It cast his own inability to grow in far too harsh a light.

He'd spent the past couple of months forcing her out of her shell—insisting she evolve into what he knew she could be—even when it had meant stretching her to the very limits of her capabilities. Forcing her to acknowledge her innermost fears and expose them for the fraud they were. And what had he done? Reverted to old patterns—to a knee-jerk reaction to end things between them instead of taking a good look at himself. Instead of facing his own fears.

Chloe had been right. If he didn't allow himself to care about another person, if he didn't allow himself to *feel*, no one could destroy him like that ever again. Burying himself in his work, *providing* had been the only way he'd known how to survive. It was the way he'd operated since he was fifteen years old.

Which had been fine until Chloe had battered through his defenses with her courage and fire. Until she'd made him question his limitations. Made him want *more*. Until she'd made him want to *be* more. And that had scared the hell out of him.

He lifted the Scotch to his lips, welcoming its low, fiery burn. He missed her. He'd told himself his knee-jerk reaction to end them had been the right one, because dragging this affair out any longer was only going to hurt her more. Had buried himself in his work with twenty-hour days, expecting its usual anesthetic effects to function as it always did. But it hadn't.

Instead, her absence in his bed at night had only illuminated how lacking his life was in the spirit and warmth she brought to it. How being programmed as a machine to do only one thing wasn't enough anymore.

The problem was, he thought, staring out at a cavalcade of lights, he might have killed the one chance he'd had of having more because of a past that had owned him for far too long.

Christmas Eve had always been the most magical night of the year for Chloe. Right from the very beginning, when her father had read her and Mireille *The Night Be-*

*fore Christmas* in full theatrical voice while they sat on his lap at the house in Great Neck and drank big mugs of cocoa laced with her mother's candy cane syrup.

Later, when they'd gotten older, and Evolution had been founded, the magic had come from her father's big heart. He couldn't stand the idea of any of his employees spending Christmas alone, so he'd rounded them up like stray kittens and invited them to dinner, which had sometimes meant forty or fifty people at the table, her mother holding her head and muttering *numbers* the whole while.

But her mother had loved those boisterous, chaotic celebrations as much as Chloe and Mireille had. It was like the whole word had come to their big, warm, happy house on the hill.

And then there'd been the year the Di Fiore boys had shown up, looking shell-shocked in the middle of the crowd. Chloe thought she might have taken one look at Nico as he'd sat through her father's traditional end-of-year philosophical rant, so serious as he'd soaked it all up as if it was the most profound thing he'd ever heard, and fallen in love with him that instant.

But, she reminded herself as an ache surfaced deep inside her, she wasn't thinking about *him* right now. She and Mireille were going ice skating at Rockefeller Center, before they had wine and fondue at home. A new tradition. And she wasn't going to cry about that either, because Be was under half of Manhattan's Christmas trees, she knew her mother would be so proud of her and she was going to hold her memories close to her heart, exactly as Nico had said.

*Damn him. He was everywhere.*

Hat planted on her head, mittens at the ready, she tapped her foot impatiently on the hardwood floor. She had just glanced at her watch for the third time when a knock sounded on the door.

"You're late," she said impatiently, swinging the door wide. "Why is it I'm—" She stopped dead in her tracks at the sight of Nico standing on the doorstep, the memory of that kiss, that *show-stopping* kiss, flashing through her head.

Oh, no. She was not doing this tonight.

"Go away," she said firmly, refusing to acknowledge how beautiful he looked in jeans and a dark turtleneck sweater. "Mireille and I are going ice skating."

"Mireille isn't coming until later."

Her eyes widened. "Why not?"

"Because we need to talk." He gestured toward the door. "Can I come in?"

"No."

He sank his hands into her waist, picked her up and moved her aside. She gasped and gave him a furious look as he closed the door. "I don't want to talk to you. Nor do I want to kiss you until I lose my head. I want to go ice skating."

"Chloe," he said quietly, eyes on hers, "I need to talk to you. Hear me out and I promise I'll go away if that's what you want."

He looked serious, so serious she relented, toeing off her boots and leading the way into the living room. Perching herself on the sofa, she eyed him warily as he sat down beside her.

He raked a hand through his hair in an uncharacteristically fidgety move. "You were right," he began, "about why I pushed you away. This time and *every* time. Because I have always felt too much for you. Because you make me *feel* too much."

Her heart lodged in her mouth. "My father *was* a workaholic," he continued. "He was addicted to the buzz, but he was also addicted to keeping my mother happy. She messed with his head, she played him for all he was worth. If he'd *had* his head fully in the game, I'm not sure he would have made the mistakes he did, taken the risks he did, and maybe the outcome would have been very different."

She shook her head. "You can't say that. It may simply be that he had an addictive personality, a disease. To blame it on your mother is unfair."

His mouth compressed. "I'm not so sure. I went to see my mother, Chloe. That's how much you've turned my head upside down. I thought maybe you were right—that it would help me to understand better. Reframe things in my head."

Shock rendered her speechless. "What did she say?" she finally managed.

"That she was to blame for most of it. That she resented losing her career. She felt unequipped to be a mother, and she took it out on my father." He lifted a shoulder. "She also said she felt a great deal of sorrow about the decisions she's made."

"And did you believe her?"

"She seemed genuine about it." He rubbed a palm over the thick stubble on his jaw. "She said my father had the affairs to hurt her. To strike back. It became a vicious circle between them."

"Relationships are rarely simple," she murmured. "Even my parents, as in love as they were, had fights that would take down the rafters. They were passionate people. But the point is, they worked through it. They loved each other enough to make it work."

"Yes," he agreed. "They did." He dropped his head in his hands. Was silent for a moment. When he looked up, she saw the glitter of an emotion she couldn't read in his eyes. "I told myself I would never go on that kind of an emotional roller-coaster ride with a woman. I made *sure*

I never did. But with you, I didn't have a choice. It just *was*. And when things fell apart with Eddie, it raised all my red flags and I mentally disengaged. A force of habit."

She shook her head. "We're better together, Nico. We are more *powerful* together. That's what held it all together. You and me."

"Yes," he acknowledged, "I know that now. But all of my baggage came into play. I started to question what I could be. Something Martino said to me." He rubbed a hand against his temple. "He saw us on the Fourth of July, Chloe."

Her jaw dropped, disbelief filtering through her. "He never said."

"He talked to me about it afterward. He told me to date you seriously or walk away."

She sank her teeth into her lip. "I can't believe he did that. It was *my* life."

"You were eighteen, Chloe. A baby. I was a hardened twenty-two. And he was right," he conceded. "I couldn't offer you what you needed. You needed to grow up and learn what life was all about. I already knew *too much* about life."

If she thought she'd been furious with her father before, she was livid with him now. Because what would she and Nico have become if he hadn't interfered? What *could* they have become?

"So why are you here now?" she tossed at him, her insides hollow and empty, as if they'd been scraped out with something sharp. "If you're so sure you can never be what I'm looking for?"

His gaze locked with hers. "Because you've always been the best thing in my life. Because I was a fool to walk away from you again, and if you give me one more chance, I promise I won't mess it up."

"How do I know?" she whispered, hurt throbbing from the inside out. "I can't go through that again, Nico. Not one more time."

"Because I love you," he said, without missing a beat. As if they weren't the most earth-shattering words he'd ever uttered to her. "Because I've been in love with you a long time and I'm tired of fighting it."

Her heart skipped a beat. Hope bloomed inside her, so powerful, potent, it would have knocked her off her feet had she been standing. But there was also fear—fear he would do this to her again.

Clearly realizing how badly he'd screwed up, he reached into his pocket and pulled out a brightly wrapped box. The blood in her veins pumped, jagged, erratic, as he sank down on one knee in front of her.

*"Nico,"* she gasped, "what are you doing?"

"Proposing." He gave her an annoyed look. "I took Santo jewelry shopping, for God's sake. Let me get there."

Her stomach fell off a shelf and crashed to the floor. Oh, no, he wasn't doing this to her on Christmas Eve. The night fairy tales were made of.

"Marry me," he murmured, eyes on hers as he held up the most brilliant sparkling diamond she'd ever seen.

"Don't you think this is a bit extreme?" she breathed, eyes glued to the ring. "I forgive you. There, I've said it."

He shook his head. "It's always been you, Chloe. Always you."

That was it. She was done for. Forever and always.

She held out a trembling hand. Watched as he slid the brilliant diamond on her finger. It was like watching her most secret, most unobtainable fantasy come true. She couldn't speak, could only fling her arms around his neck as he gathered her up and sat down with her in his lap.

"I love you," she murmured against his amazing mouth.

"So much. I've been so miserable, I think Mireille was dreading spending the evening with me."

"She's coming back. She's bringing Lazzero and Santo with her."

She pulled back. "You were that sure of me?"

He shook his head. "Willing to crash and burn."

Her heart contracted on a low pull. "I'll have one of those rather earth-shattering kisses now, thank you. You've earned it."

He gave her exactly that. When they finally came up for air, he pulled another box from his pocket. "One more."

She slid the box open to find a stunning Murano glass star nestled inside.

"So we can start our own traditions," he explained quietly. "Make new memories."

Her heart shattered. Turned to dust. But it was a good thing because with that last barrier smashed, she knew they would put each other back together again. Stronger. *Better*. Because that was what they'd always been about.

Nico stood with her in his arms. Boosted her up to set the star on top of the tree. She wrapped her arms around his neck as she stared up at it, glittering like the most gorgeous jewel in the sky.

"When did you say the others are coming back?"

He carried her toward the stairs. "*Later*. There's a tradition I'd like to start right now."

Her thoughts exactly.

\* \* \* \* \*

# THE BOSS'S WIFE
# FOR A WEEK

## ANNE MCALLISTER

For Haine, in friendship forever, and for Chuck,
who taught Ted everything he knew.
So it's the wrong book. We know life isn't fair,
but thanks for making mine so much better.

# CHAPTER ONE

IT WAS paperwork that kept Sadie Morrissey tied to Spencer Tyack. He was hopeless at it.

If paperwork were left to Spence it would never get done. And that was no way to run a business. Tyack Enterprises was an enormously successful property development business because Spence had a good eye, great insight and a prodigious work ethic—and because he had Sadie to take care of the details.

She'd been doing it for years, ever since she'd been in high school and he'd been barely twenty-one, a boy from the wrong side of the tracks with grit and goals and not much else. Now, twelve years later, he owned a multinational business and had his finger in property developments on five continents.

He'd have taken over the world by now, Sadie sometimes thought, except she couldn't keep up with the paperwork.

"You need to file faster," Spence always told her, flashing that megawatt drop-dead gorgeous grin of his as he breezed through the office on his way to London or Paris or Athens or New York.

"Not on your life," Sadie always replied, wadding up a piece of paper and throwing it at him. The grin flashed again and he winked at her.

Sadie resisted the grin, resisted the wink. Resisted Spence—something else she always did.

"I'm busy enough, thank you very much," she told him tartly. "And it's not only filing."

Of course he knew that. He knew it was Sadie who kept things organized, who could lay her hand on any piece of paper at any given moment, who could set up a meeting between people on four continents at the drop of a hat, whose address book was even more stuffed full of information than his own.

He only said it to annoy her. Then he'd grin again, rattle off half a dozen more things she needed to do, and then he'd vanish, off to catch another plane while Sadie got back to work.

Not that she cared.

Until last year she'd had a reason to stay in Butte. She'd been determined to care for her elderly grandmother, to make sure Gran would be able to stay in her own home as long as possible.

Now that Gran had been gone six months, her parents were urging her to come to Oregon where they lived, and her brother, Danny, had promised her job interviews galore if she came to Seattle.

But Sadie hadn't gone. She liked Butte with its wild and woolly history. Loved Montana. Delighted in the change of seasons, in the wide-open spaces. It was still, as far as she was concerned, the best place on earth.

And she liked her life—what there was of it. Mostly there was her job. But that was all right. She and Spence had always worked well together, and the job was exciting and demanding, even though she was always going like mad, working insane hours as she did her best to keep the ducks in a row and the details aligned so that Spence could get on with buying up the world piece by piece.

Some days—like today—Sadie thought she ought to have been born an octopus. But even eight arms would not have been enough to deal with all the Tyack Enterprises projects she was juggling this afternoon.

The phone had been ringing when she'd opened the office door at eight-thirty this morning. By lunchtime she had talked four times to an Italian determined to encourage Spence's interest in some condominiums in Naples even though she'd assured him that Spence wasn't there, he was in New York. She'd listened to an imperious Greek tycoon named Achilles who wouldn't take no for an answer, either. And in between those and all the other calls, she'd worked on finalizing Spence's meeting in Fiji next week.

Arranging the logistics for him and his co-investors to spend a week on one of Fiji's smaller islands at a resort for stressed-out and overworked businessmen and women was, to put it bluntly, a challenge. Movers and shakers like Spence and his partners did not have schedules that permitted them to laze around for a week in paradise.

"We don't want to laze around," Spence had told her last time he was in Butte. "We just want to go, see the place, crunch the numbers and, if it works out, buy in."

"That's what *you* want," Sadie had agreed. "But Mr. Isogawa wants you to experience the peace you're going to be investing in."

That had been clear during the first conversation she'd had with Japanese businessman Tadahiro Isogawa. Mr. Isogawa wanted partners, yes. But not just any partners. He wanted partners who believed in the resort's concept—and who would experience it firsthand.

"The piece we're investing in?" Spence had frowned. "We don't want a piece. We want partnership in the whole place."

*"P-e-a-c-e,"* Sadie had spelled patiently. "He expects you to all turn up and spend a week getting to know the place—and each other—and reconnecting with your families."

"I don't have a family."

"So tell that to Mr. Isogawa. He's very big on marriage and family. It's why he works, he told me. But he believes sometimes people who work so hard get their priorities mixed up. Hence the need for Nanumi. It's Fijian for 'remember,'" she'd informed Spence. Mr. Isogawa had told her that when he'd explained his reasons for the resort development.

It hadn't impressed Spence. He had given her that sceptical brows-raised look Sadie knew all too well. She'd just shrugged. "Up to you. But he says if you want in, he wants all of you—and your spouses—there for a week to experience it."

Spence had rolled his eyes. But his desire for the resort won out and finally he'd shrugged. "Fine. Whatever he wants. Set it up."

And so she had.

Besides all the rest of her work, it had taken her days to make sure everyone had a clear schedule for the week to come and then to make all the necessary travel arrangements from the far corners of the world to the island resort. In the process she'd answered thousands of questions from astonished spouses who had rung to be sure the proposed week's holiday in Fiji was actually on the level.

"We never get holidays," Marion Ten Eyck had told her. "John is always working."

Steve Walker's wife, Cathy, had said much the same thing. And Richard Carstairs' wife, Leonie, had rung her every day, saying, "Are you sure? Quite sure? Does Richard know?"

And Sadie had assured her over and over that indeed Richard did. She was beginning to think Mr. Isogawa knew what he was talking about.

And just when she finally got everything sorted and began to go over a contract Spence had faxed her for a development in Georgia he was involved in, the phone rang again.

Sadie closed her eyes and prayed for patience. It actually wasn't eight hands she needed, she thought wearily as she reached for the phone. But eight ears certainly wouldn't hurt.

"Tyack Enterprises," she said and was rewarded by the crackle of a transoceanic connection and a voice whose first language was clearly not English. On the plus side, it wasn't Italian or Greek, either.

"Ah, *Isogawa-san, konnichi wa*. How lovely to hear from you!"

And it really was. Mr. Isogawa was the one person she hadn't talked to. "Everyone arrives on Sunday. I have all the details right here."

She happily relayed the information and smiled at his cheerful approval.

Mr. Isogawa, she had discovered, had had little experience with westerners beyond the ones he saw in films. Since Sadie was more given to hard work than car chases and shooting people to get things done, he thought she was a miracle worker. He took all the information as she relayed it, then said, "You must come, too."

"Thank you. I'd love to," Sadie replied with a smile. Who wouldn't want to spend a week in a South Pacific paradise? "But I have work to do here."

"Even so," Mr. Isogawa said. "You work very hard. You should have a holiday, too. A life."

How did he know she didn't have a life?

"You talk to Spencer," he said. "He will arrange it."

Spence didn't take vacations himself. She knew he wouldn't see any reason for anyone else to, either. Officially she had two weeks a year. She couldn't remember ever taking them.

"Maybe someday," she said to Mr. Isogawa. When hell froze over.

Still, after Mr. Isogawa hung up, she thought about what he said.

Not about going to Fiji. There was no chance of that. But maybe she ought to consider getting away. Moving away. For years she'd assured herself that she thrived on the variety and busyness of her life.

But was it really a life?

Rob McConnell, the man she'd been dating for the past few

months, was sure it wasn't. "You never have time for anything but your damn job," he complained over and over. "You're not getting any younger, Sadie."

Usually Rob wasn't quite that blunt, but she knew he was getting irritated at her refusal to want more than a casual relationship. She didn't blame him. He was a genuinely nice man. He wanted to marry and have a family. He'd said as much. And he was right, she wasn't getting any younger. She was twenty-eight. If she was going to get serious, she needed to start.

Sadie wanted to get serious. Truly. But not with Rob.

And that was the problem.

Maybe she should move on. She'd been thinking about it ever since her brother, Danny, had come home from Seattle to visit last week, bringing his wife and their one-year-old twins with him. That had been a shock. Danny had always been as footloose as Spence. Seeing her brother as a devoted family man had jolted her.

It seemed to have given Danny pause for thought, too.

"Who'd have thought I'd settle down before you," he'd said the night before he'd left. He'd been sitting in her living room with a twin in each arm, looking exhausted but content. And then he'd considered her slowly, making her squirm under his gaze as he'd said, "But then, you are settled, aren't you, Sadie?"

"What do you mean?"

His mouth twisted. "You're settled in as Spence's drudge."

"I am not!" Sadie had tossed down the copy of Spence's itinerary she'd been going over, making some last-minute adjustments, and jumped up to prowl around the room. "Don't be absurd."

"It isn't me who's being absurd, Sade. It's all work and no play with you. Always has been as been as long as I can remember."

"I play," Sadie had protested.

"When you work seventeen hours instead of eighteen? Hell, you're as driven as Spence."

"We have goals!" she informed him loftily.

"Spence does," Danny had corrected with an elder brother's ruthlessness. "You're just hanging on."

Sadie had whirled around to glare at him. "What's that supposed to mean?"

Danny met her glare head on. "You know damn well what it means"

"I have a great job!"

"But do you have a life? Come on, Sadie. You're the one who always used to name your kids when we were growing up. You're damn near thirty and you barely even date!"

"I'm twenty-eight, not *damn near thirty!* And Rob—"

"You're not serious about Rob McConnell. If you were you'd have invited him over while Kel and I were here. You didn't. So find someone you are serious about. Get married. Have that family you always wanted." He threw the words at her like a gauntlet, and Sadie couldn't pick it up.

"I'm fine," she'd said stiffly.

"Yeah. Sure you are. You could get a job anywhere. Come out to Seattle. Kel will find you a hundred dates. Believe me, you're wasted on Spence."

"I'm not dating Spence."

"And thank God for that," Danny said. "He's my friend, but he's not exactly marriage material, is he?"

He wasn't telling her anything she didn't know. But she shook her head. "I work for him, that's all," she said.

"So quit."

"I can't."

"Why not? Does Spence own your soul?"

"Oh, for heaven's sake. Of course not!" But her face had burned and Sadie had hoped Danny wouldn't notice.

Fortunately he'd just shaken his head. "Well, it makes a guy wonder. You've been working for him for years! Since high school."

"Because he needed the help. You know Spence. He's great at wheeling and dealing. Great at finding properties and renovating them. Great at potential. He can see the big picture. But he's not great at paperwork. Not at details."

And Sadie had always been marvelous at both. She could organize anything.

"Anyway," she'd reminded her brother. "I didn't stay. I left, remember? I went away to college. Four years at UCLA."

"And then you came back, you idiot. To him."

"To the job," Sadie insisted. "He pays me a mint. And I get a percentage of the business, for heaven's sake. And where else could I possibly go and manage a global property-development business at my age? And still live in Butte?"

"Oh, yeah, that's a real plus. Butte! The hub of the western cultural world."

Of course it was anything but. But the old mining city was making a comeback. Long depressed, Butte was making a slow climb back toward prosperity, thanks in large part to Spence and a few other guys like him who were determined to turn things around.

"Don't be sarcastic. And don't knock Butte." Sadie's voice had been frosty at his dismissal of their hometown. "It's home. Spence doesn't knock it, and he has more right than you do."

She and Danny had had a good childhood with stable, loving parents. Spence had not. For all that he was now a real-estate tycoon of international scope, Spencer Tyack hadn't been born with a silver spoon in his mouth.

"Not even a copper one," he'd once said with a wry grin, a reference to Butte's copper-mining past. "But I survived."

No thanks to his own parents, that was for sure. Sadie remembered Spence's grandfather as kind and caring, but the old man had died when Spence was ten. From then on his life had been hell. His alcoholic father hadn't been able to keep a job and rarely turned up at home except to fight with his mother or take a swing at Spence. And his mother's bitterness toward her husband found its most convenient target in their only son.

Sadie, whom Spence had never permitted to set foot in his house while she was growing up, had still got close enough on occasion to hear her shrieking at him, "You're just like your father!"

He wasn't. Not even close.

Unlike his father, Spence had always been driven. Even when he'd been something of a juvenile delinquent in high school, he'd been determined to be the best delinquent of the bunch.

A probation officer who had insisted they meet not in his office but in the cemetery by Spence's grandfather's grave had put an end to the delinquency. After that Spence had been determined to do the old man proud. To succeed. To achieve. To become the best man he possibly could.

He'd gone to work wherever he could. He'd saved and scrimped and had bought his first house the week he turned twenty-one. To call it a "fixer-upper" would be kind. It had been little more than a hovel with a leaky roof.

As soon as he could, he'd gone to work in the mine, making better money driving those behemoth trucks all day. Then he'd come back and work on the house all night. Several months later he sold that house at a profit, bought another, then did the same. He did it again and again.

By the time he was twenty-two he'd been able to apply for his first commercial-property loan. And that's when he'd hired Sadie to create order out of the paperwork chaos—in his truck. He hadn't had an office.

"I can't waste money on an office," he'd told her.

So for the first year she'd worked out of the back of his truck camper, using a shop light run by a battery, and a filing system that she carried around in a cardboard box. It was primitive. But it worked.

And so had Spence. Constantly. Within the year he'd had a building. Then two. During her senior year in high school, Sadie finally got an office to call her own. Spence had even bought her a silly plaque that said, "Sadie's office."

And he'd been furious when she'd told him she was leaving to go to college in California.

"I got you an office," he'd protested. "I thought you were going to work for me!"

"Not forever," Sadie had replied.

Because she couldn't. It was more than her sanity was worth, the thought of working for Spence forever—because she was in love with him. Had been for years. As long as she could remember, in fact.

Not that he knew it. God forbid. He'd have been appalled, because he certainly wasn't in love with her.

Sadie knew that. She didn't like it, but she accepted it. She'd tried a little flirting with him, and he'd completely ignored it. So she'd gone to UCLA to get away.

She'd hoped she would learn a lot, get wonderful job offers and meet a man who could make her forget Spence. That had been the plan at least.

And if she'd come home every summer to help Spence out, it was only because he refused to hire anyone in her place while she was gone.

"No need. It can wait for you," he'd said. "You'll be home, anyway."

Which was true. She'd come back to spend summers at her parents' house, to see Gran, to visit Butte. But she hadn't intended to come back permanently. Ever.

Everything went the way she'd planned. She'd learned a lot, graduated with honors and had lots of wonderful job offers—including one from Spence.

He'd come to her graduation. "Why not? I feel like I have a

vested interest in your business degree," he'd said blandly. And he'd offered her a job that very afternoon.

He'd promised her a remarkable amount of money, a completely refurbished office in one of Butte's historic landmark buildings that he was painstakingly renovating, and a percentage of his business empire.

"A percentage?" Sadie's eyes had widened in surprise.

But Spence had just shrugged. "Why not? You've worked almost as hard to put Tyack's on the map as I have. You deserve a share. So, what do you say?" The characteristic Tyack impatience was all too clear.

Sadie hadn't known what to say. The truth was she still hadn't gotten over him. His killer grin could still make her knees wobble. His hard-muscled body could still make her quiver all over. And when his steely-eyed stare grew softer and gentler, as it did on rare occasions, her heart seemed to simply turn over in her chest.

She was hopeless, she'd thought grimly. What she needed, she'd decided, was shock therapy. She needed full-scale immersion into Spencer Tyack's world. That would undoubtedly cure her of all her starry-eyed fantasies.

So she'd said yes.

She'd been back for almost six years.

A lot had happened in those six years. She'd done her best to get over him. Told herself she *was* over him. She was dating other men. Just because she hadn't found one yet who set her heart to pounding the way Spence had didn't mean she wouldn't.

She knew Spence wasn't for her.

"I like working for him," she'd told Danny. "It's exciting." Spence was a mover and a shaker. He now had properties in seven countries. He owned apartment complexes, office buildings, condominiums. He always had new ideas. And he always talked about them with her. He sought her opinion. They discussed and analyzed—and argued—together.

"You've got a stake in it," he always said.

And that was true. She did. She might not have a life, but she had a stake in an exciting business. Last week Spence had been in Helsinki finalizing a deal for an office building. This week he was in New York looking over some apartments with father-and-daughter investment team Tom and Dena Wilson, who had done deals with him in the past. And next week, with luck, he would be part owner of a South Pacific resort.

And, as first Danny and now Mr. Isogawa had reminded her, she would be in Butte. Sadie sighed.

It was nearly five. She could leave at five. If she left at five, maybe she would get a life—even though she had piles more work to do.

The phone rang again and unhesitatingly she answered. "Tyack Enterprises. This is Sadie."

*"Say-dee, case-me, meu amor."* The voice was like rough velvet.

Sadie grinned, recognizing it. If there was ever a man— besides Spence—who could send a woman's hormones into overdrive, Mateus Gonsalves was that man. Trouble was, he knew it. "Hi, Mateus. *Obrigada.* But no, I still don't want to marry you. And Spence is in New York."

He sighed. "I don't want to marry Spence." Mateus Gonsalves switched to perfectly clear, though accented, English. "I want to marry you—and take you away from your slave-driving boss."

It was a conversation they'd had a dozen times at least. From the first time Spence had brought his Brazilian friend to Butte, Mateus had been full of Latin charm, flirting like mad with her, always asking her to marry him.

"She won't," Spence had said cheerfully, not even looking up from the file cabinet he was riffling through. "Sadie's a man-hater."

"I am not!" she'd protested, pushing him out of the way and plucking out at once the document he'd been looking for.

Spence had grabbed it. "See, she's a genius. Knows where everything is," he'd told Mateus happily. Then he'd turned to her. "You don't date."

"I do, too," she'd said. "When the mood hits," she qualified, but that was the truth. She certainly didn't hate men.

"She will date me," Mateus had said with complete assurance.

But she never had. "I don't mix business and pleasure," she'd told him.

"You should," Mateus had rejoined irrepressibly. And he hadn't stopped asking her to come to Rio and marry him every time he called.

"Life is a party in Rio," he said now. "We know how to live down here. You should dump that workaholic and come to work for me."

Sadie laughed at that. "You work almost as hard as he does."

"But I hide it better. And I take holidays. What do you say?"

"Maybe someday I'll come to Rio for a visit," Sadie placated him. "Now, what can I do for you?"

Mateus shifted gears as easily as he always did. "I need to talk to Spencer about a building in Sao Paulo."

"I'll tell him."

"Give me his cell phone number."

"He never turns it on." Unless he was expecting a call, Spence kept his cell phone off. But he always expected her to keep hers on so he could reach her. "When he checks in, I'll have him call you."

"*Obrigado,*" he said. "Tell him I've got a proposition for him. And one for you."

"I'm not marrying you, Mateus," she said firmly.

"No marriage," he agreed sadly. "But seriously, Say-dee, you should come work for me. I'm opening an office in Texas. You could run it with one hand tied behind your back."

And have a life besides, Sadie reflected for a brief moment. But then she sighed and shook her head. Battling Mateus off could make life even more difficult than working for Spence who didn't seem to remember that she was a woman. "Thanks. But, no, Mateus."

"Think about it."

"I'll think about it," she agreed because it was easier than arguing with him.

"We will talk later," he promised. *"Adeus, carinha."*

*"Ciao, Mateus."* She hung up, then picked up the contracts, determined to take them home and read them. At least that way she could say she'd left the office by ten past five. But her cell phone rang as she did so. She saw who it was and glared.

"It's after five," she said irritably when she picked it up.

"So?" Even when she was annoyed at him, the sound of Spence's rough baritone could cause her pulse to speed up. Damn it.

"I have a life," she snapped.

"Whoa. Who ticked you off?"

You, she wanted to say, even though it was really herself she was annoyed at. "It's been a madhouse here today."

"Well, good. Glad to hear it." Which she supposed he was. "Need you to do something for me," he went on briskly.

Sadie grabbed a pen, ready to write, but he didn't say anything. "Spence?"

"Yeah." He sounded suddenly distracted. His normally quick speech grew even quicker. "No big deal. I just need you to get my birth certificate and the divorce decree and bring them to New York."

Sadie stopped dead. "What?" She felt as if she had been gut-punched. "Do what?"

"You heard me. My birth certificate. The divorce decree. I need them. Tomorrow. In New York."

She'd always thought that breathing was in involuntary reflex. Now she wasn't sure.

"Sadie? Are you there? Did you hear me?" His voice was sharp now.

"I heard you." She managed that much. Couldn't manage any more.

"Great. So just get them and hop on a plane tonight. Or tomorrow. I don't care which. Just so long as you're here by 2:00 p.m."

She didn't speak, just stared mutely at the pencil she'd broken in her hand.

"Sadie!"

"Yes!" she snapped back at him now. "I heard you!"

"Well, good." He paused. "You could congratulate me."

"Because…?" she said, though she knew without asking the reason, even though it stunned her.

"Because I'm getting married." He said the words almost defiantly as if expecting her to argue.

She knew better than to argue. But she couldn't help the sarcasm. "Tomorrow? Isn't that a little precipitous? I mean, considering your track record and all?"

*Shut up*, she told herself. *Shut up. Shut up. Shut up.*

"It'll be fine this time," he said flatly. "Not like Emily."

"It wasn't Emily I was thinking about," Sadie said, unable to help herself. "You didn't marry Emily."

"I remember who I married." He bit the words out.

Sadie remembered, too. He'd married her!

A wedding on the rebound. When society belle Emily Mollineux had stood him up for their Las Vegas wedding, he'd been gutted. His desperation had reminded Sadie of his boyhood pain when his father walked out and his mother had unleashed her fury on Spence.

So when he'd slammed out of the chapel with a fearsome look in his eyes, Sadie had gone after him, unsure what he might do. She'd never imagined that half a dozen whiskeys later he'd decide the answer was to marry *her!*

But he had. He'd been most insistent. "You'd marry me,"

he'd said firmly, but there had been just a hint of doubt, the tiniest question in his words, in his gaze. "Wouldn't you?" he'd persisted when she hadn't answered.

And Sadie, because that moment if no other seemed to call for absolute honesty, had to admit she would.

"If you asked me," she'd replied because it was only the truth.

And then, heaven help her, he did.

"Marry me," he'd said. And he'd met her gaze with all the intensity Spencer Tyack was capable of in those midnight eyes.

And so she had married him. Within the hour.

They'd got a license, done the deed. And they'd gone back to the honeymoon suite and made love. Passionately. Desperately. Dazedly. It had been the most amazing night of her life.

And she'd awakened in the honeymoon suite the next morning to find Spence already awake and fully dressed, pacing furiously, raking his hands through his hair and saying, "It was a mistake."

Sadie had barely got her eyes open when he'd come and loomed over her, all harsh expression and anguished bloodshot eyes. "It never should have happened. We never should have— *I* never should have— Hell!" He'd shaken his head as if he didn't believe it. "I'm sorry, Sadie. I never meant— Damn it! I don't know what I was thinking! But it'll be all right. Don't worry. We'll get a divorce."

"A d-divorce?" She'd managed that much. Had simply stared at him slack-jawed.

Spence had nodded vehemently. "Well, we can't get an annulment," he'd said grimly. "But it won't be a problem. I promise. I'll handle it."

He'd been adamant, determined. Just as determined to divorce her as he had been to marry her only twelve hours before. It might be some sort of record, Sadie had remembered thinking. She'd blinked rapidly and tried hard to swallow against the boulder lodged in her throat.

Had it been that awful? That wrong?

Apparently it had.

At least it hadn't seemed like the time to declare her undying love. She'd simply nodded. "Right," she managed, though she'd nearly strangled on the word.

Spence peered at her closely. "Are you okay?"

Oh, yes, terrific. Never better. Having been married and found wanting in the space of half a day was exactly the sort of thing to give a girl a heap of self-confidence!

"I'm fine," she said as steadily as she could. "Why?"

"You don't look fine."

"Thanks very much."

"I didn't mean— I just—" he shuddered visibly "—sorry. I don't know what I was thinking. I'm sorry. Sorry about the marriage. About…" His voice trailed off. His gaze shifted southward, away from her face. Down her sheet-draped body.

Sadie felt immediately self-conscious. So he was sorry they'd consummated the marriage? Sorry he'd made love to her?

He was sorry, apparently, for everything.

"Don't think about it," he said. "I'll handle everything. You don't even have to mention it."

*Was he afraid she might?* Stand on the rooftops and announce that her husband of twelve hours was dumping her? She stared at him, speechless.

"You're tired. You have to be. Go back to sleep. The room is booked through Wednesday. Stay until then if you want."

As if she would stay on in the honeymoon suite by herself while her husband was divorcing her!

"I won't be here," Spence said quickly, misinterpreting the appalled look on her face. "I called Santiago this morning. I'm just going to head to Barcelona a few days early. But I'll arrange for the divorce before I go. Okay?"

Sadie shrugged. What else could she do?

Seeing the shrug, Spence gave her a strained smile. "It'll be okay. I promise." He paused, then said, "It won't change things, will it? You'll stay on."

"Stay on?"

"Keep working with me. It doesn't have to be awkward. We're friends." He said this last almost insistently and with complete seriousness. And why not? Last night had meant nothing to him—beyond an error in judgment. He wanted her as a friend, not a wife. And he was remedying that as quickly as he could.

She didn't know what to say.

"No" would undoubtedly have been smart. But she had been afraid that saying no would make him think their marriage mattered far more to her than he wanted to believe. And if he thought it did, would he change his mind? Stay married to her because he felt sorry for her?

The very thought made her squirm.

"I'll stay," she said. "For now."

He'd grinned then, that perfect, sexy drop-dead gorgeous Spencer Tyack grin that Sadie had spent years trying to resist. "That's all right then," he'd said happily. "You're a pal, Sade."

Wasn't she just?

"I knew you'd agree. I'll ring a lawyer from the airport and get him to do it. I'll give you a call tomorrow from Barcelona. But don't worry. Consider it taken care of." And grabbing his suitcase, he'd bolted out the door.

And that, basically, had been that.

Except that when he'd called her from Barcelona the next day, he'd said, "Are you okay?" in a worried tone completely unlike any he'd ever used with her.

"Of course I'm okay. What do you think?" Sadie had retorted. She was damned if she was going to let him think he'd cut her heart out.

She must have been convincing because he'd never asked

that question or sounded that worried again. And the first morning he was back in the office, which was a month later, he'd said, "Don't worry. It's sorted. I've got the papers. It's all taken care of."

And so her short, better-forgotten marriage to Spence had been over.

He'd never mentioned it again.

Neither had she. She'd thought of it again, of course. Plenty of times in those first few months. Minute by minute almost. But eventually she'd managed to put it aside. Not to forget, but to consider it with detachment, as if it had happened in some alternative universe. Like a dream. Or a nightmare.

It had faded over the past four years. Until now. Now she said, "I don't know where the papers are."

"In my safe deposit box. You have a key."

"Yes, but—married?"

"It's business, Sadie. Did you think I'd fallen in love?"

She didn't know what to think. "Business?"

"I'm marrying Dena Wilson. Who'd you think I was marrying? Someone I just picked up on the street?"

"I—"

"It's perfect. A great idea. Dena and I joining forces. I don't know why I didn't think of it sooner. Together we've got twice the clout. Twice the expertise."

"Yes, but—tomorrow?"

"So we'll be married before I head to Fiji. Which reminds me, can you book a flight for Dena?"

She was going to kill him.

"You don't have to do it tonight," he said, all magnanimity. "You can do it tomorrow from here. Just bring the papers and show up at the courthouse tomorrow afternoon. Ceremony's at two. I'll book you a room in a fancy hotel for tomorrow night for your trouble, okay? The Plaza? The Four Seasons? You name it. Think of it as a vacation. Right. I've got to run. Tom and Dena just came in the door. See you tomorrow."

There was a click—and a second later, a dial tone.

Sadie stood staring at the phone in her hand and felt as if the bottom had fallen out of her well-ordered world.


Where the hell was she?

Spence checked his watch for the tenth time in five minutes and raked fingers through his already disheveled hair. He'd been pacing the hallway of the courthouse, just outside the judge's chamber for three-quarters of an hour.

He'd got there an hour before that, wanting to be there when Sadie showed up and not certain when she would arrive. Last night he'd kept his phone off, not wanting to get any calls from Sadie telling him he was making a mistake.

He wasn't making a mistake.

The Emily fiasco had been a mistake. No doubt about that. Four years ago when he'd intended to marry Emily Mollineux, he'd been out of his mind—a victim of his own youthful enthusiasm, infatuation and hormones—not to mention a misplaced determination to wed a beauty whose family was all about Old Money.

And marrying Sadie for God-knew-what insane reason after Emily hadn't shown up—well, that had been an even bigger mistake.

He should never have imposed on her, never proposed! Never put her on the spot like that.

But at the moment he'd been out of his mind. Insane. Rejected. The word still made him wince. But Emily's defection had seemed to confirm his deepest fears—that, as his mother had always claimed, he was worthless.

And so he'd turned to Sadie—had used her unwavering friendship to restore, however briefly, his shattered self-esteem.

It had been easy enough to do, damn it. For all that she would argue with him forever about business propositions, Sadie was putty when it came to people—when it came to him.

And in the morning when he'd awakened to find her in bed beside him, when he remembered how they'd spent the night, he'd been appalled at what he'd done.

Christ, she'd even had a boyfriend! And he hadn't given a damn.

He'd just turned to her and said, "Marry me," and he knew that that night he wouldn't—couldn't—have taken no for an answer. But in the morning's harsh light he knew regret. He knew he'd made a mistake.

And so he'd done his best to make it right.

He wasn't making that mistake again. This marriage was business, pure and simple. He and Dena both wanted exactly the same things. It would be fine.

Provided, he thought, shooting back his cuff and glaring at his watch again, Sadie showed up.

He didn't know where she was or what time her flight had been expected to get in. He might have known, he reminded himself, if he'd turned on his mobile phone last night. But he hadn't. He hadn't wanted to talk to her last night—just in case she tried to talk him out of this marriage.

Sadie was, after all, an idealist, a romantic. As long as he'd known her, she'd been deluded by the notion that someday she would meet "the one." It was one of the reasons he'd known he had to divorce her as quickly as possible—to give her a chance to meet her Perfect Man.

So he hadn't wanted to hear how Dena Wilson wasn't his Perfect Woman. She was all about business—not at all about home and family. She didn't want them any more than he did. And that, to Spence, was about as perfect as she could get.

So he'd shut his phone off and, consequently, he had no idea where the hell Sadie was or when to expect her. He'd tried calling her, but her own phone was shut off.

He knew, of course, that if she was still in the air, she couldn't have it switched on. But good God, she'd better not be in the air now. The ceremony was due to start in less than fifteen minutes.

"Well, Sadie is certainly cutting it a little close," Dena said, appearing at his side. She was smiling her usually imperturbable smile, but there was a hint of strain around her mouth.

"She'll be here."

"Of course. Just give me a heads up. I have some papers to go over," Dena said. "I'll work on them."

She went back into the room, and Spence continued to pace the hallway. He cracked his knuckles. He tried her number again. And again.

Ten minutes later the door to the judge's chambers opened and Dena's father, Tom, appeared. "I'm meeting Sawyer in Savannah at nine. Let's get this show on the road."

"Sadie's not here."

"You're not marrying Sadie."

"She's bringing my papers. Birth certificate. Divorce decree." He hadn't wanted to mention the divorce, but of course he'd had to.

Dena had raised her eyebrows at the news, but then she'd shrugged. "Makes no difference to me."

"Get married now. Worry about the paperwork after." Tom suggested.

"Without Sadie?"

"Why not? No big deal, is it?" Tom said with the air of a man who bent the rules to meet the circumstances. He checked his watch pointedly.

Spence shrugged. "Of course not."

It was sensible. Sane. Logical. It was making the best use of time and resources—just as their marriage would be.

As Mr. and Mrs. Spencer Tyack, they would improve their business standing enormously. Dena's considerable assets alongside his would add to their portfolio and their viability on the property-development front in the long run. And in the short run it would solve a problem with Mr. Isogawa and his "happy family" scenario. One of Spence's partners had a wife with a wandering eye. In Barcelona last month it—and she—had wandered in Spence's direction. Into his bedroom, in fact.

The last thing he needed was her pulling a stunt like that at the resort. Having a wife along, he'd determined, would make sure it didn't happen.

He understood that Tadahiro Isogawa was, as Sadie had said, all about happy families. So was he, even though his personal experience of them was negligible. Marrying Dena, though, could solve his problem and create enormous opportunities for them in the future. He could certainly be happy about that.

And Dena, when he proposed the idea, had understood at once.

"Smart," she'd said after only brief consideration. "We'll do it—for the business. And sex, of course. But no kids. Those are my terms."

"No problem," Spence had agreed promptly. Those were his terms, too.

So here they were now—all of them, except Sadie.

Where the hell was she?

"So, are we ready?" Tom said briskly.

"Sure. Why not?"

Tom smiled. "I'll get Dena."

The clerk went to get the judge. Tom reappeared moments later with Dena, still carrying her briefcase. Spence put his suit coat back on and straightened his tie.

The door opened and the judge swept in. "I'm in recess," he announced. "Not much time." He glanced at Spence and Dena. "You're the couple? Come up here."

Spence took Dena's arm and went to stand in front of the judge, who cleared his throat and began to speak rapidly in a monotone. It was all legalese. Mumbo-jumbo. Not real estate law so Spence didn't understand any of it. It didn't matter. What mattered was saying "I do," at the right moment. And finding Sadie.

Suddenly he heard a door squeaking open behind them. His head whipped around.

Sadie!

But hardly the calm, centered, settled Sadie he'd been expecting. This Sadie's hair was windblown, her eyes bloodshot with dark circles beneath. Her skin was so pale that her normally golden freckles seemed to have been splashed across her cheeks by an impressionist run amok. And the look she gave him was of a deer caught in the headlights of a semi. A deer clutching a red leather portfolio against her chest.

"Don't just stand there, young woman!" the judge barked. "Sit down! I don't have all day."

"I need to—"

"Shut the door and sit!"

Sadie shut the door and sat.

Clearing his throat, the judge began again. More legalese. Something about the power vested in him by the state of New York. Blah, blah, blah. Behind him Spence heard someone— Sadie?—fidget in her chair.

"…must ascertain if there are any legal impediments or reasons why this marriage should not take place. Any objections?" Then without pausing, the judge continued, "No. So we'll move on then and—"

"Yes." It was Sadie.

Spence jerked around to stare at her. So did Dena and Tom.

"You object, young woman?" the judge demanded.

"I, um, yes."

The judge's brows drew down. "On what grounds may I ask?"

What the hell was she playing at? Spence scowled furiously at her.

Sadie shot one quick unreadable glance at him, then turned her gaze back to the judge again. "He's already married. To me."

## CHAPTER TWO

"WHAT!" Spence stared at her.

The judge's jaw sagged, Tom Wilson's eyes bugged, Dena's mouth flew open, and Sadie understood perfectly. She'd done all of the above.

Now she wet her lips and made a faint and fairly unsuccessful attempt to smile. "I'm afraid it's true," she said apologetically to the judge and Tom and Dena. But by the time her gaze reached Spence, she hoped there was no apology left in it at all.

"What are you talking about? That was years ago! The divorce papers—"

"We need to talk about that," Sadie said. And she hoped they had reached the point in their years-long relationship where non-verbal communication was a no-brainer.

"Damned right we do," Spence said. He shot a quick glance at Dena—also apologetic, Sadie noted—and one that seemed to say, "you just can't get good help these days," to the judge and Tom. And then he stalked over and took her arm none too gently. "Come on."

"Don't be long. I've got a plane to catch," Tom called after them.

Spence didn't reply. He hustled her out of the room and into the hallway, looked around at the various people in the corridor and opened the door to a room across the way. "In here." He kicked the door shut behind them, then spun her around to face him. "What the hell do you think you're doing?"

"Trying to stop you committing bigamy," she suggested.

"Don't be ridiculous. That was hardly a marriage we had and—"

"It was quite legal in the state of Nevada."

"And I filed for divorce the next day."

"Correction," Sadie said, "you called a divorce lawyer and told him to handle it."

"Which he did! I got the papers!"

"You got an envelope," Sadie corrected him. "You didn't open it." Which was pretty much Spence all over. Delegate and assume it would be done.

Too bad he hadn't delegated arranging their divorce to *her!*

Spence's jaw tightened. "I didn't want to look at them," he growled. "Would you?"

"No." She had to admit she wouldn't have wanted to see their folly in black-and-white, either. It had been far too painful in those days. "But I would have made sure it was done."

He shook his head. "So what was that?" He frowned as she withdrew the envelope from her portfolio. It was a bright-red portfolio, one he had bought her after she'd complained that she couldn't find things in her office if he came in and dumped papers on them.

"Put them in here," he'd said, brandishing the shocking-red leather case. "You won't mislay them, then."

Sadie forbore telling him she never mislaid anything, he just covered things up. Instead she'd thanked him—and made good use of it. Now she took the papers out of the envelope and showed them to him. The first one was the cover letter thanking him for contacting them and telling him they would be happy to handle the case if he would simply fill in the forms enclosed and create a Nevada residence which he needed to maintain for six weeks before filing. Another six weeks after, and if the divorce was uncontested, it would be finalized.

"No problem," the letter had concluded. "We are specialists at correcting such mistakes and we will file your papers as soon as you verify your Nevada address and fill in the necessary forms."

Spence stared at them. He flipped through them. Read them once—and then again. And then he lifted his gaze. He looked furious. "Bloody hell." He slammed the papers down on the desk and spun away, prowling the room. "They could have called! Did they think I'd changed my mind?"

"That is apparently exactly what they thought," Sadie told him. "I rang them this morning."

It had been too late last night by the time she'd gone to the bank and searched for the papers he wanted. She'd found his birth certificate right away. But the divorce papers weren't there. In desperation she'd opened the only thing she thought they could be in—the unopened envelope from a Las Vegas law firm. And when she'd read the letter, she'd stood there stunned, realizing that Spence had never read it, hadn't even bothered to open it.

And then, she, too, had thought that surely he must have had some other contact with them.

"I called the courthouse to check, when I didn't find the papers. They said there was no divorce on file. By then it was too late to call the lawyer. So I did it this morning on my layover." That had been another disaster—a plane with mechanical problems that had landed for an unscheduled maintenance stop in Detroit. But at least she'd been able to confirm her worst suspicion.

"They checked their records. They had nothing beyond a note of your initial phone message. They said it happens more often than you would think," she added, "people changing their minds."

Spence just stared at her.

Sadie shrugged. "So, it appears we are still married."

The notion had had her brain buzzing all night. *Married?* She was still *married?* To *Spence?*

"Bloody hell," Spence said again, then raked a hand through his hair so it stood up in dark spikes all over his head.

Good thing she hadn't expected him to be thrilled. "Sorry," she said with some asperity. "I realize it upsets your plans."

"Damned right it does." He ground his teeth, then sighed. "Not your fault," he muttered grudgingly. He slanted her a glance. "You would have seen it was done."

"Yes," Sadie agreed.

They stared at each other. In his gaze Sadie could see he knew it was true.

"But I didn't want to put you to the trouble," he muttered. "It was my screwup. My mistake."

"I'd say we both made a mistake," Sadie replied. She, after all, had been idiot enough to agree.

There was a light knock on the door. Before either of them could say, "Come in," it opened and Tom poked his head around the door. "Sorted?" he asked Spence.

Spence shook his head. "We have a small…hang-up."

"How small?"

"Not very," Spence said grimly.

Tom's eyes widened. He looked at Sadie. "You're still married to her?" His astonishment—and disapproval—were obvious.

"So it seems. Just go to your meeting, Tom. I'll talk to Dena. We'll sort things out."

"But the wedding—"

"Is off. For now."

"But what about the island resort project?" asked Tom. "What about Carstairs? Leonie? What will Isogawa say?"

Sadie frowned at these references to the people she had just lined up to attend the meeting at Nanumi. What did they have to do with his marriage?

"What *about* the island resort project?" she asked. "What about Mr. Isogawa and Richard and Leonie Carstairs?"

"Why? What do you know about Leonie?" Spence demanded, fixing her with a hard look, as if he thought she'd been prying.

"Nothing," Sadie said. "Well, nothing much," she corrected herself. "She just seems a little insecure."

Both men stared at her.

"She keeps ringing me," Sadie said, "very worried that Richard will come to the meeting without her. I assured her he wouldn't, that Mr. Isogawa wants couples, that she'd be very welcome."

Spence's jaw tightened. Tom gave him an arch look that Sadie didn't understand.

"She would be," Sadie said. "Mr. Isogawa said wives were welcome. Encouraged, in fact." Was that why he'd wanted to bring Dena? But she couldn't ask—not in front of Dena's father. Even though Tom Wilson was as much of a businessman as Spence, it didn't seem like the thing to say.

"Right," Spence muttered. "It's just—never mind." He broke off and turned to the other man. "Just go on now, Tom. I'll be in touch."

"What about Dena? What are you going to tell my daughter?"

"I'll explain."

Tom just looked at him doubtfully, then shook his head. "If this blows up—"

"It won't."

Tom looked doubtful. But Sadie knew that Spence didn't do doubt. He stared Tom down until finally the latter pressed his lips together and gave a curt nod. "Fine. Handle it, then." And he was gone.

In his absence there was silence.

"We can get a divorce," Sadie felt compelled to say.

"Not in the next half hour."

"Well, no. But—"

"Forget it. For now," Spence amended. "I need to talk to Dena."

"I'll come with you."

"No, you won't."

"But—"

"No. This is between me and Dena. Our wedding may have been business, but she's my friend. And I owe her the courtesy of telling her what's going on personally. Privately."

"I just thought it might help if—"

"It wouldn't," he said harshly. "And I think you've helped enough for one day, Sadie. Just wait here. I'll be back." And he stalked out the door, banging it shut behind him.

She'd helped? As if this were all her fault?

Well, it wasn't. But some of it was. She needed to make a break. She would see about the divorce this time—and get it done properly. And then she would leave. Find a new job. Sell Spence back his percentage of the company. That would certainly make it permanent. She needed to stop waffling around, trying to make a life for herself while all the while she hovered on the edge of Spence's.

Enough Spence.

There would be a time, as Danny had said, when she would finally need to grow up and take control of her life—to *get* a life.

"And the time," she told herself firmly, "is now."

Dena didn't even look up when he came into the judge's chambers. She was reading some legal documents, completely absorbed. No one looking at her would ever have imagined she'd just had her wedding cut out from under her. As always, she was immaculate and composed. Not a blond hair was out of place. The lipstick she'd put on right before the ceremony still looked fresh, not gnawed.

Spence, on the other hand, felt as if he'd been dragged through the New York subway system backward and shot point-blank with a stun gun.

He was *married?* To *Sadie?* Had been married to her for the past four years?

Dena finished the page she was reading before she looked up at him expectantly and smiled her own cool, self-possessed smile. "Well," she said. "That was interesting."

He knew she didn't mean the papers in her hand. His jaw clenched and he had to make an effort to relax it. "Yes." But he couldn't keep from biting the word off, and apparently that was the only clue she needed.

"So, it's true?"

"Apparently." He explained haltingly. Not about Emily. He just said he and Sadie had been in Vegas. They'd got married. In the morning he'd realized it was a mistake. It was hard not to sound like an idiot. So he tried not to go into too much detail, just hoped that sane matter-of-fact words came out of his mouth until finally there seemed nothing more to say.

"Obviously, I should have read the damn letter. I assumed it was a done deal."

Dena let the silence gather for a few seconds before she said mildly, "That'll teach you," as if it were only a minor folly, not a full-scale disaster.

"It will," Spence said. His jaw locked tight. His head pounded.

"So, okay. As long as we know," Dena said, shifting gears. "I just don't want to see the deal fall through."

He stared at her, surprised that she was taking it so calmly. But then, he reminded himself, it was just business to her. Business deals collapsed all the time. And in any case, it was his problem, not hers.

"It'll be fine," she said. "You just take Sadie instead."

"What?" Spence stared at her.

Dena gave him a completely guileless look. "Well, she's your wife."

"Yes, but—" He couldn't finish. It would never be "just business" with Sadie. It couldn't be.

Sadie was businesslike, but she didn't see the world the same way he did.

"Well, what else are you going to do?" Dena said reasonably. "It won't look very good to Isogawa and his 'happy family' theme if you show up having just filed for divorce."

"No." He was trying to think. He was usually so damn good at it. Solutions were always at his fingertips, always on the tip of his tongue.

"You've worked too long, too hard on this resort. It's a once-in-a-lifetime opportunity," Dena reminded him.

"I know that," Spence said tersely. There were bigger in-vestors in the deal—Richard Carstairs for one—but Spence was the one who had made the initial contact with Mr. Isogawa. He was the one whose reputation was riding on it. Richard and John and Steve, the other three investors, were old hands at this sort of deal. This was Spence's first resort, first foray into business in the Pacific. He had more stake in it than anyone.

"So you have to make it work," Dena said simply. "And if once upon a time you couldn't keep your jeans zipped and Sadie made you make an honest woman of her, so be it. At least you're married. That's what's important."

Spence barely heard the last part. His brain had ground to a screeching halt at the words *You couldn't keep your jeans zipped.*

All of a sudden memories of a naked Sadie Morrissey were alive and well and rising like a phoenix in his brain.

He pressed his palms to the sides of his head, feeling as if it were going to explode.

"What's wrong?" Dena asked. "Headache? I wouldn't be surprised."

"No. Yeah. I need to think."

"Yes. And thank your lucky stars Sadie showed up."

Spence blinked, then goggled at her. "Lucky?"

"Well, it certainly wouldn't have done any good if you'd turned out to be a bigamist, would it?" Dena said impatiently. "With Isogawa being Mr. Propriety. Let's face it, if he'd discovered you were married to two women, the deal would be in the trash faster than you can say 'bigamist.' And Leonie would have been thrilled. She might have steered clear of you seeing one wedding ring on your finger. But I'm pretty sure two would have allowed her to put her scruples aside." She smiled.

Spence didn't. He was usually pretty good at taking whatever life dealt him and making the best of it.

But he couldn't see how he was going to make the best of being married to Sadie Morrissey.

Dena kept smiling. "You'll be fine. You wanted a wife, didn't you?"

"Yes, but—"

"You've got one. And she knows your business. You'll be fine. Just do what you do best."

He looked at her blankly.

She stood up, put the papers away, then closed her briefcase and patted him on the cheek as she turned toward the door. "Improvise."

Sadie could hear Spence bellowing her name up and down the hallway.

It was tempting to stay right where she was—in the ladies' room. But that would be cowardly, and she'd faced the worst already, hadn't she?

Of course she had. Now they just had to sit down and work out how to get divorced for real. She could do that. And Spence would *want* to do it. He had probably already filled out the paperwork.

"So get on with it," she told herself. "Nothing's changed."

Not really. It wasn't like they were a real couple who had

loved each other. She had loved him—still did, she supposed. But that had been foolish. She should have tried harder to get over it. She should have left years ago.

Well, better late than never, she thought. That was what Gran always said. She sent a prayer winging heavenward, a little divine help—or a little encouragement from Gran—wouldn't come amiss right now.

*Please*, she added as she pushed open the door and stepped out.

Spence was standing with his back to her, punching his cell phone furiously. Then he raised it to his ear and waited. Tapped his foot. Ran his fingers through his hair.

Sadie approached quietly, knowing better than to interrupt his call.

He glared at the phone, punched another button furiously, then snarled into it, "Damn it, Sadie. Where the hell are you?"

"Right behind you."

He whipped around. He glared at her, then at the phone. Then he flicked it shut and stuck it in his pocket. "Where have you been?"

"I went to the ladies' room while you were talking to Dena. Is she all right?"

"Who? Dena?"

"Of course. Was she very upset?"

"Not a bit." He shrugged as if it didn't matter, but there was an edge of annoyance in his voice. Had their proposed marriage, perhaps, not been totally business, after all?

Sadie didn't want to think about that. She'd always liked Dena, and among the many reasons she'd hated having to announce their marriage so bluntly today was the worry that, despite Spence's assurances to the contrary, Dena might really be hurt. "I'm so glad. I wouldn't have wanted to hurt her."

"Hurt her? What about me?" Spence said indignantly.

"It was just business for you!"

"My business could be hurt."

"How?" Sadie cocked her head. "Were you counting on maybe a Caribbean island from Daddy for a wedding present?"

"No, I damned well was not!" His indignation was very real now, and Sadie felt small for having made the remark.

In his entire life Spencer Tyack had never got anything the easy way. No one had given him anything. And it had always been a matter of honor for him to earn everything he had.

"Sorry," Sadie said now and meant it. "I'm sure it's…difficult. And for all that it was business," she added quickly, "you must care. We'll get a divorce as quick as we can and then you can marry Dena."

"No," he said flatly. "I can't."

"Why not?"

"Because I'd have to divorce you first."

"Well, yes, but—"

"And Isogawa's not going to like that. He's as old school as they come. He believes in the sanctity and stability of marriage."

"So do I," Sadie muttered. "Appearances to the contrary."

"You shouldn't have said yes, then," Spence snapped. He looked as if he'd like to hit something.

No, she certainly shouldn't have. But it was too late for self-recrimination now. "Fine," she said. "If you don't want to get a divorce right now, we won't. We can wait until you're back. Until your deal is done. Isogawa doesn't have to know. After all, until less than an hour ago, *you* didn't know! Let him go on thinking you're single."

"Can't."

"Oh, for God's sake, stop being cryptic! Why can't you?" Sadie scowled, perplexed by his stubbornness. "I've talked to him. Yes, he's very into marriage and family. But he doesn't think the whole world has to march two by two." She knew enough of Mr. Isogawa's views to be sure of that.

But Spence just shook his head. "No. Look, I—" He started

as if he were going to explain further, but then looked around at the people wandering up and down the corridor, some of them giving the two of them speculative looks, and instead abruptly he took her by the arm.

"I don't want to discuss this here," he said. "Let's get a cab."

"A cab? And go where?"

"To my place." And as he spoke he steered her toward the elevator.

His place? Sadie knew, of course, that he had a pied-à-terre on the Upper West Side. In the past two years, he'd spent so much time in New York that he kept a studio apartment here as well as one in the Caribbean, one in Greece and one in Spain. Sadie had seen pictures of them all, but she'd never been to any in person. In fact she could count on the fingers of a single hand the occasions that she had ever been in Spence's house in Butte!

For all that she had grown up with him running in and out of her house with Danny, the reverse had never been true.

When they'd been children, life in Spence's house—with his bitter mother and unreliable father—had been unpredictable at best. She knew he hadn't wanted anyone to witness it.

But even now that he was master of his own destiny and domain, and lived in one of the old Copper King mansions he'd restored himself in uptown Butte, Spence kept his home separate from the rest of his life.

"It's the way he is." Danny had shrugged with complete indifference when Sadie had asked him about it. "Besides," he'd added with patently bossy big-brotherliness, "you don't want to go there."

Which hadn't been true at all.

Being seriously infatuated with him, Sadie had wanted to very much. But in all the years she had known him and worked for him, Spence had remained a good employer—and a good friend—but a man with definite boundaries.

"You're taking me to your place?" she echoed now, surprised.

"Where the hell else," he said gruffly, "since you're my wife."

He could snarl the words "my wife" easily enough. It was less easy to think about the reality of it. In fact, it was damn near impossible.

Spence sat in the backseat of the taxi carrying them to his Upper West Side apartment and studied Sadie out of the corner of his eye.

His "wife" was sitting in the backseat, too, but as far away from him as she could get, as if she were trying to avoid contamination. She wasn't looking his way, either. Instead she was deliberately staring out the window, feigning complete absorption in the traffic as they hurtled, then crawled, up Eighth Avenue.

That wasn't like Sadie. Sadie usually paid no attention at all to where they were. She was normally focused on him, waving papers in his face, pointing at fine print, rattling on a mile a minute.

Now she wasn't saying a word.

Of course, he knew she wasn't happy, either. This situation—this mess!—was no more normal for her than it was for him, though she'd had a few hours longer to get used to it.

What was she thinking? Usually he had no trouble figuring that out. Usually she was telling him without his having to ask. It was what they did—discuss, argue, debate, clarify.

But now she was as still and silent as a stone. He wished he could see inside her head. Then again, all things considered, it was probably better he couldn't.

This was all his fault. No doubt about it.

He accepted that. Spence was never one to deny responsibility. He should have made sure it was taken care of. Should have faced his demons and his momentary foolishness and made sure it didn't come back to haunt them.

But he hadn't. His mistake.

So it was his job to fix it. Properly. Completely. Unflinchingly.

And he would.

But first he had to deal with the resort. They'd worked too long and too hard on it—both he and Sadie—to risk letting the deal fall apart now. He wasn't sure exactly how to handle it, though. His intuition, normally brilliant—if he did say so himself—seemed to have completely deserted him.

Dena's notion—that he take Sadie—was impossible. She would never agree. And he understood completely. But he couldn't think of any other options.

Sadie would. He was sure. That was the joy of having her working with him. They battled things out. He proposed and she contradicted. Usually he was right, or close enough. But sometimes she had a better idea.

She'd better have a better idea today.

He started to say something, then shut his mouth again. He didn't want to start the argument in the taxi. So he would wait. He would get her back to his place and then he would tell her what they needed to do.

And she could argue him around to something else. Yeah. He smiled at the thought, the first smile he'd managed since Sadie had dropped her bombshell an hour ago. Then he shifted against the back of the seat, flexed his rigid shoulders, took a deep breath and felt considerably better.

They finished the cab ride in silence. When they reached his apartment, Spence paid off the driver and gestured her ahead of him up the stairs to the brownstone in which he owned a floor-through apartment.

He unlocked the door and said, "Third floor," and waited until she started up the steps, then fell in behind her.

"You don't have to bring up my case," Sadie said.

Spence didn't bother to reply. He wasn't getting them sidetracked on another argument. Instead he just jerked his head toward the stairs. Sadie scowled at him, but began to climb.

He went up after her—and found himself at eye level with a curvy female backside that sparked a memory. He tried to resist it.

But his eyes were glued to the view—and the word *wife* was suddenly pounding in his brain. Not just *wife* but *my wife*.

He hadn't seen Sadie as a woman in years—hadn't let himself even consider her that way, except obviously for one very intense night. And now, damn it, was not the time to start!

So he stopped where he was and let her get half a dozen steps ahead of him.

Sadie glanced back over her shoulder. "Something wrong? I told you not to lug it up. It's heavy."

Did she think he couldn't carry her damned suitcase? "It's fine," Spence snapped. "I've got…something in my shoe. Go on."

Sadie raised skeptical eyebrows, but shrugged, then turned and kept on going. Spence waited until she had reached the next landing and had disappeared from view. Only then, when he was no longer treated to a vision of her backside, did he continue up after her.

Wordlessly he unlocked the door and pushed it open, then waved her in ahead of him.

"Not going to carry me over the threshold?"

He stared at her. "Do you want me to?"

"No! Of course not." She scurried into the apartment. "I'm just being—" she grimaced, then gave him a quick self-conscious smile and a little awkward shrug "—inappropriate."

Spence followed her in and kicked the door shut behind him. "Not as inappropriate as you might think," he said, dropping her suitcase on the floor.

Sadie frowned. "What do you mean?"

"I mean that, as apparently we're still married, on Friday you're coming to Nanumi with me—as my wife."

# CHAPTER THREE

GO WITH him to Nanumi? As his wife?

Sadie stared.

"Why not?" Spence persisted. He began pacing around the room. It was a small room, relatively impersonal, exactly the sort of anonymous place she'd expected he would have. "We're married. You said so."

"Yes. I did. But—" She looked at him more closely. Was he suggesting…? Surely he couldn't mean…?

Her heart seemed to kicked over in her chest as her brain entertained a possibility that had never occurred to her—that Spence would want to continue their "marriage", that he saw her as a woman at last.

He stopped dead square in front of her. "For better or worse, Sadie," he said, as if she needed the reminder, "right now you're my wife. And Isogawa is all about family. You said so yourself. He wants couples at the resort. We're a couple. It makes perfect sense. Right?" He was grinning now, looming over her, daring her to contradict him, to argue.

And Sadie suddenly knew it had nothing to do with wanting to stay married to her at all. He wanted to argue.

This was Spence in confrontation mode. Spence looking for a fight. A challenge. It was the way he worked.

Spence's gut-level instinct picked up and proposed things continually. Sometimes, Sadie thought, his brain worked faster than the speed of light.

It was the way he began each deal. He would spot a possibility, then—using some sort of sixth sense, some intuition that she could never quite catch up with—he would analyze whatever he was considering at warp speed, consider the options, calculate the odds, then fling some sort of outrageous idea at her.

Like now.

Usually, of course, he didn't do it with the edgy fierceness she heard in his voice now, despite the grin. But even with the granite-jawed, I-eat-sharks-for-breakfast glitter in his eyes, the look on his face was decidedly familiar.

He was daring her to confront him, to stop him. He didn't expect her to agree. He was, to put it bluntly, looking for a fight.

And, she was quite sure now, hoping she would provide him with half a dozen other options. It was the way they worked. One of Spence's tests of his intuition, Sadie had realized long ago, was to spring a decision on her, then wait for her to argue.

And Sadie always embraced the opportunity. She loved arguing with Spence. It excited her, exhilarated her. It made her feel as if she were a vital part of his decision-making process, a real member of the team, because Spence really did listen to what she said. And he was, if she was convincing enough, quite willing to revise and reconsider as a result of their battles.

Now she just smiled and said, "All right."

The sudden silence in the room was deafening. Spence stared at her, eyes wide. "*All right?* What the hell do you mean, *all right?*"

"I mean, I agree."

His dark brows drew down, and he scowled furiously at her as he rubbed a hand against the back of his neck. "I wasn't asking you," he said sharply. "I was telling you."

"Yes. And I agreed with you."

"You do? I mean, of course you do," he blustered. "It only makes sense."

Sadie nodded. "Yes."

"You think so?" He was eyeing her narrowly.

What made real sense, Sadie thought, was for her to turn tail and run for the hills. She wasn't used to Spence looking at her like that—with that intense gleam in his eye. But she'd backed down, gentled, calmed and gone on far too much in the past. It was time to stop, for her own sake as much as his.

"Yes," she said firmly, "I do."

"Why?"

She shook her head. She wasn't telling him that. She wasn't even sure she had worked out all the reasons yet herself. But she knew what she had to say.

"It's just business."

He blinked. Then nodded. "Yes."

"So, no big deal." Hahaha, her brain chortled at her naiveté, but she ignored it. "I'll go to Fiji with you. And after, I'll resign. I'll come home. We'll get the divorce. A real one this time—with paperwork completed. All i's dotted and t's crossed. Official. Legal. And then I'll get out of your life."

"Don't be ridiculous. I mean, the divorce, yeah. Sure. Fine. But you don't have to get out of my life!"

"Yes, I do."

Dear God, yes, she absolutely did. She certainly did not want go through this again, get *another* divorce from Spencer Tyack and then go back to being his office manager. She'd been foolish enough and self-deluded enough to try it once. And to a degree it had worked. But she hadn't ever got over him. And if she stayed she never would.

She looked up and met his eyes with as steady a gaze as she could manage.

"I'll be your wife for the week. And then I'm gone."

Spence's jaw tightened. He glared at her for a long time, then shrugged. "Suit yourself."

"I am."

It would, she decided, serve her right. She would go to Nanumi with him as his real, honest-to-God wife for a week. And she would let herself act like a wife. She would have a week of the dream that she'd always wanted. And then she would leave. There would undoubtedly be a bit of shock value in it. Maybe it would wake her up sufficiently to force her to get on with her life.

Spence didn't look completely convinced. And she wasn't going to stand there and argue with him about it now.

"I'm filthy," she said. "And I've been up all night. I need a shower. May I take one?"

He looked startled. His scowl deepened. "A shower? Here?"

"You have a bath, I think. Indoor plumbing? I know I've never been to New York before, but surely—"

"Yes, damn it." He jerked his head toward a door beyond the small kitchen area. "Go for it."

"Thank you." She shrugged, glad now to have her suitcase and fresh clothes at hand. "I've been on the road since yesterday evening."

"Then why were you late?"

"Plane trouble. We had a wiring problem. Spent five hours on the ground in Detroit. Just think, if the plane had gone down, you would have been a widower and all would have been well." She smiled up at him brightly from where she knelt and opened her suitcase.

"Don't be an ass!" Spence snapped.

She was trying hard not to be. She pulled out a pair of linen slacks, a scoop-necked T-shirt and some clean underthings, and got a grip on her wayward emotions. Only when she was sure she was in control again, did she stand up to face him.

He was standing in her way, staring at her. "Do you mind?"

she pressed when he didn't move. "A shower?" His gaze seemed fixed on the clothes in her arms and she wasn't even sure he'd heard her. "Spence?"

He gave a quick shake of his head. "No, of course I don't mind." And as if he suddenly realized why she wasn't moving—because she couldn't—he moved out of her way.

"Thank you." She slipped past him. "I'll hurry."

"Take your time," he muttered. "I'll get…us some food."

"Sounds good," she lied, certain she couldn't eat a thing. She went into the bathroom, then turned and gave him one last bright determined smile.

He was still staring at her when she closed the door.

Sadie wore silk underwear!

Those were peach-colored silk panties she had in her hands, not to mention a lacy scrap of a bra that looked as if it had come right out of some Hollywood lingerie catalog. Not the sort of underwear she could have bought in Butte!

Spence's mind went straight from the sight of those lacy garments in Sadie's arms to a vision of her wearing them. He sucked air.

The unexpectedness of it had him gasping. Not just the unexpectedness of the peach-colored lace and silk—which was astonishing enough given Sadie's sensible matter-of-fact demeanor—but even more his brain's almost immediate and very vivid notion of what she would look like wearing it.

Somewhere back in Sadie's teenage years, Spence had begun to notice that Danny's kid sister wasn't built like a stick insect anymore. He'd even found himself, more than once, lying in bed thinking about her curvy body and her long long legs and imagining what they'd be like bare and wrapped around his waist.

One night he'd actually made a remark about her feminine

attributes in front of Danny—and found himself knocked off the bar stool.

"Don't even think it," Danny had warned, standing over him, breathing hard. "Sadie's the marrying kind. Or she will be when she's old enough. She's a good girl and she's going to stay that way. So you keep your eyes—and hands—off and your zipper welded shut. She's not for the likes of you! Got it?"

Spence had got it.

And even in his hormone-driven lust-filled early twenties he had known that Danny was right. Sadie *was* a great girl. A good girl. And when she grew up, she would deserve a good man. The best.

God knew that wasn't him. With his alcoholic, here-today gone-tomorrow father and his bitter hard mother, not to mention the chip he carried on his shoulder that was the size of all the rock they'd ever taken out of the Berkeley Pit, Spencer Tyack was no man for a girl like Sadie Morrissey.

So he had kept his hands to himself—and his zipper, around Sadie at least, firmly zipped. But he had still known she was gorgeous, just as Danny undoubtedly knew it—though Spence didn't think Sadie herself ever had a clue.

She had certainly never flaunted her assets. And at an age when lots of teenage girls were determined to practice their feminine wiles on susceptible males, Sadie had never done that.

If anything, as she'd grown older and more beautiful, she'd got quieter and less forthcoming. As a kid she had always been easy to talk to as she'd tagged around after him and Danny. But by sixteen or so, that had ended. And far from flirting with him whenever he came around with Danny, she became almost distant and remote.

"What'd you do to her?" Danny demanded, seeing her reticence himself and deciding it was because of something Spence had done.

"Nothing! Not a damn thing!"

He'd have spilled blood—even his own—to prove it to Danny. But his protests apparently were enough.

"See that you don't," Danny had said.

"Count on it," Spence had replied. He just figured she didn't like him anymore. As a kid, she'd tagged after him, but as a young woman, she'd evidently seen him for who he was and decided he wasn't worth bothering with.

Better that way, Spence had thought. Better that he not think about Sadie anymore at all.

But then one winter afternoon when he had been in the Morrissey kitchen talking to Danny and tearing his hair over the state of his office and his paperwork, Sadie had walked though, listened a minute, then said, "That's silly. Just file it."

"I would if I could figure out a system!" It wasn't the easiest thing in the world.

"I could figure out a system," Sadie had said blithely, as if she held the answers to all the mysteries in the world.

Spence had snorted. "I doubt it."

"I'll prove it," Sadie had countered.

And the next day she'd shown up at his truck. "So where do you work?"

He'd jerked his head toward the camper top on the truck. "Here."

She'd blinked, then goggled at him, but then shrugged and said. "Fine. Show me."

"You don't want to mess with it," he'd said because he certainly didn't want her poking her nose in his living quarters.

"Afraid I'll be able to do something you can't?" Sadie had challenged.

And of course then he'd had to let her in. So he'd opened the hatch to show her the heaps of paper—notes and scraps and abstracts and legal documents—all tossed around on top of the sleeping bag and mattress he slept on and thrust under the platform where he kept his gear. "Still think you can file it?" He'd given her a lazy smug grin.

"Out of my way." And Sadie had pushed him aside, then clambered in, making him swallow hard as he'd got a good full look at her pert curvy backside disappearing into the back of his truck.

Then she'd turned and looked back at him. "Are you going to help?"

"If I were I'd do it myself," he told her honestly.

She'd nodded. "Then go away."

He had. He'd gone out for a run, determined to wear himself out—and get all thoughts of Sadie's bottom out of his head.

When he came back, exhausted, that evening, he felt more in control of his hormones. Sadie didn't look any more in control of the mess in the back of his truck than she had before he'd left. The paper was still all over the place—in different piles now, but not better piles.

He'd been relieved. And since the next day he had been going to L.A. to a business seminar, he'd said, "Nice try. See. It isn't as easy as you thought. Just forget it."

But Sadie hadn't. She'd shaken her head and held out her hand. "I'm not finished. Give me the key to your truck."

"You're insane." But he'd handed her the key.

When he came back a week later, the mess was gone, the camper was bare except for the platform, mattress, sleeping bag and four filing boxes. He felt a moment's panic.

"Where—?"

"There." Sadie pointed at the filing boxes. "Everything is sorted and in its very own place. I can show you how it works," Sadie had offered.

But the one thing Spence had learned at the seminar was the value of delegating. He didn't want to know how it worked. He just wanted Sadie there making it work. He'd hired her on the spot.

As his employee, Sadie had stopped being quiet.

She would come every afternoon after school to his truck and sit in the cab, making him go over papers with her, filing them, discussing them, arguing about them. Sadie, for all that she'd been only sixteen, had definite opinions. She'd asked questions about things he'd never even considered.

It wasn't long before he'd realized she wasn't just a genius at organization, she had a good instinctive mind for business—one that complemented his—and he was damned glad she was working for him.

She was gorgeous. She was fun to have around. And she'd become an incredible asset to his work.

The second two he could deal with easily. The first was a problem. Or it would have been if he hadn't learned long ago how to compartmentalize his life.

Dealing with his parents had taught him that. And just as he'd built a "family box" around his parents to keep their anger and bitterness and failure out of his life in order to survive, so he isolated Sadie.

He built a mental "employee box" around her. And then every time he'd found himself even remotely thinking about the physical Sadie Morrissey, he'd slammed the lid on that box.

Until the night Emily had jilted him and the lid had come off. At his rawest, lowest point, Sadie had been there. She'd been gentle, warm, caring, supportive.

Loving.

A word—an experience, let's face it—that Spence knew damn little about. And he'd given in to it. He'd needed her warmth, her care, her love that night. He'd needed Sadie. And he hadn't been able to resist that need.

And so he'd asked her to marry him. Asked? How about

coerced? That was closer to the truth. He'd resisted temptation for years. Had resisted Sadie for years. But that one brief night he had succumbed.

He'd married her. He'd made love to her. He'd—God help him!—taken her innocence that night. At the time he'd been shocked and, perversely, delighted. And of course, faced with her beautiful sleeping face in the morning, he'd known what he'd done was wrong.

Then he'd done what he thought was right—divorced her. Or tried to. Even that, it seemed, he'd done badly. The only thing he'd done right was to stuff Sadie and all his intimate memories of her back into that box and slam the lid on. In the past four years he had never once let himself contemplate her big green eyes or her lovely golden freckled skin or her long long legs or supremely kissable mouth. He had resisted all thoughts of the night he had made love to Sadie Morrisscy.

And he sure as hell wasn't going to get through a week of sharing a *bure* at Nanumi with her if he was fixating already on what sort of underwear she wore!

The trouble was, now that he knew—and knew that he was still married to her, knew that legally at least he had a right to her—he couldn't get the vision out of his mind. And he couldn't get his mind out of the bathroom where it had gone to watch her strip off her clothes and get in the shower!

The lid hadn't simply come off, the whole damn box he'd put Sadie Morrissey in for years and years—minus that one fateful night—had crumbled to smithereens.

And his imagination, unleashed, was a fearful thing.

"Get a grip," he muttered furiously to himself. "It's Sadie, for God's sake. It's business."

But his mind—and even more important, his body—were busy reminding him that Sadie wasn't only business; she was his wife.

"For a week," he reminded himself. "Only a week."

Or until the contracts were signed and the resort was a done deal. A week. He could build another damn box and jam her back in for a week.

His body begged to differ.

"Hell!" He stalked over to the door of the bathroom and pounded on it. "Sadie!"

The water shut off. "What?"

He squeezed his eyes shut as if that would keep him from visualizing her standing naked and wet in his shower. "What do you want for dinner?"

What if she said, "You?"

Of course she didn't. "Surprise me," she called back through the closed door.

Spence tried not to think about surprises.

And Sadie must have had second thoughts because she suddenly called, "Just get something they don't have in Butte." And then the water went back on again full force.

Spence stood there drawing in ragged breaths and trying to drag his wits back from wherever they had scattered. "Right. Focus," he commanded himself. "Something they don't have in Butte." Shouldn't be hard.

And certainly a lot simpler than trying again not to think about Sadie Morrissey naked in his shower.

Sadie came out of the bathroom, showered and dressed in clean clothes, feeling better—and warier at the same time.

While she'd been showering, she'd tried to pull herself together, to come to terms with what he'd asked her to do, to convince herself that she could do it without making a fool of herself. She knew she had to or die trying.

At the same time she wasn't even sure how she was going to get through dinner.

Spence was in the kitchen setting out containers on the table.

"It's Burmese," he said. He didn't even look her way, just unloaded white cardboard containers of piping-hot food that made her mouth water, then turned to get plates out of the cupboard. He was moving with customary quick efficiency and he didn't sound angry any longer. Was that good?

"Smells wonderful." Sadie smiled, still a little uncertain.

Spence laid out silverware, then added chopsticks from one of the bags, then filled glasses with ice water and set them on the table.

"Do you want wine?" There was an unopened bottle on the countertop.

"No, thanks. I'd fall asleep." She was fresher than she had been, but still feeling the effects of the night on the plane and the stress of the past two days. "You go ahead."

He didn't open the bottle, however. He just nodded toward the chair closest to her. "Sit down. Dig in."

Sadie sat. "It *looks* wonderful, too."

"Usually is." He opened a container of rice and handed it to her. "I eat at this place whenever I'm in New York. There's beef satay and chicken curry and something with pork that I never remember the name of. Prawn salad and some kind of fritters. You won't get it in Butte." He was talking quickly and shoveling food onto his plate as he did. He still wasn't looking at her.

She dished up some of everything, then picked up her chopsticks. She took a careful breath, then let it out again. Things felt almost…normal. Like the business lunches she and Spence often shared. Only those were accompanied by sheaves of paper, contracts, diagrams, and nonstop talking.

This meal had no paper, no contracts, no diagrams and, right now, no talking. What it had was a big fat determinedly unacknowledged elephant in the room.

The "marriage" elephant. *Their* marriage elephant.

And how it was going to work. Clearly he saw this as a business effort. But ordinarily when they worked on a project and had agreed on what needed to be done, they sat down and strategized how to do it. They divided up the tasks. They worked out how to support each other. They each had their jobs, and they knew what to expect.

Sadie needed to know what to expect.

But Spence didn't tell her. He didn't say a word. Kept his mouth full or was busy chewing all the time. The whole meal passed in silence. They ate doggedly, determinedly. Until finally there was nothing else to eat. The cartons were empty. Their plates were clean.

And then, when she hoped he might finally speak, he jumped up and began clearing the table.

Sadie stood, too. "Let me help."

"No. It's all right. I'll do it. Kitchen's pretty small." And it was clear he didn't want her anywhere in it. "Coffee? Tea?" He had his back to her again, rinsing off plates in the sink. Since when had Spence become so determinedly domestic?

"Tea, then, please." The cup would give her something to hang on to when at last they came to grips with things. And coffee, she was afraid, would make her already-frayed nerves even more so.

"Okay. Go sit down. I'll get it."

She would have liked to offer to help with that, too. But Spence was already filling the kettle with water and it didn't take two to make tea. So Sadie crossed the room to where she could look out over the back gardens of the block of brownstones.

It was a clear spring evening, already gone dark. And even with the window closed, because it wasn't warm enough yet to leave them open, she could hear the sounds of the city, although muted a bit now. The trees were just coming into leaf. One neighbor's window box was filled with bobbing heads of something that she expected would, in daylight, turn out to be daffodils.

Her own daffodils growing against the wall behind her house

back in Butte weren't blooming yet. It was still too cold in Montana. But Montana in the winter felt warmer than this room.

All right. Enough. If he wouldn't bring it up, she would. She turned to where Spence was pouring out cups of tea. "You said it was business, marrying Dena. But you could have married Dena anytime. Why now? What's going on at Nanumi that you need a wife for?"

"You said it yourself. Isogawa wants couples."

"But he wouldn't expect you to marry just to please him. So what else?"

Spence scowled, and Sadie actually thought he wasn't going to answer. But finally, after a long moment, he said, "Leonie."

Sadie blinked. "Leonie? Carstairs?" She didn't follow. "Richard's wife? I don't understand."

Spence's scowl deepened, and something that might have been a tide of red seemed to creep up to his jaw. But he didn't speak as he carried a mug across the room and handed it to her wordlessly.

"Thanks." Sadie accepted it and took a sip, then asked, because she still didn't get it. "Why on earth would you marry Dena because of Richard Carstairs's wife?

"Oh, use your head!" Spence snapped. "Because she doesn't put much stock in being Richard's wife!"

"Doesn't…?" Sadie's voice trailed off. "What?" She considered the implications of what Spence was saying. "You mean… but she's so nice on the phone!"

A harsh breath hissed between Spence's teeth. "How the hell many times has she called you?"

"Three or four. She seems very…nervous. Like she's not sure she's welcome. Not wanting to get in the way."

"Yeah, right," Spence muttered. He hunched his shoulders, looking hunted.

"What's that mean?" Sadie asked. Mentally she ran through the conversations she'd had with Leonie Carstairs. The other woman had seemed perhaps a little overly bright and bubbly when they'd talked, but sometimes a little wistful, too. Richard was always so busy, she'd said. She never knew what she should do.

"She seemed very concerned about whether her husband would have time for her."

"Her husband?" Spence's tone was suspicious.

"Who else?"

He didn't answer, but the fierce red along his jawline and up into his face answered the question for her.

"*You?* You think she's after you?" Sadie gaped at Spence.

"I don't think!" he snarled, dark eyes flashing angrily.

Sadie's eyes widened as she considered the implications. "What's going on?" she finally asked, hoping that inviting him to simply spell it out would get the answers she was missing.

"Leonie Carstairs is a desperate, pushy little tart! A guy is single, she hits on him!"

"She hit…on you?"

"She did." The answer was flat.

"But she's married."

"How naive are you?"

"Oh." Sadie felt her cheeks warm. "Um, I see. But…isn't marrying Dena a little drastic just to get her to stop? Couldn't you just say no?"

"No, damn it, I couldn't!" Spence smacked his mug down on the counter with more force than was necessary, slopping tea everywhere. "I tried that," he added grimly.

Sadie tried not to look agog with interest, just matter-of-fact. But she couldn't help saying, "What happened?" with far more curiosity than she'd intended.

Spence scowled and raked a hand through his hair. "It's a mess. I've been doing business with Richard for years. Knew his first wife."

"Margaret. Yes, I remember her." While she'd never met either Margaret or Richard Carstairs, she'd enjoyed conversations with them during Spence's dealings with them. And she remembered well when Margaret died five years ago.

"They were perfect together. And then three years ago Richard met Leonie." Spence shook his head. "She's young. He's in his fifties. Hell, his kids are her age! But he wouldn't see reason. He wanted her, and he married her. And now—now it's a hell of a mess." Spence prowled the room like a trapped jungle cat, then flung himself into one of the chairs and looked up at her from beneath hooded lids.

Sadie waited, knowing there were times to prompt Spence and times not to. This was one when she needed to wait him out.

"Now that he's got her, he…doesn't pay a lot of attention to her. Frankly I think she scares him. She scares the hell out of me! She…flirts. To get his attention, I think. At least I thought. Now I don't know. After Barcelona…" He scowled and abruptly stopped talking.

Well, there were some things you couldn't just wait out.

"What about Barcelona?" Sadie demanded. She knew Spence had gone there last month for a meeting. She was the one who'd set it up. And she remembered now that Richard had been scheduled to be there, too. "Leonie was there?" She hadn't scheduled that.

"She was," Spence agreed. "Insisted on coming along, Richard said. But he couldn't take her to all his meetings. So one night she was on her own at the hotel. I didn't pay much attention. It wasn't anything to do with me. I was working. And then, that night, I played poker with some of the guys. Later, when I went back to my room—" he grimaced "—she was in my bed."

Sadie stared. *"In your bed?"*

"You heard me!"

"She was in your *room?* But how…?"

Spence shrugged. "Pretended it was hers. Told a maid she got locked out. She was giggling. Bragging about it. 'A few pesetas is all it takes,' she told me. She thought it was great fun. And she was intent on having more fun. She was—" he rubbed a hand against the back of his neck "—not inclined to take no for an answer."

Sadie felt her mouth go dry. Was he saying he'd slept with Leonie Carstairs?

"I packed her right back out, protesting all the way," Spence answered the question she couldn't ask. "But she wasn't happy about it. 'He'll never know,' she said. 'And if he did find out he wouldn't care.'" Spence shook his head grimly. "Not true. Richard would have damned sure cared. He might leave her for a few hours—she might drive him mad—but as far as he's concerned, she belongs to him. It would have killed our working together. It would have ruined that project. But beyond that, I don't sleep with other men's wives."

Sadie swallowed a surge of relief. "Of course not," she said, happier than she had any right to be.

"When the Nanumi deal came up, I could see Barcelona happening all over again."

"You don't think she got the message?"

"No. She doesn't hear what she doesn't want to hear. But I remembered she tried to hit on Dan Fitzsimmons a few months ago, and then he got married and that was the end of it. She apparently doesn't respect her own wedding ring, but she doesn't poach on other women's husbands."

"So you decided to get married?"

"It sounded like a good idea," he said tersely. "I know you think marriage is all about love and romance and flowers and whatnot, but it's not." He bounded out of the chair and began pacing again. "Marriage, throughout history, has more often been an economic alliance than a hearts-and-flowers romance. I understand that. So did Dena. It would have worked." He turned and faced her, his look challenging her to deny it.

"It still seems…pretty drastic."

"Yeah, well, if you were trying to pull off a several-hundred-million-dollar deal that could be scotched by some floozy with boobs for brains, you might do something drastic, too!"

"And now?"

"Now," he said heavily, "there's you."

Right. The marriage elephant. Front and center.

"So, what are we going to do?" she asked.

"Show up and act like a married couple. In front of everyone else," he qualified quickly. "I don't expect anything else. Don't worry."

Yeah, Sadie had pretty much figured that. But then their gazes met and, for one brief instant, she didn't think that at all. Something vivid and intense and extremely personal seemed to flicker in Spencer Tyack's eyes. Something hot. But before she could be sure, he jerked his gaze away again.

"Come on," he said abruptly. "I'll take you to your hotel."

"Hotel?" Sadie said stupidly, still feeling singed by that momentary heat.

"Hotel. Got you a room at the Plaza. Told you I would, remember?" He was already on his knees, stuffing her pile of dirty clothes into her suitcase and zipping it up as if he couldn't wait to be rid of her.

"I—yes. But I thought that was supposed to be a treat for my having brought your birth certificate and our…divorce papers. I didn't," she added, though she supposed she didn't need to remind him of that.

"Doesn't matter. You've got to sleep somewhere. It's paid for. No sense in it going to waste. Come on." He picked up the suitcase, opened the door and stood there, waiting for her to precede him down the stairs.

And Sadie could hardly say, *I want to stay here.* Could she?

No. Of course not.

But the scarier question was: Did she? Was she fool enough to want that?

And if she was honest, then yes, a perverse part—an exceedingly stupid part—of her wanted just that.

But clearly Spence didn't.

He didn't want her. He didn't want to be married to her. And whatever he might have said one night four years ago—those hungry, desperate words he'd murmured that had given her hope that night that she meant more to him than he'd ever let on—had obviously been an aberration, not a heartfelt desire.

Now she sucked in a breath, shoved away all romantic notions of happily ever after, and said what she needed to say. "Very well. Thank you. I'm sure I'll enjoy it." Then, chin held high, she went out the door and down the stairs.

She thought she'd be rid of him then. She'd expected he would hail her a cab and she could crawl into it and stop trying to pretend it didn't matter, that she was indifferent, that she didn't care.

But he didn't just see her into a cab. He got in with her. He accompanied her all the way to the Plaza, where she thought he'd leave her at the door.

But, damn it, he came in with her there. He took care of her registration and then walked her to her room.

"You don't need to," she said desperately.

"I do," Spence said. And she wondered if she heard any irony in his words. Probably not, judging from the studied determination on his face.

She wasn't used to a studiedly determined Spence. She was used to a quicksilver man, a brash, outspoken, clever, wild man. Proper and polite had never been Spence's way—not, at least, around her.

But he was proper and polite tonight. He acted like someone had shoved a copy of Emily Post right up his back.

*Go away!* she begged him silently. *It's settled. We'll do it. But I need some space. I need some time. I need to be alone.*

The last thing she needed was Spence acting all stiff and so-
licitous, like this was a duty he was performing—which, of
course, it was. It was far worse than being treated in the offhand,
breezy way he ordinarily treated her.

At least then it had felt as if they were actually friends. Now
that they were still married, there was this terrible tension. It felt
awful. Neither of them spoke all the way up in the elevator. He
didn't look at her. She didn't look at him.

When they reached her room, he took the key and opened the
door for her, then held it so she could precede him. Very stiff,
very proper. She felt like kicking him.

The room was big and beautifully decorated and it must have
cost him a fortune, not that money was an issue to Spence anymore.
He barely seemed to notice the room at all. He'd put her suitcase
on the luggage rack, then backed toward the door. There he stopped
and looked at her intently. "Are you going to be...all right?"

And what would he do if she said no?

Sadie didn't want to find out. "Why shouldn't I be?" she
snapped.

He grimaced. "No reason. It's just...I know it's as awkward
for you as it is for me. I'm sorry. About everything and—"

"Well, you don't have to keep going on about it!" She had
reached the end of her rope. "Just go!"

"I'm going," he said. "I'll be back in the morning to take you
to the airport."

"Don't bother. It's entirely unnecessary, and I can certainly
get to the airport by myself." Sadie was grateful that her voice
sounded cool and composed. She felt like screaming. "I'll want
to get an early flight. That way I can be back home by noon. I
have work to do."

He looked almost relieved, as if he could hardly wait for her
to be out of the city. "I've got to work in the city all week. I won't
have time to get back to Butte before we head out to Fiji."

"I know."

"Right. So get yourself a ticket on my flight to Fiji and I'll see you in L.A. The charter from Fiji won't be a problem. I'll let them know you're coming." He started out the door, then stopped in the hallway. "I just thought…can you get someone to cover while we're gone?"

Cover the office, he meant. They were never both gone at the same time. Or they never had been before. Except once. In Vegas four years ago.

Sadie met his gaze. "I can get someone. Don't worry. Thank you for seeing me here. I won't keep you."

"They have to be competent. No air heads," he went on as if she hadn't spoken.

"I know that." Did he think she was an idiot? "I'll take care of it." *Just go, damn it!*

"Good." There was another pause. He shifted awkwardly. "Thanks." Then he cleared his throat. "I meant what I said earlier, Sadie. You don't have to quit."

*That's* what all this hemming and hawing was about? He was stalling until he found a way to work that into the conversation.

"It can be like before. We can just go back to—"

"Good night, Spence," she said abruptly.

And she shut the door in his face.

# CHAPTER FOUR

IN HER FANTASIES Sadie had spent nights at the Plaza. It was what came of being a bookish child, one who spent hours in the library and who read every single book in the children's section over and over.

She'd loved *Eloise*. She'd read the story of the little girl who lived in the Plaza Hotel until the book cover nearly fell off. To Sadie the Plaza had always seemed more distant than the craters of the moon. She could see the craters of the moon from Butte, Montana. She could only imagine the Plaza.

And now here she was. In her very own room—one that Eloise would have enjoyed immensely. She'd have bounced on the bed and hung by her knees from the shower curtain rod. She'd have rung up room service and ordered whatever she wanted.

Sadie could do that. Spence had said so.

"You didn't eat much at dinner," he'd said when he'd been standing at the registration counter with her. "If you get hungry, order room service. Get whatever you want."

Very magnanimous. Thoughtful. Very proper. A good boss.

Not much of a husband. But then he didn't intend to be.

It shouldn't bother her. She should have got over Spencer Tyack years ago. In fact, she rather thought she had. She had dated other men in the past four years, hadn't she? Just because she hadn't found the right one didn't mean she wasn't looking.

But yesterday, the minute she'd discovered she was still married to him, her world had turned upside down—and all those old desperate completely unreciprocated feelings came right back.

And she couldn't help thinking that, while his wedding with Dena might have been no more than taking their "business" relationship to a new level, no doubt he had planned to spend a wedding night with his new bride. He certainly would not have married her, then packed her off to a hotel by herself while he went back to his apartment alone!

But he'd packed Sadie off to a hotel. He'd acted like he could hardly wait to get rid of her!

She shouldn't be surprised, of course. In fact she wasn't. But it would be so much simpler if she didn't love him, if she never had loved him, if she could just smile carelessly and walk away.

But she couldn't walk away for another week. He wouldn't let her. She sat in the middle of her big bed in the Plaza and felt like crying.

At the same time, she emphatically did *not* want to cry!

She had far more important things to do—like figuring how on earth she was going to survive next week knowing that she wasn't pretending—that she was, in fact, Spencer Tyack's wife.

Wedding nights, according to everything Spence had heard, were supposed to be memorable.

Theo Savas, whose wife, Martha, had painted the murals in Spence's office building, hadn't been able to stop grinning when he'd mentioned his. He'd been completely discreet, of course. Theo would be. But you only had to look at the guy to know that he and his wife had had a very satisfactory time, even though Martha had been in the last stages of pregnancy by the time Theo finally got her to wear his ring.

Lucky Theo, Spence thought grimly.

He could have told Theo a thing or two about memorable wedding nights! He'd had more than his share.

It was mortifying. Humiliating. First Emily's defection four years ago. Then his desperate marriage to Sadie.

And now this! He hadn't had a wedding today—but apparently he still had a wife!

He had tried so scrupulously for four years to forget that night—to forget holding Sadie in his arms, to forget making love to her—that to be hit again with the memories was like being gut-punched.

He might have been all right if he hadn't seen those wispy underthings. When the hell had Sadie started wearing sexy underwear like that?

What he remembered had been cotton and serviceable. Nothing that would stir a guy's libido. Of course, she could have been wearing a gunny sack and it wouldn't have mattered. Once he'd got her out of her clothes, it was all about Sadie.

And his libido had taken over completely.

It had been hard work to walk away from that night—to know that forgetting it was the best thing to do, the only thing to do to be fair to Sadie.

And now it was like all his efforts were for naught.

Why in hell had he had to see those flimsy lacy panties when she'd taken them out of her suitcase? Why couldn't he have been left to contemplate having gone to bed with a Sadie with no more "come hither" attraction than a nun?

Trouble was, he knew Sadie was no nun. Now that he couldn't seem to help but think about that night again, he remembered very well how un-nunlike she had been. Shocked him, really.

She'd always seemed sort of buttoned-down and demure in the office. Well, not demure exactly. But he hadn't counted on a woman who could make his blood run thick and hot.

He'd got one. And so he lay there in his wide lonely bed, twisting and turning, hard and aching—remembering his wedding night!

And, worse, thinking about what it would be like to have Sadie here now—a Sadie in silk and lace. And worst of all, thinking about taking the silk and lace off her. Thinking about running his hands up those long, smooth legs and tugging the scrap of silk down and tossing it aside. Thinking about unfastening that wisp of lace she would call a bra, and letting his hands learn the curve of her breasts, letting his mouth feast on rosy peaks and tease nipples with his tongue.

"Damn it!" He shot out of bed and began pacing the room, his body protesting because walking was *not* what it wanted to do right now. What it wanted was release. Inside warm, wet, willing…Sadie.

Damn it, yes, he remembered!

After years of neatly sticking her in her employee box, her announcement that they were still married had blown the lid right off. It boggled his mind.

He didn't think things like this, or hadn't since he was a hormone-fueled teen. He certainly didn't *do* things like this! He was logical. Sensible. He'd been going to marry Dena, hadn't he?

He was passionate about his work. *Not* about women.

He tried to think. To understand. Was this sudden preoccupation with Sadie because he couldn't have Dena tonight?

It seemed likely. He'd been expecting to have sex with her, and now he couldn't. Even though he admittedly wasn't in love with her, he didn't need love to enjoy a night in bed with a willing woman. He would have enjoyed it.

Enjoyed it a hell of a lot more than he was enjoying this!

He prowled the length of the apartment. It wasn't really big enough for much pacing. But Spence frankly doubted if all of Manhattan was big enough for the pacing he needed to do tonight.

He flicked open the blinds and stood glaring out into the darkness. There were a few lights in other windows. A few others were up at 3:00 a.m. New York never slept.

But he bet Sadie was asleep.

She'd practically nodded off during dinner. She'd sat there with her head bent over her plate, not saying a word. Totally not like Sadie. He was used to her talking his arm off. Tonight he'd got nothing. She couldn't even look at him!

He flung himself down on the bed again and sprawled, staring at the ceiling. Then he rolled over and punched his pillow and kicked the duvet into a heap. It didn't help. He was wired. Strung out.

Sex would help. It would ease his frustration. Relax him.

If Dena were here—

But it wasn't Dena he imagined having sex with! It was a lissome dark-haired woman in peach-colored lace he could see writhing beneath him. It was the same woman he could imagine straddling his thighs, running her hands over his chest, settling lower, taking him in.

"Hell." Spence dragged the pillow over his face. He flung it aside and got up again, then stalked into the bathroom and turned on the cold tap in the shower full blast. Then he stripped off his shorts and stood underneath it, let the frigid water course down his overheated body and cool his ardor.

He stood there until his teeth chattered, until there were goose bumps all over his body. Until he couldn't stand it any longer. Then he got out, dried off and went back to his bed.

And the first thing he thought was that Sadie had been damn lucky he'd been gentleman enough to take her over to the Plaza instead of making her spend the night with him. If he had, he could have peeled those tailored black slacks off her, pulled that burgundy sweater over her head and found the peach-colored tease she wore beneath them.

And damn it to hell, the shower had been useless. Here he was back thinking about Sadie's damn underwear again!

There was a bottle of scotch on the fireplace mantel. It promised solace, consolation. Oblivion. He got up and poured himself a glass, then sat down and stared at it. The fumes tempted him, teased him. Promised him forgetfulness. He'd used it before, right after he'd got the divorce. Or thought he had.

He'd needed to forget. And so he had—until one morning when he actually couldn't remember the night before and it had scared him spitless that he was, exactly as his mother had claimed, just like his old man.

Not that John Tyack had wedding nights he couldn't remember. But the old man had sure as hell had spent plenty of other nights in drunken oblivion. Nights that Spence remembered—and hated—all too well.

He'd stopped drinking right then. He only drank after that if he drank in company, and then only a little. Now, tempted as he was, he turned away from the scotch in disgust and flung himself into the armchair and willed himself to calm down, to cool off, get a grip.

He wasn't his old man. He could find another way out of his pain. Surely he could find another way to forget Sadie and the promise of peach-colored silk.

Of course he could. He had plenty of time. He had the whole rest of the night.

"Are you okay?" Martha Savas poked her head into Sadie's Butte office the next afternoon, frowning and giving her a quizzical, slightly worried glance.

"What? Oh, yes, of course I am." Sadie jerked her brain back to the present and tried to paste a cheerful smile on her face. "Why wouldn't I be?"

"You tell me." And instead of waggling her fingers and

heading down the hall to her studio where she was painting gigantic panels to be hung in a recently renovated bank, Martha marched into Sadie's office and settled into Spence's chair. "You look awful."

"Thank you very much." Sadie kept her tone light, even as she shoved a hand through her hair in an effort to make it look better. But she knew she couldn't do much about the circles under her eyes and the lack of color in her cheeks. "I'm just tired."

"When did you get back?"

"Yesterday afternoon. And I leave again tomorrow."

"Leave? Again? Twice in one week?"

Everyone knew that Sadie never went anywhere. She could get away with explaining that Spence wanted her in New York for a meeting one time. But twice in one week was unheard of.

Martha grinned. "Don't tell me you're finally going to take a vacation."

It was tempting to say she was. After all, a trip to Fiji could be called a vacation, couldn't it?

But she didn't want to lie to Martha. Sadie liked all the artists who had studios or showed their work in the gallery downstairs or the co-op on the second floor, but she liked Martha the most.

When she'd first met Martha, a muralist who had come to Butte just last year, Sadie had felt mortifying twinges of jealousy. After all, Martha had only come because she'd met Spence on a plane coming back from Greece and in his cheerful offhand way, he'd said she ought to come paint a mural for him.

Whether he'd actually ever thought she would or not, Sadie didn't know. But he'd been delighted to see Martha when she'd shown up a few weeks later. And he'd told Sadie to help her find a place to live and suggest places she might look for a job.

"Seattle," Sadie had suggested when she and Martha were alone.

Martha had laughed. "Don't worry. I'm not interested in Spence," she'd said, though Sadie had never once implied she had any interest in Spence, either. She remembered saying so vehemently.

"You don't have to say so." Martha had shrugged. "I'm not blind."

Was it obvious, then? The panic must have shown on her face because Martha had smiled sympathetically and shaken her head. "I see it because I feel the same way—about someone else."

About Theo, it turned out—the man who was now Martha's husband.

But it hadn't been all smooth sailing. When Theo Savas had turned up, determined to marry her, Sadie had watched the drama unfold, enchanted by Martha's tough Greek sailor.

But even though Martha loved him, Theo hadn't had an easy time convincing her to marry him.

"He's being responsible." Martha had dismissed Theo's determined pursuit. "He thinks because I'm pregnant, he needs to marry me."

Well, yes. That had been a complication. And Martha hadn't wanted Theo to marry her out of duty. She'd wanted love.

Sadie understood that feeling. Shared it. Had for years wanted Spence's love. And didn't stand a prayer.

"It's not vacation," she said slowly. "It's…I'm going with Spence to Nanumi—you know, that resort in Fiji—for a week."

Martha's eyes lit up. "Well, hallelujah! He's finally seen the light." She was grinning broadly. "And I didn't even have to hit him over the head with a frying pan." She was absolutely gleeful, and Sadie hated to spoil her good cheer.

"It's…business," she said.

"Oh, right. Business? No. If it were business you'd be here. You're the home front and Spence is the traveling circus."

Sadie wouldn't have put it quite that way, but she understood Martha's view. "Ordinarily, yes," she agreed. "But this time I get to go, too."

"And not because he's finally interested? He's taking you to a private resort—" Martha invested the words with oodles of innuendo "—to make you work?" She shook her head again. "He's in love."

"He's not. He just…needs a wife."

The minute the words were out, she would have called them back. But it was too late. Martha was staring at her, aghast.

"You're not! Have you lost your mind, Sadie? How manipulative can he be? You are not going to let that bloody man pass you off as his wife!"

Sadie swallowed. "He's not."

"Well, then…" Martha frowned, confused.

"It's true." Sadie shrugged. "I am his wife."

Martha looked as if she'd choked on her tongue. Her mouth opened, but nothing came out. Then she snapped it shut, her eyes still wide and unblinking, and profoundly disbelieving, which had the effect of making Sadie feel about two inches high.

And then quite suddenly Martha's whole expression changed. Her outrage softened. Her features gentled. And she reached for Sadie's hand and squeezed it between her fingers. "For how long?"

Sadie swallowed. "Four years."

She expected Martha to yelp in astonishment. But Martha only sighed and squeezed her hand again. "Oh, you poor dear girl."

The other woman's acceptance and sympathy were very nearly Sadie's undoing. She gulped against the lump in her throat. "It's…my own fault."

"Oh, I doubt that," Martha said dryly. "I know Spence. He can manipulate with the best of them."

"He…well, yes, he can," Sadie admitted. "But he didn't. I mean, he didn't intend to. It's just—"

And then Sadie had to explain. Not all of it. The bare minimum. She knew Spence would hate her dragging up the past and talking about Emily's jilting him. But in order to make sense of what had happened, Sadie roughed out the general sequence of events, ending with, "He said, 'You'd marry me, wouldn't you?' And, I should have said no."

"I'd like to know how," Martha said tartly. "When Spence gets a notion, he doesn't back off. He's like a bulldozer. Besides—" her tone softened "—you loved him."

"But he didn't love me!" Sadie protested. "You wouldn't marry Theo when you thought he didn't love you!"

"That was different," Martha said. "I didn't know Theo. Not really. We hadn't known each other for years like you and Spence. We'd had a fling. And that was my fault, not his."

Sadie stared at her. "Your fault?"

"Long story," Martha said with a wry smile. "Suffice to say I was the one who pushed Theo into the fling. No strings, I said. Just mind-blowing sex—" She reddened. "Stop looking at me like that. I was crazy, all right? Anyway, he agreed. So I knew he only wanted an affair. So when he turned up demanding to marry me after I got pregnant, I certainly didn't think it was because he was in love with me."

"But he was," Sadie said with satisfaction, remembering Theo's determined courtship, his last desperate gesture. "It was so romantic."

"It was insane," Martha said.

"But he convinced you. You knew he loved you then. And so you married him. Not like me. I married Spence because I thought...I hoped..."

But she couldn't even bring herself to voice those desperate hopes. Instead she blinked furiously, hating the tears that welled up in her eyes. "Because I'm an idiot," she muttered.

"He's the idiot," Martha said without hesitation. She crossed one leg over the other knee. "So what happened?"

"He was going to marry Dena Wilson. He wanted me to bring him his birth certificate and the divorce papers. He called, told me, then hung up. And I went looking where he told me to look—and he hadn't got them. He thought he had and tossed the envelope in the file. But it was a preliminary letter, not even close to a decree. And I couldn't reach him because he never turns his phone on. So I had to go to New York…and tell him."

"What? At the wedding?" Martha grinned when Sadie nodded. "Well, that will teach him to keep his phone on!"

Sadie grimaced. "I guess. And we will get a divorce, but we can't yet. He…needs a wife in Fiji this coming week."

"Needs a wife?"

"It's business," Sadie said firmly. "And perfectly legitimate. He's just making the best of a bad situation."

"Did he *say* that?"

"Not precisely."

"Lucky for him. I'd have killed him if he had," Martha said bluntly. She sighed. "This is difficult."

"I know," Sadie agreed. "But I have to do it."

"Why?"

Confronted with the question that bluntly, Sadie couldn't find the words. Finally she mumbled something about owing him.

"You don't owe him a damn thing," Martha said indignantly.

"I agreed to marry him. And I'm still…his wife." Sadie actually managed to get the words out. "I can do this," she said in the face of Martha's doubt. "It will be all right. Then we can divorce. And…and I can walk away."

"Oh, for heaven's sake!" Martha stared at her. "Are you listening to yourself? You *love* him. How can you walk away?"

Sadie knew better than to deny it. "You walked away from Theo."

"Actually, I didn't. Theo left me."

"What?" Sadie stared in astonishment.

"He left Santorini and went to the States. And then I left, too, because it hurt so much to be there without him. And maybe that's when I was really an idiot, because before I was due to go home, he came back."

Sadie's eyes widened further. "Really?" She wanted to hear more. It was far better to hear a story with a happy ending than to contemplate her own miserable one.

But Martha said, "What happened between Theo and me doesn't matter here. What matters is that if you love Spence and have loved him for years—not to mention having spent *four years* married to him!—you can't just walk away. You have to fight for him."

Sadie stared at her.

"You do," Martha said. "Unless you're giving up. And frankly, I never thought you were a quitter." The words dripped challenge.

But Sadie resisted. "And how am I supposed to do that? Arm wrestle him? If I win, he has to stay married to me? No, thanks. Besides—" she sighed "—I wouldn't win."

"So, you're going to give up? Just go for a week in paradise with the man you love, and then turn tail and run?"

"It isn't what I *want* to do!" Sadie protested, realizing the truth even as she said it. "But it's not going to work! I've known him forever, I've worked for him for years, and he's never *ever* even asked me out!"

"But he asked you to marry him," Martha reminded her. "And not for business. Think about that."

Sadie did. She thought about something else, too—the one thing that had kept her hopes up all these years. She thought about what had happened on their wedding night when they'd come back to the honeymoon suite where he'd intended to bring Emily.

Sadie had been wary and worried, waiting for Spence to come to grips with the realization that he had married the wrong woman.

But Spence had been completely intent on her. They'd barely got in the door when he'd kissed her deeply, passionately, with all the fervor of a man in love.

Sadie had been stunned—and delighted. And she'd responded

with all the eagerness she'd held in her heart for so long. She'd returned the kiss, had deepened it, had pulled his shirt out of his trousers and run her hands over his heated skin. She'd encouraged him when he'd moved to pull her top over her head. She'd leaned into his hungry embrace, ravenous herself.

And when he'd taken her to bed, she'd gone willingly, eagerly, as desperate for him as he'd been for her—even though she feared he was pretending she was Emily all the while.

Their lovemaking had been fast and frantic and delicious. It had ended with them clinging to each other, shattered and spent.

And then Spence had drawn her tight against him and whispered raggedly, "It always should have been you."

She thought about that now. Had he meant it? Had he even known he'd said it? He'd certainly never said it again, nor anything remotely like it. But still, if he had…

"You're very quiet," Martha said now.

"Just…thinking."

"Finding a reason to fight?" Martha speculated.

Sadie ventured a tentative smile. "Maybe so."

He didn't call Sadie the rest of the week.

Why should he? She'd be in L.A. on Friday. They'd have hours on the plane to catch up on work. He didn't need to talk to her every day, even though it was a rare day he didn't. Or used to be a rare day. Now it wasn't that important. She knew her job. She was clever. She was competent.

*She was his wife.*

And Spencer Tyack didn't have a clue what to say to a wife. Not a wife who was Sadie, at least.

If he had married Dena, talking would have been no problem at all. They could have discussed work, upcoming projects they might pursue, the logistics of the resort financing.

Of course he'd always talked about business with Sadie, too.

Often. But not now. Not when he kept remembering her peach-colored silk. Not when his tongue seemed welded to the roof of his mouth. Not when his memories of the night they'd spent together all crowded back into his brain and wouldn't let him think of anything else.

That Sadie he couldn't talk to at all!

Which didn't matter, of course, because she had never rung him, either. Not once.

She'd never called to say she got home. Had never updated him on any of their current projects—not that there were any in immediate need of his attention—but she might at least have let him know the status of things. She'd never even called to tell him when her flight to L.A. was arriving.

Their only communication all week was when he'd sent her an e-mail or a text message telling her what he needed her to do.

Far more efficient than phone calls, he assured himself. They should have been doing this for years. But that was infuriating, too, because the only response he ever got was the single-word reply, "Done."

He'd sent her five texts today, though, all updating his progress across the country. He never got a reply to those. He'd sent her another as soon as he'd landed in L.A. Again no answer. Of course she might be en route herself.

But he didn't like not knowing.

They were going to have to sort things out as soon as she got here. It damned well wasn't going to work if she ignored him at Nanumi. Mr. Isogawa was sharp. He wasn't going to be convinced that they were a solid stable couple if they snarled at each other or avoided each other the whole week.

And even if Isogawa didn't notice a rift, Leonie undoubtedly would, and there was a good chance she'd try to exploit it.

Spence knew he'd been lucky to get her out of his room in Barcelona without Richard's ever learning that she'd come calling in the first place. And he didn't want the same thing happening again. He liked Richard. He actually even liked Leonie, when she wasn't behaving like a tart. And Richard's millions were an absolute necessity to the resort investment package.

Leonie could destroy that—and her marriage—and that wouldn't be good for anyone.

So no matter whether he and Sadie felt like talking or not, he was going to have to spell out what he expected of his wife. And, God help him, he was going to have to behave like a husband.

"So," a familiar voice said behind him, "I'm here."

Spence spun around at the sound, and yes, she was—right here in front of him: Sadie Morrissey looking exactly the way Sadie Morrissey always did neat, professional, appropriate, in control. Thank God.

And yet, even so, his heart did a weird kick-thump in his chest at the sight of her because his first thought was, what sort of underwear was she wearing?

His eyes screwed shut as his brain tried to get his hormones under control. But did they listen? Not on your life. He steeled himself against his reactions, scowling at how inappropriate they were.

"Obviously you're glad to see me," Sadie said dryly. "Did you change your mind, then?" There was an edge to her voice that said she wasn't any more thrilled than he was.

"What? No, of course not. I'm just relieved you finally got here." He made a point of glancing at his watch. "Cutting a little close, weren't you?"

"Was I? I don't think so. I had things to arrange," she reminded him loftily. "Anyway, I'm here now."

And without another word, she turned, walked straight over to a bank of seats and sat down.

Spence stalked after her, annoyed at what seemed like blatant dismissal, "So you got 'backup'?"

"Of course. I wouldn't be here if I hadn't."

"Who?"

There was a split second's hesitation. Then, "Grace."

*"Grace?"* He stared at her. "Grace Tredinnick? Have you lost your mind? Grace is eighty if she's a day!"

"Eighty-two, actually," Sadie said, her chin coming up, her gaze steely. "Her birthday was in January. The eleventh. I sent her a card." Subtext: you didn't. "Did you know she graduated from the Butte Business College? She was valedictorian."

"No," Spence said through his teeth. "I damned well didn't know it. And I'll bet you didn't either until yesterday."

"The day before, in fact."

"I don't care if you knew it last month! That doesn't qualify her to run my business. What the hell were you thinking? Tyack's is a multimillion dollar international firm and—"

"—and you insisted that I come with you. And I couldn't answer all the correspondence and deal with the day-to-day stuff from the middle of the Pacific Ocean, so I had to find someone who could. On short notice. I found Grace," she added belligerently.

"Grace can't—"

"Grace certainly can! And in case she wants some help, she won't be doing it alone."

"Oh." He breathed a sigh of relief, still annoyed that she'd just been winding him up to annoy him, but glad she'd got competent help. "Well then—"

"I also found Claire and Jeremy."

*"Jeremy!"* Now he really was apoplectic. "Claire's all right, I suppose. At least she's not a criminal, though she is about fifteen. But Jeremy! For God's sake, Sadie! He's a juvenile delinquent!"

"Was. And of course, no one who's ever been a juvenile delinquent could possibly do anything constructive with his life!"

They both knew that Spence had been a far bigger delinquent than Jeremy in his time.

He scowled furiously. "I paid my dues."

"As has Jeremy. He did a fantastic job on the mural and you know it. Besides, Theo and Martha both vouch for him. They think he'll do a terrific job. And you know he won't cross Grace."

"How do I know he won't mug and murder Grace?"

"Because he got sent to juvie for painting graffiti, not for knocking off old ladies! For heaven's sake, Spence! He got an A in bookkeeping last semester. And Claire is in the Future Business Leaders of America."

"Bully for her. Is Grace in the *Past* Business Leaders?"

"I wouldn't know. I do know they'll be fine! And if you don't want them, say so now and I'll turn around and go straight home!"

Her eyes flashed fire, her freckled cheeks were big blotches of red, and she was glaring at him the same way she always did when they were battling it out, and quite suddenly Spence felt a real overwhelming sense of relief. She was still his Sadie after all.

He grinned. And then felt an instant stab of panic as he realized that *his* Sadie might at this very moment be wearing scraps of silk and lace. And was his wife!

His grin vanished. He needed to talk to her about that. But not now. Not when he was beset by a sudden vision of peach-colored underwear. He took a shaky breath. "Well...we'll see, won't we?"

He was talking about Grace, Claire and Jeremy. Really, he was. He was *not* talking about seeing Sadie—his wife!—in her underwear. It didn't even occur to him. Not consciously.

Not then.

Well, so much for that.

All her hopes and dreams and professed determination to make Spence sit up and take notice and want to stay married to her—the ones that had actually seemed possible when she'd been sitting in Butte, encouraged by Martha—didn't stand a chance.

He was treating her exactly the way he always had. Barking at her, arguing with her. And she was instinctively barking back. Of course she knew that her choice of Grace, Claire and Jeremy would rile him. But she truly hadn't had any choice. Not if she was going to come along. And despite her fretting, the more she thought about it, the more she knew she had to.

As Martha said, she couldn't just walk away without a fight. But fight over Grace wasn't exactly what she'd had in mind.

"Sorry," she said now as they boarded the plane and settled in spacious business-class seats. "It was the best I could do. And I do think everything will be fine. She does have the number at Nanumi in case there's a problem."

Spence grunted, which she hoped meant he was mollified. She wasn't sure. He had stowed her carry-on in the compartment overhead, but he kept his own briefcase with him and took out a sheaf of papers.

"We need to go over these," he said.

"Now?"

"Of course."

So much for any plans for a heart-to-heart. Obviously in Spence's eyes she had only come along as his wife to play a part.

Sadie ran her tongue over her lips and tried to swallow hard to dislodge the lump of disappointment that seemed to be stuck in her throat. "Fine," she said, with all the equability she could muster. "Let's."

It was back to normal with a vengeance then, as Spence talked nonstop. He seemed to have stored up a week's worth of things to discuss with her, letters he wanted her to write, research he wanted her to do.

While she had spent the last three days gearing herself up for the coming week—trying to imagine how she would deal with life as Spencer Tyack's wife, how she would share a *bure* with him, smile lovingly at him, kiss him—Spence seemed not to have thought about it at all.

"...paying attention, Sadie?"

"What?" Her cheeks reddened as she tried to jerk her mind back to whatever he'd been saying. "I'm sorry. I'm feeling a little cramped. My feet are going to sleep. Maybe if I walked around. I'll be right back."

Spence looked disgruntled, but obligingly folded up the papers and pulled his legs back against his seat so she could slide past his knees to get into the aisle.

At least she had far more room to do so than in coach class. Even so she was acutely conscious of the brush of his knees against the backs of her legs. "Sorry," she murmured. "Back in a minute."

It wasn't a minute. She took her time, walked the aisle, went to the rest room, splashed a little water on her face. When she got back, the flight attendant was just bringing her meal. And after the meal, just as Spence was about to drag out his papers again, the in-flight movie began.

"Oh, good! Hugh Jackman!" Sadie was delighted. And she made more of her delight than was absolutely necessary because, even more than Hugh Jackman, she liked not having to try to deal with Spence for a couple of hours.

"I suppose you want to watch that. Be my guest. I'll get some work done."

And he got out his laptop and began tapping away furiously on it. The film was good. Even so, it took Sadie a while to lose herself in it and not in the mess that was her life. Sometime later, though, she noticed that Spence had stopped typing.

She glanced his way, expecting to see him caught up in the film, too. Instead he was frowning at her.

"Something wrong?" she asked.

He jumped, looking startled, then quickly shook his head. "No." His tone was abrupt, and he immediately went back to his laptop.

Sadie sighed and tried to lose herself in the film again. But all she could do was hear Spence typing furiously next to her. What was that all about?

When the movie ended and the lights came back on again, he stopped typing and looked at her.

"We have to talk." He was looking very dark and grave. Very un-Spencelike.

"All right," Sadie said cautiously.

He didn't, though. Not for a moment. He seemed to be weighing what he was going to say, which was also totally not like Spence. With her, Spence always said the first thing that came into his head and then they argued about it.

"I know why you married me," he said at last.

*He knew?*

*Knew she loved him?* Sadie felt her marvelous first-class meal climb into her throat. She clamped her teeth together and prayed it would go right back down again. And she didn't open her mouth until she was sure it had.

Then she said, "Do you?"

She wanted to sink into the earth—a difficult feat at any time but particularly when one was 38,000 feet above it.

He nodded, still dead serious. "And I want you to know I do appreciate it."

Appreciate it? She frowned. What?

*She loved him and he appreciated it?*

"I realize now that you were only trying to help," he went on solemnly. "To do what needed to be done, what was best for the company." He leaned toward her earnestly.

She stared at him, stunned. *That* was why he thought she'd married him?

"And I'm very grateful. I know it was hard on you. The

marriage. After. And the divorce—well, the nondivorce," he said, his mouth twisting "has only made things worse. But we can make the best of a bad situation. We're adults. Right? Mature, sensible, sane."

Were they? Then why was she feeling like killing him? She didn't say a word, just stared at him.

"We can handle this," he went on. "Can't we?"

He was looking at her expectantly, as if she was supposed to be saying something in response to his comment.

Like what? *I love you, you stupid idiot?* He had no clue.

Spence's expression grew impatient. "Fine. If you don't want to discuss it, we won't. I'm sorry you feel that way. I'm just trying to say I understand. I'm…grateful."

Oh, good, just what she wanted—gratitude!

"I also hope this isn't going to be too difficult for you—what I'm asking you to do," he added stiffly.

"What *are* you asking me to do?" she said, irritated. "Exactly, I mean?"

Might as well get it all spelled out. She was reasonably sure that "loving him forever" wouldn't come up.

At her question, something that might have been a flush climbed into his face. "Nothing compromising," he assured her.

"Compromising? What sort of word is that?" She couldn't stop herself. She'd battled with him too often.

And Spence knew a challenge when he heard it. "You know damn well what sort of word it is! I'm not expecting you to sleep with me!"

Well, she'd asked. *Take that*, Sadie said to herself. "Of course you aren't," she murmured, more to herself than to him.

But he heard her and his gaze narrowed. "I do expect you to act like my wife. My happily married wife."

Deliberately Sadie widened her eyes, goading him. "Which means?"

Spence ground his teeth. "See if you can pretend to like me. Just a little."

"I do like you," Sadie said truthfully. "When you're not acting like an ass."

His brows drew down. "What's that supposed to mean?"

"It means that you trust me to do everything else. Trust me to do this."

He looked momentarily taken aback. Then he nodded jerkily. "Of course. I do. I…just want it clear. So Leonie knows," he added. "And Isogawa."

"They'll know," Sadie promised heavily, suddenly tired.

All her initial determination to make this work was gone. Spence was all about pretending. He didn't want anything real she had to offer.

"Okay, then." Spence let it go for a minute, then added, "You realize we are going to have to share a *bure*, though. One of those thatched cottages. They have a bedroom and a living room. Two beds."

And that was more than Sadie had any desire to discuss right now. Maybe it was because she'd been operating on adrenaline ever since Spence had said he was marrying Dena. Maybe it was because her dreams had suddenly come back to life only to be mocked by Spence's determination to pretend. She didn't know. She just knew she couldn't deal with it—with him!—any longer.

"Right," she said. "Two beds. Fine. Whatever. I will do my best to convince Leonie and Mr. Isogawa and everyone else that I am a deeply devoted wife. Now, if you're finished explaining my duties, I'd like to go to sleep."

And without giving him a chance to reply, she wrapped herself in the blanket the attendant had given her earlier, reclined the seat as far as it would go, turned her back on him and shut off her light.

# CHAPTER FIVE

SADIE slept the whole rest of the flight.

Spence knew that for a fact—because he couldn't.

He tried, God knew. He was used to grabbing forty winks wherever he could—in a bank lobby, on an airplane, standing up in a hallway. A man who'd slept in his truck for two years could sleep anywhere.

Except, apparently, when Sadie Morrissey was sleeping next to him.

He watched her for hours in teeth-grinding frustration, wide-awake, wired and ready to chew glass, while Sadie, having frozen him out when he'd been trying to be understanding, damn it, slept like the proverbial baby.

The trouble was she didn't look like a baby. Babies didn't have tousled dark hair that brushed against their cheekbones. They didn't smile and sigh erotically in their sleep. They didn't twist and turn and flip the blanket away so that bits of bare midriff peeked out.

Spence didn't want to see bits of Sadie's bare midriff. Not if that was all he got to see. He didn't want to feel the temptation to reach over and run his fingers lightly along those few inches of soft, pale skin. Not if he couldn't just hook his fingers right under the edge of her shirt and tug it over her head. Not if he couldn't unzip her slacks and slide them down her end-less legs.

"Damn it!" The words hissed through his teeth. He jerked his gaze away and clenched his hands on the armrests of the seat.

"Sir?" The flight attendant appeared at his elbow. "Is every-thing all right?" She bent down and was peering at him worriedly.

Spence dragged in a harsh breath. "Everything's fine," he said in a low controlled voice. "I just…remembered something."

What it was like to have Sadie naked in his arms!

"Can I get you anything?"

Knockout drops? A stun gun?

"Coffee," he said at last. "Lots of coffee. I need to work."

There was always plenty to be done. And he'd always done it, using work to put his life's circumstances out of his mind. To forget his jerk of a father, to blot out his shrewish mother. He'd used work earlier on the flight, talking about the projects to Sadie because when they talked about work, he had things under control.

The flight attendant brought him coffee. He booted up his laptop again. He opened a file, focused on the specs of the Sao Paulo building Mateus Gonsalves was recommending that they buy.

Tried to focus. It didn't work. He muttered under his breath.

"Mmmm?" Sadie shifted and turned his way.

Swell. Now if he shifted his eyes even slightly he could see her face, feast his gaze on her slightly parted mouth. He had kissed that mouth. Really kissed it. Not just given Sadie the duty peck that he had allowed himself to bestow as a part of their friendship-business relationship.

She had a generous mouth. A kissable mouth. And he was going to have to kiss her again this week. Not just brush his lips over hers but—in the interest of their convincing portrayal of a newly married couple—drown himself in her kiss. And bury himself in—

*Stop! Just stop!*

Wanting Sadie Morrissey was the last thing he should do.

She didn't want him. She'd married him out of kindness, damn it!

He'd told her he understood why she'd done it—out of care for the company—because the truth was worse. When Emily jilted him, Sadie had felt sorry for him. He'd said gruffly, "You'd marry me. Wouldn't you?" And she had because what the hell else was she supposed to say?

She'd married him out of pity!

The very thought made him cringe. It made him squirm.

He didn't want pity. Never had. He had hated it when the teachers had tsked and murmured about his father, about what a hard life he'd had. Sure, his life might have been easier with different parents, but he'd done fine.

He'd survived, hadn't he? He always would.

He didn't know what the hell she'd got mad about, either. He had only been trying to do her a favor by reassuring her that he didn't intend to jump her bones. He could control himself. He hoped.

Besides they wouldn't be sharing a bed. Only a *bure*. They would be fine.

He glanced her way again, determined to steel himself against the attraction. But there was more midriff showing.

He shut his eyes. Heard her move, then mutter. She flung an arm out and it landed on him. His eyes flew open. Sadie's fingers curved around his forearm, warm and possessive.

They were long and slender fingers with sensible short nails, well-trimmed and neat—just like Sadie. Looking at them a guy would never think they belonged to a woman wearing lacy peach-colored silk. There was nothing particularly sexy or erotic about them—until all of a sudden her thumb began to stroke his sleeve.

At her touch Spence jerked, then looked at her suspiciously. Was she awake? Having him on? Or reading his mind?

But her breathing didn't change. She just smiled. He swallowed and barely breathed, but he didn't move his arm, didn't pull away, because beneath the cotton of his shirt, his skin tingled at her touch.

Once upon a time, four years ago, he remembered burning under Sadie's touch. He shut his eyes and tried not to think about it. He should have had his head examined for insisting she come along.

But it had seemed perfectly sane and sensible at the time, no different than taking Dena.

Ha.

Sadie hadn't expected to sleep. She certainly hadn't expected to be refreshed by it. So she was amazed to wake up to hear the sounds of a breakfast cart rattling nearby and to feel almost human and hopeful again.

She stirred and shifted, keeping her eyes slitted as she turned so she could catch a glimpse of Spence.

He was slouched in his seat, looking stubble-jawed and rumpled, his hair a little spiky, his eyes a little tired as he stared at some papers in his hand. She doubted he had slept at all.

She sighed and stretched and slowly opened her eyes the rest of the way. Spence didn't look up until she sat up and began to fold the blanket. Then he glanced her way.

"Sleep well?" he growled.

"I did, actually," Sadie said. She took a brush out of her purse and ran it through her hair, then fished out a lipstick and a mirror. "Almost human."

Spence grunted and went back to his papers.

When she'd finished to her satisfaction, she straightened and looked over at him. "Did you work the whole flight?"

"I had things to do. Work to catch up on. And I wanted to be prepared." His tone was gruff and he flexed his shoulders as if trying to get a little of the tension out of them.

"You don't think a little sleep might have done more for you?" Sadie said lightly.

"I said I had work to do," he said sharply.

"Sorry," Sadie said lightly. She paused, then decided maybe she'd been a little too abrupt earlier. He couldn't help what he didn't feel.

"I'll do my part," she assured him.

He looked over at her. "What?"

"When we land. I'll do my part. You don't have to worry. I'll…be your wife."

He stared at her a long moment. There was something there in his gaze again when it connected with hers that seemed, to Sadie, almost electric.

*Don't*, she warned herself. *Do not read anything into this. It's your brain. Your emotions. Your dreams. It's not real.*

And then, "Right," Spence said, and gave her a jerky nod just as the flight attendant appeared with their breakfasts.

They ate. And then after, as the dishes were being removed, the captain announced that they'd begun their descent and they needed to put everything away in preparation for landing.

And suddenly Sadie felt the shiver of nerves all over again. It felt oddly like childhood piano recitals when all of the expectations of her teacher, Sister Catherine Marie, came to rest on her thin shoulders. She trembled briefly.

Spence stood up and put his computer and files away, then rummaged in his carry-on and sat back down again. "Here," he said, almost offhandedly, and a small black velvet box landed in her lap.

Sadie jumped as if it were a grenade.

"It's not going to blow up," Spence said gruffly. "Open it."

But Sadie couldn't. She couldn't even pick it up. Her breath seemed caught in her throat. She regarded the box warily, wordlessly.

"Too awful to contemplate?" Spence growled. "Come on, Sadie. You can't be my bride without rings. What are you waiting for? Me to put them on you?"

His rough tone galvanized her voice at least. "Of course not!" It was just a shock. So...unexpected.

She guessed she shouldn't be surprised. Spence believed in covering all the bases. That's what had made his screw-up of their divorce such a shock. Now she prayed that her fingers wouldn't tremble as she picked up the box and carefully eased open the spring closure.

"It's not booby-trapped, either," Spence said irritably.

"No." She barely breathed the word as the lid opened and she simple stared. Didn't move. Didn't speak.

"You don't like them," Spence said after a moment. His voice was flat. "They aren't exactly...traditional."

No. That was what was so remarkable about them.

Sadie had seen the ring he'd bought Emily—a showy elegant diamond with little rubies all around it. She didn't know what he'd done with it after Emily hadn't shown up. At least, thank God, he hadn't given it to *her*.

She'd glimpsed the engagement ring Dena had worn—a diamond solitaire on a white-gold band. Polished and sophisticated, like the woman who had worn it.

"I suppose I could've just given you Dena's," he said now. "But I didn't think—"

"No," Sadie said, the word torn from the depths of her soul. "No," she said again. "Not those. These." She tipped the box to allow more light in. There were two rings—a thin gold filigree band with an exquisitely cut piece of jade inlaid for an engagement ring. And the wedding ring was pure jade inset into a bead of Celtic knots. Her Morrissey ancestors would have approved. A circle of green and gold fire. Primitive and perfect. Completely her.

"Dena's rings were worth a hell of a lot more, moneywise,"

he said. "But they didn't...look right. Didn't look like something you'd wear."

Numbly Sadie shook her head. "No. I wouldn't."

If he'd brought Dena's for her to wear, she would have turned the diamond into her palm, clenched her fingers around it and never opened her fist. But it's what she would have expected.

After all, what difference would it have made, if they were only going to be married a week?

These rings, however, were so completely "her" it was spooky. How had Spence known? She shot him a quick probing glance, amazed.

"I didn't buy you one the first time," he reminded her.

"I know. But you gave me that old pipestone ring you used to wear."

He stared at her.

"Don't you remember it? The one that belonged to your granddad."

*"My granddad's ring?"* He looked stunned. "I thought I'd lost it."

Sadie shook her head. "No. You took it off and gave it to me. Put it on my finger," she told him. "Until you got me something better, you said." She shrugged. He still looked poleaxed by the news. "You really didn't remember?"

He shook his head, looking almost dazed.

"Well, you were gone a month, you know...after. And then I guess I forgot. I should have given it back to you."

The truth was, she hadn't forgotten. And she never would. She'd loved that ring. It was precious to her. And she'd kept it on a chain around her neck for the next month. Only after Spence had come in and told her the divorce was final had she removed it.

She would have given it to him if he'd asked, but he never had. So she had put it in the drawer of her bedside table. More nights than she liked to remember she opened that drawer right before she went to sleep. She touched the ring and thought about what might have been.

"I still have it." She swallowed, then made herself say words she never wanted to say. "You can have it back if you want."

"I'd…like that." His voice had a ragged edge. "It's the only thing I had that belonged to him. We can trade. If you want," he added quickly. "If you don't like these I can get you something else. I just thought—"

"I *do* like them," Sadie said fervently. "They're…beautiful. Truly. That seems like such an overused word, I know. But they are. They're…perfect." And as she spoke, she reached out a finger and touched them with something almost like reverence. She felt tears well up.

"Good God, you're *not* going to cry!"

That only made her blink even faster. But at least she took a deep quick breath and said, "Of course not. I'm just…I think they're wonderful. Thank you."

"Well, good," he said gruffly. "So, aren't you going to put them on?"

Carefully Sadie took the wedding ring out of the box and slid it onto her finger.

"It might be too big," Spence said.

But it wasn't. It fit perfectly.

"It's the color of your eyes," he said suddenly, surprising her even more. She might have known him for most of her life, but she'd never have imagined he'd know what color her eyes were.

Now she turned them on him and saw that there was a definite flush of red over his cheekbones.

"They're like that forest pool in that kids' book," he told her. And even as he said so, the color got deeper. "The one you made me read you when you were little. That fairy tale." He looked completely embarrassed now.

"I remember that!" When Spence had been in fifth grade she'd talked him into reading her a storybook fairy tale in which there had been a picture of a magical pool like that. Danny wouldn't have been caught dead reading her fairy stories. But Spence had no little sisters pestering him all day, so he'd indulged her. And if he hadn't already, he'd won her heart by telling her that the pool in the forest was the same color as her eyes.

She remembered now that she'd been amazed. "Really? The magic pool? Are my eyes magic?"

"Sure," he'd said then. Now he insisted, "They were that color. It's not like I was making something up."

"No. Of course not!" Sadie grinned. She felt suddenly deliriously happy. She took out the other ring and felt a moment's fleeting temptation to ask Spence to put it on her finger.

But he'd come much further than she'd ever believed he would already. It wouldn't do to push. So she slid it on herself. It, too, fit perfectly.

She lifted her gaze and met his. "Thank you. They're beautiful."

He cleared his throat. "Glad you like 'em. You keep them. After, I mean."

"After?"

"After the week is up," he clarified.

She was still smiling, but it froze on her lips.

"I don't want them back," he went on. "They're for you."

For her? But he was still planning on divorce at the end of the week? She could hear Martha now saying, "I don't *think* so!"

Sadie didn't know what to think.

The ring thing had shaken him.

Not just the rings he'd bought her, which he was very glad she liked and which suited her—though he couldn't quite make out why she'd blown warm and then very cold right at the end—but even more than Sadie's new rings, what shook him was realizing she had his grandfather's pipestone ring, and that he had given it to her the night they'd wed.

It just proved what a daze he'd been in. He couldn't imagine having given that ring to anyone.

It was big, awkward, homemade. His grandfather's father had carved it out of pipestone he'd found when he'd first come to Montana to mine as a young man. The ring was a heavy dark red inlaid with a piece of mother-of-pearl in the rough shape of a heart.

"He always said he reckoned he'd give the heart to my ma when she got here," his grandfather had told the young Spence. It had taken the young miner three years to save up enough money to bring over the family he'd left behind in Cornwall.

But only the children—a boy and a girl he barely recognized—had got off the train in Butte that summer morning. His wife had died on the voyage.

"So he wore the ring," Grandpa had said. "And the heart."

The red pipestone with its mother-of-pearl heart had stayed on his finger until the day he'd died, though the mother-of-pearl heart had cracked and a chip was missing.

Grandpa had worn it that way, too. "To remember," he'd said.

When he died, it had gone to Spence's dad who had never worn it.

"Don't like rings," he'd always said. He'd never worn a wedding ring either. So the pipestone ring used to sit in the saucer on top of his bureau. Spence would put it on his own finger when no one was around. Then his father left, but the ring stayed, and he tried it on more often. His hands grew bigger. The ring wasn't quite so loose. It didn't feel so heavy.

Then, one day when he was fifteen, the ring, like his father, was gone.

"Got rid of it," his mother said. "Ugly old thing. And with that broken heart." She shook her head. "Bad luck, if you ask me."

"Where'd it go?" Spence had demanded, furious, desperate.

"Took all your father's stuff to the junk shop on Galena," his mother said. "Good riddance."

Spence hadn't cared about anything else, only the ring.

The lady in the junk shop had sold it back to him. "It's not really worth much," she'd said doubtfully when he'd insisted on buying it.

"It is to me," Spence said. It was the only thing he had that connected to a good family memory. The only thing that connected to his grandfather.

And he had given it to Sadie the night she'd married him?

What had he been thinking?

He didn't have time to figure it out, though, because at that moment the plane jolted down onto the runway.

And as it slowed, turned and taxied toward the terminal, Sadie took a deep breath. "All set?"

Spence nodded. He hoped to God he was. He still felt shaken.

Then everyone was getting up and moving out.

"Here," Sadie said as they edged toward the door. And he felt her press something into his palm. "You'll need this."

"Need what?" But he could feel the answer even as he asked. A wedding ring.

His fingers instinctively closed around it. The edge of it dug into his palm. The rings he'd got for Sadie had been a token of appreciation. He never expected to receive one in return.

"It's called rose gold. It has copper in it," Sadie said when he stopped in the air bridge to stare at it, blocking the way for the other passengers trying to move around them. "It's not a big deal," she added. "But I thought maybe you'd want to—considering Leonie and all."

He hadn't been going to with Dena. But now he nodded. "Good idea."

Leonie would see it and know he was taken. Isogawa would

see it and understand that he and Sadie were a pair. It made perfect sense.

He slid it on his finger.

He suddenly felt married.

And not a moment too soon, he thought, once they'd cleared customs and were headed to the charter-plane departure lounge.

Everyone else was already there. He knew both New Zealand couples, Steve Walker and his wife, Cathy, and John and Marion Ten Eyk were getting there the night before. And Richard and Leonie were there, too. The four kiwis were talking among themselves. Richard was, as usual, deeply engrossed in something on his laptop. But as soon as Leonie glanced up from a magazine and saw them coming, she squealed with delight.

"Spence! Darling!" She leaped out of her seat and rushed toward him, arms open wide.

He braced himself for the onslaught, ready to catch her and hold her at arm's length when other fingers suddenly slid into his hand, and Sadie was right there next to him saying smoothly, "Aren't you going to introduce us, dear?"

Dear? Spence opened his mouth and nothing came out.

It didn't matter. Sadie went right on. "Oh, I recognize your voice." She beamed at Leonie, who, apparently seeing Sadie's hand in his, had stopped inches from launching herself into Spence's arms. "You must be Leonie! I'm Sadie."

And she intercepted the hug meant for him and gave Leonie an enthusiastic one of her own.

"S-Sadie?" Leonie sputtered, stepping out of the embrace to look Sadie up and down. "You're *Sadie?* Spence's—"

"Wife," Spence said smoothly. He had his bearings now. "Sadie is my wife," he told Leonie, sliding his arm around Sadie's waist as he did so. "And you can be the first to congratulate us."

Shock, confusion, consternation and a whole host of other expressions skittered across Leonie's face.

"But Sadie...works for you." Leonie's wide blue eyes fastened on Sadie who withstood the scrutiny and didn't give an inch.

"She does. She did."

"It's like out of a romance novel," Sadie told the other woman cheerfully. "You know the ones—years go by and finally the boss wakes up and sees the woman underfoot all day for the woman she really is."

Leonie's eyes went wider still, then just a little doubtful. But at Sadie's determined pleasantness she could hardly do more than smile wistfully.

"Wow. Congratulations." Then she turned a half-sceptical, half-accusing gaze on him. "And you never said a word. Not a single clue. Richard!" She turned to call to her husband, "Guess what Spence has brought with him!"

"Contracts, I hope," Richard said vaguely, not glancing up.

"I'm sure he has, darling," Leonie said impatiently. "But he's also brought a wife!"

Richard's head came up then. "A wife? Tyack's got a wife?" He set the computer aside then and came straight over, his eyes studying Sadie all the way. From the appreciation on his face, Spence thought with annoyance, he apparently liked what he saw.

Richard offered Sadie a hand, kissed her on both cheeks, then beamed at her. "Married the boss, did you? Smart girl. Beautiful, too." He turned to Spence. "Got eyes in your head," he said approvingly. "And you're not stupid, either. This girl's the one who keeps the wheels turning at the home office, isn't she?"

"She does a good job," Spence said stiffly, wondering why Richard was still holding on to Sadie's hand. He scowled.

Sadie smiled and deftly extracted her hand and laid it on Spence's arm. "I try to keep him thinking that," she told the other man.

Richard laughed. "I'm sure you manage." He rubbed his hands together. "Glad we've got a week on the island. Great idea of Isogawa's. It'll give us lots of time to get to know each other better."

Spence stared. Was Carstairs hitting on Sadie?

"I'm sure we'll have plenty of opportunity to visit," Sadie replied easily. Her smile included Leonie, too. "I'm looking forward to it. And to meeting everyone else in person as well," she added as the Ten Eyks and Walkers came over.

Spence made the introductions, but Sadie already seemed to know them all.

"Of course I do," she said. "I made all the reservations. Marion and Cathy and I have spoken on the phone. Cathy's a weaver and Marion paints. She's done some murals like Martha, and next time Theo and Martha go to New Zealand they're going to visit Marion and John."

"They are?" Spence just stood there, somewhere between bemused and stunned, while his wife chatted with everyone as if she'd known them for ages—which apparently she had.

# CHAPTER SIX

MR. ISOGAWA was at the dock to meet the seaplane when it landed.

A dapper man in his late sixties with steel-gray hair and a small bristly mustache, he was exactly as Spence had pictured him—a strict, soft-spoken field marshal—a man with Standards and Expectations.

He bowed and shook hands with Spence, but before Spence could introduce everyone, he said, "Come. We will go to the lodge. I will introduce you to my wife. She looks forward to meeting you. It is good you are all here. Nanumi is a place for families."

He made another bow, then he directed a small army of silent, smiling staff members to carry their luggage to various lodgings, then turned and led the way up a plank walkway toward a thatched roof Spence could see in the distance.

He turned and caught Sadie's eye. See?

Sadie smiled slightly and gave an infinitesimal nod in return.

The lodge when they came up on it, was a low-slung, sprawling, native wood, glass and thatch building that overlooked a crescent shaped bay. Spence had seen pictures of it, of course. But in person it was even more impressive than the pictures—not just a beautiful structure, but a harmonious extension of the picture-postcard, Pacific-island paradise in which it was set. Beside him, Sadie seemed to draw in an awed breath.

Dena would barely have noticed it. She'd spent so much time in the Caribbean—her father owned an island there—that tropical beauty held no novelty for her.

But Sadie was clearly dazzled by the island, the resort and the lodge they were entering. It was a spacious high-ceilinged room, one side all glass and open air, facing the bay. A bamboo bar curved around one end, and groupings of chairs and sofas all upholstered in brightly colored Polynesian designs were arranged around low tables.

"Here we will sit," Mr. Isogawa gestured toward them. "And now you will introduce us, Spencer-san?"

Spence did. Mr. Isogawa smiled and bowed and, for good measure apparently, shook hands with each of the men and their wives. It was very cordial, very proper. And then Spence took Sadie by the hand and drew her forward.

"I would like you to meet my wife, Mr. Isogawa. This is Sadie."

"*Sadie?*" Mr. Isogawa's distant politeness vanished. He stared first at Spence, and then abruptly turned his gaze on Sadie. "This is Sadie? You are marrying *my* Sadie?"

"*Your* Sadie?" It was Spence's turn to stare as Mr. Isogawa reached out and tapped Sadie on the arm so that she turned to face him squarely.

Sadie was smiling broadly but almost shyly as she nodded. "Yes, he is. Married to me, I mean."

At which Mr. Isogawa clapped his hands together delightedly, then broke into a wide welcoming grin. He bowed now to Sadie—a much deeper bow than anyone else had merited—and then he grasped both Sadie's hands in his and began talking rapidly to her.

In Japanese.

Spence stared. "She doesn't—"

But apparently she did, because Sadie began talking, too. In Japanese.

"Since when," he demanded, "do you speak Japanese?"

Sadie finished whatever she was saying to Mr. Isogawa before she turned to him and shrugged lightly. "Remember Tammy Nakamura, my roommate at UCLA?"

"No." The most he remembered about Sadie at UCLA was how damned inconvenient it had been the four years she was there. Coming home in the summers had never been enough. What he remembered about UCLA was going down for her graduation and hauling her back to Butte!

"Tammy was Japanese-American. But her dad made sure all the kids could speak the language. I made her teach me. When you started doing business with Mr. Isogawa, I tried it out on him." She grinned. "He thinks I'm very clever."

Mr. Isogawa's head bobbed in agreement. "Sadie is very smart. Works very hard. Beautiful, too," he murmured. And he still, Spence noted, hadn't let go of Sadie's hands.

What was it with men and Sadie's hands?

Just then Mr. Isogawa said something else to her in Japanese, and she blushed and held out her left hand for his inspection.

Spence felt a prickling between his shoulder blades as Mr. Isogawa even lifted her finger to scrutinized them in silence. They were only simple jade rings. Folk art. Nothing valuable or even particularly beautiful. And it was obvious that Mr. Isogawa thought Sadie was both.

Spence suddenly wished he'd kept the rock from Tiffany's and had insisted that she wear it. Dena had known what she was doing. He, on the other hand, had let his business sense be blinded by knowing Sadie.

But then Mr. Isogawa smiled. And this was different than his earlier smiles. This one reached his eyes. It seemed to come from the inside out. He held Sadie's hand out for Spence to take.

Slowly Spence took it.

Then Mr. Isogawa looked at Sadie. *"Sono yubiwa, o'suki desuka?"*

"Do I like them?" she translated. "Oh yes!" She nodded vehemently. "I mean, *hai.* I certainly do."

The smile on his lined face deepened as Mr. Isogawa nodded. "I, too." He turned his gaze on Spence, his gaze searching. "I see you chose well."

And Spence didn't think he was talking about the rings at all.

His face felt suddenly hot. "I think so. I'm glad you agree."

Still smiling, Mr. Isogawa nodded. Then he turned and beckoned to a woman hovering in shadows on the far side of the lounge. She was about the same age as he was, very petite and beautifully dressed in a silk sarong that seemed to reflect all the colors of the sea.

"My wife," Mr. Isogawa said, "Toshiko."

One by one he introduced her to all of them. And when he got to Sadie, the woman's eyes lit up and Sadie's did, too. They bowed and smiled very properly, and then they were holding hands and talking like old friends.

"I suppose you've met Mrs. Isogawa, too," he muttered.

Sadie laughed. "Sort of. We met on the phone. She's learning English. When Mr. Isogawa told me, I offered to help. We practice together, don't we?" she said slowly in English so the other woman could understand.

"Sadie is a good teacher." Mrs. Isogawa's voice was soft but her pronunciation was clear and precise. "Very smart."

"So I see." Spence was seeing more than he'd ever imagined.

While he'd been putting this deal together, he'd been all over the world, keeping tabs on other deals, as well. He'd sent Sadie the specs and the background and what he hoped to accomplish, and then he'd said she should keep track of things and get in touch with the various people he'd contacted. Then he'd left her to it.

He'd never considered how much contact she'd had, how

much work she'd done. He'd just assumed everything had fallen into place because of his intuition and groundwork. Now he saw that Mr. Isogawa's willingness to consider a bunch of western investors was more because Sadie had provided such diligent hands-on care and friendship than because he was a brilliant strategist and had put together a good group.

"We'll practice while I'm here," Sadie was saying now, and Mrs. Isogawa nodded happily.

But then Mr. Isogawa began speaking rapidly to his wife in their own language. Her eyes widened and she looked from Sadie to Spence and then to the rings on Sadie's hand as if seeing them for the first time.

"You are married?"

"Yes, we're married," Sadie agreed.

"Newlyweds," Leonie drawled. "So sweet."

"On their honeymoon," Mr. Isogawa decided happily.

"Well, not really." Sadie shook her head and wrapped her arms across her chest.

But Mr. Isogawa had other ideas. He called to the barman for champagne, then spoke to another man who nodded and disappeared quickly out the door. In a matter of seconds bottles of bubbly appeared, were opened and poured, and everyone was handed a flute.

"And now we will toast your happiness," Mr. Isogawa said. He raised his glass and spoke first in Japanese, then in English. Spence had no idea what he'd said in Japanese, but in English he wished them a long life, great wealth, deep happiness and many children.

"Many many children," he heard Mrs. Isogawa echo, then she smiled at Sadie and giggled.

Sadie blushed.

"Many many many children," Leonie agreed sotto voce. "Wouldn't you love lots of little kiddies, Spence?"

Sadie looked like she wanted to disappear through the floor.

"You're embarrassing the girl," Richard said brusquely. "Let them decide how many they're gonna have in private. But I'll drink to the rest of it. To Spence and Sadie. Congratulations and best wishes."

Fortunately, once the toast had been drunk, attention shifted. Sadie asked about the building, and Mr. Isogawa began to talk about the concept, the furnishings, the native artists whose work was displayed on a rotating basis, the local woods and textiles that were used as much as possible in the upholstery and bedding.

"We try," he said, "to give our guests the very best of this world. We do not let the outside intrude. We make a haven of beauty, as you say?" He looked to Sadie for affirmation that he had the right words.

"Indeed you have," Sadie agreed, running her hand lightly over the back of one of the sofas.

"And your quarters even more, I think. You will see." He glanced up as the young man who had disappeared through the doorway now reappeared. "And as soon as you are ready, Jale will show you to your *bures*." He turned to Spence. "We did not know you were bringing a new wife. This is special."

"Anything is fine," Spence assured him. "Sadie and I don't care."

"I care. Toshiko and I had moved into the honeymoon *bure* because it is small. Intimate. Only for two. Not for families. We did not realize we would have real honeymooners with us. So we'll make a change."

"We don't—" Spence began.

"It's not necessary—" Sadie said quickly.

But Mr. Isogawa raised a hand to silence them both. "It is necessary. *Shinkon-san ni, tekishite imasu.*"

Spence blinked, then looked at Sadie to see if she understood.

"He says it's appropriate," Sadie translated quietly. "He wants us to stay there because it's the appropriate place for newlyweds."

"But we're not on our honeymoon," Spence protested. "We're here on business. We're here to come to terms on the resort."

"But why is the resort at all?" Mr. Isogawa asked simply.

Spence shook his head, confused. "What?"

"We make the resort for couples. For families. To come together," Mr. Isogawa explained. "To remember, yes? Nanumi. To remind ourselves of what is most important. Business, yes, of course we do business. But business is only a part of life," Mr. Isogawa said. "The less important part. You understand?" His dark eyes seemed to bore into the depths of Spence's soul.

"I— Yes."

He understood the concept, at least.

His family had had no idea. The ring he'd given Sadie had been his only experience of that sort of connection. It had been a sign of his great-grandfather's love. A love which had endured loneliness and then death. But his own father had ignored it, had left it sitting in a saucer on the bureau. His mother had, typically, thrown it out.

But Mr. Isogawa was smiling at Sadie—and Sadie was smiling, too, just like she was thrilled, like she was his real wife.

"All right," Spence said. "But we are here for business."

Mr. Isogawa bowed. "Later we will talk business. Now you must share the beginning of your marriage with your beautiful wife."

The honeymoon *bure* was like *Swiss Family Robinson* meets *Modern Bride*.

Sadie stood in the open doorway and looked around in amazement. All of the resort's *bures* or native bungalows had looked beautiful as they'd passed them. But this one, inside and out, was spectacular.

It was a *bure* and not quite a *bure*. A thatched island cottage, yes, but it was built in a tree—like a treehouse. Not cobbled on, either, but exquisitely interwoven so that the *bure* seemed to flow between the branches. The room seemed carved out of the tree, not perched in it.

"Not traditional," Mr. Isogawa had apologized. "But we think, nice."

*Nice* didn't being to cover it.

The *bure* was nestled a dozen steps up in the spread of a vast tree that Sadie couldn't identify. From the frond-covered front porch with its gently swinging hammock to the interior native hardwood floors and *kiao* mats, from the vast king-size bed—"Almost as big as Kansas," she murmured—to the private open-air waterfall shower and spa hidden from the beach by carefully placed bamboo screens, it was elegant and spacious. With its stunningly printed tapa cloth wall hangings and the airy wicker table and chairs under the window and a pair of sturdy upholstered kauri chairs, it was exotic yet homey and welcoming at the same time. With views of a sand-and-sea paradise out of every door and window, it was beyond anything she had ever imagined.

"I hope you will be very happy here." The young man who had brought them along the wooden pathway that threaded through the trees now bowed slightly and left them alone. Together.

In the honeymoon *bure*—with one room. And one bed.

"Well, isn't this nice?" she said brightly when Spence didn't say anything at all.

He hadn't said a word since they'd left the main lodge. He'd followed the man called Jale—which Sadie had figured out was the local version of Charlie—down the path in silence. Ordinarily Spence peppered people with questions. He rarely had a thought he didn't share. But he'd taken in all the *bure's* amenities in complete silence. And even after Jale left he didn't speak.

Now he said abruptly, "We'll have to share the bed. I can't sleep in the hammock." He jerked his head toward the one swinging lightly on the porch outside the door.

"I know."

"Isogawa would notice. Or the help would. They'd comment. We can't take the chance."

"I know."

He didn't seem to hear. He cracked his knuckles and began to pace. "All the other *bures* have two beds!"

"Don't worry about it," Sadie said. "I'll stay on my own side. I promise I won't molest you."

He stopped dead. "What?"

"I said, I promise not to attack you!"

It was Spence's turn to blink. "That's not what I meant," he said gruffly. "I promised you two beds."

*You promised to love, honor and cherish me for the rest of our lives, too,* Sadie thought. But she didn't say it.

"I was there the whole time. I could almost see what was going through Mr. Isogawa's head. He was determined to make this special for us."

"You don't mind?"

"I'll live," Sadie assured him. "Will you?"

"Of course! It will be fine."

But even as he spoke, he moved away from the bed, as if determined to put as much space as he could between it and himself for as long as possible.

Sadie tried not to notice. With her thumb she turned the rings on her fingers. The rings proved that on some level at least Spence understood her, cared about her. And the *bure*—well, she was going to take it as a sign that someone, besides the Isogawas, wanted her and Spence to be together.

She kicked off her sandals and flexed her toes against the cool wooden floor. "How about a swim?" she suggested.

Spence glanced at the bed. "A swim sounds fine," he said quickly. "You go ahead and change. And I'll— Oh, hell, I left my briefcase up at the lodge. I'll go up and get it."

"You'd better be sure not to stay up there and work."

"No." He went out, then stopped on the porch and turned back. "Sade? Thanks."

She cocked her head. "Thanks?"

"I knew everything on this deal was coming together smoothly. I never realized how much of it was thanks to you. Your connections with all of them—the Isogawas, the Walkers, the Ten Eyks, even Richard and Leonie—are what has made this work so far."

"I've enjoyed it all," Sadie said truthfully. "It's been fun. They're interesting people."

"Yeah. They are. But I want you to know I appreciate it." He hesitated, as if he might say something else. Then he just muttered, "Thanks," again, and turned and hurried up the path.

She watched until he disappeared among the palms and then she sank down on the bed and sighed. He'd noticed her relationships with the Isogawas, the Ten Eyks, the Walkers. He *appreciated* them. He *thanked* her for them!

He probably even thought she'd developed them for the good of the company and for no other reason at all.

Sometimes Spencer Tyack was too stupid to live. And before the week was over, she just might kill him.

But—Sadie smiled—since he'd brought her to paradise, she might as well take a swim first.

Sadie swam.

John and Marion joined her. They found the water warm and inviting. Waves were almost nonexistent. It was like a gorgeous peaceful turquoise bath, breathtakingly clear and beautiful.

Spence never came.

"Working," Marion guessed.

"Damn fool," John said.

Was he? Sadie wondered. Or was he just avoiding her? She swam or lazed on the sand for over an hour. He never appeared.

"Richard probably got him," John said. "Trapped him some-where. Doing ten-year projections. He's even a bigger worka-holic than Spence."

Richard? Or had Leonie waylaid him on his way to the lodge?

All of a sudden Sadie thought she'd better go check. "I'll just go have a look," she said.

"You do that. Grab him by the ear and bring him down," Marion suggested.

"Or find something better to do." John grinned and gave her a conspiratorial wink.

Sadie blushed. "Yes, um…maybe I'll do that."

She waggled her fingers in farewell, wrapped the towel around her middle and made her way up the pathway to the tree-house. She could see the door was open when she reached the steps. So no Richard and, presumably, no Leonie.

He was either working or avoiding her.

"Spence? If Mr. Isogawa finds out that you're up here working—" She stopped dead.

He wasn't working. He was fast asleep.

Apparently he had actually intended to come down to the beach because a pair of black swimming trunks lay on the bed beside him. His feet were bare, his shirt unbuttoned. His lips parted slightly. And through them Sadie heart the faintest of snores.

"Spence?" she said, quietly this time, more to be sure that he really was sound asleep than to try to wake him.

He didn't respond. Not even an eyelash flickered.

She shouldn't be surprised, Sadie realized. While she had slept on the flight, he had apparently worked the whole time. And before that flight, she remembered, he'd already flown into L.A. from New York, a longer journey than hers, over more time zones. No wonder he was exhausted.

And damnably hard to resist, Sadie thought, as she stood looking down at him, drinking in the sight.

He might have been a different man from the one she knew awake. The fierce intensity that so characterized his every waking moment was gone. His mouth was softer. The rest of his face, too, seemed more relaxed. Gentler.

His five-o'clock shadow had gone another twelve hours and was rougher and darker than ever. Sadie remembered the brush of his whiskered jaw against hers when they'd made love the night they'd married. She hadn't touched that stubble since. She felt a compulsion to reach down and brush her hand against his cheek now.

She didn't. Couldn't let herself. This week was roller-coaster ride enough. She didn't need to make it worse. So she tucked her arms across her chest and trapped her hands in case they got the best of her.

*Just look, don't touch.*

But this Spence was so much more clearly the person she knew was inside the one the world saw that she almost couldn't help herself. In him now she saw hints of the boy she remembered—and of the man she'd married that night four years ago.

When they'd got back to the room, they had made love eagerly, desperately, frantically, barely making it to the bed as they'd torn each other's clothes off as they went. Their lovemaking had been scorching.

And afterward he had murmured, "It should always have been you." And then, almost instantly, he had fallen asleep in her arms.

And Sadie had watched him sleep.

She had lain awake, astonished at the sudden turn in direction her life had taken, afraid to close her eyes lest when she awoke it would all turn out to be a dream.

And when she finally did go to sleep, she'd awakened a few hours later to find that it had become a nightmare.

Still, she remembered this part as vividly as if it had happened only hours before. Remembered how she'd held him close, relishing the brush of his soft hair against her nose, loving the feel of the rough whiskers on his jaw against the smoothness of her cheek.

She'd feathered kisses there. And Spence had sighed and smiled, had moved his mouth as if to kiss her back, but in the end had slept on.

She saw that man asleep here now, and she could only remember the night—not the morning after. It was all she could do to hug her arms against her chest to stop them reaching out for him.

*Go on,* Martha whispered inside her head. *What are you waiting for?*

But as much as she would have loved to lie down beside him and wrap her arms around him, Sadie couldn't do it.

He had to want it; he had to want her; and she had to know it.

She started to move away, but couldn't quite do it. Not without, for just a moment, freeing a hand to reach down and let it drift lightly over his ruffled dark hair.

"I love you," she whispered.

It was only the truth—as much as it hurt to think her love might never be returned.

Spence smiled. And he slept.

There was a regular tub in the bathroom that would afford her privacy. But just beyond the sliding glass doors there was a small, screened outdoor patio with a rainforestlike shower that fell into a rock pool.

Sadie had been able to resist sharing the bed with Spence—at least for the moment—but a rainforest shower was too much temptation. He would never know. He was dead to the world. So she fetched a towel from the bathroom and one of the thick terry-cloth robes there, too. Carrying the rose-colored robe and the towel, she padded back quietly through the bedroom to slide open the doors.

Spence had rolled onto his side. But his breathing was still deep and even.

Sadie watched him, assessed the room on the bed and decided that, if he stayed where he was, there would be room for her to slide into the bed when she'd showered. That shouldn't offend his sensibilities too much.

She stepped out onto the decking and eased the door shut behind her. With a quick self-conscious glance back at the sleeping Spence, she wriggled out of her swimsuit. Feeling even more self-conscious and enormously decadent, she stepped into the pool and beneath the shower.

It was heaven. The spray was soft and full, the water lukewarm—absolutely perfect. She tipped her head back and let the spray hit her face, slide down her neck and over the rest of her body.

"Ah, yes." She smiled, turned, let it course down her back. Reaching for one of the tubes lined up along the rock shelf, she squeezed out a dollop of the pineapple-scented shampoo and worked it into her hair, then rinsed it and watched as blobs of lather slid down her arms and over her breasts and plopped into the pool which seemed to be filling with bubbles.

*Decadent* didn't even begin to describe it. She would never take a shower again in her utilitarian claw-foot tub back in Butte without remembering this one.

Once more she lifted her face into the spray and let it wash over her whole body. A gentle sea breeze stirred the air and the surrounding tree leaves. In the distance she could hear people's voices on the beach. Marion and John seemed to have been joined by Steve and Cathy and Leonie. They were laughing about something. It felt odd to be able to hear them so clearly, be so close—and so naked—and know they couldn't see her.

Or could they?

Sadie craned her neck to look over the top of the screen to

make sure. But they weren't looking her way at all. She was completely hidden.

No one saw her.

Except Spence.

# CHAPTER SEVEN

SPENCE was dreaming.

They were vibrant vivid dreams in which he was undressing Sadie, then kissing his way up her arms and across her shoulders, along her jawline, all over her cheeks, the tip of her nose and, finally, her luscious beautiful mouth.

And all the while he was kissing her, he was running his hands over her and dispensing with her clothes, her proper tailored blouses and jackets, eager to get to the peach-colored scraps of silk he knew were underneath.

Then, just when he reached the silk and began to unhook her bra, he heard the faint click of the hook.

Click? Of the hook?

He jerked. His eyes opened as Sadie clicked open the sliding glass door to the enclosed shower room. Then the door clicked shut again. And through it Spence beheld a reality more vibrant and vivid than all his dreams and fantasies of Sadie in peach-colored underwear.

As he watched in dazed but dazzled fascination, the real-live Sadie Morrissey hung her towel and robe on a hook by the waterfall, then with a quick glance toward the door, turned and peeled down her swimsuit and stepped naked into the water.

His mouth went dry. His eyes didn't blink as he stared at a peach-colored Sadie wearing nothing at all!

He groaned at the sight, at the instant reaction of his body, already primed by his dreams. Sucking in a harsh breath, Spence shut his eyes.

"Damn." He swallowed, then opened his eyes a fraction, hoping against hope that he'd imagined it all, that jet lag and stress and overwork and sexual frustration—not to mention Sadie frustration—had combined to create hallucinations.

Not so.

She was still there. Standing in the shallow rock pool beneath the spray, then doing a little hop-skip, a little dance step, like some water sprite. Her breasts bounced lightly, the water made her skin glisten. He swallowed again.

He couldn't close his eyes now. There was no point. Why bother? He was never going to be able to forget this. He might as well enjoy the show.

She was, after all, his wife.

So he was entitled, right?

He could get up off this bed and strip off his clothes and join her there in the pool under the shower. As her husband, he could run his hands over her soap-slicked body. He could kiss her neck, could kiss his way down across her breasts, could touch his tongue to her navel, kiss lower, touch her—there.

His jaw clenched and he rolled onto his back, his body screaming a protest at not being allowed to do exactly that, at not being allowed to do more.

Why *not* do more?

Was she going to fight him off? She hadn't been as upset about there being only one bed as he had. And he'd been upset because he thought it mattered to her.

Didn't it?

Did she *want* him to make love to her?

She'd married him, hadn't she? his body argued.

But she'd only married him under duress, his brain replied. Because he'd made it impossible for her to refuse. Because she'd cared about him as a friend, because he'd been at the end of his rope and, knowing it, she'd done him a favor. Because she'd *pitied* him!

And why would she want to be married to him, anyway? She knew his family. She knew his background. She knew as well as Danny ever had what poor husband material he was. She was a forever woman—a woman who had always wanted a husband, a home and a family.

She deserved a far better man than him.

So the least he could do was keep his mind on business. He just needed to remember that.

But right now he needed to get out of here.

Spence knew human nature—especially his own—well enough to know that all the rational resolutions in the world could fail in the face of too much temptation.

His father hadn't taught him much. But he'd damn sure taught him that.

He wasn't there!

Sadie had finished her shower, dried off and wrapped herself in the soft rose-colored terry robe. She'd combed her fingers through her hair so she didn't look like a complete scarecrow, and then, taking a deep breath, carefully and quietly as possible, she'd slid open the glass door, hoping Spence had left her a corner of the bed in which to nap.

And he wasn't there! The bed was empty, the coverlet rumpled, but Spence was gone.

Heart slamming against her chest, Sadie ran to the bathroom. He wasn't there. She peered out onto the front deck. No Spence. She even went out and looked down toward the beach. But everyone had gone. It was empty now, too.

She couldn't see or hear a single soul, only the sound of the sea as it washed against the shore and the rustle of the breeze in the palms.

Where had he gone?

And why?

His swim trunks were missing. The clothes he'd been wearing were hanging in the closet. Had he awakened and grabbed his trunks, thinking she was still down at the beach?

Had he not seen her in the shower?

*Naked* in the shower!

How could he not? Her face burned as she realized there was simply no way he could not have seen her. While the view from the waterfall into the room was obscured by the sun's reflection on the glass, the view of the shower area was crystal clear.

He couldn't have missed her.

Her whole body was hot now. Burning from humiliation, not the possibility of embarrassment.

He had seen her and looked the other way. *Run* the other way!

She wanted to die. How could she spend a week with Spence in the same room—in the same bed—if he couldn't even bear to look at her?

And she'd hoped to make a real marriage out of this?

What had she been thinking? The very thought seemed laughable now.

And the joke, Sadie knew, was on her.

The sound of drumbeats, deep and hollow, echoed off the wall of the *bure* late that afternoon. Sadie knew what they meant—that the lounge and bar were open, that dinner would soon be served.

And of course she had to be there. It was her job.

For the past two hours she had sat huddled in one of the wicker chairs in the *bure* crying. It was stupid. Pointless. She told herself that over and over. But it didn't help.

She hadn't any idea where Spence was. Wherever he had gone to, desperate to get away from her nakedness, he had never returned.

He would have to show up at dinner, though. It was a command performance, one of the places Mr. Isogawa was sure to expect to see them together. So Spence would turn up, expecting her to act the part of the loving wife.

"How about the spurned wife?" she muttered, scrubbing at her eyes with a tissue. She wondered if this was how Leonie felt.

Probably. Damn men, anyway.

Still furious, Sadie wiped her eyes, then carefully applied a bit of makeup, hoping it would mask the worst of the blotchiness on her face. Her eyes were still red, but she could always say they were bloodshot from swimming. It wasn't a great excuse, but it was good enough.

Then she went to the closet and took out the red-orange wildly printed sundress Martha had brought over the morning Sadie had been leaving.

"It's seen Greece," Martha had said, thrusting it at her. "I wore it there when Theo and Eddy and I went back a few months ago. Theo thought it was *trés* sexy." She'd wiggled her eyebrows and grinned. "Maybe Spence will, too. Anyway, it should see the South Pacific before it retires."

And so it would, Sadie decided. She would do her job, and she would enjoy herself as best she could. The hell with Spence. But she owed it to Martha to give her dress a whirl.

She arrived by herself, and Mr. Isogawa, who with his wife had been visiting with the Ten Eyks, rose quickly and came over to bow and invite her to join them.

"You are enjoying yourself?" he asked.

"Yes, thank you. *Arigato*," she repeated in Japanese, making Mrs. Isogawa smile. "I'm having a wonderful time. The tree-house *bure* is magnificent. And I've been swimming already. The beach is beautiful, the water was so warm. And the waterfall in the spa—I loved it."

She must have been convincing because he smiled. "And Spencer? Did Spencer enjoy? Where is Spencer?"

"Spencer fell asleep," she reported with absolute honesty. "He was so tired after working on the plane all the way down here, he just collapsed. I went swimming without him. And when he woke up, I guess he went out exploring on his own."

And when he showed up, he could damned well tell Mr. Isogawa all about it. What she'd said was the truth—minus her own interpretation of it.

Mr. Isogawa nodded. "I will be interested to hear what he found."

What Spence found, they learned, when he arrived just before dinner was served, was that there was a track up the hill through the bush to a lookout area at the top from which you could see virtually the whole island.

"It has amazing 360-degree views. Blows your mind." He looked bright-eyed and handsome as sin, well rested and completely at ease.

Sadie hated him.

He must have gone back to the treehouse after she'd left, because he had changed clothes and now wore a pair of tropic-weight khaki-colored trousers and a deep blue polo shirt that exactly matched the color of his eyes, though she was sure he had no idea.

"You had a good time, then?" She did her best to sound as cheerful and upbeat as he did, determined that she would do what she'd signed on for.

"Yep." He paused. "Sorry I didn't make it down swimming. I conked out. I was going to join you, but you weren't swimming anymore when I woke up,"

*No, I was naked in the shower. You could have joined me there.* But of course she didn't say it. She just pasted a bright smile on her face and hoped she looked sincere.

"I'll take you there tomorrow," he said "You'll love it." And smiling down at her, he slung an arm around her shoulders and drew her hard against him.

The self-preserving part of Sadie wanted to stiffen and resist. The furious part wanted to kick him where it would do the most good. He was such a convincing liar!

But she'd given her word, and to fight now would be disastrous not just for the deal, but it would make everyone uncomfortable. So she leaned into his embrace and smiled. "I'm sure I will."

Then, because she was damned if he was going to be the only one who showed how devoted they were, she turned her face toward his, and kissed him lightly on the jaw.

It was Spence who stiffened then, and she saw a flicker of confusion in his gaze, followed by something that looked like determined challenge. And the next thing she knew Spence bent his head and kissed her full on the lips!

It wasn't a passionate kiss, one that should have been saved for the privacy of a honeymoon *bure,* but it lingered long enough to be possessive, and it promised a host of things that left Sadie startled—and shaken—when at last Spence stepped away.

He smiled at her.

She shot him a furious glare, then looked up to see Leonie Carstairs watching.

The meaning of the kiss was suddenly perfectly clear. It was a "keep your distance" kiss, meant for Leonie. He'd intended it to mean nothing to Sadie. Nothing at all.

"Come," Mr. Isogawa said. "It is time for dinner." He took his wife's arm and led her toward the dining room.

Spence, still smiling, held out his arm to her.

And Sadie, after one careful steadying breath, slipped her arm through his and, ignoring her heartache, walked by his side to the dinner table.

* * *

"Well, that went well," Spence said briskly as he opened the door to their *bure* after an excellent dinner and an evening of general "getting to know you better" conversation.

"Do you think so?" Sadie said ironically, because, while she'd done her best, she didn't think *well* described it. *Hypocritcal* came closer.

Now she brushed past him into the room, then immediately wished she hadn't.

The bed, which had seemed Kansas-size a few short hours ago, now appeared only slightly larger than a postage stamp. And it was one thing to go to bed with a man you loved if you thought he might find you appealing, and another to go to bed with a man who had turned and run when he'd glimpsed you naked.

And now there was no beach to escape to, no grounds to wander about it. It was all darkness—velvety black with amazing stars and constellations she had enjoyed learning about from John Ten Eyk. But she couldn't stay out there all night.

"Didn't you think so?" Spence sounded surprised. He shut the door and kicked off his shoes. "Everybody was having a good time. The place is in terrific shape, a lot better than I expected. The service seems very good. The food was fantastic."

"Yes."

"Leonie left me alone," Spence said with supreme satisfaction. "And when you get past the starchiness, Isogawa's a nice guy. So's his wife. And they obviously think you're wonderful. So do I," he said cheerfully.

"Why? Because I scared off Leonie? Because your clever plan is working? Isn't that just great."

Spence's forehead furrowed as his brows drew down. "What's the matter with you?"

"Nothing's the matter with me! Nothing at all."

"I can tell. You're so full of sweetness and light tonight." Spence rolled his eyes.

"You don't know anything about me!"

"So, tell me. Why are you mad?"

His simple question infuriated her even more. "Who said I was mad?" Sadie spun away, putting the bed between them, as he came toward her.

"Lucky guess," he drawled. Their gazes met across the bed, his stony and furious, hers equally mad. He raked a hand through his hair and scowled deeply. "So, let me venture a guess."

She lifted a shoulder indifferently. "Suit yourself."

"It's about this afternoon. Isn't it?" he prodded, when she didn't reply at once.

"What do you think?"

"I think I'm doing the best I can, damn it," he snapped. "All right, fine, I apologize! But I'm not blind, Sadie! If you don't pull the drapes across the windows, I'm going to get an eyeful. I can't help it! But I left, didn't I?"

Sadie's jaw dropped. *"What?"*

Still Spence glowered, eyes flashing. "If you didn't want me to see you naked, why the hell did you leave the drapes open when you took your shower?"

*That* was what he thought she was mad about? That he had seen her naked? Not that he had been so disgusted by the sight that he'd left the room?

"Well?" he demanded when she didn't reply.

Numbly Sadie shook her head, still trying to fathom that, make sense of it. Finally she could only ask dumbly, "That's why you left?"

"Did you want me to lie there staring at you? Is our Sadie an exhibitionist now?" His tone was mocking.

"Of course not! I needed a shower. I'd come in from swimming in the ocean. It was beautiful, inviting. Not like the bathtub I can use every day. And *you* were *asleep!* I wasn't trying to seduce you!"

"Which is exactly what I figured," he informed her flatly. "And I didn't imagine you would be any less enticing when you came back in the room." Hard blue eyes met hers. "So I left."

But Sadie was stuck a sentence earlier. "Enticing?" She echoed the word as if she had never heard it before. Was he saying. "You thought I was…?" She stared at him in wonderment.

"You're enticing as hell, Sadie Morrissey," he bit out. "And while I would have loved to lie there watching you cavorting under the shower—"

"I was *not* cavorting!" she protested.

"No? Well, dancing then. Hopping around. You hopped." He made it sound like an accusation.

God, how long had he watched? Sadie felt herself go scarlet.

"You enticed," he said again, very firmly. "And I wouldn't have been content with looking. I would have wanted more. And that wasn't part of our bargain. So I left."

Oh.

"So I apologize," he said tersely. "It was all I could think to do at the time."

"All?" Sadie said before she could stop herself.

Their gazes met again, locked this time. Electricity arced between them. Desire. Hunger. Frustration. Need. Sadie certainly felt all of them. She had no idea what Spence felt at his end.

He gritted his teeth. "Don't tempt me, Sadie. Little girls who play with matches are likely to get burned."

It was as if she'd been cut free, her fears banished, her heart hammering. "Is that a promise?"

"Cut it out," he said, his voice sharp. "Get ready for bed. I've already apologized for the bed, and I'm damned if I'll do it again."

"I don't care," Sadie said.

He ignored her. "I'll go out and walk on the beach while you're changing. Flick the light when you're decent and all tucked in." Then, without letting her reply, he opened the door and stalked out into the night.

He stood outside looking up into the night sky, telling himself it would be all right.

He'd survived the evening. He'd played his part well and so had Sadie. Yes, there had been a few tense moments, but he'd handled things well. He'd apologized for this afternoon—not that it had been his fault, damn it—and he'd got out before Sadie could misinterpret anything else.

If he was lucky, she'd just go to bed and fall asleep at once. She hadn't had any rest as far as he knew. Maybe she'd slept this afternoon after her shower, but the bed looked pretty much the way it had when he'd decamped. So she ought, by rights, to be exhausted.

Spence prayed that she'd be exhausted. He certainly was. By design. It was the only way he knew that he could get any sleep in a bed with Sadie Morrissey. He'd left the room this afternoon and he'd walked miles. Literally. He doubted there were many trails on the island that he hadn't explored.

So he could spend the night with her. Of course he could. It wasn't like he was a teenager anymore. He had control.

Then, out of the corner of his eye, he saw the light in their *bure* blink on and off—and all of a sudden his control didn't seem so certain.

*Quit,* he told himself sharply. *You never get anywhere by anticipating disaster. It will be fine. Give it five minutes. She'll be sound asleep.*

So he waited. He tried very hard not to think about peach-colored underwear and naked Sadie Morrisseys. He directed his mind firmly *away* from whatever Sadie might be wearing, tucked under the covers.

Mind over matter. He could do that. He climbed the steps and opened the door.

She wasn't under the covers at all!

"I told you to get in bed!"

Sadie smiled and stretched languorously. "I don't work for you 24/7. Sorry, but it's after hours."

He glared at her, furious at the enticement she provided sitting there on the bed in some flimsy little short yellow nightgown, all smiling and sweet, as tempting as Eve and her damned apple.

"What are you trying to do?" he demanded.

"To do?" She looked at him guilelessly.

He didn't believe the pose for a minute. "You're flaunting yourself! Trying to tempt me!" He flung words as accusations.

She smiled slightly. "Is it working?"

"What the hell do you think...? Damn it, Sadie! Do you want me to attack you?"

There was a half-second's hesitation. Then she gave him an impish smile. "As a matter of fact, I would."

# CHAPTER EIGHT

'SADIE?" HE LOOKED as if he hadn't heard her right. As if he doubted his ears. She couldn't repeat it. So she said nervously, 'Unless you'd rather not."

He stared at her. "You're kidding, aren't you?" His voice was ragged. And without another word, he dragged her into his arms, gathered her close, fastened his lips on hers.

He kissed her.

And instinctively Sadie kissed him back.

It was like coming home.

It was an echo of that earlier night—their wedding night—but infinitely better. Those kisses had been hungry and anxious and desperate. Frantic, almost. This kiss was hungry, too. Maybe even a little desperate.

But the similarity ended there. It didn't plunder; it explored. It didn't demand, it sought a response. And even more than that, it offered. It offered her Spence the way she had always dreamed of him. This kiss said he was hers.

Sadie, of course, had been his for as long as she could remember. But until now—until this moment—she'd been afraid that she had given herself wholly and completely to a man who, except for one brief night, would never want more from her than casual friendship and a lot of hard hours at work.

But in his kiss now, in the fine tremor of his hands as he touched her, she knew her fears were baseless. He wanted her every bit as much as she wanted him.

"Sadie." He whispered her name against her lips. She could taste it, taste the mingling of her name and him.

She smiled. "Mmm." She murmured, heady with pleasure as she tugged his shirt up and over his head, then let her hands roam over his arms, his shoulders, the hard muscular breadth of his back. "Yes."

"Yes? Like this?" he asked. His own hands were busy learning her. Touching her. Delighting her.

But he had much more access to her than she did to him. And she reached for the buckle of his belt, but fumbled it. "Lack of experience," she muttered as he undid it for her, then quickly shucked them and the rest of his clothes, and she could see him in all his naked glory.

"Oh yes," she whispered, pulling back to look, then reaching out to touch, to run her fingers lightly over his chest and across his hard abdomen, to brush lightly against his erection.

He tensed. "Sadie!" Her name hissed between his teeth.

"Mmm?" But he didn't answer as she pressed kisses against his jaw, his neck, his shoulders, his chest. His breathing grew faster, shallower. His skin was so hot she wondered if he had a fever. Against her hand she could feel the gallop of his heart. Still no answer, just a strangled sound from deep in his throat. Worriedly Sadie asked, "Are you...all right?"

The sound turned into something between a laugh and a moan. "I'm dying."

The ragged tone of his voice had her pulling back, horrified. "Dying?"

"For you, idiot," he muttered. "I've *been* dying for you."

Sadie didn't believe that for a minute. But she didn't mind him saying it. Actually she loved him saying it. "You're sure?"

He pressed her back onto the bed, his body coming full length against hers, settling in, fitting perfectly. "What do you think?"

"Oh." She understood now. She smiled, wriggled against him.

"Stop that." Spence's lips were against her mouth. "You're going to push me over the edge."

"What a shame," Sadie murmured, a delicious smile curving her mouth.

"Tease." Spence's lips moved from her lips over her cheeks. They touched, they pressed, they stroked, they nibbled. They teased and made her burn, too. There was a fine tremor in his fingers as they skimmed up her legs and caught hold of the night-gown, then tugged it up and over her head and tossed it away.

"Spence!"

He raised his head. "What? You wanted to wear it?"

"Yes. No. I don't care, Spence. I—"

He kissed her. "Shh. Lie back and think of Montana."

"No." She was absolutely not going to do that. She was going to participate. Completely. "I get to…to do things, too."

"Oh, really?" His mouth was so close she felt his breath on her cheek.

"Yes, really."

"I thought I was the boss."

"Only in the office. We're not in the office now."

"Now, wait a minute!"

But Sadie was done with waiting. She kissed him to shut him up, then drew her tongue along his lips and dipped it inside. At the same time she ran her hands down his back and over the solid curve of his buttocks, reveling as she did so in the fact that she finally felt free to touch him the way she'd wanted to touch him for years.

"Got a problem with this?" she asked him, wriggling again.

"I think I could get used to it," he muttered, then buried his face in her breasts only to lift his head a moment later and grin at her. And she could hear the awe in his voice when he said, "It really is you, Sadie. It really is you."

"It is." Though after all these years, she could hardly believe it, either.

Then Spence stopped talking once more. He kissed her thoroughly. His hands were everywhere, learning her lines and curves and secrets, making her gasp and squirm. And even though he had her gasping, she was determined to do the same for him.

Four years ago she'd been so overwhelmed by the sudden and bewildering turn of events and their astonishing marriage that she'd done little more than give herself to him. Now she wanted to do more, have more, share more.

And so she touched and stroked. She kissed and nuzzled. And Spence's control was snapped. His breathing quickened. His heart slammed.

"Sadie! Slow—!"

"No! I want you."

"I want...you...too. But I need—" He didn't finish, just pushed away to get off the bed.

"What?" Sadie stared after him, stunned.

But in a moment he'd found what he was looking for in his suitcase. Protection. They didn't need it, Sadie wanted to tell him. She'd be thrilled if she conceived here in this wonderful place.

But Spence had already accomplished the task and was settling between her legs again, finding the center of her, stroking, nudging, probing.

And Sadie took him in.

It had been so long. Sometimes she had despaired of ever having him again, of ever knowing this feeling of completion, of fulfillment. Sometimes, in fact, she thought she'd dreamed it.

But she hadn't. Oh, dear heaven, no, she hadn't! And she knew it now as she drew him into the heart of her being and wrapped him in the wonder of her love.

And then she knew nothing more—only the hot shuddering release of passion and tension and the sensation that at last the two of them had finally become one.

He owed her better than this. More than this. And Spence knew it.

He should have been slower, gentler, more thoughtful. He felt boneless, weightless, though he was sure he must be pressing Sadie into the mattress. Flattening her. But even though he willed it, he couldn't seem to move.

Sadie wasn't moving, either, though he felt her heart beat against his chest.

"That…" Sadie said breathlessly from beneath him, "was amazing."

Spence didn't move. "Yeah?" In what way amazing? Amazingly awful?

Sadie's lungs expanded. He could feel her drawing in a deep breath. "Oh, yes! It was wonderful."

His heart skipped a beat. He could almost feel it expand in his chest, as if the weight of the world had suddenly been lifted.

"Mmm." And then she looped her arms around his neck and tugged his face down to plant a kiss on his lips. "The best."

He grinned. He laughed. He couldn't help it. "You think that was good?" he said gruffly. "I'll show you good."

"Now?" Sadie squeaked.

"In a few minutes. How about that?" He rolled off her and drew her against him, marveling at how right she felt in his arms, against his side, as if she belonged there.

"I think I could stand it again in a few minutes," Sadie said after a moment's consideration.

"Good." He settled a hand in her hair. Turned his head to kiss her brow. Could barely believe this was happening. Was he going to wake up and have it all be a dream?

But the night passed…with more lovemaking. Lots of lovemaking. Spence was determined to show Sadie every kind he could think of. And it wasn't a dream. He was exhausted at dawn. Eyes bloodshot. Body drained. Brain dead.

He didn't care. Sadie agreed it was good. Very very good indeed.

They missed breakfast.

Well, not all of it. But everyone else had finished and was sitting around the lounge drinking cups of tea and coffee when they came in together, looking flushed and distracted and as if they'd spent the night in the honeymoon *bure* doing exactly what honeymooners were expected to do.

And they had.

And they were flushed and distracted because they'd spent the most amazing night together—all of it sleepless—and at dawn they had gone out for a swim.

Spence had suggested it.

"You want to *swim?*" Sadie had stared at him in disbelief. "I'll drown. I feel boneless."

"C'mon." Spence had tugged her hand to pull her up. "It'll be wonderful. You'll see."

He was right. It had been magical. The cool morning air, the water almost warm when they plunged in. They'd romped and played and kissed—and loved.

And then, floating there in the water watching the sun rise out of the ocean, it had become even more wonderful because she'd been floating back against Spence's chest, his arms encircling her, his breath soft against her ear.

Then, once the sky had changed from navy to a stunning mixture of violets and reds and oranges, and finally to the pale yellow and bright blue of morning, they had left the beach and come back to their treehouse *bure*, where they had showered together in the waterfall where Spence had watched her the day before.

Had that been only yesterday? Not even a full twenty-four hours? How was it possible that things had changed so much?

Sadie didn't know. She only knew the joy they had today. And that she felt a little stiff and sore, as if she'd used muscles she was unaccustomed to using. Imagine that, she thought, unable to keep the silly happy grin on her face.

Spence looked equally pleased, though his eyes were decidedly bloodshot and he hadn't shaved because Sadie had decided she liked his stubbly jaw.

She'd urged him not to shave. "Unless you think Mr. Isogawa will object," she'd said, aware that there were other priorities.

"You're more important than Isogawa," Spence had said, rubbing his whiskers lightly against her cheek.

And Sadie couldn't help feeling more important as they came into the lounge, with Spence's arm looped over her shoulders.

One look at them and Sadie was sure everyone knew what they had been doing. She was far too pleased to care. And even when Mr. Isogawa asked politely if they had slept well, she hadn't been able to stop grinning.

"We had a good night," she said. It was the truth, after all, even if they hadn't slept.

"I'll bet you did," Leonie said enviously.

Richard didn't notice, but Marion jumped in and said diplomatically, "It's a wonderful place. John and I enjoyed it, too. Not too hot. Not too cold. Peaceful. And all those lovely gentle waves."

Had she seen them? Sadie wondered, knowing her face was even redder. But Marion didn't give her a knowing grin or wink. Bless her heart.

Cathy beckoned them toward a table with two empty chairs. "Come sit and enjoy your breakfast. It's marvelous. Fresh fruit. Eggs. French toast. Whatever your heart desires, really. We ate too much. Marion and I were just talking about going for a walk while they're all in meetings. Want to come with us?" Her gaze included both Sadie and Leonie.

"Not me," Leonie said promptly. "I'm going to have a massage," she said with a knowing smile. "With Jale."

Jale, the young man who had taken them to their *bure* yesterday, was a definite hunk. And obviously he had more talents than carrying luggage.

Sadie shot a quick glance at Richard to see if she could gauge his reaction to Leonie's plan. But Richard didn't even seem to have heard. He was talking to John, not paying attention to his wife at all.

"I'd love to," Sadie said to Marion and Cathy, "but this isn't just a honeymoon for me. It's work, too. I have to be at the meetings."

Spence hadn't said so, but the truth was, she wanted to go to the meetings.

She wanted to be wherever Spence was, to watch him in action. She wanted to spend the whole day just looking at him, marveling at the fact that finally, after so long, he was really hers and that finally they both knew it.

They hadn't spoken much last night. When the barriers had finally come down it had been too startling, too new, too overwhelming. There had been words, but not many. There would be time later for them.

She had said, "I love you," though.

She'd dared that much, and had held her breath after she'd said it, fearing he would laugh.

He hadn't. He had groaned and kissed her with a desperation that told her he loved her, too. And she had been willing to settle for that. She believed he loved her even if he couldn't yet say it.

But he'd surprised her by pulling back and looking deeply into her eyes and saying, "I love you, too."

She'd blinked, amazed, then exultant. She was confident now that he was the soul mate she had always thought he would be.

Spencer Tyack had always been a guarded man, who charmed others easily, who had many friends—but who loved only a few.

He loved her. He'd said so. And she had no doubt that he would demonstrate that fact again as soon as they had some privacy.

And in the meantime she could watch him. She could take notes as needed, and when they weren't needed she could mentally undress him and rehearse all the things they would do when they were alone.

The very thought made her smile again.

"Newlyweds," Marion chided her, laughing at her dopey smile. "Stop your daydreaming and order your breakfast. You're making me envious, you are."

Sadie felt herself blushing again. But hastily she sat down and one of the waitresses instantly appeared with a menu.

"If you don't see what you want," the waitress told her, smiling, "we will find it for you."

It was hard to imagine anything she might want that was not on the menu. It was as extensive and amazing as Cathy had claimed. And Sadie saw far too many things she wanted because suddenly she was starving.

Finally she settled on a glass of juice, a muffin, an omelet and a cup of tea, though she could probably have eaten a lumberjack-size meal, she'd expended so many calories during the night. But she didn't want everyone to think Spence had married a glutton. She needed to behave properly and with dignity, moderation and decorum—as long as she could be a complete wanton in bed!

A giggle bubbled up.

Cathy and Marion looked at her, shook their heads, still smiling as they sighed. Leonie looked from Sadie to Spence and back again, then turned her head to look daggers at Richard who still didn't notice.

Sadie felt sorry for her and wished she could help, especially since it was due to Leonie's attempt to seduce Spence that she owed her own current happiness. Poor Leonie.

"Ah, I see you are happy this morning." The soft, precisely accented English made Sadie look up to see Mrs. Isogawa standing next to her table.

"I'm very happy," Sadie assured her. "I think this is the most wonderful place on earth!"

"Good place," Mrs. Isogawa agreed. "Happy place. Meet my husband here."

"You did? Here?"

"Yes, yes." Then she glanced over and said something to her husband in Japanese.

"It's true," he agreed. "She was with some friends on a holiday. I was working here. Designing these buildings. Except I couldn't take my eyes off her. I found a way to get introduced to her." His smile widened. "And the rest is, as you say, history."

Sadie was enchanted. It really was a magical place.

"Every year our family comes, too. They will be here later this week. Our sons and daughter and grandchildren. Maybe," he said, "you will come in the future and bring your family, too."

Sadie could get misty and starry-eyed just thinking about it. She glanced over at Spence, but he was listening to something Steve Walker was saying.

"You do not need to come to the meetings today," Mr. Isogawa told her. "If you wish to enjoy the island, my assistant can take notes and give them to you."

"I'd like to come," Sadie replied. "It is my job. But I really want to. I don't usually get to see Spence in this part of his work."

Mr. Isogawa nodded. "Very well. Enjoy your breakfast. We meet in an hour."

Sadie did enjoy her breakfast. And Spence, who was sitting with Richard and Steve, appeared to enjoy his. He was back in business mode, deep in conversation with both of them, barely touching his food as he listened.

But every now and then he glanced up and looked her way. Their gazes would connect and a corner of Spence's mouth would lift.

And Sadie—remembering last night and thinking of all the nights to come—felt joy fill her heart again.

The guys had been on him the minute he and Sadie had reached the dining area, Richard with a sheaf of papers, Steve and John with a host of questions.

If he'd been worried that they would wonder what he was up to all night, he needn't have bothered. This morning they were all too absorbed in things they wanted to talk about regarding Nanumi.

Nanumi. *Remember*, Sadie had said it meant. And now Spence felt he had a right to do just that. The instant he had borne her back onto the bed and wrapped her in his arms, he'd had the sense that he'd been here before. All the kaleidoscopic bits of memory—sounds, shapes, touches, feelings—that he'd made himself blot out, came tumbling back. And as he'd made love with Sadie last night, he had felt as if he were assembling pieces of a puzzle he'd put together before. He heard echoes of words he'd heard before and feelings he already knew.

It was fresh—and yet it was oddly familiar, too.

Mostly it was completely right.

In their lovemaking Spence recognized a feeling he'd never experienced before that single night four years ago—a feeling he hadn't felt since. He had lost it without even realizing he'd had it—in Sadie's arms he found again the feeling of being welcome, of finally, after a lifetime of searching, finding the place where he belonged.

With Sadie.

The notion still had the power to stun him when he thought about it too long. It was like staring into the sun. Brilliant but impossible. And yet—

*Sadie loved him.*

She'd said so. Fervently. Eagerly. Even desperately, or so it appeared.

Pretty much like he loved her.

He'd even told her. And that had stunned him, too. Spence could never remember having said the words to anyone in his entire life. But with Sadie, the words had come out unbidden.

She had said them first, and maybe he'd been responding to that.

But he didn't think so. He thought he really loved her—and had for a very long time.

That surprised him, too. Of course he had always liked Sadie, even as a knobby-kneed, gap-toothed five-year-old, when she'd tagged after him and Danny all those years ago. As he watched her grow up, he'd admired her determination, her intelligence, her talents.

He'd certainly appreciated her help when she'd first come to work for him. They'd had a great time. He'd missed her desperately while she was away at college in California—because she had been such an asset to his business, he'd thought then. And for that reason, he assured himself, he had done whatever he'd needed to do to make sure she'd come back afterward.

It was the truth.

But not the whole truth.

Spence understood that now. For years he understood there had been more to his relationship with Sadie Morrissey than he'd been willing to admit. Clear back when she'd been in high school, there had been those early twinges of sexual attraction, that awareness of her curves and mile-long legs, of the feminine attributes that changed her from the knobby-kneed, gap-toothed kid to a delectable, appealing young woman.

A young woman far too good for him. And if his own good sense hadn't prevented him from acting on his feelings, Danny's fierce "Leave her alone. You've got nothing to offer her," took care of any inclinations he'd had. At least until the trauma of Emily's defection had jolted him so badly that his instincts had taken over.

Then he'd dared ask a question buried so deep he hadn't dared to even think it. He'd done what his heart had desired. He'd married Sadie.

And ruined it all again the next day.

But he hadn't been able to ruin it forever. Quite by accident he'd been given a second chance. And he was glad. More than glad. Over the moon.

Last night Sadie had made him feel alive, whole. She'd made him feel like no one had ever made him feel in his life.

She'd made him feel loved—something Spence had always recognized more by experience of its absence than its presence in his life.

Other people loved. Other families. Not his.

But none of it mattered now because Sadie loved him. She'd shown him that love last night. All night. And this morning while he was supposed to be paying attention to Richard and Steve, he kept glancing over at Sadie during breakfast. And she glanced back, grinning all over her face.

Spence grinned, too, because never in his life had he felt like this.

He was the same Spencer Tyack he had always been. The same wrong-side-of-the-tracks son of down-and-out parents who had spent his life scrabbling to try to become someone—and had.

But frankly he felt reborn. Alive. Nothing he had earned or achieved or become came close to describing the gift Sadie had given him with her love.

"...listening to a word I've said?" Richard Carstairs's rough voice penetrated the blissful fog that clouded Spence's brain.

Spence dragged his attention back briefly from far more inter-esting contemplations. "What? Yes, of course I'm listening."

But he couldn't seem to focus on anyone but Sadie. She'd finished her breakfast. Where had she gone?

His gaze didn't stop moving until he found her out on the deck, the breeze lifting her hair, the late-morning sunlight kissing her cheeks. They looked redder than usual. Probably his fault. Whisker burn had been the last thing on his mind last night. And this morning she hadn't wanted him to shave.

"I like it," she'd said, rubbing her palm over his cheek. "Very sexy." He was glad she liked it.

"—build some stables as well," Richard said. "Don't you agree?"

"Mmm."

"Let the man eat his breakfast," Steve said gruffly. "He'll listen to you soon enough."

Richard grumbled, but put his sheaf of papers away, then looked around absently. "Where's Leonie?"

"Don't know." Don't care, Spence thought. But feeling generous—and in fact feeling as if he owed Leonie something for having inadvertently prompted him to bring Sadie along, he said to Richard, "You ought to find her. See if she's having a good time. Go for a swim with her."

"A swim?" Richard looked aghast.

"It's what Isogawa wanted us to have this week for," Spence reminded him with the zeal of the converted. "Remembering what's important. Reconnecting with family."

Richard shook his head. "Leonie's my wife, not my family."

Spence didn't see the difference, but he was no expert. "Just a thought," he said mildly.

Richard grunted and went back to his papers.

\* \* \*

Sadie spent the two hours before lunch and two hours after attending the meetings, taking copious notes—and Spence-watching. And if it was possible to find more reasons to love the man she'd married four years ago, Sadie did it that afternoon.

It had been a long time since she'd seen Spence at work other than in the office in Butte working one-on-one with her. But today she saw him working with people, listening to ideas, visualizing, synthesizing, concretizing. He took a group of men with diverse agendas and individual concerns and brought them to a group agreement.

It wasn't all settled yet, of course. The deal wasn't done. But he had connected with Mr. Isogawa. The respect between them was clear. And his rapport with the others was also there. When Richard seemed about to go off on a tangent, Spence tactfully and speedily redirected his focus. When John got bogged down in the details, Spence took him back to the big picture. He had a way with words and a way with people that gave them confidence and helped them zero in on the program.

"You were spectacular," she told him after when the meeting broke up for the afternoon.

He grinned, all boyish enthusiasm. "You're prejudiced," he told her.

"But that doesn't mean I'm wrong." And then, because she dared now show her feelings, she raised up on tiptoe and kissed him.

He kissed her back, a warm, possessive kiss. And when all the men gave them a round of applause and a couple of cheers, he slung an arm around her shoulder and said, "If you'll excuse us, gentlemen, my wife and I have things to discuss."

They "discussed" for the rest of the afternoon. They made love in their bed and under the waterfall in their private outdoor spa. It was far more wickedly wonderful and erotic than Sadie had ever dared imagine.

Spence left her, boneless and replete, then had to get dressed to meet Richard and Mr. Isogawa to look at the place where Richard had suggested they might want to put in some stables.

"You don't mind?" he said.

"Of course not. It's what you're here for."

He bent over her on the bed and kissed her with lazy thoroughness. "Want to go for a swim tonight?"

"A swim?" She grinned.

"And all that that entails."

"Love to. Love you," she said, and smiled as she watched him stuff his feet into his flip-flops and head out the door.

Sadie took another shower after he left. Then she dressed and went for a walk on the beach.

Leonie was standing near a group of beach chairs, talking with Jale. He was smiling while she batted her lashes at him and ran a hand down his arm. When she saw Sadie, she waved him off, and, looking almost relieved, he hurried away.

"Just arranging another massage," Leonie explained as Sadie came up. "He's very good. Sure you don't want one?"

Sadie wasn't sure how much to read into the "very good" but she did know the answer to the question. "No, thanks."

Leonie sat down on a beach towel and stretched her legs out, wiggling her toes. "I suppose you don't need anyone else with his hands on you." She flicked Sadie a sideways glance.

"Besides Spence, you mean? No."

"He's obviously nuts about you."

A day ago Sadie wouldn't have believed it. Now she said, "The feeling is mutual."

"I can tell." There was a grudging envy in Leonie's tone.

Sadie let it go. "Are you enjoying yourself?" she asked.

"What do you think?"

Oops. Wrong question.

"I know how much you wanted to come and—" Sadie began to back pedal.

"Did Spence tell you about Barcelona?"

Sadie's gaze jerked over to meet the other woman's. The color was high in Leonie's cheeks, but she didn't look away. Nor did Sadie. At least they weren't going to have to pretend it hadn't happened. She nodded. "Yes."

"Figures." Leonie gave a bitter half laugh. "When I saw you with him yesterday morning at the airport in Nadi, when he said you were married, I thought maybe he was pretending—to avoid me, you know? To make sure Richard didn't find out and ruin the deal." She shook her head. "How's that for egocentric?"

Sadie hoped the question was rhetorical.

"Spence and I have actually been together for a long time," she said. "We just thought we shouldn't make an issue of it. You know, during work."

"I understand." Leonie grimaced. "Lucky you. I envy you. Oh, not about Spence." She paused. "Well, to be honest, yes, about Spence. He's dynamite. But it's more that he actually pays attention to you."

Unlike Richard.

Sadie understood. From what she'd seen, Richard barely seemed to register that his wife was there.

"Was that why you went to, um, Spence's…in Barcelona?" she asked, not quite finding the words to say it. "The reason for the massages? And Jale?"

Leonie nodded grimly. "I keep hoping Richard will wake up!"

"By making him jealous?"

"Why not? I want him to notice me… Remember that I'm his wife. How else can I wake him up?"

"Tell him?" It was more a question than a suggestion. God knew Sadie was the last person who should be giving advice about how to improve a marriage.

"Tell him I want a baby?"

"A baby?" Sadie stared at Leonie. "Do you?"

The leap from "notice me" to "want a baby" was substantial.

"I do, yes. I know Richard already has grown children. I know he thinks he's finished with all that. But I'm not! I love him. I want a child with him. A family. Don't you?"

"Yes, of course we do." Sadie didn't have to think an instant about that. She'd been dreaming about a family with Spence since she'd been old enough to know how babies were made. She already had names picked out for their children, though she supposed she'd allow him some input.

"But I didn't realize you did. Doesn't Richard?"

"We haven't discussed it," Leonie admitted. Then she got a mulish expression on her face. "How could we? He barely acts like I'm alive. It's weird, you know. He was all over me before we got married. I got complete attention. Once he had the ring on my finger, he went right back to work. Marrying me was like doing a deal. The thrill of the hunt. Once he got me, he wasn't interested anymore."

"Maybe you should tell him how you feel. Maybe he thinks you don't want kids."

"Maybe he's never even considered it!"

"You'll never know until you try."

"I guess I just hoped he'd realize…"

"Read your mind?" Sadie smiled.

Leonie shrugged. "Something like that."

"Trust me," Sadie said with feeling. "Speaking from experience. It doesn't work. You have to say the words."

Leonie sighed, then picked up a fistful of sand and let it trickle out through her fingers. Then she tipped her head to the side and looked at Sadie. "You are so lucky," she murmured. "Do you have any idea how lucky?"

And Sadie, thinking back over the past four years in limbo and the last night in Spence's arms, dug her toes into the warm sand and felt the kiss of the sun on her face and could only nod and smile.

"Yes," she said softly. "Yes, I do."

# CHAPTER NINE

"I TALKED to Leonie this afternoon." Sadie was lying on her side in bed, tracing a line down the center of Spence's bare chest, then following it with her lips.

"Mmm." It was an acknowledgment that he heard her, but his attention was clearly elsewhere. He shifted as her mouth moved lower, then held still, sucking in his breath.

"You're very tense," Sadie murmured, teasing his navel with her tongue, then moving lower still.

"Not tense," Spence muttered. "Wrung out."

"But obviously not unwilling to continue." Sadie grinned and kept on tracing, touching, teasing.

They had gone back to their room after dinner, a memorable meal, succulent pork and locally grown vegetables cooked in a *lovo*, or Fijian earth oven. But while almost everyone else had taken Mr. Isogawa up on his offer of drinks in the bar afterward, Spence had said he and Sadie needed to go over some papers.

"Go over some papers?" Sadie had said doubtfully,

Spence had waited until they were out of earshot. Then he'd grinned. "We'll put them under the bed."

She didn't know if they were under there or not. She and Spence had been in the bed—except when they'd been in the waterfall shower—for most of the rest of the evening.

Their lovemaking had been by turns heated and passionate,

then leisurely and frolicksome. It was everything Sadie could ever have wanted it to be. It spoke of the closeness, the trust and the intimacy that she and Spence had achieved.

And in the joy of their love, she remembered Leonie's unhappy face.

"You were right," she said now, looking up between kisses. "She did intend to seduce you."

Spence jerked halfway up, weight resting on his elbows. "She told you that?" He looked appalled.

Sadie moved her shoulders. "She did, actually. She thinks you're gorgeous," she added with a grin. "But it was really more about Richard. She was trying to make him jealous. He didn't notice, apparently."

"And thank God for that," Spence said dryly. "Or this whole thing would have fallen through. It's too bad, though, if she really does care," he reflected. "Richard tends to get pretty single-minded at times." He settled back down, the fingers of one hand playing in Sadie's hair, making her scalp tingle.

She bent her head and continued her exploratory kissing. "At one time, apparently, he was single-minded about pursuing her. Like she was some sort of trophy. And then when he got her, he forgot her." She nipped his belly.

Spence's fingers clenched in her curls. "She's not exactly destitute. She's getting something out of the marriage," he pointed out. "World travel. A fantastic house. Three fantastic houses, for that matter. One in Florida, one in England, one in Costa Rica. She wouldn't be cavorting around Fiji now if it weren't for Richard."

"I don't think it's Fiji Leonie cares about. Or the fantastic houses. It's her marriage. It's Richard. She loves him."

"She's got a damn funny way of showing it, then. Why doesn't she just say so?"

"That's what I told her." Sadie eased her way down and let

her fingers walk along his thighs, first one and then the other, then dipping between them and making him squirm.

"Asking for trouble," Spence muttered.

"No. A baby," Sadie said, kissing him exactly where she'd been aiming for all along.

Spence jerked. *"What?"*

"Leonie," Sadie said, breathing on him, tasting him, making him gasp, "wants a baby."

Spence was strangling. "Forget babies! I don't care what Leonie wants! I want you!" Hastily he sheathed himself to protect her, then hauled her up to straddle him and thrust to meet her—to make them one once more.

And Sadie met him eagerly, delighting in the way they moved together, rocked together, loved together. Shattered together.

"I love you," she breathed as she collapsed on top of him. Her head rested on his chest. His heart thundered in her ear. She turned her face to press a kiss there, then she lifted her head and smiled tenderly up at him. "Sometime soon maybe we'll have a baby, too."

He didn't respond. He just lay there with his fingers threaded through her hair, relishing its silken softness. He turned his head and pressed a kiss against her cheek. "I love you, too," he whispered and wrapped his arms around her, holding her close while she dozed. He still wanted her and it wasn't that long before his body was ready again to love her.

He ran his hands down her back, began to kiss her.

She squirmed against him, as eager as he was to love again.

He smiled. "I think," Spence whispered against her ear, "that life is plenty full enough as it is."


"Richard thought he was hearing things," Leonie reported Friday morning.

They were on the beach while the men were tidying up the last details of the Nanumi agreement.

Sadie had wondered since their conversation earlier in the week, but she hadn't wanted to ask. And nothing in Leonie's demeanor before today had given her any reason to hope. But this morning the other woman's eyes were wide and there was a light in them that Sadie had never seen before.

"You told him?"

"Well, I had to get his attention first. I tried talking, but he kept right on working away on his damned laptop. So after three tries, I finally grabbed it and threatened to stomp it into oblivion if he didn't listen."

Now it was Sadie who was wide-eyed. "You didn't!"

"Well, I didn't stomp it, but I could have," Leonie admitted. "I may not be trying to seduce Spence anymore, but I still believe in dramatic gestures. I just had to find one that got his attention. That did."

Sadie was impressed. "I'll bet. So what did he say?"

"He was surprised. Stunned, really. I guess we never did talk enough before we got married. It was very rush-rush. I told you, he acted like he had to win me. And he did. But he thought I'd married him for his money, and that was all. The idiot didn't realize I really loved him!" Leonie shook her head and made a sound that was somewhere between a laugh and a sob.

Sadie was amazed. "And now he does?"

"He's…working on it. I think I gave him something to think about."

Sadie just bet she had. "And the baby? What did he think about that?"

"He couldn't believe I meant it. He thought he was too old. That *I* would think he was too old. I told him he wasn't the one who'd be pregnant! And then he wondered what his kids would think. I said, 'Ask them,' and that surprised him, too."

"That you would offer to let them voice an opinion?"

"I suppose. I think he thinks they won't approve. I think he thinks they don't approve of his marrying me. But that's not their decision. It's his, though they could certainly have told him if they wanted to. And they won't make this decision, either. But why shouldn't he ask if he wants to know how they feel?"

It seemed like eminently good sense to Sadie. And she said so.

Leonie smiled. "I hope so. We'll see. He's told me a hundred times what a big step it is. He says I should take a good look at the Isogawas' grandchildren tomorrow and see if I really want all that hassle. But he's not saying no. He's actually interested. Tempted, I think. Mostly, though, he knows I really love him now. And—" she threw her arms around Sadie and gave her a crushing hug "—we owe it all to you!"

"She says she owes it all to me," Sadie reported, grinning.

"Huh? Who owes what?" Spence was distracted, she could tell. He'd been eager to wrap her in his arms as soon as he'd found her on the beach. And he'd spirited her away from Leonie without a backward glance. Something was on his mind.

"I said, Leonie and Richard are talking to each other," she repeated patiently while they walked up to their *bure*. "He's actually listening to her. They're communicating! They might have a baby! And she says she owes it all to me." She was sure Spence would appreciate the irony of it.

But he just shook his head. "The woman's nuts."

Well, he'd had a hard day. While Sadie had only attended the morning meetings, he'd been tied up all afternoon hammering out the last of the details so that the new resort consortium was now a done deal. So he could be forgiven not caring one way or another about Leonie's family issues.

"You must be relieved that it's over," Sadie said as they climbed the steps up to the treehouse porch. Once there she reached up to knead the taut muscles of his shoulders and back.

Spence sighed. "Yeah." He let her hands work their magic for a few moments, then straightened. "I was thinking we ought to go home."

"Home?" Sadie's hands stilled.

"We can't stay here forever. It's paradise, yes. But the work's done."

"But the week isn't. Mr. Isogawa expects us to be here. Besides, tomorrow's family day." And she'd been looking forward to that.

Spence shrugged. "Isogawa's family."

"And we want to meet them. They come back every year—all of them—Mr. and Mrs. Isogawa, their kids and grandkids. It's what Nanumi is all about. It's what we've worked on all week."

Spence's jaw tightened briefly. But then he shrugged. "Fine. If you want to stay, we'll stay." He walked into the room and fell on the bed face down. His eyes shut.

Sadie sat down next to him and began rubbing his back again. "All the adrenaline's gone, isn't it?"

He rolled over and grabbed her, pulling her down on top of him. "Don't you believe it!"

He was still sound asleep when she awoke the next morning.

And no wonder, Sadie thought. He'd kept them up most of the night. He had loved her eagerly, urgently, almost desperately, in a way that reminded her of their wedding night four years ago.

But it wasn't like that, Sadie was sure, because there was no forgetting what had happened between them here.

It was nearly eight. She'd promised to meet the Isogawas and their family for breakfast at nine. That gave her time for a leisurely shower—provided Spence didn't join her—before she had to be there. She wouldn't have minded at all if he had joined her. But she knew he was exhausted.

She looked at him now, her heart full to bursting at the love she felt for this man. She reached out and brushed a hand lightly over his tousled hair. He didn't stir. She leaned down and kissed his stubbled cheek. He sighed and smiled slightly, but he didn't wake.

She took her shower, then dried her hair and combed it, taking more care than she had all week so she would be presentable for meeting the Isogawa family. When she left at five minutes to nine, Spence still hadn't moved.

The sound of children's laughter woke him. Startled him.

For a moment Spence didn't know where he was. Then he opened his eyes and remembered. Family day.

Talk about a foreign experience.

He lay there considering the best way to avoid the whole thing, when there was a knock on the *bure* door. He frowned because in the entire week, no one had come knocking. Everyone had respected his and Sadie's privacy. But maybe Sadie had sent a messenger to see if he was ever getting up.

He pulled on a pair of shorts and opened the door, blinked when he didn't see anyone, then realized the knocker barely came up to his chest.

Two girls and three boys were standing there, hopping and jigging from one foot to the other.

"We've never seen a tree house this big. You live here?" The tallest boy asked him, eyes wide. He sounded like a Kiwi and looked like Steve, so Spence had a pretty good idea who he was.

"This week I do," he replied, as they craned their necks and peered past him into the room. Their eagerness reminded him of his own youthful curiosity. "Want to have a look around?"

Did they? He was practically trampled in the rush to explore. They were fascinated by the way the *bure* was built around the branches, that one of them was so big that it could be used as a "window seat." They were delighted with the private waterfall.

"Can we go in it?" the redheaded girl asked.

He shrugged. "Be my guests." And as they danced and hopped

and skittered through it, laughing all the while, Spence laughed, too. He told them his name and found out theirs. The biggest boy, Geoff, and the littlest, Justin, belonged to Steve and Cathy. The middle one was Keefe Ten Eyk. The redheaded girl was his sister, Katie, and the other was Mai, the Isogawas' granddaughter. She didn't speak English but the language barrier wasn't slowing them down any.

"This is amaaaazing," Keefe said. "I could live here my whole life!"

"Which is soon to end," came a voice from the door. And a very stern Marion appeared. "You know better than to bother the guests."

"We asked," Katie said. "Politely."

All the rest of the kids nodded in agreement.

"He said be his guest," Justin piped up. "Didn't you?" He looked at Spence for confirmation.

"Absolutely," Spence agreed.

"They didn't wake you?" Marion was still looking worried. "Sadie said you were exhausted, that you needed your sleep."

"I was awake. I was just coming down for a swim."

Justin grabbed one of his hands, and Mai shyly took the other. "C'mon, then."

"Leave Mr. Tyack alone," Marion said. "Out now. All of you. And say thank you for his kindness at letting you interrupt his life."

"They didn't. They were fine." And Spence took the hands of the kids who had dropped his and led them out the door and down the steps. "Hit the beach." He swung their hands up, and when he let go they all took off running, yelling whooping—even Mai who couldn't possibly have understood.

Marion lingered beside him. "Crazy children. They think they've been turned loose on Swiss Family Robinson's island. Thank you. I'm sorry they bothered you."

"It's all right," Spence said again. "They're fine."

"Glad you feel that way," Marion said, then patted him on the arm. When he raised a quizzical brow, she turned and nodded toward the group coming down from the lodge.

The group included both the elder Isogawas, a younger couple Spence presumed were their children, with two more grandchildren much smaller than Mai.

A little boy just learning to walk was holding on to Richard on one side and Leonie on the other while he took staggering steps toward the beach and Richard and Leonie laughed and made encouraging noises.

The other child was nestled in Sadie's arms.

"She's in her element now," Marion said, watching Sadie with a smile on her face.

And Spence, watching, had to agree.

He'd always known she'd doted on Edward, Martha and Theo's little boy. It was a woman thing, he figured, because every time Martha brought him in, Sadie scooped the little boy up and danced him around the office, blew kisses on his belly, made him laugh and told him nursery rhymes.

"She'll be a good mother," Marion assured him.

"Yeah." She would.

Sadie had enjoyed all the other days—and of course she'd loved the nights—but family day was the best.

She got to play with the Isogawas' grandchildren. She got to watch Spence playing with the bigger kids. She got to imagine what it would be like when they had their own children someday, even though she knew she shocked everyone when Leonie had asked her how many children she wanted and she said, "Eight."

"Ha!" John Ten Eyk had laughed.

And Marion had shuddered and said, "Rather you than me!'

"Sadie could handle them," Cathy said firmly.

But the look on Spence's face was so appalled she'd hastened to reassure him. "I don't really want eight," she said quickly. "I know how much work kids are now. So I think maybe three or four would be wonderful. Even one or two. Whatever we get, I guess. And if we don't get any we can adopt."

Something was wrong. Sadie could tell.

When the kids went to eat dinner with their parents, she and Spence ate with Richard and Leonie, who suddenly were acting more like newlyweds than she and Spence were. Leonie was bubbling with enthusiasm as they talked about the Isogawas' grandchildren.

Far from putting her off having children, the day had whetted her appetite. And Richard didn't seem to be averse to the idea.

"My kids—my *old* kids," he corrected himself, "will just have to get used to it if I have another one. It's not like they're teenagers embarrassed by everything Dad does."

"Of course not," Sadie said. "Tony Hunt, one of the artists in Spence's art co-op became a father again in his fifties three years ago. His son is his grandson's best friend. Right?" She looked at Spence.

"Yeah." He shoved a delicious piece of *lovo*-cooked pork around on his plate. He didn't say anything else.

Sadie studied him in silence during the meal. He had got more sun today than the other days. There had been no meetings, just fun and games on the beach. Maybe he'd got too much sun. Maybe he didn't feel well.

"I think," she said when she finished her own meal, "that I'd like to call it a night. I've got a lot of packing to do before our flight leaves in the morning. Do you want to come?" she asked her husband. "Or do you want to stay and visit some more?"

He shoved back his chair and stood. "I'll come."

They said goodbye to the Carstairs. Richard shook hands heartily. Leonie hugged both her and Spence hard and whispered,

"You guys are the best. We have a baby, we'll name it after one of you."

Sadie laughed. "I think you should discuss that with Richard first."

They wished everyone else goodbye, too. Their plane was leaving early in the morning. The Carstairs were staying another week for some determined "together time." And both New Zealand couples had a later flight back to Nadi and then home.

The Isogawas bowed then hugged Sadie, probably because she hugged them first. "I know it's probably not at all the proper thing to do," she told them. "But this has been the most wonderful week of my life. So thank you. Thank you!"

"Thank *you* for everything, too," Mr. Isogawa said. "You are part of Nanumi now. You will come back." And then he bowed and shook Spence's hand. "It is not goodbye. It is a new beginning for all of us. I thank you. I look forward to seeing you soon on Nanumi."

Spence bowed and shook hands, too. He said thank you as well, his voice quiet and grave. He bowed to Mrs. Isogawa. He said good night to everyone else and then he walked out into the star-washed night with Sadie.

He held her arm so that she didn't stumble as they walked down the plankway. He didn't speak. Neither did she. She was drinking in the beauty, savoring the memories, knowing she would take them out and replay them in her mind over and over again.

Spence opened the door to their *bure* and held it for her. She stepped past him inside, then turned and wrapped him tight in her arms. For a second he stiffened. But then his arms came hard around her and he just hung on.

"It was wonderful," Sadie said. "It *is* wonderful."

He gave her a little squeeze and rested his cheek against her hair. He just stood there. Didn't let go. Until Sadie finally loosed her arms and took half a step away to look up into his eyes.

"What's wrong?"

"Nothing." He swallowed. "I'm fine. I—" He stopped, took a breath, then started again. He looked pale now and there were lines of strain around his mouth. "What you said about kids…"

Sadie laughed. "I was kidding! Don't worry. We won't have eight."

"No, we won't."

"But however many we have, I want them all to look like you."

"No."

"Yes. I've had a thing for you forever. For my whole life. And I can't imagine anything more wonderful that lots of dark-haired little rascals just like you."

Spence shook his head. "No. I can't."

"What?" Sadie stared at him, stunned. "Can't what?"

"Won't," he corrected. "Have kids. I don't want any kids at all."

# CHAPTER TEN

"I DON'T want kids." He repeated the words again. "I won't have any."

And Sadie could see by the way he paced and by the ferocity with which he cracked his knuckles that, unlike her, he wasn't joking.

"Well, we might not have any," she said, taken aback by both the sentiment and the ferocity.

"But then you want to adopt!"

"What's wrong with adoption?"

"Nothing. Nothing at all!" Another knuckle crack. "It's great. Fine. Terrific. For someone else. No kids, Sadie. I can't do it."

"But—"

"I can't. I won't be responsible for giving a kid the kind of rotten childhood I had!"

"Oh, for heaven's sake. Is that what you're worried about? It won't be that kind of childhood!"

"How do you know?"

"I just know," she said stubbornly. "How can you even think that?"

"Because I lived it, damn it. It's hell—and it's what I know. I can't do it. I won't! No kids. I made up my mind years ago."

"Spence—"

He folded his arms across his chest. "No."

She wanted to argue. She wanted to pound on his thick skull and tell him to stop being an idiot.

But there was no arguing with Spence when he got bullheaded like this. What made him a great developer was his ability to be flexible, to see options where others saw only one outcome.

But he wasn't seeing any other options now. He saw only one—the life he'd had.

"Spence," she began, softening her voice, gentling, trying to get past the wall he'd built. But he shook his head.

"That's the way it's going to be, Sadie. No kids. Period."

Stubborn jackass. Mule-headed fool. She could go through a whole barnyard of obstinacy if he kept this up.

"You can visit all the kids you want. I'll never stop you."

"Oh, thank you very much." Her voice was sharper now. Gentleness wasn't going to begin to penetrate the steel he'd wrapped around his heart. "How very nice of you."

"I know you like kids and—"

"*You* like kids! That wasn't you out there today, playing with them? Jumping around in the water with them? Letting Justin climb all over you?"

"Of course I like them. But that doesn't mean I intend to raise them!"

"You can't just unilaterally lay down edicts like that."

"Of course I can. I just did."

"Spence—"

"No. And I'm not going to change my mind. Sorry. If it mattered so much, you should have asked. Emily knew. Dena knew. They were fine with it."

"Well, I'm not. And you never told me."

"I'm telling you now." Their gazes met, dueled.

"Not good enough."

He shook his head. "Sorry. That's the way it is." And abruptly he turned away. He strode over to the closet and began packing, stuffing things in his suitcase, keeping his back to her. His movements were jerky, angry. There was none of the fluid ease she usually associated with the way Spence moved. Nothing he'd said since they'd come into the room was what she would have associated with Spence, either.

It wasn't like Spence to be dogmatic. He knew what he wanted, and he went after it.

But he'd always wanted her to argue. And he'd always listened.

"Spence," she tried again. "You need to be logical about this. You need to think clearly before you make hard-and-fast pronouncements like that."

He turned, leveling his gaze on her. "I have thought, damn it. What the hell do you think I spent my life doing?"

"I—"

"No, it's you who are going to have to be logical, who are going to have to think clearly and make a decision. Because if you want kids, Sadie—one kid or eight kids or 153 kids—you don't want to be married to me! You want a divorce."

She stared, openmouthed. Stunned.

*Divorce?* He was talking divorce? Again? After the most beautiful week of their lives?

"Divorce," he repeated, in case she hadn't heard him the first time he'd dropped the word like a granite boulder into the silence of the room. "Think about it."

Then he banged down the lid of his suitcase and stalked into the bathroom. The door shut. The shower turned on.

No waterfall shower together tonight, then. No eager lovemaking. No steamy passion.

Well, there had been passion. But it hadn't been steamy. It had been angry. Passionate anger. Irrational anger. Irrational thoughts.

Because of some fear of giving their children the same sort

of childhood he'd had. No chance of that! It didn't make sense. He had to realize that. Had to.

But she didn't think he did. Sadie sat down on the bed, feeling cold and sick as the realization that he really believed that sank in.

*Don't overreact*, she cautioned herself. *That's what he's doing. Calm down. Take it easy.*

So she took a deep steadying breath and made herself get up and start to pack. Taking things out of drawers and off hangers was mechanical and mindless, but somehow calming. And packing the various clothes she'd worn during the week made her recall the occasions when she'd worn them. Good times all. And even better times when they had come back to the *bure* and Spence had taken them off her. To make love to her. To share his body, heart and soul with her.

But he'd never shared this.

How could he not want children?

He was so good with them. And they had loved him.

They'd clambered all over him today. And Spence had instinctively known how to treat each of them. He'd roughhoused with Justin and Keefe, had listened intently to Geoff's opinions, had charmed Katie and had no doubt made a lifelong devotee out of Mai by picking her for his team when they'd played ball.

How could he not want to have the chance to do that for children of his own?

She didn't know. Didn't understand. All she could think was that he would come to his senses. He had to come to his senses.

Had to.

He'd known she would be shocked. He'd known she wouldn't be happy. And he knew that marrying her without having told her wasn't fair.

Of course, the fact that he thought he'd immediately divorced her was somewhat of an excuse! He stood under the shower, letting steaming hot water pour over his head and down his body and tried to think.

It wasn't a big secret. He had told Emily, just as he'd told Sadie he had. Not that it had mattered, when she hadn't even bothered to show up for their wedding. There might have been significant things on which they differed—and there must have been, since she hadn't turned up—but his "no kids" edict hadn't been one of them.

He had been clear on the "no kids" count with Dena, too.

She'd been relieved to hear it. A consummate career woman with, as she put it, "not a single maternal bone in her body," Dena had broken off a relationship to Bahamian investor Carson Sawyer when he decided he wanted a family. She knew she didn't.

So she had been delighted when Spence had said he had no interest in one either. "I knew it," she'd said. "I knew we were right for each other."

But then Sadie had intervened. When she'd shown up at the courthouse with the news that she was still his wife, she'd thrown everybody's plans out of whack.

She'd also given him the most beautiful joyous week he'd ever known.

He couldn't forget that. Never wanted to.

But he couldn't lead her on, either. He couldn't pretend to want a future he had no intention of pursuing. He supposed he should have told her the day they'd been making love and she'd told him about Leonie wanting a baby.

But how?

Was he supposed to say, "Stop driving me madly insane with what you're doing for a minute so I can tell you I don't want children?" And then what? Tell her to go ahead and wring him out? Because that's exactly what she'd been doing.

And after, when she'd said she hoped they would have a baby someday, too, he couldn't bring himself to spoil the moment.

So, all right, he was a selfish bastard. An emotional coward. But at least he was honest. She had to give him that.

He shut off the shower and stood still in the stall, shivering. Cold clear through.

He didn't want to hurt her. He hated to hurt her. He loved her, damn it. But he'd had to tell her. He couldn't let her go on dreaming about some brood of children they were going to have.

She'd get over it. She was an adult, after all.

What if they couldn't have had children? Lots of couples couldn't. Would she hate him then? Would she love him less?

No. Not and still be Sadie. He knew it. He believed in the power of her love to the depths of his being.

She just needed time to adjust. To understand. He needed to give her time. Space. He needed to show her that he loved her— and then she would.

There were different kinds of silence. Sadie knew that. But she'd never experienced it so vividly as that night.

Spence came out of the shower, a *sula* wrapped around his waist, his chest still damp, his hair in wet spikes. He looked at her, his expression unreadable, then he turned away to stow his leather dopp kit in his suitcase. He didn't say a word.

Neither did Sadie.

She didn't know what to say. Everything that occurred to her would, she imagined, make matters worse. She knew Spence—or thought she did—well enough to know that backing him into a corner wasn't going to get him to change his mind. And pretending to give in to his demand wasn't going to help, either. She could hardly just smile and blithely say, "No problem."

It was a problem. That was the truth.

"Shall I set the alarm clock?" The question was very polite. Very civil. Very remote.

"Probably a good idea," she answered in a like tone. "We wouldn't want to miss the plane."

"Since we're going to be the only ones on it, I imagine they'll wait." He didn't smile.

They'd have laughed about that yesterday. Today she just nodded. "Do what you want, then."

He opened his mouth, as if he were going to tell her what he wanted. Or tell her something, at least. But he must have thought better of it because he closed his mouth again. His lips pressed into a thin hard line. He didn't speak.

He set the alarm and lay down on the bed, eyes hooded but watching her.

Another night she would have gone straight to him. She would have crawled onto the bed beside him and he would have wrapped her in his arms and started them down the path to bliss. Tonight, as he folded his arms under his head and watched her, she couldn't do it.

"I'll take a shower, then," she said tonelessly. And, plucking her nightgown off the hook, she disappeared into the bathroom just as he had. She shut the door.

She would have loved one last shower in the waterfall outside. She would have loved to have shared it with Spence. But there was no easiness between them now. No sense of togetherness. No "us" any longer.

And while she knew, if she did shower out there, that he would be watching her, she didn't feel like being on display. She wanted a shower in privacy, where if she cried—no, make that *when* she cried—Spence would never know.

Her eyes were so bloodshot when she came out, though, that if he'd been able to see her, he certainly would have known.

But when she returned, the overhead light had been turned off. He had left on one dim light next to her side of the bed. He was still there, but lying on his side—turned away from hers.

Was he awake? She didn't know.

He didn't say a word.

In the silence Sadie shut out the light, then slid into bed beside him. It felt like Kansas again. Maybe Texas.

No. More like Alaska. Big and wide. And cold.

Her throat ached from crying. Not because she couldn't have her way. But because he'd cut off all dialogue. He'd made a unilateral decision based solely on memories she couldn't share. And then he'd retreated behind the wall of a childhood she couldn't change.

She sucked in a sharp breath and pressed her fist against her mouth to keep from making noise. But he heard it and rolled over at once.

"Don't cry, for God's sake!" His voice was as harsh and pained as her heart.

"I'll cry if I want to, you ass," she retorted, and did exactly that.

"Oh, hell." He reached for her then, hauling her into his arms, holding her, kissing her. "It'll be all right," he promised. "Shh. I'm sorry."

She hiccupped and tried to stop. But the feel of his arms around her, of his care and his concern undid her. It was so stupid. *He* was so stupid! How could he deny this part of himself to children he could love?

"Don't," he whispered urgently. "Sadie. Please. Stop." He kissed her then, in desperation, no doubt. How else could a guy shut up a crying woman? The kiss was urgent, hungry. In it was so much of everything she loved about Spence, she couldn't help but respond.

She kissed him back, wrapped herself around him, as desperate for him as he was for her. Their coupling was silent but for ragged gasps and breathing. It was fierce, demanding.

But in the end, instead of fulfilled and complete as he rolled off her and lay there staring silently at the ceiling, mostly she felt empty and lost.

* * *

She smiled the next morning. She talked to him. Yes, there was still a certain reserve there, a little strain, maybe a hint of dullness in her eyes. He didn't blame her. He knew she was upset. But it was early days yet.

She would get used to it.

He just needed to be patient.

Their trip back to Butte was long and exhausting but uneventful. Sadie slept as she had on the way out—and he watched her as he had done then.

He loved her now, couldn't get enough of looking at her. When she shifted in her seat and her shirttails parted to expose some pale-blue lace, he smiled. He knew all about Sadie's underwear now. It was wonderful.

But she was more wonderful. He was blessed.

"So, how'd it go?" Martha had enough discretion to wait until they'd been home overnight before turning up in Sadie's office the next morning, eyes wide and curious. "Ah, I see a ring!"

She grabbed Sadie's hand, exclaiming over her rings. "They're perfect. They're you!"

And Sadie nodded. She even managed a smile. Outwardly she could do that. It was inside she was hurting.

"You look tanned and beautiful and exhausted," Martha decided. "I hope the exhaustion is from not enough sleep." She eyed Sadie speculatively. "So, inquiring friends want to know. Did you…?" She waggled her eyebrows.

Sadie nodded, but didn't meet her gaze.

Martha peered at her more closely. "Don't tell me he's that bad in bed?" She sounded appalled.

"No!" Sadie went crimson. Couldn't help it. "He was—it was—wonderful."

"Yeah. I can tell how thrilled you are." Martha's tone was dry.

"It's just…there are…there *is*…a problem."

"Shall I kill him? Or just injure him?"

Sadie shook her head. It was so good to have a friend like Martha, who always took her side, no matter what. She smiled again. "Probably not kill him. Eddie needs his mother, and you wouldn't do him much good if they locked you up."

"Okay. Tell me what to do and I'll do it."

"I don't think there's anything you can do," Sadie said. She wondered if she dared take Martha into her confidence, then decided that she had to. Maybe Martha would think Spence was right. Maybe she was the one who was being foolish. Not him.

So she told Martha what had happened. "It was a wonderful week. A perfect week," she finished. "I love him. And I know he loves me. But we can't talk about this. He *won't* talk about it. Am I crazy? Am I wrong?"

Slowly, adamantly, Martha shook her head. "You're not wrong," she said. "He would be a wonderful father. Why does he think he wouldn't be?"

"I think because his father wasn't. His parents were…pretty dismal. He doesn't want the same for his kids."

"Oh, like that would happen." Martha rolled her eyes.

"I know that. You know that. Try convincing Spence of that."

"I can't," Martha said. "But you're not wrong. If you want this to work, you're going to have to."

Easier said than done, of course, once they were home and real life intervened. Spence was on the phone all the time. He was faxing and calling and sending messages on the computer. He flung himself back into work with a vengeance. And he never once mentioned the "no kids" issue.

Sadie almost began to think she'd dreamed it. But she only had to see him around Edward to know that she hadn't.

Martha brought her son into work often. She always had, especially when Theo was away sailing, which, as it was his job, happened regularly. Whenever Edward came, Sadie had always played with him. Tickled him. Played peek-a-boo with him and, now that he could fling a ball, played ball with him.

Edward was her pal. When Theo was home, Sadie even watched him so Martha and Theo could have an evening out now and then.

"You want Eddie some night?" Martha asked her. "Theo's not home. But I could always use some time to work. At least you'd have a natural lead-in."

Sadie remembered counseling Leonie just to talk to Richard. But when the shoe was on her own foot—and Spence was pretending that everything was fine—it didn't seem so easy. It was like the marriage elephant all over again. Only now it was the kid elephant in the room that neither of them could talk about.

"Yes, let me have Eddie," she said.

The evening with Eddie was a great success. He loved Sadie. Sadie loved him. He toddled over to Spence and grabbed him around the knees. "Da," he said.

"Not me," Spence said. But he didn't turn the little boy away. He picked him up and read him a story. Then the three of them ate macaroni and cheese for supper. They had jello cubes for dessert. Eddie even ate part of a jar of peas because Sadie convinced Spence to eat some, too.

"I'll bet Theo doesn't eat mushed peas," he complained. But he ate them. And seeing him do so, Eddie did, too.

Watching them together, Sadie dared to hope.

When Martha came and got him at ten, Eddie was asleep on their bed—next to Spence. Sadie went in to pick the little boy up and stood looking at the two of them, Eddie's small fingers wrapped around Spence's big thumb.

And he didn't want children?

How could he say that?

Martha took her sleeping son out of Sadie's arms and crossed her fingers. "Here's hoping," she said. "Good luck."

"Thanks," Sadie said. And after Martha went, she said to herself out loud, "just talk to him."

"We need to talk," she said baldly the next morning.

Maybe it wasn't the best time, but he was leaving for two weeks in a matter of hours, heading out for the Bahamas to see Dena and Tom Wilson, then going on to Naples to have a look at a project there. He was coming back via Ireland because he had a notion about buying some cottages near Cork for a retirement village. He had a lot of irons in his fire.

He didn't ignore her. He was attentive at home. He was the Spence she remembered at work. But the new elephant—the "child elephant" was always in the room. And she couldn't let him leave without talking about it.

"Talk? About what?" He was still keying in something on his handheld computer, but when she didn't speak, he finally glanced up.

Sadie took a breath. "Kids."

His features grew still. He didn't say anything for a long moment, as if waiting for her to continue. When she didn't, he said almost casually, "What about them?" and to underline his lack of interest, he went back to messing with the tiny computer.

Remembering Leonie, Sadie reached out and snatched it out of his hand. He looked at her then, astonished at her behavior. "I said I want to talk," she repeated.

His jaw set. "Talk, then."

"You can't just make a pronouncement in the middle of a marriage that you don't want kids."

"I can," he said. "I did. And don't start on me about telling you beforehand. You know it was impossible."

"Well, it's not impossible to rethink. To change your mind."

"I don't want to change my mind."

"Can't Edward change your mind?"

He frowned. "What's Edward got to do with it?"

"You loved him. You played with him. You ate peas for him. You fell asleep with him!"

"So?"

"So, why do you want to deprive children of a father like that? We'd be good parents, Spence!"

"You would."

"So would you! I know it!"

He didn't answer, just sat there, a human Mount Rushmore, except for the tension making a muscle tick in his jaw. They stared at each other, gazes dueling, grappling in silence. Finally he flicked off the computer without even looking at it, tucked it into his shirt pocket and stood up.

"I love you, Sadie," he said, his tone even, steady, flat. "And I think you love me—"

"I do love you, damn it!"

"Then try to understand that I'm not going to change my mind. My parents—"

"Oh, stop hiding behind your parents!"

His whole body jerked. "What did you say?"

"You heard me! You drag them out every time you don't let yourself do something. Yes, they left a lot to be desired. They were a couple of unhappy, sorry, miserable people. And if you give in to their influence, they win."

"They never won anything!"

"If you believe what they told you, they've won your mind," Sadie argued, knowing she was saying too much, cutting too deep, but unable to stop herself. "They own it. They own you!"

"The hell they do!" He was furious now. His face was scarlet. The veins in his neck stood out in sharp relief. "They never thought I could do anything. They always believed I was just like them!"

"And you believe it, too. I love you, Spence. And I believe you love me. The sad thing is, I don't believe you love yourself."

There was no sound in the room, in the house, in all of Montana, it seemed, after that. The world stopped. Sadie knew she had spoken the unforgivable truth. Spence's face simply closed up.

She didn't know how long they stood there—the silence beating between them—until finally Spence said, "I'll be gone two weeks. If you change your mind, I'll see you when I get back. If not, I suggest you leave and file for divorce."

"He told you to get a divorce?" Martha was apoplectic. If it were possible for a human being to carom off walls, Martha might have done it. She sat down in Sadie's office. She bounced up again. She paced. She banged doors. She hit window sashes. "What kind of idiot is he?"

"A stubborn one," Sadie said flatly. She felt dead inside. Gutted. She was alive but simply going through the motions. Had been since Spence had walked out the door yesterday afternoon.

"Maybe he'll be the one who comes to his senses, who changes his mind," Martha said when she finally settled down.

Sadie shook her head. "He won't change his mind."

Martha turned and looked at her closely. "Will you?"

"Will I what? Change my mind? I can't." Sadie knew that much. She'd lain awake all night thinking about it. "It's like when you left Theo in New York and came back to Montana even though he said he'd marry you. It was for the wrong reason. If I stayed with Spence now, it would be for the wrong reason. It would be because I didn't believe in him. And I do."

"So what are you going to do? Divorce him?" Martha went pale as she said the word.

"Maybe. We'll see. But I'm not going to live like this."

* * *

It was the longest two weeks of his life.

Spence, who ordinarily lived for the fast lane of travel, new faces and new places, was desperate to get home to his wife. Not that he'd said so. He'd only talked to her once—from the Bahamas.

It had been a stilted conversation. Polite. Distant. But he couldn't hang up without asking, "So, are you leaving me?" He was glad his voice hadn't betrayed any of his fear.

"I don't know yet," she'd said.

He'd sent text messages and e-mails and faxes after that, just like he had the first week that he'd known about their marriage, because he didn't want to argue. And he didn't want to hear what she had to say. She'd already said too damn much.

He tried not to think about it. She hadn't meant it. She'd just been angry. He was sure she missed him as much as he was missing her. And even though he'd liked what he found in Ireland, he could hardly wait to get home.

He even managed to catch an earlier flight out of Newark, via Minneapolis to Butte. Then, as it was still only three in the afternoon, he drove straight to the office to surprise her.

She wasn't there.

Grace Tredinnick was sitting at the computer, adjusting her glasses, then moving her head back and forth.

Spence skidded to a halt in the doorway. "What are you doing here?"

"Well, hello to you, sonny," Grace said, peering at him over the top of her spectacles. "Didn't expect you until morning."

"I got an early flight. Where's Sadie?" He looked around, up and down the hall, but he didn't see her.

"Sadie's gone."

"Gone home?"

Grace shook her head. "Gone away. That's why I'm here."

Spence felt as if all the blood drained right out of his head.

Gone? Sadie? His stomach lurched. He felt suddenly hot and clammy, then cold as a Montana winter.

"Where?" His voice, even to his own ears, sounded like an old man's. "Where is she?"

"Texas. Austin, Texas. Took a job down there."

*Texas?* Who the hell did she know in Texas? Who cared who she knew? Why had she gone?

She loved him! She wasn't supposed to leave him!

"Left a letter and some stuff for you on your desk," Grace said.

But she'd barely got the words out before he had pushed past her into his office. There was an envelope on the desk, and next to it a small box.

Spence kicked the door shut, then sank down into his desk chair and picked up the envelope. She had written his name in her inimitable neat script on the front. He would know her writing anywhere.

Slowly he slit open the envelope and took out a single sheet of paper. More neat script. He felt a hard aching lump in his throat.

The letter said exactly what he didn't want to read—that she had taken him at his word, that she had gone. She had accepted a job working for Mateus Gonzales—starting up an office for him in Texas. It was all very simple. She never reproached him. She just said she was doing what he had suggested.

He opened the box. In it there were three rings—the two he'd given her on the airplane, the jade and Celtic gold that were so clearly her, and the one he thought he'd lost—his great-grandfather's heavy hand-carved ring.

He held them in his hand, rubbed his thumb over them, felt the smooth jade, the intricate filigree, the soft warmth of the pipestone. He rubbed them stroked them, turned them over and over, round and round. His throat ached, his eyes stung. His cheeks were already damp when his thumbnail caught on the edge of the inlay where the heart was broken.

\* \* \*

It would get easier. Sadie knew that it would. Her new job was interesting. Mateus was easy to work with. He divided his time between Sao Paulo and Rio and Austin. So, frequently, like when she'd worked with Spence, she was left to do things on her own.

He never minded what she did. He was more laid-back than Spence. He worked hard, but he actually stopped to breathe now and then. He also believed in that wonderful Latin custom, the siesta, so while Sadie worked, in theory, longer hours, she was really just out of her apartment more. That was good because in the middle of the day she could get out and see parts of Austin, get used to the city, find new things to do and places to go.

It also meant she had less time to feel sorry for herself.

She knew she had done the right thing by leaving. She truly did love Spence enough to know that she couldn't live with him if it meant agreeing with his parents' definition of who he was. There was so much more inside him. So much love that he had given to her and that he could give to their children, if only he learned to spare some for himself.

He believed in himself at work. How could he not do the same at home? With her? He could. Sadie knew he could.

But it got harder and harder to stick it out on the moral high ground when days turned into weeks and weeks turned into a month and then two—and Spence never came.

She'd been sure he would. He would read her letter and understand. He would come after her and take her home again. She certainly hadn't made a secret of where she was.

She stayed in touch with Martha. She talked on the phone with Grace. Once she'd even talked to him when he'd answered Grace's office phone.

"Sadie?" He almost choked on her name when she'd asked for Grace.

She had already done her choking when she'd heard his gruff, "Tyack Enterprises," seconds before.

"Hello, Spence," she said coolly. "How are you?"

"I'm...good. Doing fine." His cadence quickened. "Just off to Ireland again. The project there is taking off. It's going to be—" He stopped. "Never mind. I'm sure you're not interested. You've probably got a lot of equally interesting stuff going on down there."

"Quite a few things," she said airily. "Lots of excitement. We went to Rio last month. Mateus keeps me busy."

"I'm sure. Right. Here's Grace," he said abruptly, and the next thing she knew she had been handed over to the older woman.

It was the only time she'd talked to him. But it disturbed her dreams for the rest of the week. And she was only getting her equilibrium back when Mateus breezed into the office one morning and said, "Congratulate me. I'm engaged."

As he had been clearly smitten with a young *carioca* woman called Cristina when he and Sadie had been in Rio, it was not a big surprise.

"That's wonderful," Sadie said. "I'm so happy for you."

And of course she was. But it made her go home and weep for the love she'd lost. She hadn't filed for a divorce yet, but she expected any day to be served papers by Spence. There was no reason why he shouldn't. She'd left him. He could get the divorce and marry Dena now, exactly the way he'd wanted.

"Has he said anything about divorce?" she asked Martha the next time they talked. She'd told Martha about Mateus's engagement, and half expected to hear that Spence was contemplating the same.

"You think he'd tell me?" Martha said. "He doesn't talk to any of us. Not much. Oh, maybe he chats with Grace. Mostly he's gone."

Working? Sadie wondered. Or lining up a new wife?

She tormented herself with thoughts like that on a regular

basis. She wished she could get past it. Get past *him*. But some-times it felt as if she'd been born loving Spencer Tyack, and digging him out of her life—and her heart—was going to be a rest-of-her-lifetime project.

She told herself for the hundredth time this week to get started on it as she carried her week's dirty clothes down to the apart-ment complex laundry room. She took great pleasure in grabbing each piece of clothing and stuffing it unceremoniously into the washing machine, then adding the soap and dumping in the bleach. She needed bleach for her brain she thought. Something to get rid of Spence.

A shadow fell across her as she was putting in her quarters. "Sorry," she said without turning around, "I've taken the last one. You can have the washer after me."

"I don't want the washer. I want you."

At the sounds of that gruff, dear, familiar voice, she spun around, slinging quarters everywhere. *"Spence!"*

She wanted to run to him, grab him, hang on and never let him go. But he made no move toward her. He stood in the doorway, his thumbs hooked in his belt loops, looking like a gun-fighter. His throat worked. He wet his lips, then let out a shaky breath.

"If you'll have me…and my children," he said. He didn't smile, but there was a light—a fire—in his eyes as they met hers.

"Oh, Spence!" She flew at him then, practically knocking him flat. And she knew the joy of his arms coming around her, crushing her to him, hanging on to her as if she were the only thing keeping him from drowning.

"Oh, God, Sadie, I missed you!" He said the words against her mouth, punctuated them with kisses, then buried his face into the curve of her neck, his arms still clutching her as if he'd never let her go.

That was all right with Sadie. She had lived too long for this moment, had dreamed of it too many times. And had, for a long time now been afraid it would never come.

"Excuse me?" A voice behind Spence sounded tentative. A tall black woman with beautifully beaded hair was looking bemusedly at them. "I just need to get to the dryer, please."

They stumbled apart, but Spence hung on to Sadie's hand as they stepped out of the way. "Come on," she said, "come upstairs."

Ordinarily she stayed and read a book while she did her laundry. Not today. She hauled Spence after her up the steps. The apartment was boring, nondescript, lonely. Not today.

"Why?" she asked him when she had him inside the door and their arms were around each other again. "After all these months, why now? What happened?"

"Mateus got engaged."

*"What?"* Sadie's jaw dropped. She couldn't believe her ears. "Mateus? What does Mateus have to do with it?"

"I…I thought you…and he…" Spence shook his head. "You left me. You went to him. He's…a catch. He probably wouldn't mind having a dozen kids." He shrugged. "I couldn't stand in your way."

Sadie was speechless. Mateus? She and Mateus? If it hadn't been so painful, it might have been funny. "No," she said at last. "We've never—"

"I didn't know. I wasn't fair to you, Sadie. I know that. And you're right. You would be a good mother."

"If we couldn't have kids, Spence, I could live without them." She already knew that. It would hurt. But she would survive. If she had him, she would always survive.

"If we don't, we can adopt some," he said.

"You changed your mind." It wasn't a question. She didn't need to ask the question. She could see the answer—the transformation—in his eyes. In the way he looked at her. In the way he smiled.

He loosed his grip on her and held up a hand for her to see. Next to the rose gold of the wedding band he still wore—the wedding band she'd given him—was the pipestone ring she'd returned.

"Grandpa changed my mind," he said. "And Richard Carstairs."

Sadie gaped. She pulled him over to her lumpy secondhand sofa and pulled him down on it, holding his hand, looking at the ring, running her finger over the inlaid heart. "It isn't broken anymore."

He shook his head. "I fixed it. Got a new piece. It's whole now." He didn't say the words, but she heard them anyway: *whole...like me.*

"The ring brought back a lot of memories. More good than bad," he said quickly. "My granddad was the one good part of my childhood. When I had it, when I started wearing it again, I started remembering him. He used to tell me not to listen to them—my parents. He used to say they tried to hurt me because they were hurting inside. He said they were sad and he wished he could do something to change who they were but he couldn't. 'They have to find it in themselves,' he said. 'It's inside you,' he used to tell me. 'You can be who you want to be.' I always thought he meant about business. I never thought beyond it. Not to my life, to the people I love. Now I realize it's about us, too."

He lifted her hand to his lips and kissed them lightly. "I got a call from Richard a few weeks ago. He and Leonie are having a baby."

Sadie didn't know whether to laugh or cry. "That's wonderful."

"It is." And he sounded like he meant it. "He said thanks, by the way. He said you woke them up, made them talk to each other, made him think about decisions he'd already made without even consulting his wife. Made him realize he'd made them because he was scared. A lot like me," Spence told her.

"I didn't want to be like my parents. Mostly I didn't want to not be the man I wanted to be, that you believed I could be. I was terrified. Still am." He smiled shakily. "But I figure Grandpa might be right, that if I work at it and take the risk, I can be the man I want to be—your husband, the father of your children, the man you love and who will love you—for the rest of our lives."

She was crying then, and hugging him, kissing him, wiping away tears that she thought were hers but might have been his. "I love you so much," she whispered, her voice breaking. "I thought I'd lost you. I thought you'd never come."

"I came as soon as I thought I had a chance. Do I?" His eyes searched hers.

"Oh, yes," Sadie answered. "Oh, my love, yes!"

It was the best Christmas Spence had ever had.

The snow was flying. The temperature was far below zero. The winds were howling out of the north, and the scene was as far as one could imagine from their Fijian honeymoon. It was a long way from Austin, too, where five months ago he had gone to bring her home.

But it was the best place in the world to be this morning, lying on the sofa with Sadie wrapped in his arms, looking at the Christmas tree—the first one they'd shared—which they had decorated together with ornaments they'd made to symbolize places they'd been, people they'd known.

Sadie had made a tiny papier-mâché house that looked like Spence's Copper King mansion. He'd carved a little birch canoe. They'd gone to Ireland and brought back a shamrock and to Cornwall and brought back a flag of St. Piran. Mateus had sent them a miniature map of Texas and, of course, one of Brazil. They had a plaster of paris circle of Edward's tiny hand, and a Statue of Liberty to recall their New York courthouse experience, and half a dozen others, including an exquisitely detailed copy of their Nanumi treehouse *bure* which Mrs. Isogawa had made for them.

"It's lovely, isn't it?" she said, snuggling close and leaning up to kiss his stubbled jaw.

"Perfect," Spence agreed. "Couldn't be better." Life couldn't be better as far as he was concerned.

"No, not quite perfect," Sadie said. "That one Grace made is out of place."

"What one?"

"There. Behind the *bure*. I can't think how it got there. Could you move it? Then it will be perfect."

"It's fine. Don't fuss." He kissed her.

"But it would be better…" She looked at him hopefully and grinned.

Sighing, he got up off the sofa and padded across the rug to the tree. "Which ornament Grace made?" Grace made a lot of god-awful ornaments. Knitted things like tiny antimacassars and dangly things that were supposed to be stars but looked more like Martian antennae.

"Behind the *bure*. See it?"

He plucked out another of Grace's knitted efforts. "This?" But when he got a closer look, he realized it wasn't an ornament. "Why does Grace knit booties for Christmas ornaments?"

"She doesn't," Sadie said, smiling. "She knits them for babies."

Spence stared. He swallowed. He looked at Sadie, dazed, disbelieving, and yet… "Is she—I mean, *are you*—sure?"

Sadie nodded, still smiling.

He felt oddly breathless. "Are you…all right?" He looked worried, nervous.

"I'm fine. Are you?" She was still smiling, but there was a hint of apprehension in her tone.

Was he? Spence thought about it. He thought about the burden, the stress, the responsibility, the potential for disaster, the sleepless nights and all the times his child would cry and he would not understand.

And then he thought about sharing a child with Sadie—about the honor and joy of being allowed to be a part of someone else's life—and a slow delighted smile spread across his face.

He crossed the room and wrapped his arms around his wife and kissed her. "Thanks to you, Sadie my love, I've never been better in my life."

# LET'S TALK
## Romance

For exclusive extracts, competitions
and special offers, find us online:

f facebook.com/millsandboon

🐦 @MillsandBoon

📷 @MillsandBoonUK

**Get in touch on 01413 063232**

For all the latest titles coming soon, visit
# millsandboon.co.uk/nextmonth

# MILLS & BOON

## THE HEART OF ROMANCE

## A ROMANCE FOR EVERY KIND OF READER

**MODERN**

Prepare to be swept off your feet by sophisticated, sexy and seductive heroes, in some of the world's most glamourous and romantic locations, where power and passion collide.
**8 stories per month.**

**HISTORICAL**

Escape with historical heroes from time gone by. Whether your passion is for wicked Regency Rakes, muscled Vikings or rugged Highlanders, awaken the romance of the past.
**6 stories per month.**

**MEDICAL**

Set your pulse racing with dedicated, delectable doctors in the high-pressure world of medicine, where emotions run high and passion, comfort and love are the best medicine.
**6 stories per month.**

*True Love*

Celebrate true love with tender stories of heartfelt romance, from the rush of falling in love to the joy a new baby can bring, and a focus on the emotional heart of a relationship.
**8 stories per month.**

*Desire*

Indulge in secrets and scandal, intense drama and plenty of sizzling hot action with powerful and passionate heroes who have it all: wealth, status, good looks…everything but the right woman.
**6 stories per month.**

**HEROES**

Experience all the excitement of a gripping thriller, with an intense romance at its heart. Resourceful, true-to-life women and strong, fearless men face danger and desire - a killer combination!
**8 stories per month.**

**DARE**

Sensual love stories featuring smart, sassy heroines you'd want as a best friend, and compelling intense heroes who are worthy of them.
**4 stories per month.**

To see which titles are coming soon, please visit

## millsandboon.co.uk/nextmonth

# MILLS & BOON
## *True Love*
### Romance from the Heart

Celebrate true love with tender stories of
heartfelt romance, from the rush of falling
in love to the joy a new baby can bring,
and a focus on the emotional
heart of a relationship.

# MILLS & BOON
## MODERN
# Power and Passion

Prepare to be swept off your feet by sophisticated, sexy and seductive heroes, in some of the world's most glamourous and romantic locations, where power and passion collide.